THREE WOMEN

AND

THE RIVER

OR

THE ENGLISHMAN WHO FORGOT HIS OWN NAME

A LOVE SAGA
OF THE GREAT WAR

WILLIAM HARRY HARDING

LYMER & HART
GARDEN OAK PRESS
RAINBOW, CALIFORNIA

Lymer & Hart
Garden Oak Press
1953 Huffstatler St., Suite A
Rainbow, CA 92028
760 728-2088
gardenoakpress.com
gardenoakpress@gmail.com

First published by Garden Oak Press on November 11, 2018

ISBN-13: 978-1-7323753-0-7
ISBN-10: 1-7323753-0-5

Library of Congress Control Number: 2018906453

Printed in the United States of America

Lymer & Hart is an imprint of Garden Oak Press

The views expressed in this work of fiction are solely those of the author and do not necessarily reflect the views of the Publisher and the Publisher hereby disclaims any responsibility for them.

THREE WOMEN

AND

THE RIVER

OR

THE ENGLISHMAN WHO FORGOT HIS OWN NAME

A LOVE SAGA
OF THE GREAT WAR

WILLIAM HARRY HARDING

ACKNOWLEDGEMENTS

FOR
GENEROUS RESEARCH ASSISTANCE:

THE AMERICAN RED CROSS
JEAN SHULMAN, RN
VOLUNTEER,
HISTORICAL PROGRAMS AND RECORDS

THE QUEEN'S OWN WEST KENT REGIMENT
HISTORIANS AND ARCHIVES

C.T. ATKINSON
LATE CAPTAIN, OXFORD UNIVERSITY O.T.C

BRIGADIER GENERAL SIR JAMES EDWARD EDMONDS CB CMG

COMBAT SCENES CONCUR WITH HISTORICAL REPORTS,
AND OCCURRED ON DATES AND TIMES
AND IN WEATHER AS DEPICTED,
WITH CASUALTIES CONFIRMED BY OFFICIAL RECORDS.

Prologue
The River

19 February, 1918

Through the wire, between gaps in the curls of barbs and tilting posts, he could see them moving – a helmet glinted under the half moon, then another. And another. They were sneaking toward the tree line and the big bend in the river. Barry would be smoking near those trees.

Reg nudged the new recruit. "Tell sergeant we've company."

The lanky boy, a '99er yet to fire his rifle at the enemy, turned and started coming out of his crouch. Reg shoved him back down. "Keep your napper down. Low, the full way."

With a gulp, the teenager nodded, made his way in a squatty duck walk toward the place the others had tied up the main raft at the high bank, 50 meters downstream. The recruit, whose uniform still looked new, should never have been tagged for this foray.

At least it was dry here, not the sticky mud of Ypres. On hands and knees, Reg scurried to the river, reaching the boulder – a chunk of the Dolomites the current had sent down. He made out the glow of a cigarette short of the trees, where the little raft had been secured.

Barry had his feet up on a rotting stump. He was blowing smoke rings at the river. Reg swatted the cigarette from his lips.

"My last fag," Barry said.

Holding a finger to his lips, Reg pointed at the tree line. Barry squinted into the darkness, brought his rifle up to the ready. "Bloody suicide squad."

"Better than a Flanders trench," Reg told him.

"We finally get some cushy quiet and we go looking for trouble? With this moon? We're idiots." Barry shook his head. "How many?"

"At least three. Cheeky clan – paint their helmets."

They listened for footsteps in those trees. "Sending us back to France. It's certain." Barry used the stump to steady his aim. "Captain got it straight from Sergeant Major."

"When?"

"A week. Two at most." Something splintered down river. Barry swung his aim from the trees. "Half a mind to wander off and hide in the woods back there. This war never ends."

Heavy footsteps pounded the trail along the bank. Capt. Rodgers and Sgt. Jeffs led the others at a crouching run. Reg signaled with his hand for them to get lower, but they kept coming. The snap of a rifle blasted out of the trees. The Captain stumbled, fell. Sgt. Jeffs hit the ground face first, the others behind him doing the same. In that instant, the tree line came alive with the crack of rifles.

3

Barry had already swung his aim back at the trees. He began shooting. On his back, the barrel-chested Sergeant yanked a Mill's grenade from his webbing, armed it, then rolled and threw from a lying position, all in one motion. Seconds later, the small bomb exploded in the trees.

Reg crawled behind the saplings where the little raft was tied up. He took aim, waited for muzzle flashes. He could hear them in the trees, shifting positions. More than three. Maybe a whole company out there. The rope felt slick. And it had already begun to freeze. He used his bayonet to open the knot. "Bar, let's cross back."

Barry nodded, then crawled on his stomach. "We'll take Captain with us." Without waiting for an answer, he grabbed the officer's uniform collar and began lugging him toward the saplings.

The rest of the squad began firing at the trees. On his knees, Barry rolled the officer's motionless body onto the raft. Something made Barry jerk forward. His arm twitching, he slumped on top of the Captain. Reg slid hand over hand down the rope line, holding the raft fast against the bank. The weight of the two men and the slippery rope were too much to fight. He coiled the rope around his hand, dug his heels into the slick earth. The raft slipped into the icy water. The current caught it instantly.

Holding onto the rope with both hands, Reg felt the last part of the river bank rip the rifle from his grasp. A second later, he was in the river, dragged under by the building speed of the raft.

In water so cold his fingers felt as though they were burning, he worked his way up the rope, feeding it around a wrist with each pull. He tried to climb aboard, but the raft bumped off a big chunk of river ice, tossing him back in. He got a boot onto the long side of the wood poles, used leg strength to get into position, then he grabbed a handful of Barry and pulled himself onto the raft. Shivering, he rolled over, came face to face with Capt. Rodgers. Against the protests of everyone in the 11th Battalion because it would surely bring bad luck, the young officer had made good on his promise to shave off his thin moustache once they left France and reached Italy. He bragged that shaving his face clean had brought the good weather, the dry ground, the cushy encampment at The Montello, scented with pine, swept by fresh water − the Piave River − and no enemy in sight. Even the artillery fire stopped the day the battalion arrived to relieve the Italians, who moved up to support the Australians on the front line.

Only one of the Captain's eyes was open. The other eye was gone. Blood leaked out of the dark hole.

4

The strong current carried the little raft past the main one, wet and shiny from the waxing moon, still tied up at the high bank. The Sergeant and the rest of the patrol would have no trouble finding it. If they could get to it. Down river, small islands were coming up. A leg might be enough of a rudder to steer this raft into one of them.

Barry coughed. Reg started pulling him off the Captain. Blood saturated the front of Barry's uniform. His? Capt. Rodgers's? Barry blinked.

"Finally got your blighty." Reg told him.

He must have seen Reg in the dim light. With a small smile that turned up a corner of his mouth, he said. "I'm napoo." Then gurgling: air and blood bubbled out of the gaping wound in his throat.

The raft had already picked up so much speed, it was swirling sideways in the current. No way to steer it. Reg uncoiled the rope from his wrist, tried to get to his knees. The raft careened into what was left of an old stone column. The wood poles cracked, the raft flipped over. Barry and the Captain splashed into the water, floated away. Struggling against the current, Reg grabbed a section of splintered raft poles, but the river ripped it out his hands. He slammed into another wide stone column, bouncing off it into another. His helmet snapped off. The current cart wheeled him head first into something smooth and hard. Dazed, he held on to the stones.

Losing feeling in his fingers, he pushed off with legs to swim his way toward another group of rocks closer to the bank of an island. The river picked up speed here, propelling him downstream, past those rocks and into stone rubble at the bank with such force that he didn't have to roll out of the water − the river hurled him onto the island as if he were a Mill's bomb.

Something heavy inside his chest. Breathing hurt. It felt as if he was still moving, but the pebbles here were dry, and much warmer than the river. He blinked at the stars, patted down his arms for broken bones, bent his legs at the knees, tried to wiggle his toes in his boots. Everything worked. He drew a breath against the pain, rolled onto his side. Numbed by the cold, he started crawling toward the edge of the island closest to the north bank. No trees. No cover. *Sitting duck.*

He wiped the wetness from his right eye. Blood. Sticky. His fingertips felt the gash near the hairline. He dug into his webbing, found the extra pair of socks and used one of them as a compress, the other as a towel to clear blood from his eyes.

He shut one eye, then the other, testing his vision. The inlet between the island and the north bank was less than five meters wide, but the current raced through it with the same gurgling sound Barry had made. He glanced down the river. No hint of what remained of the little raft, no sign of the two bodies.

He tried to sit up, but dizziness forced him back onto his stomach. The sound of rifle fire and grenade explosions floated downstream. The inlet got wider to the south. Or was that the east? He didn't have the strength to roll onto his back and check the stars for Polaris or The Plow, what Yanks called The Big Dipper. It didn't matter which way he went. Unless he got across that inlet and found cover by first light, he'd be easy to spot.

The sound of his body against the pebbles felt soothing − a sign he was making progress, foot by foot. With one hand holding the sock against his head wound, it was slow going to the stone piling near the edge of the island. It looked like a rampart − old stones fitted together, maybe three feet above the water level. He needed both hands to pull himself up so he could start climbing. His left pinkie was sticking straight out to the side. Broken? Dislocated? Why didn't it hurt?

And why didn't his head ache? All that blood, and no pain. He rested his face against the smooth stones − so cool, like hugging a glass of iced lemonade. He swallowed that remembered taste, got something sour instead in his throat. With his tongue, he checked to make sure he hadn't lost any teeth. He started climbing.

At its high point, the ancient rampart was over five feet above the river, but only two feet above it from where it ended, halfway across the inlet. In a sitting position, using his legs and boots as stabilizers, he bumped his way down over jagged edges to the ledge of stones nearest the bank, less than five feet away. If he could stand, it would be like leaping off the rocks in Denny Bottom. One good push, a shoulder tuck, a back roll, and it would be over.

It took a series of painful breaths to gather the strength to get his feet under him. He couldn't stand. Pushing off from a squat might be better anyway. He scanned the bank for something to grab onto. Nothing there. He was shivering now, no way to stop it. Staying here, exposed to the wind, would only make it worse. He shoved the bloody socks back into his webbing, leaned forward, readied his leap.

His legs betrayed him. The best push he could get threw him flat into the current. He could feel the force moving him downstream. But his boots were on the bottom. With footing, he let the river push him,

6

kept his legs moving, running inside the current, straining sideways, angling for the bank. The water started to come off him. Waist deep, then knee deep. He lurched toward the bank, landing on his side. The river let go of him. He could hear it race by. He dug his heels into the muddy bank, grabbed a handful of that mud and turned sideways, his back against the slope.

Every breath hurt worse than the last. His teeth chattered. He watched the dark water, that invisible current. Moving sideways and keeping his back to the mud, he inched his way downstream to where the slope shallowed out. After a short rest, he rolled onto his knees and crawled up the bank.

Checking his webbing to make sure he still had his emergency supplies, he scanned the long field laying fallow along the flood plain. No lights. Nothing moving out there. No trees, either. Only craters made by German artillery shells. One of them might be big enough to hid in.

He pulled out the socks, put the bloody one back on his wound. It stung now. Just above right temple, in the hairline, a big piece of scalp had been torn off.

Beyond the island, the river widened. It was empty of everything except ice chunks. On his hands and knees, he crawled toward the nearest shell crater.

It didn't look big enough to be from a Black Maria, one that had fallen short of the river and the town of Nervesa, and well south of the trees of The Montello on the other side, where the rest of the 11th was settled in. They wouldn't send out another patrol even if Sgt. Jeffs and the others got back. Odds were the '99er wouldn't have made it. Reg kept moving, toward the other craters up the field.

Moonlight bounced off something yellow in the field. An unexploded shell. This field must have been farmed once. The top was all dried out, but underneath, where the artillery explosions had exposed it, the earth was black and sweet smelling. He reached a big crater halfway up the field and slide down into it. He reached for his emergency ration, but his dislocated pinkie kept getting caught in the webbing. He grabbed the finger – it looked dead – and snapped it back toward the others. The pain he had expected never came. It wasn't straight, but it moved. It wouldn't bend, but it moved. *Progress.*

He untied the webbing, dug inside for the tin of bully beef. Maybe just the biscuit now. The beef for breakfast. Better to get out of these clothes first and air dry his body before the shivering got worse.

All those buttons, the heavy wet wool, the weight of it, made stripping down an exhausting chore. Even unwrapping his puttees was difficult, especially the final windings near the ankles. And the laces on his boots were impossible to unknot. Too wet. With no bayonet, he used the tip of his trenching tool to cut the knots, stabbing them the way his father used to dig up potatoes. His father could grow anything in this soil. It was darker and richer than anything back in Rusthall.

Getting the boots off took so much effort he had to rest in between pushes and pulls. His socks felt glued to his feet. But it was working. He could feel warmth on his skin when he rubbed it. Protected from the wind, he used his grey shirt to tie his uniform into a bundle. He peered over the lip of the crater. Still nothing out there. And he could stand now. The cold ground was warmer than the air. He found the biscuit in a pouch in the webbing. It was too hard to bite into. He snapped off an edge, put it into his mouth, waited for saliva to soften it, scanned the horizons.

Using the bundled uniform as a pillow, he lay on his back, staring beyond the four-foot walls of the crater. The Plow put the North Star to his right. The sun would come up on the downriver side of the crater, warming him from toe to head. He kept rubbing his arms and chest, his thighs, rubbed his feet and ankles together. If it didn't get any colder, if it didn't snow, he might survive the night.

He finished the biscuit, thought about losing Barry. No way to survive back in France or Flanders without him. They were the only two, along with Sgt. Major, left in the 11th who had not been wounded or killed. *Suicide to return with no Barry.* Lt. Col. Corfe would understand. Reg and Barry had helped pull the badly wounded OC back to safety at Ridge Wood.

He rubbed dirt over his skin, using the friction to chase the chill. He kept his feet off the ground by placing them on top of his boots, now lying on their sides. He got the tin of matches from the webbing, set it on top of his chest, beside the identification disc on that grimy string around his neck. If it got any colder, he would have to search for kindling and a place to build a fire. For a moment, he thought he could smell smoke. It must have been left over from the gunpowder in the shell that had made this crater.

His thoughts turned to Mr. Quaite at *The Rusthall Gazette*. What a dispatch this would make. The little man would be grinning the whole time he set the type. He would take care of telling Barry's father at the old hotel in Tunbridge Wells.

The warmth of tears on his cheek surprised him. He tried to focus on the stars. *Missing, presumed killed.* His mother would drop into her chair in the kitchen. His father would walk outside and get back to work. Mr. Quaite would head back to the newspaper office and write the article. That's probably how Madge would hear about it.

He couldn't imagine her face anymore. The stars started spinning. It got black in a hurry.

•

A hard sun woke him up. His whole body ached. The sock compress had stuck to his scalp, the blood dried. It hurt to touch, and the pain got worse when he tried to peel the sock off. It was like a new growth sprouting above his temple. "You put them on your feet," Barry would have joked if he could have seen this. "But you have a future in the circus freak show: Sock Head − born in the bowels of West Kent!"

The tin of matches had slid off his chest, onto the webbing at his side. His knees and arms looked scraped up and bloody. No bones were sticking through the skin. And it was warmer. He sat up. The dizziness returned, but it wasn't bad enough to force him back down. His mouth was stone dry. He pulled himself up to the edge of the crater, checked the field: empty. A drink from the river would hold him long enough to lay out his clothes in the crater to dry. There might even be some brush near the bank dry enough for a fire. He climbed out the shallower end of the crater, carrying his boots, then dusted the drying soil from his skin and stepped to the smaller crater a few feet away. He aimed his urine stream at the bottom of the pit.

She was coming up from the river bank, water buckets in a yoke over her shoulders. Willowy. Blonde. Young. She stopped in her tracks. Her face tightened. Morning light reflected off her skin and hair. Instinctively, he turned to hide his nakedness, then looked back over a shoulder. His head started thudding. His legs got wobbly. He felt the boots slip out of his fingers. Dizzy, he tried to back away from the crater, but his feet were no longer feeling the ground. A heel started sliding. He watched it moving, but couldn't make it stop. He tumbled into the hole. The perfect death: drowned in his own hot piss. Even that little laugh hurt. He rolled onto a side, tried to get up.

The last thing he remembered was that sweet black ground smacking him in the face.

BOOK ONE

HER GARDEN

THE NEXT DAY

1

Some sort of small house. A stone cabin. One room. Slender timbers joisting the roof. The bed was low enough that his fingers could touch the smooth hide on the floor. The blanket covering him smelled of fish and smoke. Someone had washed him: no dirt on his skin anywhere. Sunlight ran in through the lone window, painting the wide plank table against the far wall. A fire crackled in the rock-faced hearth. Evergreen. Young, still full of sap. By the door: a shotgun. An old muzzle loader? The bandage wrapped around his skull felt like a cap. Nothing hurt, except that problem pinkie. It throbbed. And he still couldn't bend it.

He tried sitting up. His ribs ached when he moved. No sign of his uniform or the webbing. His tongue felt swollen. No saliva. Only five or six steps to that shotgun. If he could walk. If he could get up from this bed.

The door opened. A small gray-haired man came in, his arms full of cut saplings. His back curved at the shoulders like one of those smooth stones at the river. He went straight to the hearth, fed the fire. A black-haired woman followed him inside. She saw Reg moving, grabbed the shotgun, aimed it at him. Her eyes looked darker than her hair. "Zio. È 'sveglio."

The old man man dumped the rest of the wood onto a pile near the corner. "Vai fuori."

The woman backed out, but her shadow and the shadow of that shotgun painted the threshhold.

Keeping an eye on Reg, the slump-shouldered man stepped to the table, poured water from a jug into a small cup. "Inglese, no?"

Reg gulped down the water. Surprisingly not cold. The little man took back the cup — he had light blue eyes — then dangled the string and the identification disc from a crooked finger. "Mi chiamo DaPonte." He jabbed a thumb into his chest. "Luigi DaPonte."

Reg reached for the disc, tumbled onto the floor. The angry-eyed woman ran back in, shotgun at the ready. Luigi laughed, then eased the shotgun out of her hands. She started talking — a low-pitched growl. It sounded like swearing. Then the flat of his hand slammed the table so hard the water jug jumped. In a soft voice, he said, "Basta, Teresa."

The woman – Teresa – glared at him, then at Reg. She would have shot him, no doubt about it. She looked as though she still wanted to.

Behind her, two little girls ran inside. They had that same dark eyes and hair, but they didn't look angry, or scared. They started giggling when they saw the naked man on the floor. The woman spun on a heel, every part of her a sharp angle, and with her dressfront ushered the girls back outside, past a light-haired woman, who dumped an apron full of carrots on the table. This couldn't be the same one who carried water from the river. Reg turned away, used the low bed to get off the floor. She smiled when he pulled the blanket to cover himself. It was tucked under the short foot of the bed frame and he didn't have the strength to free it. He tugged, but fell back onto the bed.

"Non è mai vestito." She had the same soft blue eyes the gray-haired man did. She began rinsing the small carrots with water from the jug.

Reg draped his legs over the edge of the bed, covered himself with part of the blanket. "My uniform. It's in the shell crater."

She acted as though she hadn't heard him, ladled liquid from the pot hanging in the hearth. Steam rose from the clay bowl. "Si mangia ora. Sono sottili."

Her fingers were cold, the bowl warm. No spoon. He sipped it. Some kind of broth. Tangy and sour, like cabbage. If she had not been watching, he would have dumped it out. He sipped the soup. "Awful stuff. Cheers."

She nodded, smiled. "Bene."

"Worst I've ever had. Truly."

That dark-haired woman came back in holding an old hoe like a weapon. The two girls crouched behind her at the threshhold, sunlight making them look like a photograph. She pulled the tin of bully beef from the pocket in her wool dress. His emergency ration. "Manzo, sì?"

The light-haired woman ripped the tin out of her hand: "Hai rubato quella."

Another argument. The smallest of the girls, probably no more than two, jumped to chase the tin as it danced back and forth in the grasp of the two women. They had to be related. Sisters? The older one, the black-haired snarling one, won the battle. She probably always won. She stormed out with the tin and the hoe, followed by her girls.

14

"Ladro!" The blonde woman lowered her head. With the edge of her apron, she wiped a carrot and handed it to him. "Mi dispiace."

His jaw felt sore. It hurt to take a bite. Chewing was worse. Swallowing wasn't so bad. The carrot tasted sweet.

"Gabriella." The old man pointed to her, then to himself. "Luigi." He handed the identification disc to her. "Leggi lo."

She stared at the small letters. Her lips formed the sounds: "Reg-i-nal-d Ol-cutt."

"Il tuo nome?" Rough weathered hands took back the disc. "Non è vero?"

Reg finished the carrot, took another from her. She checked the bandage on his head. Moving in closer, then nodding with satifaction, the stoop-shoulder man rapped his knuckles against his own temple. "Testa dura. Bene." With a short laugh, he turned and stabbed the fresh wood in the hearth with an iron rod.

It might have been the smoke, but the room started spinning. Reg steadied himself on the bed. His mouth tasted salty. Something was churning in his gut. He leaned forward. Sharp pains ran up his sides. Bits of chewed carrot spewed onto the floor in a puddle of warm broth as if self-propelled. His nose stung, his head started pounding again. His vision got blurry, then dimmed. His lungs hurt, every short breath a razor cut. "Sorry," he tried to say, but never got the word out. It felt as though he was falling backward, with no one there to catch him. Those roof timbers got smaller. He could feel more bile ready to come up, but he couldn't turn his head to keep if off the bed.

They were talking. It sounded like singing in whispers.

She washed out his puttees every day and rewrapped his head
with them after cleaning his wound with cold water. Somehow,
she had got them clean enough to be all one color again. How
long had it taken to scrub out the mud stains, the blood? He could
feel the long dent − a raw, sticky channel − running front to back at
his hairline where the scalp had been torn off. The river had eaten
that, too.

She washed where he couldn't reach − his legs and back. So many
bruises, now coloring legs and chest, his upper arms in blotches of
black and blue. He wondered what his back looked like. The swelling
around his jaw and cheek was going down, but that pinkie was never
going to be right again. Against the burning pain, he forced his head
as far as it would go to each side, then up and down. He was able to
keep food down, but he didn't feel like eating. Only the things she
didn't cook were edible. But it was more than that. He had no
appetite, not even for the bully beef that Teresa had stolen.

Gabriella kept him covered, added a knitted shawl − alternating
diagonals of red and brown − on top of the wool blanket. One
morning, it snowed. She came in with a handful, placed it directly on
his gash. He tried to hide the shock, but when he pulled back, she
grabbed his hair and pulled him forward, shaking her head.

She hardly ever spoke to him, or to the man she called Zio, either.
She hummed outside, the sound of her throaty melodies drifting in
when it wasn't raining or when the gusts weren't blowing off the
Alps. On those days, the roof made its own music, tap dancing in
rain, whimpering in wind. The sound of artillery was now so far
away, it wasn't even thunder anymore, just a soft thud, as if a book
had fallen from shelf to floor. That had to mean the Germans were
going backwards. *Finally.*

She spent most of her hours at the fire or outside. Several times a
day she carried hot embers in a pail out to the garden. What she did
with it was a mystery. Working at the table, she kept her back to him,
her stare fixed on the landscape through the little window, as if
expecting someone − a boyfriend come calling, a brother coming
home? − to magically appear out there. She cooked the rabbit and the
fish the old man brought in. Everything in a pot, stewed, with carrots.
Luigi always took the old shotgun with him, but Reg had never heard
it fired. Each time he brought the weapon back inside, fingers with

swollen knuckles unloaded it, rolling buckshot from the wad into a blistered palm, then into a jumper pocket. Each time, she asked, "È davvero necessario?"

Old shoulders shrugged, hard hands tended to the fire. She spoke to his back, waving a hand at Reg in the bed. A stream of words, clipped by anger. Maybe she was cursing him. It didn't matter. The sounds she made, the shapes her lips made, these were enough.

•

It took him days to find the courage to touch her hand. It was warm from cooking. She was handing him a bowl of soup. He squeezed her fingers. "Thank you." Slowly, she withdrew her hand. But she was smiling.

•

There were no books in here. They wouldn't do him any good – he couldn't read Italian – but it had been a long time since he had slept in a place without books. Even on the front line, in those soggy trenches, stinking of men and gunpowder and filth, he had books: a travel-sized copy of Kipling's *Jungle Book* that fit snugly in a trouser pocket and his own diaries, kept in his kit when he wasn't copying the entries to send back to *The Rusthall Gazette*, always beginning *Somewhere in France* or *Somewhere in Flanders* to keep Sgt. Major and the censors happy. What would Mr. Quaite be reading these days? Or the boys at Rusthall School? Probably *The Boy's Own Paper*. A monthly now. Back when he read every issue, he had to wait for summer for the new weeklies to come out. They stopped as soon as the school term started again, and there would be another whole year to wait for new issues. What great adventure were they writing about now?

He wasted one entire day bending and unbending his left pinkie, hearing it *pop* – like his mother's oatmeal bubbling to a boil – when he formed it into a curve, then *snap* – like a piece of rotted-out shed wood – when he put it back straight. The cruel game fascinated him. With his eyes closed, he couldn't feel if the finger was straight or bent. It was worthless when straight, not much more useful when curved. It seemed important to make a decision about whether it should be bent or straight. Just after dark, he decided to use a ripped piece of his puttee head bandage to tie the pinkie to the next finger, keeping it out of harm's way.

When he woke up the next morning, that tiny bandage was gone. Not in the bed, not on the floor. She must have unwrapped it. His own private nurse. *As cushy as it gets.*

17

The clothes were at least two sizes too large. They smelled of mildew and old potatoes. She didn't laugh at him, though. She had tears in her eyes. She ran outside. It was freezing out there — ice frosted the lower window pane.

"I vestiti del marito." Some of that gray hair was thinning in the back. He stoked the fire, sighed. "Forse è morto. Forse no."

"Forces?" Reg said. "Who?"

"Sì, forse." Those slumped shoulders shrugged. "Chissà?"

Hopeless. He tucked in the tail of the long tan shirt, rolled up the dark brown pant legs, tightened the thin rope around his waist to hold the trousers up. They were in much better shape than the frayed blue pants the old man wore. Reg stood, found his balance. At least they had not stolen his socks and boots. The first step was easy. The second wasn't. Wobbly, no strength, like a punch-drunk fighter.

"No, no." Luigi dropped the iron rod and grabbed him under the armpit. "Pagliaccio."

It still hurt to breathe. With help, he made it from bed to table, to wall to door, to chair and back to bed. No sign of his uniform anywhere. The frost on the window pane distorted the view, like one of those sideshow mirrors at the summer fair on Rusthall Common that made everyone look taller or fatter. He was glad he couldn't see her out there.

•

He decided to tell her everything. About the patrol, the Captain's missing eye, Barry's bloody throat, how they had been each other's good luck charm since that first day at Aldershot, how they had saved Lt. Col. Corfe from what would have been a mortal wound and had been awarded a Distinguished Conduct Medal for it, how dragging the OC to safety was easier than going house to house in Hollenbecke — yet they got only Military Medals for that — and how he couldn't go back to France or Flanders, not without Barry, so he was going to hide here, with her, until the war was finally over.

He was going to get strong again and take care of her garden. He knew about gardening, growing up on a farm, not like Barry, who had a posh life in the old hotel in Royal Tunbridge Wells where his father ran the bell staff. Barry couldn't grow weeds. But Reg could grow all sorts of crops: turnips, cabbages, potatoes, tomatoes by the bushel, carrots, squash as big as your arm, pumpkins, even flowers, like the tiny blush pink roses his mother loved. Heirlooms, she called them. She kept them in a bud vase on the kitchen table, a fresh one

18

each couple of days during their bloom. In the soil here, he could grow anything.

"Imagine that field in fruit trees," he told her. "Apples and pears, they'd do well here. You'd have a winter's worth of preserves and a year's worth of jam."

She was watching his lips move, too. She had probably never worn a corset. Did these people even wear underwear? They had not given him any. He forced himself to stop looking at her breasts, swaying under the heavy fabric of her dress when she moved.

"And those trees could be planted down one side of the broad field," he said, "so you could still see the river from here." With the long wooden spoon, he stirred vegetables stewing in the pot. Why didn't she use salt and pepper? "You could walk between the trees, in the shade, smell the blossoms, pick fruit for breakfast."

He tasted the stew, concealing its bitterness with a grin. "Fabulously terrible. You could win the war with this." He raised his arms. "I surrender."

She laughed. He had never heard that sound before. Like the whimper of a puppy. "Sembri comico."

He bowed. "Thank you. Merci."

Her eyes widened. "Ah – grazie!"

It was his turn to laugh.

""Merci significa grazie," she said with a pout. "In Italiano. Grazie."

"Grat-zee."

"No – grat-zee-eh."

"Grat-zee-eh," he said.

"Sì, grazie!"

They took turns saying the word, in different inflections, as if challenging each other to see which one could be the loudest or the funniest or the saddest.

"Our first game," Reg said.

"Mmm?" she said. "Grazie?"

He nodded and watched her pick up a head of cabbage and start ripping it apart.

•

Back in Rusthall, his mother would be at her cooker. How wide she got when she bent to crack open the cast iron door to check on biscuits. Madge never baked biscuits. She had made him a sandwich once. Cheese and cucumbers. No onion, no mustard. Maybe she had used the last two-plus years to visit the farm and learn how to cook

19

something. Anything. No, she hated the place, especially the smells – manure, dank soil, the outhouses, the too-sweet rot of compost. She felt the same way about all of Rusthall, even though her house was on the same street and less than a five-minute walk from Dornden, the former home of Princess Louise, Queen Victoria's daughter. "The Princess Royal left," Madge liked to remind him. "So should we."

She wanted to live in Tunbridge Wells – since 1909, Royal Tunbridge Wells, though it had been over 40 years since the great Queen had paid a visit. For some reason, her grandson, George V, whose image graced the front of the Distinguished Conduct Medal, authorized the *royal* title – "an appellation," Mr. Quaite called it. Something to do with the spa there, a place the King had visited exactly once. Madge was sure Reg could work at a newspaper there – *The Royal Tunbridge Wells Gazette and Fashionable Visitors List*, followed in very small print directly under the banner: *Not affiliated with The Rusthall Gazette*. Mr. Quaite sniffed a laugh at that, never failing to add: "It certainly is not."

"Andrew Quaite is no gentleman," Madge liked to remind him. "He pokes his nose into private matters."

"That's his job," Reg would tell her. "To get the actual story."

"It's uncouth."

"It's the news."

"He has ink on his fingers," she said. "No husband of mine is doing that."

"They use ink in Tunbridge Wells, too."

"They have people for that there."

She was right. They had typesetters and apprentices in the neighboring town. Mr. Quaite had no one. Just Reg. And he wasn't allowed to set type. Not yet. But working for the paper – writing – was the only thing he could remember ever wanting to do – the only way he could see to make his way. There were nice cottages along Rusthall Road. A few of them, just inside outside the eastern border of Rusthall, still overlooked Denny Bottom. The best of both worlds: village life out the front door, wild land out the back. Great for children.

Madge wouldn't settle for that. A shack in Tunbridge Wells would be better than a solid house anywhere in Rusthall. She won those arguments – in person, in letters. He had stopped offering his opinion. There was no point, no winning.

He woke up in a sweat. The small room was dark and quiet. Was he hiding here the same way he had been hiding from Madge? *Another escape.*

He added a handful of saplings to the smoldering wood in the hearth, put on his boots and walked outside. With the yoke of water buckets across his shoulders, he headed down the dark field, toward the river. Starting today, this would be his chore. He could imagine her surprise, hear her say, "Grazie," and tell her, "Di nulla," the same way the Luigi did, then lead the way out to the garden where their mornings would really begin.

He would show them both how to dig a well so no one would have to haul water from the river. If parts could be found, he could show them how to put in a hand pump. They had to hit water less than three meters down: just two days of digging, even with his trenching tool, once the ground softened.

He could hear the night river singing before he could see it.

•

Gabriella was a good listener. She seemed to like the sound of his voice, because she never shushed him. When she talked, it was only to offer him food or water, or a choice between this or that — "questo o quella?" Watching her carry water up from the river had been the best part of his mornings. She still made that walk, her dress wet in patches on the front. She must wash herself in that ice cold water. There was no cover, nothing to hide behind down there, no way to spy on her.

On the coldest days, stepping outside was a challenge — the hard chill instantly filling all the spaces his loose-fitting clothes left open, the mist of his breath stealing whatever remained of his warmth inside. He needed a coat. Or his uniform tunic. Something woolen. How did she manage without one? And sometimes her uncle went without a shirt inside. How thick was their blood?

On the warmer days, being outside was like being caught inside one of those landscape paintings decorating the lobbies of the hotels in Royal Tunbridge Wells: snow-capped Alps — "Dolomiti Bellunesi," according to Luigi — spiking above the greening foothills rolling in swells like an ocean, the darker green of the piny woodlands, the long sideways run of the valley, in patches now wild with white-flowered trees. It was as if the war had never come to this place. A glance at the fallow field leading to the river, pock-marked with bomb craters, made another kind of painting: wounded soil.

"A real mess," he said, pointing at those holes.

21

"La golena del Piave." Her free hand swept across the wide plain. "Bella, no?"

Watching her pull the curtain closed over her bed in the corner nook was the best part of his evening. Before her uncle started snoring under the hides by the sapling pile near the hearth, Reg could hear her whispering her prayers, breathing. For the first time since leaving Rusthall, he was going to sleep with his jaw relaxed, his whole body floating.

•

He told her about the Flanders mud, so sticky it got inside the pores, only to come out weeks later after a hot bath and a hard scrubbing – it smelled bad even then – and the best way to keep a rifle clean, and how to get a short sleep on the fire step in a trench, and how easy it was to tell a Whiz Bang from a Black Maria, and how a Jack Johnson could leave a crater big enough to live in, and how quickly you got so used to the rumble of artillery all day long that you actually thought something had gone wrong when it stopped. That quiet was the scariest part, because everyone knew that it could not last.

Those deep craters in the field had become little swamps, filled with snow melt, rain water and the muck leaching into them. Insects had taken them over. And frogs. The old man might have thought about trying to catch some for dinner, but they were probably too much for him, especially when they spent their days and nights down the steep crater walls at the edge of those gloomy puddles.

In one of the biggest craters near the north bank, a doe had stumbled in and drowned. The water around it was dark brown, almost black, like the flies swarming on the exposed flesh, the blistering hide. He tried his best to describe it to Luigi, but when that didn't work, Reg took a rope with him the next morning. Something had already beaten him to it. Half the carcass had been chewed away. Crows pecked at the rest. Gray maggots burrowed through flesh. Flies fought for places to land.

"You're lucky that none of those shells hit your house," he told her. Every man in the Queen's Own West Kent Regiment knew better than to take shelter in a farm house – they were always targets Fritz used to calibrate range, always getting blown to bits.

At first, these one-sided conversations felt silly, as if he was just rattling on, the way Madge did when she saw a dress she liked in a shop window near The Pantiles. That dress cost three month's wages and, as pretty as it was, it wasn't a possibility, so he let her keep going on about it because her nattering would be the only way she would ever touch that dress. Did she feel as alone with that dream then as he did with the flood of war images now?

Most of the time, Gabriella paid no attention, not even looking at him. Now and then, she shot him a glance, as if to make sure he was still there. He could have been the wireless, on in the background: static. She said so little, he decided to call her Gabby. The first time he called her that outloud, she squinted with surprise. She sighed out of the corner of her smile and shook her head each time she heard it.

•

She owned two dresses. The one she wore every day, faded brown, like sun-baked soil, restitched near the hem. The other one, black, hung on a peg in the wall of the curtained alcove where she slept, a small wood crucifix and a string of rosary beads beside it. That dress looked heavy. It was smaller than she was, too. Maybe it was her mother's. He wondered if Gabby had ever worn it, if she could fit into it, why she kept it.

Why were things like this so simple to understand back home, so impossible to figure out here? Luigi always left his shoes outside by the door, unless it was raining or snowing. Gabby never did. When not on her feet, her shoes were always next to the curtained nook. It made no sense. Reg had half a mind to leave one shoe outside, the other by his bed, and see what these two would make of that.

•

The 11th Battalion would be back in France by now. The Australians might still be near the river at The Montello. He could find them when he was sure all the fighting had stopped. They would see by the hard scab on top of his head that he had been injured. They would believe how he had been swept down river, how lucky he was to have been nursed back to health, how there was no way to get back to them until now. He could claim that he had lost his memory for a while. They would believe that, too. He might even get another DCM. But then they would send him back to wherever the 11th was, where he wouldn't know more than a handful of men in the re-made battalion, where he'd be the perfect target for Fritz: an infantry man who couldn't even walk fast let alone run.

Had the War Office sent word to his parents? Would Madge know? Would Mr. Quaite make inquiries when he didn't recieve news from Reg by post? Would anyone find Barry's body floating in the current? That river flowed south into Venice Bay and the Adriatic Sea. Is that where Barry and the Captain were now?

Or had they been washed ashore, only to be eaten by the same animals that had taken most of that deer?

What kind of fish lived in the Adriatic? Were there sharks? Would there be anything left to identify? Did flies make it out onto open water?

He tasted the tears in the crook of his mouth and turned his face so she couldn't see him. But she found him, knelt beside him, stroked his hair as if he were an injured child and started humming. He laid his cheek against her, shut his eyes.

The shouting made him sit up straight. Teresa had Gabby by the hair, scolding her and pulling her toward the door. When the smaller woman tried to break free, the black-haired bully slapped her. Fighting tears, Gabby slumped to the floor. Teresa's glare turned into a flat grin. She grabbed the shotgun, turned and aimed it at Reg, pulled the trigger. *Click,* then silence.

Surprised, she didn't see Gabby get a hand on the barrel. They played tug-of-war with the empty gun. Beyond them, through the open door, he could make out Luigi coming up the garden path. The two little girls pulled at the bundle in his arms. Teresa heard them clamoring out there. She let go of the useless shotgun and marched toward the stoop-shouldered man, shouting and pointing back at the little house.

Both girls stopped. Luigi made his way inside, set his bundle on the table. Fresh bread, a wheel of yellow cheese. He sat in the chair, catching his breath, surveying the room will a dull stare, unable to make sense of the woman sobbing on the floor hugging his shotgun, the other pacing side to side at the door like a crazed animal ready to pounce.

On a knee beside Gabby, Reg touched her shoulder. She jerked away as if stabbed.

And Teresa was screaming again. Her daughters were taking small backward steps. Rubbing his face, Luigi searched the roof timbers as if there was some answer hidden up there. Gabby stood and flung the shotgun into the heap of saplings by the hearth. She shoved her sister aside and strode out, barefoot. An instant later, she was moving toward the river, dragging the yoke of water buckets.

"Hey, that's my job." Reg aimed his shout past the dark-eyed glare, but Gabby didn't stop. He picked the shotgun out of the twig pile. Teresa gasped. He leaned the barrel against the table next to the bread and cheese. The aromas made him hungry. Through the window Gabby was still walking fast, getting smaller. He found her shoes where she always left them and took them to the door. Teresa spat at him as he walked outside.

The girls were hiding in the cabbages. He waved at them. The smaller one waved back, but her sister stopped that little hand.

"Your mother tried to shoot me!" he told them. "She's mad as a hatter!"

He quickened his pace to get out of range, in case the dark-haired woman found the buckshot hidden in that worn jumper pocket.

He could imagine his father's face, reading the telegram that described how his son had died: shot by a crazy woman, in the back, for no reason. *Somewhere in Italy.*

They didn't hand out medals for that.

3

He started helping cut and bring in firewood. His head was still sore, but it didn't ache anymore. Only his ribs still hurt. And a sharp pain, like something burning inside his right hip, flared up when he was lying in bed or sitting. It encouraged him to stay on his feet, exercise with knee bends. The sound of artillery was so faint these days, he only paid attention to it in late afternoon, when the wind weakened and the ground animals burrowed in for the night.

When the snow stopped and river ice began to melt and the ground softened, he helped her in the garden. The head of the old hoe wobbled on the handle it was nailed to. Didn't they know his trenching tool would be better? Why wouldn't they tell him what they had done with it?

The soil was even better than he thought. In spots, it smelled like licorice. Each morning, a blue jay darted in from nowhere to perch on a garden stake, waiting for Gabby to put down her water bucket. The second she stepped away, the bird would fly to the bucket, plop in on its belly and thrash around, bathing. It made her laugh.

On one of his firewood hikes, he found a rusted cart wheel hub lying against what remained of a low stone wall near the rubble of a bigger house. Artillery had made quick work of it. Parts of chairs lay among the stones and slate. No stench of decaying bodies, only the scent of the splintered evergreens that hid this place from the view of anyone walking down the road. "They were lucky," he told her. "That could have been your house."

That rusted metal hub made a perfect bird bath. The first time Reg filled it, the jay – she called it, "ucello azzurro"– looked confused. It didn't take long for the noisy bird to figure it out. Gabby watched it bathe from her own perch on the low planting bench, about the width of fire step in a trench. Reg wasn't sure his back could take stretching out on that anymore.

"I piccoli uccelli torneranno," she said, her light eyes scanning the trees on The Montello across the river.

"Se i Tedeschi non hanno ucciso tutti." Luigi sank the hoe into moist soil and pretended to be eating something. " Li mangiano."

Germans eat – what – blue jays?

Eyes a blue five times lighter than the jay's feathers focused on the happy bird. "Così bella, e li uccidono. Uccidono bellezza. Tutto."

26

Gabby threw down a handful of sopping wet dirt, startling the jay. A flash of color from the hub of water to the sky, then gone. "Non Paolo," she said.

That bent old body leaned on the hoe handle. He pretended to be out of breath. "Naturalmente, non Paolo."

She was staring at ripples in the hub of water, her eyes unfocused, as if willing that blue jay to return.

"He'll come back," Reg told her. "He loves this place."

She bit her lower lip, reached up and took his hand, squeezed his fingers. Then she let go and took the hoe out of those rough, quiet hands. "Riposa ora," she said.

Wheezing, Luigi trudged out of the garden. His thick hand waved Reg to his side. "Al'altra casa."

She stopped digging. "Non prendete il fucile."

The old man started laughing. He put a hand on Reg's shoulder, used it to steady himself, like a crutch, aimed a finger back at her smirk, his thumb in air like a pistol hammer: "È 'un fucile, no?" That blistered thumb snapped down, then back up. With the same hand, he slapped his heart − "Boom!" − and he wobbled as if he had been shot. Then he started laughing again and led the way up the dirt road.

●

It was a bigger house − four windows, newer stone − about a kilometer north and behind the only real hill in the flood plain. If flat stones had not been set down to show the way, no one would have known it was there. Inside, plates and cups littered the floor to catch rain dripping through the roof. A minefield of them. The two little girls darted between them with ease. Luigi found a ladder at the side of the house. He gestured for Reg to climb up after him.

They walked the slate roof, hunting for leaks. It felt like being home, walking the slate, checking for loose pieces. A slater, even one from Rusthall or Speldhurst, would cost a small fortune, his father would say every time they got up there. A hammer and copper nails, a trained foot to detect the loose pieces, were all that were necessary. Reg found several loose pieces and renailed them before Luigi could climb back up with new slate. "These are fine," Reg told him, "just loose." Probably from the vibrations caused by the artillery crumps.

No one had scraped these tiles in years. Moss had taken root in the seams. Reg pointed to the yellow-green growth, peeled some back with his finger nails, scraped the tile edge with the splintered handle of the hammer. Luigi nodded, pulled a small knife from his waistband, handed it to Reg. The moss came up with ease, long cool strips of color, almost too pretty to hurl off the roof.

It took the rest of the day to finish. The girls had been sent out with lunch – sweet cheese and goat's milk – the first fresh milk he had tasted in two years. Teresa stayed hidden somewhere inside. He was grateful for that.

From up here, he could see a distant tower in the foothills. It looked like a castle in Kent and for a moment he felt as though he were looking across the countryside of his boyhood, where kings and queens actually had strolled, where knights had roamed. He pointed at the tower.

"Il Castello di San Salvatore." Luigi flung moss straight up with both hands and made the sound of an explosion. "Distrutto. Dai Tedeschi."

Even the Germans wouldn't shell a beautiful old castle, would they? And where were the goats the milk and cheese had come from? Why was no one using the road leading to the river? Where had all the people gone?

The two-year old gave him a handful of small yellow nuts when he came down off the ladder. For the first time, her big sister smiled at him. "Dai pini," she said, nodding at the stand of evergreens that followed the shallow slope toward the river. She showed him where to store the ladder – on its side near the hand pump of the well and the overgrown rosemary. Both girls walked part of the way up the hill with him, sharing the pine nuts. Suddenly, they turned and ran back down to the house and the dark figure in the doorway.

"Fu-chilly." Reg said.

The old man glanced over a shoulder, then laughed so hard he started coughing.

•

It rained off and on for a week, a warmer drizzle this time. Steam rose from low patches in the field and stretched out in long strands on the wind, like wisps of clouds over some far away landscape. At the table, Gabby used a crescent-shaped chopping tool to hack the joints of a rabbit. That skinless body had been hanging head down from a roof timber outside for the last two days. Still sinewed and deep red, the meat looked shiny, like jelly on a plate. No sign of buckshot. It must have been caught in a snare. In Rusthall, hares made their warrens in berry brambles. Nothing like that here.

"Where does he trap them?" Reg said.

She separated a hind quarter, tossed it into a pot of water at her feet and went to work on the other leg. What would she do with the head? He didn't want to see that. He stood and picked up his boots, took them to the door.

"Piove," she said, punctuating the word with a sharp chop through the leg joint.

"Grazie." He caught her little laugh, the quick shake of the head that made her light hair fly around her shoulder. He opened the door.

Teresa looked shocked to see him. She took a quick backward step, wiped rain from her face. "Giorno."

He checked the wall, ready to grab the shotgun before she could. Luigi must have taken it with him. Reg pulled the door open wider. The wet-haired woman pushed her daughters inside. They carried milk and cheese, but couldn't find a place on the blood-slick table to put them down. Gabby pointed to the bed with the chopping tool, grubby with stringy meat.

Teresa met her stare. " Posso entrare?"

After a glance at the spot the shotgun usually rested against, Gabby nodded and dumped the other hind quarter into the pot.

Her sister untied the blue head scarf, shook rain from her hair and stepped inside. She pointed to the roof. "La pioggia non cade dentro." When he squinted at her, she took a cup from near the hearth and held up it, again pointing at the roof timbers, her fingers fluttering in a downward motion to the cup, like rain. "Rimane fuori." She smiled at the milk and cheese on the bed. "Per te. Grazie."

She might as well have shot him. He had to brace himself against the back board holding the door slats together. He set his boots by the bed, picked up the paper holding the cheese, offered it to the girls. They looked at their mother, who nodded and smiled at him again. Little fingers dug like worms into the soft cheese, scooping it into their mouths. She patted the two-year old's head − "Sancia" − then moved behind the older girl, put her hands on her shoulders: "Nicoletta."

Reg pointed to the older girl − "Nicoletta" − and then the little one − "Sancia." The girls giggled with their mouths full. He tasted the cheese, said, "Mmm," and offered some to Gabby, who shook her head. But she was smiling, too.

"Dolce." Teresa smelled like rosemary. "Come il fiore di erba."

Setting the chopper on its side, Gabby wiped her hands on her apron, opened her arms. Her sister ran into the hug. They kissed each other on the cheeks and started talking, two machine guns never stopping to listen to the other. As if hypnotized, the little girls didn't stop staring at the women until Reg offered some the milk. They didn't bother looking at their mother before taking sips.

The tiny one, Sancia, squeezed in next to him on the edge of the bed. "Dormi qui?"

He offered her more cheese. Teresa saw them out of the corner of her eye. Those hard eyes had a glint of yellow in them now. She blinked, stopped talking long enough to nod at him. She set a tied bundle of rosemary across the top of a bowl on the chair: tiny blue flowers still dotted the green needles. A few minutes later, she was at the door, calling her daughters to her side.

Sancia jumped down, took three steps, then turned and ran back to hug him. Those tiny arms hurt his ribs. He covered his wince with a grin. Teresa wasn't smiling anymore. Her eyes looked watery, her lips trembled. She cleared her throat, barked something at the older girl, who might have been five, then spun on a heel and led her daughters back out into the drizzle, re-tying that blue scarf as she walked.

In the new silence, Gabby went back to work on the rabbit, dropping a long sprig of rosemary into the pot, humming what sounded like a lullaby under her breath. He stoked the fire. Dry, warm, full – safe. It didn't seem possible. Through the doorway, ground mist shrouded the garden and carried the weakening sound of footsteps slapping wet dirt.

"I know how to farm," he told the open door. "I can help. Teresa. Luigi. You." The hand chopper stopped moving. She turned, squinted at him.

"I'm not leaving," he said.

She kept staring at him. He started sweating. Maybe it was just his closeness to the fire. Then, with a single blow, she severed the rabbit's head, left it wobbling on the table. She handed him the blackened pot, nodded at the hearth. "Per favore, cucinarlo."

It was heavier than it looked. He placed the wire handle over the hook, steadied the pot to stop its swing. When he turned back, she was carrying the rabbit head to the garden. He watched her bury it in dark soil, the drizzle darkening her hair, new green surrounding her feet.

He laid on more wood, jabbed at the fire with the iron rod that felt warm from the stones it had been resting on.

Dry, warm, full, safe. Happy. *Possible.*

30

23 May, 1918

Fish stew simmered in the pot. The last drop of daylight faded up river. With a leg tucked under her on the chair, she was sipping tea made from steeped flowers – awful stuff that even smelled sour. He studied the wood pile by the hearth, wondered if they would actually need a fire tonight, the first really warm evening this year. Flecks of dust caught the dying sunlight, a ribbon of it running low over the table, less than the width of a cup from her fingers.

The door swung open so fast it banged into the wall. Luigi went straight to her, grabbed her wrist: "I Tedeschi. Sulla strada."

Pulling her toward the bed, the old man put a thick hand under the frame, pulled straight up, setting the bed on its edge. The rough wood slats supporting the mattress had spider webs of dust clinging to them. He kicked back the hides, grabbed the knot of a rope sticking through a floorboard, tugged on it. A small door cut out in the floor came free. He steered her to the opening, waved for Reg to join her.

It looked like an old root cellar. His uniform lay in a dark corner. On a knee, Reg grabbed it. It had been washed and folded. When was the last time it had looked like this? And it felt softer than he remembered. He stripped off his baggy clothes, kicked them into the hole Gabby was squeezing herself into – his webbing was down there, too, the trenching tool leaning against a side wall – and stepped into the uniform trousers.

"No, ti sparano!" Luigi jabbed a pointed finger at the root cellar. "Subito!"

The long tails of the grey shirt were still difficult to tuck in at the waist. The tunic felt bigger. He stepped into his boots, looked for the puttees as he went to the window. Nothing in the field. Yet. He turned and grabbed Luigi by the back of his shirt, pulling that bent back toward the hole in the floor. "Get in with her."

The old man tore free, went straight to the shotgun, began loading it. Outside, the scattering of pebbles. Age-damaged ears didn't hear it – he was too busy now fitting the little door over the hole, sliding the hides over it, reaching for the bed to pull it back into place.

Reg stopped him. "Wait!" He ran to the curtained alcove, snatched her shoes from the floor.

The old man nodded, moved the hides, opened the trap door. Reg tossed the shoes in beside her. She was sitting on a small pile of

31

clothes, shivering. Luigi slid the trap door into place, kicked the hides back over it, lowered the bed frame. He studied the uniform for a moment, shook his head, then went to the doorway, glanced outside, shut the door, his hands trembling as he aimed the shotgun at the wood slats.

The Germans would make quick work of him. Still nothing out the window. Reg gripped the gun barrel, stared into those sky-blue eyes, then eased the shotgun out of those quivering hands. "Trust me."

He opened the door, placed the gun barrel against that crooked back and prodded Luigi outside, forcing him to raise his arms.

Off the road and heading toward the garden, a small patrol – he counted six – stopped the moment they spotted him. All but one dropped to a knee and took aim. Reg pretended to be surprised. He took a step back so they could see him clearly. Slowly, he set the shotgun on the ground, then raised his arms.

The German still standing didn't have a rifle. He kept a hand on a hip holster as he walked toward the house. Even in twilight the silver on his uniform glinted. A Lieutenant. With the side of his boot, he nudged the shotgun toward the house. "Namen!"

"Don't speak Bosh," Reg said.

As the rest of patrol moved in, rifles at the ready, the skinny young officer tapped his own chest. "Oberleutnant Rommel."

The gray-haired man smiled and lowered his arms. "Luigi. DaPonte." He pointed to the open door. "Casa mia."

Lt. Rommel narrowed his shiny eyes and waved toward the house. Two from the patrol rushed inside. Things rattled in there: her tea cup, the chair. The mattress thudded against the floor.

"Non romperlo!" Luigi took a step toward the doorway, but a Corporal with a bayoneted rifle blocked his way.

The other two in the patrol – both Privates with no sleeve markings – had the old shotgun. They were laughing at it. One of them aimed it at the garden, pulled the trigger. Scatter shot made the old cart wheel hub jump. Water leaked from tiny new holes in it.

The Germans inside ran out, rifles poised to shoot. The Corporal ripped the shotgun from the Private, glanced at it, then flung it toward the craters in the field, glinting until it hit the soft earth.

Lt. Rommel hadn't flinched. His fingertips drummed the grip of his holstered handgun. He kept staring at Reg: "Namen, Engländer."

Reg tucked his chin to his chest, pointed at the scabbed over gash in his head. "I don't remember. Anything."

Long hard fingers undid the top button of Reg's tunic, felt for the neck string that held the identification disc. "Wo ist ihre identifikations," the officer said.

"Identification?" Reg patted his neck. "Must be lost."

Those shiny eyes narrowed into slits. The Lieutenant stepped to the doorway. His boots were muddy, but the soft black shafts were freshly oiled. He must have spotted something because he disappeared into the darkening room. The swoosh of material moving. Slow boot steps on the floorboards. A hand appeared in the doorway, holding the small black dress. Lt. Rommel peered around it: "Wo ist die Frau."

The Corporal found the little knife in Luigi's pocket, slipped it into his own. "Dov'è la donna?"

Sad blue eyes stared past the field to the river: "Lei è morta. Annegato nel fiume."

The stocky translator said something that sounded like "fluser drunken" and used the tip of his bayonet to move Reg and Luigi to the doorway. The Lieutenant let the black dress slip out of his fingers. Weathered fingers caught it as it hit the floor. The old man clutched it to his chest as if it were a treasure.

Testing their reactions, Lt. Rommel stepped carefully around the room. He put a boot on the mattress, now laying sideways off the bed frame, then knelt to check under the bed. He got up as cautiously as he walked. He glanced under the table, picked up the cup of tea, smelled it, dipped a boney finger in it, had a taste, frowned at its bitterness.

"Del fiore," Luigi said over his shoulder to the Corporal. "Tè."

At the wood pile, the skinny officer nudged small logs with the toe of a boot, picked up the iron rod, leaned it against the hearth wall. He looked into the pot, stirred the stew with the wooden spoon, tasted the broth. He spat it out as soon as it touched his tongue. Broth spattered on the fire. He jammed the big spoon back into the fish chunks. "Keine Frau machte dieses."

The Corporal laughed, then shoved Reg aside to clear the doorway. The Lieutenant strode outside: "Gefangenen. Die beiden."

The patrol formed two ranks. The Corporal nudged Reg and Luigi in between them. "Prigionieri," the Corporal said, nudging Reg and Luigi in between the two ranks the patrol had formed. "Tu e l'Inglese." And they all started walking around the side of the house.

The road had hardened, most of Spring already draining from it into the lower fields. The crunch of all those boots at march speed

33

reminded him of Catford and the first time he had drilled with the other new recruits. That sound had made him proud then, important even. He took a last look back at the garden, the small house.

Luigi was looking at it too. He had tears in his eyes, but wore a knowing smile. "Grazie."

•

In moonlight, the snowcapped Alps didn't look real. Silent now, they had a fairytale quality about them − something a writer might conjure for a bedtime story. He would never be able to write anything to match those mountains.

The road climbed north. Luigi started having trouble keeping up. Half a kilometer later, he stopped, bent over, out of breath. "Nessun respiro," he said. "Momento."

The Corporal, shoved him with the butt of his rifle.

Lt. Rommel barked at him: "Bleiben sie mit ihm."

The rifle lowered. The Corporal muttered something and took a few steps to catch up to the patrol that was already back up to marching speed. He pled his case to the Lieutenant. In that moment, the old man, still bent over, still wheezing, pulled a string from a trouser pocket. The identification disc glinted. Just as quickly, he jammed the necklace into his shoe. straightened up, smiled.

Reg turned away before the old fool could do something else daft, like wave. The Corporal stopped and walked back toward the sound of wheezing. The patrol kept to the road, climbing the long slope toward the castle tower.

•

It was only about three kilometers, but it took the better part of an hour, thanks to all the detours. The road was wider here, though segments of it had been blasted away. Chiseled stones lay scattered beside the rims of shell craters. Buildings reduced to rubble still had recognizable rooms. In one of them: a rag doll, singed brown and missing a leg, stuck between two vertical rails of what was left of a crib. Teresa's girls weren't safe anymore, not if this or another German patrol was roaming through the river valley. She would fight them. They would shoot her as soon as they saw her coming. There would be blood on her floor, flooding over the old stains of rain water. Did they shoot children, too? Part of him hoped they did. He didn't want to imagine what might happen to the girls if Fritz kept them alive.

A stone sign pointing east had *Susegana* carved into it. They got off the road there and headed straight toward the castle tower. It was

34

a fortress, a real medieval castle, pockmarked by artillery, but still there, still massive. Maybe that sign was wrong and the city was behind those high stone walls.

They never got inside. Taking a rutted cart path paralleling a castle wall, they trudged through an old cemetery and wound up at a makeshift pen, fenced by barbed wire that had been nailed to tall pine poles. All the others inside the wire wore the uniform of the Italian Army.

The three guards at the narrow gate treated Reg like a prize. They grabbed handfuls of his uniform, yanked on the buttons, pushed him, turned him, jabbed at him bayonets, pulled his hair, then shoved him toward the Italian soldiers, kicking him in the seat of the pants for good measure. Those guards stopped laughing when the skinny Lieutenant came over at a run.

Inside the wire, and suddenly realizing where he was, Lt. Rommel drew his pistol, then helped Reg to his feet. Backing away, his gaze fixed on the other prisoners, he got through the gate and glared at the big guard who smelled of cheese and looked as if he had been stealing everyone else's rations: "Dieser Engländer ist mein gefangener. Mein! Oberleutnant Erwin Rommel. Verstanden?"

The guards snapped to attention and saluted. The Lieutenant holstered his pistol and strode away. The shaky wire gate closed. Two chains secured it with padlocks.

One of the prisoners, just as thin as the others, their uniforms no longer fitting – how long had they been trapped here? – slipped a mud-stained brown blanket from his shoulders, held it out to Reg: "English, yes?"

Hearing his own language came as a shock. He swallowed road dust all those boots had kicked up. He felt the scratchy wool, handed back the blanket. "You need it more than I do."

Another soldier offered him a dented metal cup of water. It smelled of iron, like the hard water in the spa at Tunbridge Wells. It tasted slimy. But it was wet. He drank it all. "Grazie."

"Prego," the little man said, refilling the cup. "Tu parli Italiano?"

The soldier with the blanket was grinning. "You say the Italian?"

Reg shook his head. That skinny Lieutenant had already reached the cemetery, his capped head and narrow shoulders bobbing among the headstones, as if walking in a maze of jigsaw puzzle pieces. Near the gate, the fat guard sat on a barrel, leaned against his rifle. He looked hungry.

"Does he ever shoot anyone?" Reg said.

35

"No, no. He is – come si dice – grullo. Eh – idiota."

Reg laughed. He stepped away from the wire, sat in the dirt, stretched out on his back and studied the night sky. While the Italians whispered among themselves, he shut his eyes. She would be out of that root cellar by now, hanging that tiny black dress back up in its special spot in the nook. In the morning, she would sit in her garden and watch the confused blue jay hunt for water in its shot-up bird bath. His mother would be nipping off a rosebud or two, a low sun running down through the dark folds of Denny Bottom. Mr. Quaite would be standing at the curb, checking his pocket watch, waiting until 8 a.m. on the dot before unlocking his office door. Barry on top of Capt. Rodgers. All that blood leaking from his throat, that slow gurgle. The speed of the little raft, the sting of the icy river.

The stars here seemed farther away. How could they be the same ones he used to stare at from Toad Rock? He hoped Luigi had sense enough to get rid of the identification disc before that stocky Corporal found it on him.

"You are. . .good?" The blanketed soldier knelt beside him, a chunk of crusty bread in his hand. "Food?"

A clean, dry uniform, no lice. It wouldn't take long before those trouser rabbits found their way from the Germans and the Italians back to him. Reg let out a long breath. A clean, dry death wasn't the worst thing he could imagine.

He shut his eyes: "I'm fine."

BOOK TWO

THE QUEENS OWN

LETTERS, DIARY ENTRIES, AND DISPATCHES

30 DECEMBER, 1915
- 17 FEBRUARY,1918

Catford, Lewisham: Thursday, 30 December, 1915

Dear Mr. Quaite,

Full train yesterday after Bank Holiday. Thank you again for the Kipling. Perfect pocket size. Reading the mongoose story. Sorry I had no present for you.

Issued *Field Service Regulation* and new *Infantry Training* manuals. Tented until billets open up. Colour Sergeant Major Tranter has 18 years in and said we will have uniforms next week.

Catford, Lewisham: Monday, 10 January, 1916

Dear Mr. Quaite,

Thank you for the birthday cookies, shared with a new friend from Tunbridge Wells – Barry Yorke. His father manages the bell staff at The Lenton near The Pantiles. Still no uniforms. Drill 10 hours until 4:15, marching on parade ground. Shoes are the worst for it. Sergeant Major Goulds expects boots to be issued before week's end.

Catford, Lewisham: Thursday, 13 January, 1916

Dear Mr. Quaite,

As requested, here are the particulars: 5:30 a.m. bugled reveille, tea at 6:30, Jubilee Parade Ground drill until breakfast (8 a.m.). More drilling until lunch (noon). Back to marching drills until 4:15 p.m. Today's drill was on the Right Turn. Our primary instructor is someone our Regiment Commander (Lt/Col. Searles) met at cricket field. At least 60, the fellow wears a bowler. We call him Grandy – Grandpa and Dandy fitted together – a nickname Barry created, following the lead of his father who does the same thing with hotel guests as shorthand for the staff.

Some of us are assigned to work party chores, usually those who do poorly at drill. Most of us tend to mending clothes and shoes. Tent smells foul, like our grazing lowlands after a big downpour.

Catford, Lewisham: Sunday, 16 January, 1916

Church service at St. Laurence's. A cathedral. The old hand pump at Rushey Green still works! Entire battalion on parade ground to hear Maj. Corfe, A Company Officer in Command (OC) and new battalion number two. Served under Gen. Botha in German Southwest Africa. Uniforms now to be issued in Aldershot. We arrive there by month's end.

More foul language heard here before morning tea than in a year in Rusthall.

Catford, Lewisham: Tuesday, 19 January, 1916

Full moon last night and tonight. Happy to have enlisted and avoid assignment to a non-West Kent regiment, now a likelihood once the Military Service Act takes effect next week. All of us here are proud of The Queen's Own and cannot wait to pin on the Great White Horse of Kent insignia.

My shoes stitched up with cat gut from orchestra supply of fiddle strings. Not from cats at all, but sheep. First touch of football this afternoon. Short match called on account of corner kick beaning a senior officer walking past the part of the parade ground that serves as the pitch. Knocked his cap off and broke his eyeglasses.

Catford, Lewisham: Friday, 21 January, 1916

Even old hands like CSM Tranter grumble about the drudgery of drilling. Can march in ranks with eyes shut now. Allowed on tour of city after church this Sunday. Subaltern Rodgers leading. He is from here. We were scheduled to be billeted in town at private residence, but no longer, due to a big ruckus over a landlady who is now with child. Word is, one of ours is the father.

Catford, Lewisham: Sunday, 23 January, 1916

Grandy passed us off the square yesterday. Marched us out to Black Horse and Harrow, a pub since 1700. Not room enough for all of us.

Catford, Lewisham: Sunday, 23 January, 1916

Dear Mr. Quaite,

Our lead instructor told me that at first he mistook me for a Public Schooler because I was so well-spoken. I informed him that you were responsible for my true education and vocabulary. He tipped his hat to you.

Today we passed the guard and Lieut. Rodgers showed several of us St. Dunstan's College and Iona Close Orchard in city centre. Victorian gardens surrounded by grand homes, much like Dornden House. A heaven of ash, maples and fruit trees – apple, pear, plums, mulberry – impossible to be engulfed by city.

Saw *The London Gazette*. Mr. Kipling is cited for his argument in support of conscription. Finishing *The White Seal*. My favorite to date. Barry likes the *Parade Song of the Camp Animals*. He does not believe that you correspond with Mr. Kipling. He also does not agree that Rusthall or Royal Tunbridge Wells are part of the High Weald as he finds nothing high about them, though he has climbed Wellington Rocks like all of us have and explored our sweep's caves.

Catford, Lewisham: Tuesday, 25 January, 1916

Officially moved from the 118th Brigade, 39th Division to the 122nd, 41st as a result of losing local battalion status. The 11th is now the last to be added to the 122nd Brigade in the New Army.

Word from SM Goulds is that a new OC will take the reins in Aldershot owing to the poor state of Lt/Col. Searles who has not been medically cleared for combat.

Aldershot, Hampshire: Saturday, 29 January, 1916

Moved with the 10th Battalion. The garrison here is enormous. Barracks a relief from tent life. Hampshire resembles West Kent, but flatter. Train trip shorter than Tunbridge Wells to Catford Station. Also less crowded, our cars being added.

Aldershot, Hampshire: Tuesday, 1 February, 1916

Lt/Col. A. F. Townshend is our new OC, straight from the Scottish Rifles. Maj. Corfe remains our number two. CSM Tranter confided that Maj. Corfe's promotion to Lt/Col. has come through, effective upon our move to France.

Aldershot, Hampshire: Friday, 4 February, 1916

Uniforms issued this morning. New tunic, very stiff. Old pair of trousers. Boots to be fitted out tomorrow. The RWK insignia is the horse atop the crown. Horse on right lapel faces left, on left faces right. Some cannot keep that straight.

Lucky for me, I didn't put on the pyjamas my mother sent. One of our fellows, a bank clerk from Hawkenbury, was mercilessly ridiculed for wearing his. Most of us sleep in our greybacks, its flannel the only soft thing here. Some sleep in the buff. Warm in the barracks with all the bodies at close quarters. Noisy as well.

Aldershot, Hampshire: Thursday, 10 February, 1916

Rifles to be issued next week. Sgt. Maj. announced the 11th officially taken over by War Office. We will get new mess tins now. And socks.

Aldershot, Hampshire: Friday, 18 February, 1916

Rifles today. Refitted Magazine Lee-Enfields. Mine is new and in need of oiling. First drill with them. The sling buckle cuts into the shoulder. CSM had us remove them midway through drill. There is no manual for the rifle.

41

Aldershot, Hampshire: Monday, 21 February, 1916

Conformity being at the centre of everything here, any breach is treated with Field Punishment No. 1: the offender is tied to any immovable object and left for hours. SM Goulds says we should be grateful we aren't flogged, as is still the case with Indian troops. Barry came close to being disciplined this morning when he overcrowded the man marching ahead of him in ranks, causing both to tumble. Even CSM laughed, so neither got shackled. Had our rifles been loaded, it might have been deadly.

Aldershot, Hampshire: Thursday, 24 February, 1916

Rifle range this afternoon in groups of four, for safety. The kick of the MLE is substantial. The shells − .303 calibre − are longer than expected and sharp enough at the tip to puncture skin when touched. They get warm in our chest webbing even on cold days like today. Chamber jams are uncommon. Noise of the range is constant. My right shoulder is sore and my headache remained even after lunch. All this for an hour of missing the target. Not cut out for this.

Aldershot, Hampshire: Monday, 3 March, 1916

A demonstration by sharpshooters reveals how far we have to go to master the MLE. One of them trained by Sgt. Instructor Snoxall managed 34 rounds in his "mad minute," all striking the target, just one foot wide, at 270 meters. The record is 38, set by SI Snoxall two years ago. The cock-on-closing of the shorter bolt is responsible for the high rate of fire. You would swear you were hearing a machine gun.

We are all properly humiliated.

Aldershot, Hampshire: Saturday, 25 March, 1916

Dear Mr. Quaite,

Apologies for not writing. We are now allowed access to Smith-Dorien Soldiers Home. They have billiards, private baths and best of all a library. I'm reading Thackeray. You were right about his being from Tunbridge Wells but writing like a Londoner. Maples are in leaf. RWK has its own newspaper: *Invicta − The Queen's Own Gazette.* Col. Brock of regimental staff keeps it as an official diary. Linotype machines have their own building here. Noisy as the rifle range. Digging trenches and filling them in for the last week. Soggy ground makes for heavy lifting. And mud fights.

Aldershot, Hampshire: Wednesday, 29 March, 1916

Marksmanship testing began after lunch. Barry stands at the top of
A Company with no missed targets. He never fired any model Lee-
Enfield before either, but I cannot hit the target with even half my
rounds. Discouraging. Not looking forward the balance of testing.
Lt/Col. Corfe, just promoted, observing for most of the day. Without
his hat, he looks a completely different person. Very high forehead
with balding dome. Even smiling, he looks serious. They say he
thinks like a sergeant, not an officer. If true, we won't be in battle peril
from the Second Lieuts., all Public Schoolers and paid no attention to
by CSM Tranter or our squad Sgt. Jeffs.

Aldershot, Hampshire: Sunday, 2 April, 1916

Dear Mr. Quaite,
I am certified as a Marksman! Only 6 in A Company have to undergo
re-testing. A very low bar according to Sgt. Jeffs. Barry received
Expert certification, one of only 3 presented. Lt/Col. Corfe shook his
hand.
The buffet at Smith-Dorien costs 3 day's pay. Real bacon and fresh
berries. Fits your definition of "good value." Little else to spend on,
not being permitted to pass the guard yet.

Aldershot, Hampshire: Wednesday, 12 April, 1916

Noticed at breakfast of our moving to the front. No date yet.
Began bayonet training, with plungers – spring-loaded and dulled to
preserve the heavy bags. The MLE gets heavy after an hour of low
carry. Not allowed to shoulder a bayoneted rifle. Ears get lost.
They call our helmets "tin hats." Wish they were that light.
Everyone's neck is aching from the weight of the steel. We are
required to cinch the strap to prevent slippage. Sweat sharpens the
leather into a cutting tool. No salve for raw necks.
Drill with full packs and webbing – 90 pounds – for two hours daily,
going nowhere around the perimeter of the parade ground, while
new recruits drill in the middle portions. "We have them surrounded"
has become our battalion slogan.

Aldershot, Hampshire: Monday, 17 April, 1916

Gas masks today. Hot and sticky. The straps loosen with movement.
Holding a mask fast by hand is not permitted. Several disciplined for
this, most during bayonet drill. My mask fogs when tightened. A
blind man with a bayoneted rifle. Should scare Fritz at the first sight
of me.

Aldershot, Hampshire: Thursday, 20 April, 1916

Lectures this afternoon on the Chlorine gas. Lung burn is felling most
on the front exposed to the stuff. A new mask is already in use. Better
design than ours and longer lasting. But ours are effective. Have yet
to attempt firing with them on. Not keen to try that.
Good Friday tomorrow.

Aldershot, Hampshire: Saturday, 22 April, 1916

Dear Mr. Quaite,
St. George's Day tomorrow and we passed the guard. Barry and I saw
the city. Streets full of lorries unloading goods and the shouts of
drivers. Dogs eat everything that falls into the street. It reminded
Barry of Tunbridge Wells when the spa season begins.
The younger women must be in hiding. We saw only old men and
matrons. No one says hello to us. No doubt the town will be glad to
see us leave. We have no desire to take another tour.
We are to be given a half day for Easter Monday. The buffet will be
busy.

Aldershot, Hampshire: Tuesday, 25 April, 1916

Dear Mr. Quaite,
New helmets, mess tins, actual bayonets, webbing and extra socks
issued today. We are required to lunch on mess tin rations. The
corned beef – Bully Beef to all here – is tasty even cold. The
Maconochie is horrible stuff. A stew with only peas identifiable.
Inedible cold, not much improved warmed on the small alcohol
burners, yet some finished up the entire can. The evaporated milk
with jam spooned from Tickler tins are the only decent food in the kit.
Plum and apple. Strawberry promised. The No. 9 biscuits are good
only when dipped in tea. Tooth breakers otherwise. We might as well
be chewing bullets.

Aldershot, Hampshire: Thursday, 28 April, 1916

Dear Mr. Quaite,
Measured for new uniforms but no one expects to receive them.
Winding puttees from ankle to below knee. The cotton tape stronger
than expected. If too tight, the likelihood of trench foot is increased.
There is a manual on puttees but not on the MLE rifle. Typical
infantry logic
There are mulberry trees off the cricket field. They are strictly off-
limits.

Aldershot, Hampshire: Saturday, 30 April, 1916

Dear Mr. Quaite,

No one is permitted off grounds until further notice. CSM says that means our move up is imminent.

The new uniforms did arrive after all. Trousers stiff, the seams much stouter than my old pair. More weight for the pack. Still, the finest suit of clothes I have ever owned.

Moolenacker Farm, near Strazeele, France
Wednesday, 3 May, 1916

Dear Mr. Quaite,

My first sighting of an ocean! Only the Channel, but rough and choppy. Several down with sea sickness, including Barry.

The train ride inland was a nightmare of jostling until past HQ at St-Omer. People filled the streets to cheer us as we marched through Strazeele to a farm close enough to the front to hear the rumble of artillery.

France is full of rolling hills turning into short plains then back again. Fewer trees than back in Blighty — what the Army regulars call England. We are now back in tents. I ate French cheese. Hard as pebbles.

Moolenacker Farm, near Strazeele, France
Sunday, 5 May, 1916

Dear Mr. Quaite,

The constant thunder of the big guns sounds like a distant storm always approaching, never arriving. It is only quiet for a few hours at night. Some are already shaking from the noise and jump when a Big Bertha goes off. SM Goulds says our artillery is the equal of Fritz's. Sgt. Jeffs disagrees. "Out-calibered" is how he put it.

Live bayonet drills tomorrow, in half packs. So much different training being conducted that in every direction there are men flinging themselves into frenzies. A circus.

Moolenacker Farm, near Strazeele, France
Thursday, 11 May, 1916

Mills bomb training after breakfast. Sgt. Jeffs is a master at it, even in a gas mask. Most of us can hurl the grenade 15 meters. Sgt. throws it like a cricket ball 30 meters and more, with a high arc. Truly inspiring for such a small man.

Advanced gas mask drilling requires map reading and signal flag recognition. Impossible tasks once the mask begins to sweat.

Sniper qualifying tomorrow. Barry excited. The rest of us have no chance.

Moolenacker Farm, near Strazeele, France

Tuesday, 16 May, 1916

Dear Mr. Quaite,

Aircraft flew close enough to hear and see today. We hoped they were ours.

Full battalion addressed by OC and SM to boost morale. Extra portions at lunch, with a ration of rum. We are to be given one each morning and another each afternoon for the duration. Sweet and dark brown in the communal mug Cpl. Wiggins keeps a hand on after dispensing from the jug. Better than Navy grog we are told.

Trenching techniques have been fitted to the chalky soil here. Pages and pages of manual on it. Engineered like bridges. Once past the surface crust, the earth is crumbly, nothing like our sandstone. Going down more than a meter is a trick, using shoring-up boards that require a firm back to hold in place while digging. Pity us if it rains.

Moolenacker Farm, near Strazeele, France

Wednesday, 24 May, 1916

Dear Mr. Quaite,

Half moon tonight, beautiful anywhere else. Still mastering trench making. Complicated for a ditch. Communication trenches are straighter than Fire trenches, which follow a Grecian Key pattern of zigzags. Parapets are bags of anything, including old jam tins, set to the front firing side. Parados are berms at the rear. The manual specifies each must follow a natural contour. Barry strutted about like an instructor, pretending to be an art critic while complaining of our shortcomings as trench makers. A good laugh.

The fire step here has to be braced off the slope or it will sink to an unusable level. Ladders are kept on their sides until readied for climbing, to prevent use by the enemy – one of Fritz's favorite stunts according to Sgt. Jeffs.

Going out of the trench in full gear is no longer done. Too slow. Webbing only is the approved style, and no bayonets fixed unless so ordered when climbing out. Going over is like a queue none want to stand in. We are 3 on the ladder at all times until the last is over the top. CSM times each company. Ours is not among the leaders.

We get to wire cutting in the morning.

Between Armentieres and Ploegsteert, France
Sunday, 28 May, 1916

In trenches to relieve the 9th Division, 2nd Army after a full day's march in full pack. The nearest town is famous in song for its women. Unlikely we will get to see it or them. Did see a working windmill, as yet spared from shelling. A noisy contraption. Constant groaning, like children with stomach aches.

I thought the sound of artillery would be louder, but it is still in the near distance to our north. The OC toured our line, bent over to keep his cap below the parapet the entire way. He passed directly by me. Grey haired with a fringe brown moustache and dark eyebrows, a questioning look on his face, like a judge. Very proper in every regard. An honour to serve under his command.

Our caps, not worn in the trench, bear the abbreviated RWK emblem: horse rampant over a banner containing *Invicta* – our motto. Lt/Col. Corfe wore his when he assumed command of the trench down our line. He was scolded by SM Goulds and promptly strapped on his tin hat. Our No. 2 never stands idle and arrived at our post unannounced like an ordinary soldier reporting. He barked at Barry for having his helmet pushed back while sitting on the fire step. Not a man to cross. It is now so quiet we can hear Fritz singing.

Somewhere in France: Tuesday, 30 May, 1916

Dear Mr. Quaite,

New censorship rules are in effect. Some parts of this and future letters may be blacked out.

We are in trenches south of Ploegsteert, called Plug Street by everyone here. Have yet to fire a shot or see the enemy, though artillery explosions – crumps – are all around us.

No Man's Land is a garbage dump, littered with discards from trenches on either side. One part looks like a bomb went off in a laundry – bits of clothing trapped in the barbed wire and snagged on the support stakes.

Lt/Col. Townshend ventured out before dawn to test the footing. Did not draw fire. Sgt. Jeffs advised against it. This is a well-dug trench, fully shored up and with duckboards lining the bottom. Very happy we did not have to dig it.

Between Armentieres and Ploegsteert, France
Friday, 2 June, 1916

Shelled this morning. Spent most of the afternoon rebuilding parapets. A Fritz machine gun is active to our right flank, where the 10th Battalion is holding the line. Sentry duty tonight. No moon. Will not be able to see more than 20 meters.

There is a 2nd Lieut. Yorke in our battalion. No relation to Barry.

Somewhere in France: Tuesday, 6 June, 1916

Dear Mr. Quaite,

A 3-inch Fritz shell − a Whiz Bang, for its sound − hit so close it caused Cpl. Wiggins to drop the rum jug. The single greatest calamity in battalion history, according to Sgt. Jeffs. He and Capt. Rodgers went over to cut wire and lob grenades in retaliation, but were forced back by a barrage. We were all up on fire steps and shooting over their heads. Not certain any of us hit anything but air.

Rain in late afternoon. The trench is already a swamp. And no rum!

Somewhere in France: Saturday, 10 June, 1916

Dear Mr. Quaite,

Had 2 letters from my mother, plus yours. Thank you. Please visit her if you can and convince her I am well. So many coming down with coughs − a trench sickness, brought on by the damp and close quarters.

Our supply of rum was replenished straight away after SM Goulds learned of Capt. Rodgers' foray into the wire with Sgt. Jeffs. The SM is the last person to anger. He is said to have killed a man with a single punch in a pub near Sevenoaks − and the victim was reportedly once his friend! SM promised to shoot the next man who went over the top without orders, regardless of rank.

We have not seen Sgt. Jeffs in 3 days. Capt. Rodgers has not spoken to any of us since the incident. Cpl. Wiggins acts as though nothing happened, going down the trench dispensing from his jug morning and afternoon.

Sentry duty is the most frightening assignment. The silence and the gloom of night drizzle make me feel as though I'm watching a graveyard, waiting for the dead to rise.

Between Armentieres and Ploegsteert, France
Tuesday, 13 June, 1916

A small raiding party came at our position last night. Repelled by volley fire. Barry thinks he got one, but no bodies in the wire this morning. Fritz tests our line routinely, usually with Whiz Bangs. For such a small shell, the speed of it creates a shock wave that jolts even the biggest of our troops. The enemy is not able to bring up the heavier guns. Fortunate for us. Many of those big shells hitting north of Plugstreet. Loud as locomotives in the air.

Between Armentieres and Ploegsteert, France
Sunday, 18 June, 1916

Chaplain unable to perform service. Being taken back to field hospital. Trench fever fells another. Lice a problem now. Chatting seams with candle flames. A dozen men without trousers in the trench at any given time, all chatting cuddies, but otherwise ready to take the fire step and shoot. L/Cpl Doverton said he'd rather kill a trouser rabbit than a Fritz, but he's unwilling to get shot with his trousers off.
The 10th Battalion lost 3 of theirs in a wire cutting raid yesterday. One is still out there, to be taken off tonight. Stretcher carriers may be the bravest among us all.

Somewhere in France: Saturday, 24 June, 1916

Dear Mr. Quaite,
Thank you for your long letter and congratulations on your new linotype machine. I am anxious to see it in action.
We have had our most uneventful week to date. Barry suspects Fritz has abandoned his trenches opposite or moved farther north. Impossible to tell until we send a raiding party out. I hope I am not selected for it.
When the sun shines, steam rises from the trenches and from No Man's Land. This soil is reluctant to give up the rain it collects. Changed my puttees – ankle wraps – and put on clean socks to avoid trench foot, which CSM Tranter claims is worse than trench fever because with the former a man can lose a foot. There is nothing pleasant about trench life, even when the wind freshens and the air is not filled with Whiz Bangs.

Between Armentieres and Ploegsteert, France
Wednesday, 28 June, 1916

First time going over. Barry, Sgt. Jeffs, me and 3 others from another company, one of them a subaltern, went under the wire, bayonets fixed. No sign of Fritz. He must have slid away to the north. Sgt. Jeffs wanted to lob in a grenade for good measure, but the 2/Lieut. countermanded him. The crawl back was worse. Worried the entire time that snipers would have heard us and hurried down to use us for pot shot target practice. Did not happen, thankfully.

My tunic and trousers completely soaked and muddied. Even a long shakeout can't dislodge the stuff. MLE clean, though. Never touched the ground. Got high marks from Sgt. Jeffs on that.

Between Armentieres and Ploegsteert, France
Friday, 30 June, 1916

Plastered with everything in Fritz's local arsenal in retaliation for the raid two days ago. Pinned down all day. Several direct hits with a dozen or more killed within 10 meters of me and Barry, including a 2/Lieut. Shrapnel from Whiz Bangs injured many more. Fortunate that the enemy's heaviest guns are too distant to be targeted at us, or there would be no more 11th Battalion.

Between Armentieres and Ploegsteert, France
Saturday, 8 July, 1916

Over a week now and we have still not been ordered to take the empty trench opposite. Trench talk full of insults for the OC and battalion staff.

When the mud dries, it comes off in clumps, but some always remains in the wool, staining it a lighter color. I was called "Dapple Boy" more than once. Kinder, I suppose, than "Spotted Pig," which I feared might also be coming my way.

Our trench cookers are going day and night. No need to conceal the flames or smoke.

Between Armentieres and Ploegsteert, France
Thursday, 14 July, 1916

Barry got his helmet shot off by a sniper this morning. Stood up on the fire step to add a bag of jam tins to the parapet. Knocked down to the duck walk. The moment he got back up the entire trench erupted in laughter. He cursed us all more than he did Fritz. The bullet only dented his tin hat on the side. Several of us offered him more jam tins.

Capt. Rodgers lectured on the wisdom of the OC not sending us over to the trench opposite. We would have been easy targets and could not have sealed off an assault from the north end.

Somewhere in France: Sunday, 16 July, 1916

Dear Mr. Quaite,

The copy of *The Gazette* your letter said you put in the post did not reach me. CSM Tranter restricts all publications, including books, which he hates because they weigh so much and would slow us down if and when we actually move out. I have secreted my Kipling. This would be the week of festival on Rusthall Commons. Your letter did not mention it. Has it been cancelled on account of the war? Madge was to bring you a pudding for it.

The chief problem here is boredom. We listen to the thunder of artillery all day, the air rattles with the heaviest of the explosions. Sgt. Jeffs can distinguish a Coal Box − very large shell, not quite as big as the Jack Johnson − by its sound and the heavy black cloud of gas it produces. Fortunately for us, these are crumping well north, above Plug Street.

Got to use my Hussif to mend a sleeve tear. Good thread and needle and thimble. L/Cpl Wiggins calls it our most valuable tool and is constantly after our Regimental SM to restock the Finnigans No. 6 Comfort Boxes the "housewife" comes in, along with other essentials, including a tin of worthless anti-fly cream.

Between Armentieres and Ploegsteert, France
Wednesday, 19 July, 1916

Major assault planned. The 11th will support with enfilading fire directed at a specific spot along a salient. Our goal will be to prevent Fritz from taking that ground. A frenzy of MLE cleaning. Not easy in rain.

Between Armentieres and Ploegsteert, France
Monday, 24 July, 1916

No one knows when we move up. The trench opposite has been silent for such a long while now we no longer walk stooped over in the fire trench. Got my first look at a dugout. A dank cave, shored with ribbed metal. Actual bunks inside. Supposedly safe from artillery, but SM says a Flying Pig would cave it in on a direct hit and a Jack Johnson would obliterate it. Have yet to see either.

Somewhere in France: Thursday, 27 July, 1916

Dear Mr. Quaite,

I will do my best to translate the trench talk. The inconsistent shorthand the infantry uses confuses all of us. Sgt Jeffs calls one type of trench mortar a "sausage," while L/Cpl Wiggins calls it a "Rum Jar." Everyone else calls it a "Flying Pig." It is 5 feet long and weighs 298 lbs and has a lighted tail fuse that goes out as soon as the shell begins to descend. That's our cue to run for cover.

When we first arrived in this trench, we were told "new loot" was headed our way. Most of us thought it would be tins from home. Turns out it was a new crop of 2/Lieuts, replacements for those lost up the line. The 11th got one, but nobody has seen him yet. Rumored he went missing en route.

I learned to cook on a brazier – a sort of short chimney that stands up like a bucket. Heats Bully Beef in no time, much faster than our small Tommy cookers. Also very nice to stand next to in rain.

Our position occupies the-flank. No direct fire in weeks. A new push is rumored. We spend all our time cleaning and outfitting. Gas mask drills every day. The moment the gas mask is removed, the stench of us returns.

Between Armentieres and Ploegsteert, France
Tuesday, 1 August, 1916

Moving day. We take the most roundabout route to remain out of sight and convince Fritz we are still in our old positions.

Communication trench crawling with rats. They swim through the mud puddles and scamper over the duckboard faster than we can. CSM said the only reason we don't see them in our Fire Trench is because the rats are smarter than we are.

Permitted a half day for sleep in a dug-out, all of us rotating through every two hours. Feels odd to be standing outside of a fortified space, listening to snoring so close inside and the explosions of heavy artillery too close outside. Discussed with Barry, who called this our own private No Man's Land.

The ground shakes with the heaviest explosions. We must be less than 10 km from the main action.

Dear Mr. Quaite,

We have been told we have arrived, but no one knows where we are actually. The horizon is constantly exploding. Giant black clouds darken the rainy gloom, then the shockwaves reach us, rattling our mess tins and occasionally worrying the fire steps loose. What must it be like up the line, where the trenches are being bombarded? Lt/ Col. Townshend ordered a special additional ration of rum for today only. He sent Lt /Col. Corfe through to accompany the post. Sgt Jeffs said this was infantry ritual to make sure each of us got what might be the last letter we would ever receive. I got two from Madge, plus yours. As I look about me at all of us reading notes from home while the ground shakes and the air shatters, I now think of war as an actual place, not only between enemy lines, but also between what lives inside us and what waits for us under those black clouds. No wonder then that when reading the post, we all look to be in a trance, suspended in personal No Man's Lands for that instant, and foolish enough to feel safe.

Here, tomorrow is a swindler.

Between Armentieres and Ploegsteert, France
Thursday, 17 August, 1916

Our guns have begun a major barrage up the line. The thunderous noise is without stop. We are moving up, again by side routes. Each time I brace myself against the concussion of an explosion, my hand feels the tremors in the trench walls. Some walls have collapsed despite the shoring. We dig detours, scavenge duckwalk and sand bags, fashion new parapets, then walk on to find the same situation. SM said this is the job of all those on the flanks.

Barry is anxious to get to the point of attack. So are a few others. Impossible to have a conversation without shouting. We stuff our ears with the wool patches from our Hussifs, but the blasts get through. The small shells make a dull thudding. The larger ones sound like trains overhead, their iron wheels screeching on the track. At the junction of a Communication trench and the Fire trench we now occupy, a signpost reads, *Somme 3 km*, with arrows pointing in every direction. Another signpost, less than 10 feet away, reads, *Blighty ???*, with no arrows. We have found the wide middle of the battleground now, not quite at shooting distance, but not out of range either.

Between Armentieres and Ploegsteert, France
Sunday, 20 August, 1916

Answering letters from Madge and Mother. Nothing to say that
would not cause them worry. Stretcher carriers come past in both
directions, full of wounded one way, empty the other. Capt. Rodgers
says this is the only way to know for certain where the fighting is.
We will take up a new position in the morning, moving with gas
masks on and bayonets fixed. It doesn't feel that we are actually that
close to the action.

Somewhere in France: Tuesday, 29 August, 1916

Dear Mr. Quaite,

I have marched more miles in trenches over the last two weeks than I
have walked during the rest of my life. Yet our progress, by the
calculations of those who have experienced this before, amounts to
less than 4 km as the crow flies. "Circuitous" has entered our
vocabulary as an obscenity.

The rain halted 2 days ago. We were turned back on our advance.
Every place we go is damaged. There is a giant crater visible behind
us now, as much as 20 feet deep, the result of a Jack Johnson. It might
be the safest place here.

Have yet to take aim on Fritz. Wondering if we are chasing ghosts.

Near the Somme, France: Friday, 1 September, 1916

Took support positions and began relieving the 55th Division at the
front line. The 10th is moving out ahead of us. Conditions stark.
Everyone solemn now, even Barry, who has refrained from his
pranks and jokes. This worries all of us.

Near the Somme, France: Monday, 11 September, 1916

After two days at Montaubon Alley, we followed the 10th Battalion,
passing through the 23rd Middlesex, to the support line N.E. of
Delville Wood yesterday. The 10th is now taking heavy shelling to
our right.

Near the Somme, France: Saturday, 16 September, 1916

OC Lt/Col Townshend died today of wounds sustained yesterday, our first encounter with the enemy. Heavy barrage from our side at 6.0 (6 a.m.), followed by mechanical machines on continuous track treads moving toward the German positions. We followed on, taking cover behind the machines, joining the 15th Hampshires and taking the Flers trench, full of Germans. Most surrendered. Some ran off toward the village. Not able to tell if those I aimed at were felled by my bullets or another's. Did not feel real.

Somewhere in France: Monday, 18 September, 1916

Dear Mr. Quaite,

By now you have read of our first full action and the loss of our OC. Lt/Col Townshend led a small group back to Switch Trench, which we had successfully cleared in the first two hours of battle. There he was struck by shrapnel.

The field we advanced over was filled with flattened men. Our newest weapon − "tanks" − drove directly over many of them, whether still alive or dead. Our own artillery was directed in progression as we advanced, at times falling short and causing us to halt out in the open, with no cover except the bodies of our fallen. Two men in front of me were there one second, then disappeared the next, falling away like laundry sacks. I could not tell if that was the result of enemy artillery or our own.

Bullets striking a soldier make a thudding sound, similar to my mother punching down bread dough on her kitchen work board. The report of individual rifles cannot be distinguished through all the crumps and the awful noise of those "tanks."

Our casualties numbered over 350, including 13 officers. We fired blindly during our advance and later took careful aim at the retreating enemy. The exuberance I had expected was absent. I felt numbed, yet able to see detail, overtaken by something unfeeling, perhaps because we have been trained to focus on targets, not people. The village of Flers is half-demolished. What is left standing has been ransacked. Most of the people have left or are in hiding. Once the smell of gunpowder drifts off, the stench of waste and the corpses takes over. No one will be able to live here again.

Mericourt l'Abbe Somme, France
Wednesday, 20 September, 1916

Lt/Col. Townshend buried in Heilly Station Cemetery at Mericourt l'Abbe Somme. A handful assembled around our new OC Lt/Col. Corfe and adjutant Lieut. Puttick. SM Goulds reported new drafts coming our way from the Royal Fusiliers and at least 8 officers coming from HQ Base. This must mean we will be put back in action shortly.

Somewhere in France: Monday, 2 October, 1916

Dear Mr. Quaite,

The 11th has been remade and now does not resemble the battalion we trained with. We are subject to orders of unfamiliar officers. Moon waxing tonight to half. The growing brightness does not benefit us as we are without overhead protection. Fritz has fortifications in place and is well concealed.

I have two letters from you regarding previous posts and will answer them as soon as we are resupplied.

La Barque at the Somme, France: Wednesday, 4 October, 1916

Relieved the New Zealanders on the flank of Gird Trench and the redoubt they called the Circus, near Eaucourt. The ridge before us overlooks La Barque and a portion of the Gird Trench that Fritz still controls. Barry went out on a scout patrol and said he could see the Germans moving in the trench behind their barricades. He was not permitted to sharpshoot. We all take that as a signal we will launch a surprise assault, devised by Lt. Col. Corfe.

The shelling continues. We lose men just sitting idle. There is no way back.

La Barque at the Somme, France: Sunday, 8 October, 1916

Over the top at 13.45 yesterday. Hit straight away by machine gun fire from both flanks. Advance stymied almost instantly. Sunken road leading to La Barque impassable. Cannot determine our losses, but we remained pinned down through nightfall.

Barry and I built a parapet out of bodies, of which there was no shortage, and helped drag the wounded behind it. Blood continues to seep out of the dead for hours. It goes yellow, then dark brown as it dries. One of the men must have worn cologne into battle. That odd sweet odor floated over us, along with the reek of body fluids, until the 12th East Surreys rescued us.

Stretcher carriers still moving the wounded. One was Capt. Richardson, with us for less than a fortnight.

Somewhere in France: Thursday, 12 October, 1916

Dear Mr. Quaite,
A full moon tonight over Ribemont. We fell back here two days ago, relieved by the 23rd Middlesex. There are fewer than 100 of us remaining and only 4 surviving officers. All of us would likely have perished had the 123rd Brigade not arrived in support during the early evening hours.

I look at the faces of those who survived the assault and do not recognize even those I trained with. Barry Yorke (of Royal Tunbridge Wells) has not spoken to me or anyone in two days. Some men are now startled by any sound in the trench – a dropped mess tin or a boot slipping – but remain unaffected by the crumps exploding a few kilometers away.

My tunic looks as though I had been shot 20 times or more for all the blood of others dried into it. My trousers are mud-caked stiff to the point that it actually hurts to walk in them. I do not have the bottle to unwind my puttees and remove my boots. No one grooms himself – easier to scratch than to wash up.

Lieuts. Henderson and Bainton are to be put forward for the Military Cross. Lieut. Bainton, a Transport Officer, brought up rations and water despite the enfilading fire.

Though we could see the machine guns firing on us, we were unable to return effective fire. Barry devised a blind of corpses to sharpshoot from, but the bodies kept getting shot away. One of them was Lieut. Prior, whose body came apart in the heap, held together in an unrecognizable shape by strands of his uniform.

Even Sgt. Jeffs could not hurl a Mills bomb far enough to reach the gun line. The action was hopeless from the start, though we are told now that important progress was made. The field we left resembled a cemetery of the unburied.

Lt/Col. Corfe sat with us in silence for over an hour, offering and dispensing rum himself to any who wanted it, finding few takers. The 11th now resembles the village of Flers and equally as irreparable.

Ribemont, France: Sunday, 15 October, 1916

250 new replacements arrived from the 2nd line of the Royal East Kent Mounted Rifles. A proud bunch, led by a Major Beadle. Sgt. Jeffs has served with him and gives him high marks. Barry and I wonder how many of them will still be with us after the next battle.

It is quiet here. The food is good, even the wine. It feels like being a private room in the middle of a noisy bash. If only we could stay.

Reninghelst, Flanders: Friday, 27 October, 1916

Moved under new moon with the 10th by rail to Reninghelst, S.E. of Ypres. Horrible conditions. Trenches left in shambles by our 1st Batt. Difficult to repair with Fritz on the crest above us, overlooking all approaches. The mud is slime and it is everywhere.

Somewhere in Flanders: Thursday, 2 November, 1916

Dear Mr. Quaite,

There is a trench newspaper here, *The Wipers Times*, named for the pronunciation of the Belgian town nearby (Ypres). Mostly "Tommy Talk" and satire. Barry intends to contribute copy to it.

We await materiel for repairing the trenches. The more wood and sand bags they provide us, the more we seem to need. The trench walls continue to give out. We dare not lean against them. The fire steps sink the moment we stand on them. Sand bags frequently slide down of their own accord from the parapet and bury anyone in their path. It is worse when Fritz bombards us. Rivers of mud spew down onto us off the slope our trench is built into – the worst spot imaginable. For hours afterward, mud seeps through the trench walls, filling the bottom above ankle deep. Walking is a chore and shifting positions is work. Shoveling is pointless.

They call this place "the Salient." We have a different name for it – not fit for publication.

I had three letters from my mother, who said she had seen you at market. Prices are firm and rising, so income from the farm is steady, but necessities are in short supply. Is it true that bread is now over 8d? Over a week's pay for me.

There is rumor that a Brown Bess musket from Wellington's 1815 assault was found buried in mud back at the Somme. I thought you especially would delight in that, and I will try to confirm. Enjoy the bonfire on the Commons this Sunday for Guy Fawkes Day. We will all have our cookers going, rain or no rain.

The Salient, Ypres, Flanders: Saturday, 25 November, 1916

The moon is gone. So dark it is not possible to see Barry's face next to me. Perfect night for Fritz to attack. My skin is clammy from mud and worry. A scream inside me claws at my throat. Eating plum jam in the midst of a nightmare.

The Salient, Ypres, Flanders:
Wednesday, 13 December, 1916

Only 4 lost to shelling to date – all on the north end where Capt.
Rodgers is in charge. Advised of a promotion to Lance Corporal.
Doubles my pay. Nowhere to spend it.
New wood hauled in last week. A relief to stand on something dry.
The betting odds are these boards will sink by Christmas.

Somewhere in Flanders: Thursday, 21 December, 1916

Dear Mr. Quaite,
A happy Christmas to you in advance and thank you for the muffler.
It will help fight the trench fever felling so many. I am enclosing a
cheque made out to you drawn on Capt. Rodgers' account to cover
the cost of a new hat that Madge has picked for herself and one for
you. If the 12s/6d is insufficient, please let me know and I will send
the balance. Officers here carry cheque books in case of capture. Capt.
Rodgers' account is at Cox & Kings Bank in Germany, but assures me
the funds will be routed through Switzerland.
My promotion to Lance Corporal will be announced at the New
Year's Honours. Barry Yorke is also getting his chevron. CSM Tranter
is presenting. Sgt. Jeffs will pay the Regimental Tailor himself to sew
them on – he claims he does not trust either of us to do that job well
enough, but we know he is proud of our advancement.
There are now only 22 of our original group left.
The Wipers Times has Barry's contribution in it. It is quite good:
"Building Land For Sale: Build That House on Hill 60. Bright, Breezy
& Invigorating. Commands Excellent View of Historic Town of
Ypres. For Particulars, Apply: Bosch & Co. Menin." You are welcome
to reprint it in *The Rusthall Gazette.*
The Sherwood Foresters started the magazine earlier this year and
change the title each time they move to a new location. It is presently
The Salient News.

The Salient, Ypres, Flanders:
Sunday, 24 December, 1916

Almost midnight. No moon. Doggo, except for the rain. Doing stag –
one of a dozen sentries, all privates. One week until I become a Lance
Jack. With the doubling of pay and all I'm owed for the cigarettes I
get issued but trade, should be able to have a few real dinners of roast
beef and potatoes if we ever leave this trench. Or don't drown in it.

Thomas Warren of Hawkensbury taken away yesterday to field hospital. Took a flake of shrapnel in his arm back at the Somme and was given the No. 9 pill. Wound festered over the last two months from a piece of muddy uniform trapped under the skin. Gangrene now. Will lose the hand for certain. But going home.

CSM Tranter now requiring a wound check with every duck's breakfast – face wash and drink of water.

Somewhere in Flanders: Thursday, 28 December, 1916

Dear Mr. Quaite,

My first Christmas away from Rusthall spent sleeping in a leaky dug-out. I can only hope my first New Year's will be as uneventful.

We had extra pozzy – Tickler's plum and apple. Never strawberry.

We eat in a haze of smoke from all the fags constantly going. Several men here eat and smoke at the same time!

Fritz must be celebrating as well. Doppo – trench lingo for quiet – for the last 4 days and nights. New replacements are unaware of how rare this is.

We are promised rest time in Pop – Poperinghe, a town near here out of artillery range. I have saved the Black Cat English-French Dictionary cards in the fag packets they issue, and hope to use them at the Toch-Talbert House – an everyman's club in Pop.

The Salient, Ypres, Flanders: Monday, 8 January, 1917

Extremely bright full moon. My first night as a Lance Corporal, the chevron the only unmuddied part of my uniform, spent checking the sentries. All alert. One or two unsteady from the shelling. The screams we hear come from horses hit by shrapnel up the line. Like banshees.

Snow coming on.

Somewhere in Flanders: Tuesday, 23 January, 1917

Dear Mr. Quaite,

Another night without the moon. The enemy feels closer to us in this darkness. What is unseen becomes the true danger and the thing we are all most frightened of. Looking out into the wire, the knife rests lean toward the mud. It is only from the weight of the wire in the soggy ground, but the wood looks wounded. Nothing here is in perfect condition. Every piece of metal is dented or marred. Every uniform patched or fraying, all boots scuffed and splitting. Even my helmet, which has never been struck by any object, is scratched and pinged. The chin strap, once so stiff the leather cut into skin, is now worn smooth, like the best gloves. I actually fear having to replace it when it finally ruptures.

The only thing in pristine condition is my MLE. Trading my issued fags for bits of wool – "4x2s," owing to their size – to pull through the barrel has ensured the cleanliness of the rifle. I trade the excess wool bits for pozzy and tea, and for extra needle and thread to keep up my uniform. Compared to Barry, also now a Lance Jack, I look like a swell. This might be the first time a Rusthall lad dressed finer than one from "Royal" Tunbridge Wells. I enclose a photograph of the two of us with our new chevrons.

I will do my utmost to send you a list of trench slang words and their translations. The lingo here is more than shorthand. It is the common thing that ties us together, especially now that so many of our original battalion are gone ("crumped" would be how we describe it).

Somewhere in Flanders: Tuesday, 30 January, 1917

Dear Mr. Quaite,

Last evening, the last night before the half moon, we responded to heavy shelling by sending a raiding party over, getting as far as the German trench opposite in the Spoil Bank Sector near the canal. Cutting the wire was the most difficult task as even the loosest coils have some tension on them, requiring one man to cut, another to hold the wire fast to prevent injury. We caught Fritz dossing. Not a single shot fired on our approach, though we surely made noise slogging through freezing mud. Sgt. Jeffs took Barry and two others down into the trench, followed by Lieut. Levitt and three men. The rest of us guarded the flanks. No prisoners or IDs found, no weapons, but some ammo, which is useless to our side except that it can no longer be fired against us. Our retreat was equally uneventful and much faster thanks to the trail through the cut wire.

I was shivering the entire time – no more than 20 minutes – and not entirely from the cold. Taking aim at the parapet, waiting for a helmet or face to pop up, and listening for the telltale sound of boots against mud and boards, is nerve-wracking. It was not until we returned to our trench that I discovered I had forgotten to pack Iron Rations – a 24-hour food supply – in my webbing. I would be reprimanded if it was discovered I had neglected to pack them in.

We lost 6 in the shelling and upon our return, we began rebuilding the length of trench damaged. Barry found a boot with the foot still in it among the debris. He laughed at his discovery, but I could tell he, too, was horrified.

Somewhere in Flanders: Friday, 9 February, 1917

Dear Mr. Quaite,

We were shelled relentlessly yesterday, presumably in response to our earlier raid last week. In the middle of it, 2/Lieut. French led us over again. I was glad to be out of our trench, which was collapsing all around us. We got into the German trench at the same point again. Barry killed three guarding that area, using the shine of the full moon off their helmets as aiming points. I followed Sgt. Jeffs up the trench – my first time in one dug by the enemy and not nearly as well engineered as our own, but deeper. We encountered Fritz coming our way and captured 12 of them. One of them charged at me with bayonet fixed, but he stopped some distance away and dropped his rifle. For an instant, I thought I might have shot him, but he was simply surrendering to those coming up behind me.

2/Lieut. French shot 3 himself and took two wounds in return. I fired several rounds, but none hit their marks. We lost 4, including Tilsley from Lewisham who started with us. A dozen were wounded, including Sgt. Jeffs, who cursed all the way back to our trench that his wound was too minor to be even a "soft one" that would send him home. He seemed more distressed at his bayonet-sliced sleeve than the cut on his forearm.

My first face-to-face combat made me feel like a gladiator running up the trench at Fritz and I would surely have shot that first fellow had he not surrendered. Part of me wishes I had pulled the trigger a few steps earlier, if only to see him fall.

Sgt. Cozens directed our return under fire. It is he we all thank for getting us and the prisoners back alive.

The Salient, Ypres, Flanders:
Wednesday, 14 February, 1917

Near half moon. Still rebuilding the partially demolished trench sections. Reports from Regimental Staff state our last raid was the most successful to date. 2/Lieut. French put up for the M.C., Sgt. Cozens the D.C.M. Sgt. Jeffs recommended for the M.M., but took his name off the list, not wanting to have a medal that reminded him his bad luck at being wounded but not badly enough to wear hospital blue. He even volunteered for the next raid, 6 hours later. Fritz was ready for us, and we all withdrew before hitting the wire. No casualties.

Somewhere in Flanders: Sunday, 25 February, 1917

Dear Mr. Quaite,

We have had two weeks of lull. The stillness is unsettling. Most of us think it is an omen of worse things to come. At service today, we remembered those lost in the recent shelling. As the names were read, one of our rank began commenting on their demise — one was "blown to buggery," another "plugged by shrapnel," another "hit by a Hissing Jenny." Cpl. Wiggins slugged him with the rum jug, which we all applauded. When CSM Tranter came on the scene, he threatened to crime Cpl. Wiggins, but Barry explained the situation, prompting CSM to grab the bleeding man by the scruff of the neck and drag him up the trench to the dressing station. Much laughter and more applause greeted his going.

Regimental reports list our casualties as "moderate wastage." I wonder what Mr. Kipling would make of that awful phrase, as heartless as the No Man's Land we constantly scan.

We are told that spring will come early, meaning more rain and more mud. Even the weather conspires against us. If sunshine exits in Flanders, it is as well concealed as Fritz is.

Somewhere in Flanders: Tuesday, 6 March, 1917

Dear Mr. Quaite,

I accompanied CSM Tranter to Field Hospital west of Armentieres to visit 2/Lieut. French, who is recovering nicely. Barry and two others also made the trip south. We traveled over a familiar landscape, now quiet and still smoldering in spots. I felt ashamed of the condition of my uniform, but was happy to be out of range of the crumps.

A writer from Ledbury, Herefordshire is just up from the Somme battle area. He is writing an official account for our Military Intelligence. We were asked by a subaltern adjutant to meet with him. His name is John Masefield and he is an avid reader of Mr. Kipling's poetry. His book is *Gallipoli*, out two years now. Too old for service — near 40 — he had volunteered for the temporary hospital in Haute Marne.

Our comments about the Somme were of interest to him. He scribbled notes on his pad the entire time. When Barry asked about his background, he admitted he had jumped ship in New York City in 1895, a windjammer. The others called him a deserter and walked off. I stayed on and told him about Rusthall. A lot like his rural home on the border with Wales.

He promised to send a copy of his new book to you when it is published next year. An odd-looking man – a shock of dark hair falls on his brow like bangs, and his thick moustache makes him appear to be always frowning. He speaks in whispers.

We were to collect Cpt. Jiminez before returning, but he is not yet ready for travel. On our way back, we stopped in Pop. The sign over the entrance to the Toch-Talbot House reads, *Abandon Rank All Ye Who Enter Here.* Everyone else was in *mufti* – what the Infantry calls civilian clothes – but we were not harshly treated. I had a pale colored ale, my first pint this year. It is called a "Belgian white" and is quite bland compared to our drafts. CSM Tranter carried dispatches, so he would not permit himself any alcohol, though he had a taste from each of ours, reminding us between sips that the fine for drunkenness is 2s6d for the first offence, 5s for the second. I offered a toast to Mr. Masefield and his new book, but none of the others raised their glasses.

The Salient, Ypres, Flanders: Thursday, 22 March, 1917

Our guns continue to exchange artillery with Fritz. No shells have come our way in over a week. There are plenty of explosions to the north of our position. Being back in the mud and stench feels oddly customary, the brief respite in Pop and Armentieres the unusual. OC walked the trench this morning. Said nothing. Unnerving.

Somewhere in Flanders: Sunday, 25 March, 1917

Dear Mr. Quaite,

Fritz sent over a big disorganized raiding party yesterday. Our artillery stopped them cold. Lieut/Col. Corfe himself led us out to meet them bayonets fixed and we beat them back. We lost 30, including Lieut. Aylett, to rifle fire. Barry distinguished himself with sharp-shooting. I believe I hit at least two while they came toward our advance. The lack of moonlight made it difficult to know whether Fritz was coming or going. At a distance of greater than 40 yards, they disappear in darkness, even while continuing to fire at us. I was certain a few would reach us and require bayoneting, but none did. Sgt. Jeffs was left in charge of our reserves and angry about not being part of our pushback. He refused to speak to any of us upon our return.

The Salient, Ypres, Flanders: Friday, 6 April, 1917

Good Friday and a special meal promised for tomorrow. The Maconochie is improved by extra salt. Barry breaks up No. 9 biscuits into his. Every bite he takes makes a crunch, like a twig snapping. Irritating. Full moon tomorrow. No chance of Fritz coming our way without a dark sky.

Somewhere in Flanders: Monday, 9 April, 1917

Dear Mr. Quaite,

We moved up to the St. Eloi Sector on Saturday in response to an early afternoon bombardment. Fritz hit us at our center with Flying Pigs and Black Marias. Cpt. Wright got us moving quickly enough that most were able to escape the shelling. Our trenches were ruined. He will be put up for the M.C.

Fritz came over at 7 p.m. and managed to get into our trenches. We drove them out quickly. They took no prisoners or weapons. Sgt. Jeffs had one of them by the boot as he tried to escape. Barry and I ran with bayonets in hand, but the German came out the boot and ran off. As Fritz retreated, our artillery caught him. No Man's Land is still littered with dead Germans, all of them facing away from us. The boot Sgt. Jeffs took is now an official A Company souvenir. It sits atop the parapet, filled with empty pozzy tins, inviting its owner to return to retrieve it, if he remains alive.

The weather has turned warmer. This makes the soil even muddier. As I scan No Man's Land on sentry, I can see the bodies sinking inch by inch. At this rate, Fritz will not have to send out a Garden Party to bury them.

Somewhere in Flanders: Wednesday, 18 April, 1917

Dear Mr. Quaite,

My mother's Easter cookies and your chocolate never arrived. We have taken a new position in the right subsector of the St. Eloi trenches, very near a mine shaft. It is a strange assignment, away from the main action, but also a relief to be guarding something that we all know is not valued by the enemy, so our present risk is small. Lieut/Col. Corfe has been put up for the D.S.O. Cpt. Jiminez rejoined us a week ago, resuming his duties as Adjutant, relieving Lieut. Puttick who is promoted to Cpt. tomorrow. Barry has been put up for the Military Medal and surely deserves it for his action last month. He gets an extra ration of rum now, but he shares it among us.

I am happy you are finally wearing your new hat. Please send me a picture of you in it.

Somewhere in Flanders: Sunday, 22 April, 1917

Dear Mr. Quaite,

We were targeted 2 days ago with heavy shelling that lasted almost 2 hours, starting at 7:30 on a night without a moon – Fritz's favorite condition to attack. Our front trenches were completely obliterated, resulting in the loss of a complete garrison. Cpt. Frazier moved us to the flanks, with some taking shelter in the mine shaft. This proved wise, as when the bombardment stopped, we were up and ready at the support line to repel the raiders with rifle and Lewis gun fire. It was nonstop massacre once the 15th Hampshires Lewis gun opened up on our flank. Fritz attempted an all-out retreat and we were poised to follow, but Sgt. Jeffs held us back long enough for our artillery to hit them as they fled. Every one of us recorded multiple kills. It was like being on the firing range, with targets getting larger with each stride Fritz took toward us. We cheered up and down the line as we shot.

We lost 30, almost all from the initial bombardment. 2/Lieut. Rodney, here 10 days, was among them. Sgt. Jeffs will be put up for the D.C.M. and Cpt. Frazier for the M.C. There is a rumor that some us might be recommended for the M.M.

I was charged with the repair party. After 3 hours, it became clear we could not make suitable repairs. We have begun a new trench section, in advance of the former one, which will be filled in. Very difficult work in this mud. I have not heard so much vulgarity since Aldershot.

Near St. Eloi, toward Messines, West Flanders
Tuesday, 1 May, 1917

Moved entire battalion to support position on the Divisional Line, running north and south of St. Eloi. Even on quiet nights, the barrages all around us are lively. Fritz must be bringing up more heavies. A Jack Johnson hit less than 1 km away on Sunday. Dust from it still hangs in the air. The crater it left could hold half the population of Rusthall.

We are in some disarray here, uncertain of the enemy's position and movement. Sgt. Jeffs offered to take a scout group over, but was rejected. Barry cannot sleep. He goes on sentry every few hours to sight down the line. A waxing half moon provides ideal light for sniping. The lack of rain also helps.

Somewhere in Flanders: Wednesday, 16 May, 1917

Dear Mr. Quaite,

I saw my first battle map today. Hand drawn, it shows our position along the Divisional Line and the wandering trench line of the enemy. This makes us appear much closer to Fritz than we feel we actually are. The canal everyone regards as the main strategic location looks to be out of reach for either side, though we are at a disadvantage because a large part of it runs through territory Fritz holds.

Lieut/Col. Corfe put on the June 11th Honours List for the D.S.O. He is cheered each time he appears in the trench.

Somewhere in Flanders: Saturday, 26 May, 1917

Dear Mr. Quaite,

Our Brigade has moved 3 times since my last letter. How close we are to the enemy remains uncertain. In fact, I cannot tell if we are going up or down the line. Every inch of the immediate terrain looks the same. We move through a line of trenches encircling Englebier Farm, N.E. of Ooosttaverne, encountering no one.

I spend time sleeping and reading. I am starting *The Jungle Book* again. It is still in excellent condition. This time, I will read the stories in order.

The Wypers Times, now called *The B.E.F. Times,* has been our only other reading material after letters. I write to my mother and to Madge regularly, but am ashamed I have so little to tell them. Barry advises I tell Madge I love her and dream about her, but I no longer have dreams and have no idea why.

Messines, West Flanders: Sunday, 3 June, 1917

Honours List posted. D.S.O. to our OC. Barry listed for M.M., Sgt. Jeffs the D.C.M. Ceremony postponed until further notice. We are being drawn back into support. We will enjoy good moonlight for almost a fortnight and do not expect action until then.

The lice are more active in warmer weather. I am raw from scratching and spend hours chatting the seams of my uniform with candle flame. Nothing seems to discourage them. At least we are free of rats here. They are probably feasting on the dead we left. The flies lay eggs in the rotting flesh after just a few days. Thankful we do not have to witness that.

Somewhere in Flanders: Sunday, 10 June, 1917

Dear Mr. Quaite,

Our battalion has been tested once more. On Thursday last, before dawn, we started for an advance position behind the Dammstrasse, a sunken road. As we began our attack an hour later, we came under enfilade machine-gun fire. Fortunately, one of our "tanks" attended to that. Farther on, our flank was hit by machine guns in Pheasant Wood. Our small party, led by Cpt. Maltby, pushed forward and captured the gun and killed its crew, thanks to a Mills bomb from Sgt. Jeffs and a direct assault by Barry and 2/Lieut. Greenwood, who was severely wounded. The heel of my boot was shot out from under me, but the bullet drew no blood.

We swept into Oblong Trench by 7 a.m. The fighting got sharper, bayonets in full use. There is surprisingly very little resistance to the blade when plunged into the side of the torso, as we are trained. That angle also prevents an inadvertent return blow or shot and allows us to keep moving, our forward momentum withdrawing the blade with no additional effort. I shot or bayoneted at least 8, all infantry, one of them a full corporal. They were younger and thinner than I imagined, not the brawny giants of newspaper caricatures. Barry and Sgt. Jeffs took a position along the parados, sharpshooting all those still coming down the trench to us. Dozens fell to their bullets, saving many RWK lives.

We consolidated along a defensive line behind Oblong Reserve when our own artillery barrage began landing short, threatening us. Several of A Company were wounded by our shrapnel. With Capt. Rodgers taking us out in 5 patrols, we pushed forward to a pathway leading from Englebrier Farm. Three patrols uncovered enemy dugouts and captured prisoners. Our patrol made the raid without incident.

We had a short rest, thinking we had achieved our objective and would soon be relieved, when around noon Fritz counterattacked. After the initial surprise, we were able to rout him, though not without casualties on our side. We captured 25 more, which we tried to turn over to the Twenty-Fourth Division when it passed through the 122nd Brigade, but they were fast moving to seize a strategic location N.E. of Oosttaverne, made possible by the our efforts. Barry and Sgt. Jeffs will certainly be put up for D.C.M.s. Capt. Rodgers deserves the M.C. for both his leadership and fighting skills. He used captured enemy weapons to make his way through a host of soldiers racing directly at him, dodging their bayonets and somehow avoiding getting shot. I was equally as lucky.

The Twenty-Fourth officially relieved us after midnight, accepting our prisoners. We are presently in reserve near Battalion HQ in the ruins of the White Chateau. What a magnificent manor house this must have been, sitting on a low hill, its turret an ideal viewing spot. Barry counted 20 rooms, all with arched windows, on two floors. He said he felt as though he were in a hotel again. This one is considerably draftier than The Lenton. The front yard is cut short by barriers of barbed wire now and not a tree is left alive, all of them leafless charred skeletons.

Our losses totaled 100. That number did not seem possible until we all assembled here. We expect new drafts in short order. More training duties for the rest of us.

My boot cannot be repaired. I am to choose one from the piles taken off our dead.

The Salient, Ypres, Flanders: Tuesday, 12 June, 1917

Respite ended yesterday. Moved up short of the Ypres-Comines Canal, into Opal Reserve Trench. This continuation of Oblong Reserve is in horrible condition. No one knows why we are here. Even the OC questions our positioning.

•

7274 SUPPLEMENT TO THE LONDON GAZETTE, 12 JUNE, 1917

War Office,
June 11, 1917.

His Majesty the KING has been pleased to confer the undermentioned rewards for gallantry and distinguished service in the Field:–

The acts of gallantry for which the decorations have been awarded will be announced in the London Gazette as early as practicable:–

Awarded the Distinguished Service Order.
Maj. (T./Lt.-Col.) Arthur Cecil Corfe, D.S.O., S.A. Def. Fee., and R.W. Kent R.

His Majesty the KING has been graciously pleased to award the Military Medal for bravery in the Field to the under-mentioned Non-Commissioned Officers and Men:–

3/59595 Sjt. W. Jeffs, R.W. Kent R.
240333 L./C.,B. E. Yorke, R.W. Kent R.

•

Somewhere in Flanders: Thursday, 14 June, 1917

Dear Mr. Quaite,

Three companies – B, C and D – launched a surprise attack last night. We watched from the safety of the trench. Our artillery was fierce and brief. Equally swift was our assault. B and C captured the Optic Trench. D Company took the junction of the trench and Oblique Row, moving forward all the way to the canal.

It is the first battle I have witnessed without participating in it. At a distance, the men look like our toy lead soldiers. There is so much black and gray smoke in the air that it obscures the figures. At first the head and shoulders are enshrouded, then the smoke sinks and the men appear legless. When they fall, they disappear, as if melted into the smoke and haze. It is at once terrible and magical.

Cpt. Frazer was killed while rescuing the wounded. In all, 30 casualties for all 3 companies. Sgt. Jeffs called that "light."

Somewhere in Flanders: Monday, 18 June, 1917

Dear Mr. Quaite,

Hours after I posted my last letter to you, we were back on the attack to repel an enemy advance. Sgt. Jeffs and 2/Lieut. Webb led the bombers out. I was tasked to follow on. We hurled Mills grenades as fast as we could, bullets kicking up dirt all around us. Fritz retreated when our machine guns opened fire. Our wire was never breached. A late artillery barrage finished off the assault, inflicting heavy casualties. We counted over 80 in our corner of the Optic Trench. The next day was spent consolidating and digging a 1000-yard Communication Trench back to Opal Reserve. We handed over our position to the 12th East Surreys yesterday.

Our casualties now total 250, with 40 killed, including 3 officers. One of the wounded, Lieut. Gordon-Smith, lead the group supporting those of us who went over with grenades. He told me he saw me killed twice. Barry said it was the loss of blood talking. The Lieut.'s remark must have been overheard by those who rescued him because several soldiers, most unknown to me, have reached out to touch me on their way by, as if that might bring them good luck. Barry was upset they did not treat him the same way.

Fletre, France: Saturday, 23 June, 1917

Crossed back into France, arriving Fletre in the dark. No moon. Surprisingly cool. The bumps of the guns still in the distance, though well out of range. When the Forty-Seventh relieved us, we were so exhausted we could not speak. Even a pat on the back hurt. Had the ground been dry, we might have all curled up and slept there rather than trudge back in the slop.

Somewhere in France: Wednesday, 27 June, 1917

Dear Mr. Quaite,

We left Flanders last week and no man ever hopes to see it again. We are told our efforts distinguished the RWK. The cost was severe. New drafts arriving at weekend and much needed, even if our only future role is in support.

My Kipling survived the mud. I am now able to read several hours a day, indoors and dry. The moment I first realized my new situation, I nearly wept.

We are close to our first training ground in France. Barry thinks that means we will be stood down or rotated into a training battalion. He is the only one of us still taking regular firing range sessions.

Roast beef tonight. And sleep!

Somewhere in France: Sunday, 1 July, 1917

Dear Mr. Quaite,

I had a letter from John Masefield, the writer, thanking me for meeting with him in Ribemont to discuss the Battle of the Somme. His impression of the front is that of a river winding through countryside, following a logic of its own. I think he is mistaken that the land will recover in time and be unrecognizable as a battleground. Barry and I would wager two months' pay that the scarring is permanent and that each of us would be able to locate the places we held, even as old men – a stage of life we now think we might actually reach, having been drawn back from the fighting.

I have tasted several different kinds of cheeses. The soft ones are too sour, the hard ones too sharp. The beer here is softer tasting than in Flanders, but hardly beer. Barry says drinking it is like kissing your sister.

I now have three tunics in decent repair and four sets of trousers that are finally recognizable, free of mud. The blood stains do not come out, though they darken enough to become almost invisible.

New boots said to be arriving with the new recruits. In full sun, France is quite beautiful. You would like all the flowers in long window pots. Colorful.

Somewhere in France: Friday, 6 July, 1917

Dear Mr. Quaite,

I am sitting outside of a café under a full moon, in *mufti*, drinking beer and eating rabbit stew. The meat might not be rabbit, but Barry and I agree it is delicious. Weeks ago, I could not have imagined this.

71

We are almost certainly to be tasked as a training battalion. CSM Tranter has asked Barry to lead the rifle range detail. I have been asked to help with Regimental paperwork. Only Sgt Jeffs doubts the good fortune of this reassignment. He curses the new drafts and believes we would not be training them if we truly were to be stood down from the front.

Somewhere in France: Wednesday, 11 July, 1917
Dear Mr. Quaite,
We were taken hunting for small birds this afternoon. They shoot them with shotguns. I did not fire. Several in our group bagged enough for dinner. They do not use dogs here, so the real danger is searching through the fields for the downed birds with hunters all around reacting to sounds. Wouldn't that be an odd way to go out, after all we have experienced? The birds are doves mostly and a reddish brown songbird we do not see in Rusthall.

Somewhere in France: Monday, 16 July, 1917
Dear Mr. Quaite,
Sgt. Jeffs was correct. We are not being stood down or reassigned to training. There is talk of being shipped to Mesopotamia or Italy. Either would be better than Ypres. SM Goulds expects our orders next week.
I spent yesterday beside a stream reading and fell asleep near the bank. The last time I had such a non-eventful afternoon was in Denny Bottom, pretending to hunt mushrooms.
If you know anything about Mesopotamia, please send me details.

Fletre, France: Saturday, 21 July, 1917
The worst news. We will move back up to the front, taking the position we vacated astride the canal in Ypres. No one is able to voice the crushing disappointment. Barry confided he thought of disappearing into the countryside now that the moon is gone. Some of the others must have had the same idea because CSM Tranter joked that any deserter would be shot at dawn for a week. It did not draw much laughter.

Somewhere in Flanders: Tuesday, 24 July, 1917
Dear Mr. Quaite,
Disregard Mesopotomia. We are back in Ypres. The trenches have been severely knocked about. The wet conditions have turned them

into mud holes. Here less than four hours and already Fletre is a memory few of us believe we truly experienced.

The noise of artillery is constant. Making repairs is busy work, without much result.

The worst is going back on tinned rations. I had forgotten how distasteful Maconochie can be, even heated. It is not possible to keep the rain out of it, turning it into a dreadful soup.

Somewhere in Flanders: Friday, 27 July, 1917

Dear Mr. Quaite,

Fritz set a trap for us yesterday, appearing to have withdrawn from the trench opposite in response to our heavy shelling since early last week. We went over to investigate, only to find the Germans lying in wait. The ambush stopped us cold just beyond the canal. Had there been wire, none of us would have made it back. In all, we suffered 80 casualties, most lost and wounded in our retreat, which was disorganized owing to our surprise.

Half moon tonight. Not ideal for retrieving any wounded or dead left out there. Fritz will be sniping.

Somewhere in Flanders: Sunday, 5 August, 1917

Dear Mr. Quaite,

Tuesday last, we went over at 3.5 a.m. as our artillery bombarded the enemy to discourage any counter barrage. The moment we reached the canal, flares lit up the night sky. We are trained to stand motionless so that Fritzie will take us for wood stakes in No Man's Land – if you are skinny enough. This, however, took place in open lowland. As a result, we had no option but to push on through mist to cut the wire and pour into Oblique Trench, where we were met by Bavarian troops. They are fierce fighters and do not fall easily. They turn sideways as they charge, to present a slimmer target and to allow 2 to move down the trench at the same time.

I cannot describe the battle at close quarters because it was a blur, in large part because of the weather. Mud splashed into my eyes the instant I hit the trench and made me half-blind. Trying to clear my sight with my sleeve made matters worse. We used trench clubs and cut-down bayonets to make our way forward, but at the outset, I could not be certain I did not fire on one of our own. The thought haunts me.

We cleared the trench before first light and were able to consolidate 150 yards farther on. When C and D companies passed through, we began to take fire from houses along Hollebeke Rd. Lt/Col. Corfe himself came up to us and reinforced our flank, readying a new attack at 8 a.m. Barry and I were selected to go over with Cpts. Rooney and Lindsay in two patrols to push forward. We encountered heavy rifle and machine-gun fire, causing our unit to split up. The rain came down in torrents at that moment.

I followed L/Cpl Chapman and two others toward a dug-out, where we sank waist-deep in water. L/Cpl Chapman captured 5 Germans hiding there without firing a shot. We were forced to remain in that mud hole for over an hour, which was worse than being out in the shelling all around us.

When we emerged, we went house-to-house – more rubble-to-rubble. The villagers abandoned the place months ago, so we were on orders to shoot anything that moved. I stood against a field stone wall to cover part of our advance down a side street. Three sniper bullets knicked the wall before I could blink. Several times, shots splattered mud at my feet, the shooter remaining unseen. A new 2/Lieut. was shot turning a corner, with me directly behind him. I dragged him back, but blood and brains were leaking out of his wound. I hurled a Mills bomb down that alley, then advanced with Barry. We did not find any sign of Fritz there.

It became clear that the snipers were left behind to cover a retreat. Both patrols picked up pace and cleared the cement-fortified pill boxes, routed the cellars and other dugouts and established a presence in the ruins of Hollebeke by noon. The rest of the 11th moved up to consolidate almost instantly. We were told to hold our position until relief arrived. The persistent rain and shelling made us feel we were in flooded tombs. Thankfully, Fritz did not mount a counter-attack.

The Thirty-Ninth finally relieved us yesterday. In all we captured 60 and lost an equal number. We are below 300 strong again. Our retreat – just 2 miles – to Lock House looked like a death march for all the staggering, falling from exhaustion, vomiting from foul water. Two men crawled the last quarter mile, to be carried in by those of us who could still stand.

CSM Tranter announced that Lt/Col. Corfe will be put up for a clasp to his D.S.O. Cpts. Lindsay and Rooney are put forward to for M.C., L/Cpl Chapman the D.C.M. Barry and I are up for the M.M. We are all to be mentioned in Dispatches.

L/Cpl Chapman may be the bravest among us. He has developed a twitch in his cheek and does not appear to notice it, despite the clicking sound he sometimes makes along with it, as though some scrap has caught in his teeth. None of us has the stuffing to discuss it with him.

Reninghelst, Flanders: Wednesday, 8 August, 1917
New drafts arrived. Our largest number yet. Most are so young they look like our sweeper boys. We are all too tired to train them and are trying to enjoy Reninghelst near Pop while we can.
Official count from Hollebeke: 32 dead, including 5 officers. 54 are missing, 248 wounded and over 100 taken sick. Once again, I am able to recognize only a handful of faces in our company.

Somewhere in Flanders: Saturday, 11 August, 1917
Dear Mr. Quaite,
We moved up yesterday to take over from the 15th Hampshires. Their trenches are in shambles, very close to those we vacated last week. Less than 2 hours after assuming the position, we were gassed. The shell makes a distinctive dying out sound as it falls, a "futt-futt." We were alerted by the gas gongs – just empty shells the sentries bang on with their clubs – and had our masks in place. Our lone casualty was CSM Jennings, who had a defective charcoal filter. There is no tree left standing in this area. Every house we passed had been demolished, its contents buggered to bits. The Somme was a wasteland, but Ypres is a desert in heavy, hard rain.
Barry and L/Cpl Chapman are now pals. When they stand sentry, we all rest easier.

Somewhere in Flanders: Tuesday, 14 August, 1917
Dear Mr. Quaite,
We are back in Fletre after a short stint on the line. Some of us wonder why we were even sent back up. The baths here, in converted beer vats which hold 3 men at a time, are held in an old brewery and are superior to those in Ribemont, which are staged in a former dye house that still retains a sharp odor. I would guess we smell even worse to the villagers.
I am to be recommended for full Corporal. CSM Tranter called me down to Regimental Staff to discuss. He also asked me to be truthful about L/Cpl Chapman, who was also being considered for a promotion. His twitch is increasingly apparent and CSM intends to

75

stand him down for medical treatment. This is the wisest route for such a courageous soldier, but he will see it as a stain on his honor. There were several piles of folders on CSM Tranter's desk, which looks much like yours at deadlines. He was sorting through letters that cannot be delivered. One pile was marked *Invalided to England*. Others I spotted were *Not To Be Found* and *Present Location Uncertain*, which differs slightly from *Unable to Find*. By comparison, *Killed in Action* seems kinder by its definite status.

I am enclosing a brief list of trench talk at long last. Some, such as "Estaminet" (any place that serves alcohol) come from the French. Most, however, are variations on official items. The M.M. – Military Medal – is called the "Maconochie Medal" by most and "Many Muddles" by a few. The infantry sense of humor is the honest *Invicta* of our spirit. I have not included jargon I know you will not print. If we are finally finished with this front, as all of us now expect, I look forward to sharing those phrases with you in person one day soon.

Somewhere in France: Sunday, 18 August, 1917

Dear Mr. Quaite,

We have been withdrawn, so far from the front that the thump of artillery cannot be heard. A different world. Even the weather is better. We are told we are not far from Boulogne-sur-Mer and the Channel, but our encampment is near a wooded area that affords no long views.

The food is also much better. Real milk. The tins of condensed milk had begun to make me sick from the sweetness. The cheapest drink here is red wine. It is sometimes served in a bucket. There is some fresh fruit, mostly apricots, and salad greens I have not seen before. Meat is in very short supply. Villagers beg us for it.

There are living trees, with leaves. And children. Their voices mix with bird song. When I close my eyes, I can hear home.

The new drafts we expect are limited to stretcher bearers, signalers and Lewis gunners. All are specialists, which we take to mean we will not soon see more action.

The laundry here steams our uniforms. They are cleaner than at any time before. To be without lice is a luxury.

Somewhere in France: Thursday, 23 August, 1917

Dear Mr. Quaite,

The new Lewis gunners make a daily racket on the range, the only reminder that we are still at war. We are permitted private time until breakfast. Most sleep. Several of the new drafts saw me reading and asked to borrow my Kipling. Instead, I now read the stories aloud to them. The group has grown from 2 or 3 to over 20. I feel like a teacher must in front of a class. They are all so attentive, keen for the next sentence. Mr. Kipling keeps them spellbound. Even CSM Tranter stops to listen on his way to and from Regimental Staff.

Those of us who sailed over with the original 11th are permitted to wear *mufti* – civilian clothes. It has become a badge of honor. Barry refuses to go without his rifle and makes him an odd sight, like an armed villager.

In answer to your query, we are not issued trench clubs, but fashion them from whatever is available. Mine is a short length of lead water pipe. It is badly dented, but has yet to break up. It does seem strange that with all our modern weaponry we rely so heavily on heavy clubs and small knives at close quarters, where rifles and bayonets are too unwieldy.

Boulogne-sur-Mer, France: Tuesday, 28 August, 1917

Half moon waxing. Bacon this morning. Nothing else to report.

•

10684 SUPPLEMENT TO THE LONDON GAZETTE, 1 SEPTEMBER, 1917

His Majesty the KING has been graciously pleased to approve of the award of the Distinguished Conduct Medal to the under-mentioned Non-Commissioned Officers and Men:–

S/8635 L/C. F.W. Chapman, R.W. Kent R.

His Majesty the KING has been graciously pleased to approve of the award of the Military Medal to the undermentioned Non-Commissioned Officers and Men:–

7/40597 L./ C. R. Olcutt, R. W. Kent R.

His Majesty the KING has been graciously pleased to approve of the award a Bar to the Military Medal to the under-mentioned Non-Commissioned Officers and Men:–

3/59595 Sjt. W. Jeffs, R.W. Kent R.
240333 L./C.,B. E. Yorke, R.W. Kent R.

•

Somewhere in France: Sunday, 2 September, 1917

Dear Mr. Quaite,

Several of us have been gazetted. Please be sure my mother and Madge see it and save a copy for me.

The town center of Boulogne-sur-Mer is ancient. Its church belfry dates from the 12th Century. We attended services in a courtyard in its shadow. From the ridge edge, white caps in the Channel were visible, but not the white cliffs of our coast. It is difficult to believe that I am close enough to England that I might see it should the weather ever clear.

Training resumed today, though no one has the heart for it. Even Barry, who took range practice but did not shoot out his allotment. I will be temporarily assigned to CSM Tranter's desk to assist with files and sorting when the 11th is finally stood down. That announcement is expected next week. Our 8th Battalion is still in the thick of it in Ypres. Reports are discouraging.

There are 2 leave ships in port, unable to sail due to weather. I pity the souls onboard who may not get back to Blighty before their leave expires.

Somewhere in France: Thursday, 7 September, 1917

Dear Mr. Quaite,

The weather cleared. The trees still ooze as if the rain is trapped in them. On the map, Boulogne-sur-Mer is opposite our coast between Rye and Hastings. When we first sailed, the land mass narrowed to a brown and green sliver. Looking in the direction of Kent, even if we cannot see it, is a joy. We believe we are to be returned home before the month is out.

There is a castle here, which the French call a *chateau*. Strictly off-limits to us. I tasted a newly made red wine, not aged at all like the Bardos available everywhere. *Bojalay* it is called, spelled strangely in French. Too fruity for Barry and me. Like unsugared grape juice. Tea is difficult to find. Everything comes with milk in it.

A few East Surrey lads were taken in for pestering local girls who attend school in the floors above a popular estaminet. SM Goulds has forbidden us to speak to the local women on the threat of confinement. He is rumored to have had, as a young man, personal experience with this precise predicament.

The men of the village here do not wear hats or caps.

Boulogne-sur-Mer, France: Wednesday, 12 September, 1917

CSM Tranter informed us we are to march back to Ypres this afternoon. 40 miles, in full packs. The grousing among us is constant. Everyone on edge. L/Cpl Chapman refused medical attention on hearing of our return to the line. He is whistling as he stuffs his pack. This forest invites hiding. Barry says going "disparu" here would be no different than going missing in action. For a moment, I thought he might be in earnest.

We are to receive tinned rations en route. There can be no worse news.

Somewhere in Flanders: Tuesday, 18 September, 1917

Dear Mr. Quaite,

We arrived early this morning at Ridge Wood camp following a steady march the past 5 days. The segment of the Salient we find ourselves in splits two divisions and faces a ridge just beyond a swollen stream. We are held in reserve, which affords little comfort as we are well in range of Fritz's big guns.

The stench of the front is overwhelming after the fresh air of the Channel. Wind carries a putrid mix of gunpowder, cooking smells, excrement and filthy men in filthier uniforms. To stand sentry in this condition is a challenge. To eat without vomiting is difficult. We are all half-mad with rage at being forced back to the muck all around us. Our OC is to address us after tea. There is nothing he will say that will soothe us. I began to feel less than human the instant we hit the Salient. We feel betrayed by the mindlessness that continues to push us in and out of battle. The only certainty we can count on is each other, and that is not enough.

Larch Wood Tunnels, Flanders: Tuesday, 18 September, 1917

A surprise late evening move up from Ridge Wood. No moon, but no cover either. Gassed several times and unable to find unoccupied shelters. Having a bad time of it in trenches as Fritz is now targeting us with shell-fire. C Company taking the worst. Why send us up when there is no place to put us?

Bodmin Copse, Flanders: Wednesday, 19 September, 1917

Insanity. Bombarded all night. Moving in trenches based on the sounds of incoming shells. Capt. Stone, commander of C Company, hit directly. No trace left of him or his subalterns. Battalion HQ sending up a Lieut. to take command.

We followed a duckboard track in pitch darkness under constant shelling to Bodmin Copse, close behind the Hampshires. Only 40 casualties. First light in less than 2 hours. Sleep unlikely.

Somewhere in Flanders: Sunday, 23 September, 1917

Dear Mr. Quaite,

On Thursday last, just after dawn, we lost our OC, Lt/Col. Corfe. He came up to take over the Hampshires, who had lost nearly all of their officers to shelling. Sgt. Jeffs, Barry and I were pulled out to support him and his second in command, Cpt. Henderson. The ditch lay 40 yards short of a Fritz strong point that had withstood our barrage. A bullet most likely intended for Sgt. Jeffs, but missing because of his small stature, struck the OC in the shoulder. He carried on, reorganizing the Hampshires while we waited for our 11th to move up to reinforce. As though uninjured, he led the rush that overwhelmed the strong point and our sweep forward just short of Basseville Brook, which we secured by breakfast. It was not until then that Barry discovered Lt/Col. Corfe had collapsed. We both dragged him back out of sniper range and began carrying him toward the rear for stretcher bearers. His face had gone white and the entire sleeve of his tunic was blood red, as were his hand and fingers.

On our return forward, we joined the push past Tower Hamlets to the ridge beyond, passing the 18th K.R.R.C. on our right flank, from where we took heavy machine-gun fire and suffered uncountable casualties from it. Following Lieut. Morley, we took Tower Trench, capturing 50 and 3 machine guns. Fritz counterattacked and we suffered additional losses from savage machine-gun fire as we tried to dig in. Our fallback the length of a pitch put us with the 12th East Surreys, who had also raced through the 18th K.R.R.C. 2/Lieut. Freeman, who had thrown back a counterattack, did not survive. Fritz came at us again. We held, with Barry sharp-shooting in a "mad minute" exhibition I can only describe as astonishing. It inspired the rest of us, as did the return barrage of our heavy guns. By night fall, we were dug in, supported by the Twenty-Third Division.

The following morning, at 4:30, Fritz began shelling. Snipers and machine guns targeted us as well. The artillery intensified and Fritz launched an attack. Cpt. Henderson, now our OC, rallied our right flank which had begun retreating. What remained of the 11th followed him and Capt. Kerr, the Adjutant, to thwart the assault. We did much better than that, managing to repulse Fritz and hold the line. Once again, Barry was a spectacle. His MLE rate of fire a certain new record setter. We would have been overwhelmed had it not been for him. Several of my rounds found their mark. The lad next to me – only up with us since Boulogne-sur-Mer – was struck in the face by a round that flung him across the trench. He stuck there, crucified in the muddy wall, for the remainder of the action. L/Cpl Wiggins actually thought him still alive and offered him rum before finally prying him off. I do not know his name.

By the time relief arrived last evening, we had lost one-third of the 11th. Below strength when we arrived, CSM Tranter estimated our casualties at 250, with 28 killed, including Lt/Col. Corfe and Cpt. Freeman, 53 missing. The wounded include 5 officers. We now number 100. The 10th Battalion suffered fewer casualties, but had more killed – 29.

My tunic looks pristine next to most, but my trousers are torn in several spots. Barry thinks at least 2 of the places are from bullets passing through without hitting skin or bone. It is not possible to be certain, given all the mud. In truth, I would prefer not to know.

Somewhere in Flanders: Wednesday, 26 September, 1917

Dear Mr. Quaite,

Lt/Col. Corfe has not been killed. He is expected to recover from his wound. The news has buoyed our spirits and was met with cheers. Cpt. Henderson allowed extra rum and ordered a toast.

Battling reports once again have us headed to Mesopotamia or re-formed into a training command at Moolenacker. We have learned that Mesopotamia is Babylon along the Tigris and Euphrates rivers. If it is the desert Barry says it must be, then we will be happy to experience a dry climate. We should both like to see a camel.

Did you know that a true camel has two humps, but a camel with one is a dromedary?

There are reports of cholera there. It is said to be worse than trench fever. My legs and torso are bruised, but my arms are not. In the bath, Barry said I looked like a rotting chicken. He is as unmarked as a new draft.

Poperinge, Flanders: Saturday, 28 September, 1917

Leaving Pop and headed back toward the Channel. We all hope it is Boulogne-sur-Mer again. Some think it will be St.-Omer, an HQ town. More brass hats there than one could count. Barry wants to lead us to #4 there, a brothel. I will remain at the bar, not wanting to display my bruises. The women there are said to speak several languages and are knowledgeable about cheeses and wine. Sgt. Jeffs said their perfume is overpowering.

La Panne, Flanders: Tuesday, 2 October, 1917

Dear Mr. Quaite,

Mesopotomia will have to continue to wait. We are at the Channel again, just east of Dunkirk, in La Panne. Fine weather. We will swim in the ocean tomorrow. The 10th Battalion is 2 miles down, across the France-Flanders border in Bray-Dunes. R.W.K. has taken the coast! And we will hold the line!

Roast beef and potatoes twice in the last 3 days. My first taste of champagne. Sour, with too many bubbles.

There is a band playing in the town. We are all going to follow the music to find it.

La Panne, France: Sunday, 7 October, 1917

Dear Mr. Quaite,

It is beautiful here. Our beach, which extends north all the way to an inlet at the Ijzer, is superior to the 10th's at Bray-Dunes. Some of the 10th come up our way to lay on the sand in peace and quiet.

We are to be billeted locally next week. At present, we are in tents. The weather is so nice we are spoiled by stars.

La Panne, France: Tuesday, 9 October, 1917

Barry is in love. He has met a uniformed WAAC driver stationed in Dunkirk. His chief rival is a 2/Lieut from the Royal Army Medical Corps. She is a dark-haired beauty and very kind.

La Panne, France: Friday, 12 October, 1917

Dear Mr. Quaite,

I visited Dunkirk with Barry and his new girl friend here, Irene, a Women's Auxiliary Army Corps driver. She looks finer in her uniform than any of us. She can operate a motorbike with sidecar. The city has an ornate Town Hall. Its name is Flemish for dune-church. The Yanks are here, skulking around for a place to locate a naval base. They are rude fellows and extremely loud, especially when eating.

Irene warned us about the VD Hospital. One brave Corporal shot himself rather than be admitted. She was at the hospital when they brought him in. The surgeon discovered the syphilis on examination and the Corporal's diary confirmed it. "Love kills," Barry joked. "Not love," Irene replied. "Just sex." She is more than his match.

There is supposedly a brothel here that rivals Rue des Bons Enfantes in Armentieres. Life away from the front line can also be perilous.

La Panne, France: Monday, 15 October, 1917

Dear Mr. Quaite,

I have been cited for the Distinguished Conduct Medal and will be gazetted this week. Please look for it. The actual citation, which arrived at CSM Tranter's desk this morning, reads:

L./ C. R. Olcutt, R. W. Kent R.
For conspicuous gallantry and devotion
to duty. He has performed consistent good
work throughout. On one occasion during
an enemy counter-attack he rescued his
wounded O.C. and greatly helped to steady
his company by his coolness and daring.

It is not as colorful as the Military Medal, which has blue, white and
crimson stripes and a likeness of His Majesty on the face, the
inscription "For Bravery in the Field" on the obverse. The D.C.M. is
crimson and blue only, with the same likeness of King George V on
its face and "For Distinguished Conduct in the Field" on the other
side. Both are sterling!
SM Goulds has the Queen Victoria version, with Her Majesty's coat of
arms on the face. He will present the medals along with our new O.C.
when they both arrive.
The Channel was cold today and windy. Swimming in white caps is
more difficult than expected.

La Panne, France: Thursday, 18 October, 1917
Dear Mr. Quaite,
Barry's D.C.M. also arrived at CSM Tranter's desk. Its citation is
similar to mine. He was not at base today and I will have to tell him
this evening.
I have been billeted with a Mrs. Lawson and her collie, Rufus, in a
modest bungalow at the border between Flanders and France. She is
an ex-patriot since the 19th Century and a widow.
My room is an attic space, full of dormer angles. I hit my head twice
the first night. Rufus, at first suspicious of me, now eats from my
hand. Mrs. L. is surprised, as am I.

La Panne, France: Sunday, 21 October, 1917
My days are now regulated by a dog. I walk Rufus early each
morning. Mrs. L. has tea ready on our return. I then report to CSM
Tranter and either work at his desk or report to training as an
instructor. My specialty is the gas mask, though I barely understand
its mechanisms.
Released after lunch, I bring scraps to Rufus, who waits at the door
for my return. Another walk – Rufus prefers grass to sand when
relieving himself – and I head to the beach to meet friends. I take

dinner with them, bringing more scraps to Rufus and my dessert for Mrs. L. She favors bread pudding.

She has a wireless in her parlor. We get some news of the Zeppelin attacks on London. Most of the programs come from Calais and are in French. A final walk with the dog, then bed. The dog sleeps with Mrs. L., but rushes out as soon as he hears me on the stairs in the morning. In less than a week's time, he has me well trained.

La Panne, France: Tuesday, 23 October, 1917

Dear Mr. Quaite,

Our new O.C. arrived. Lt/Col. Beattie. Cpt. Jiminez is now second in command. He is fully recovered from his wounds and does calisthenics with us daily. Cpt. Kerr has taken over as Adjutant.

We have received too few new drafts. The 11th is still under 200 strong. Yet we are told to be ready to be sent back to the line any day now. Rumors also have us going to India or Egypt, possibly Ireland! Mesopotamia is no longer being considered.

We are of one mind. If we are sent back to Ypres or anywhere near the Salient, we will protest – not that it will do much good.

La Panne, France: Saturday, 27 October, 1917

Dear Mr. Quaite,

The moon has returned. Its light on the Channel is soothing.

When my landlady, Mrs. Lawson, learned I was from Rusthall, her face lit up. Her brother's wife actually dined at Dornden House in Langston Green with the Princess Louise. The description she gave me of the dining room and gardens made me think she had taken ownership of her sister-in-law's memory.

Her brother disliked Tunbridge Wells and she refuses to consider it a "Royal" town. He was killed in the Sudan, serving on General Gordon's staff. Mrs. L. and her husband left England shortly after that to settle here. Her sister-in-law remarried and has never come across to visit her. Bad blood between them to this day.

The way Mrs. L. says her sister-in-law's name – Mary – makes the dog snarl.

La Panne, France: Wednesday, 31 October, 1917

Dear Mr. Quaite,

Mrs. Lawson is the first person I have met who does not like Mr. Kipling's writing. She calls it "pedestrian to a fault." I keep my Kipling hidden from her. There are several clubs in Dunkirk with libraries containing his books. I have read several of them, even his poetry, and admire *The Man Who Would Be King* for its revelations about the folly of conquest and war. There is not a single battle I have taken part of that I can say I understood. Everything is forward, retreat, advance, dig in, go over, form up – a constant shifting amid destruction so complete that one battlefield looks like every other. We distinguish them by the amount of mud and how many we lose.

I will buy my own copy of this novella as the first book in my own library, after your gift. To think it was written one year after my birth! If I could write as fine a book about my experience as Mr. Kipling has about his, I would start scribbling tonight.

La Panne, France: Tuesday, 6 November, 1917

Dear Mr. Quaite,

We are to be sent by train to Italy within a week. No one knows how that will be possible, given the state of the front. CSM Tranter has closed up his office in preparation. I am to assist him in correspondence while traveling.

The war has become fierce in Italy, so we will again find ourselves in combat. We are told the Italian mud will taste better than the Flanders variety.

Barry has asked Irene to marry him. He expects her answer tomorrow or the next day. When she learns we are leaving, I fear she will turn him down. That will make a long train ride unbearable.

La Panne, France: Friday, 10 November, 1917

Mrs. L. kissed me on the cheek and hugged me as if I were her son this morning. Rufus whined as I walked out of the yard, wanting one more of our walks. Already I miss the sharp angles of my room and the tail-wagging nuzzles. I would like to live seaside or at least near some body of water. It calms me the way the countryside no longer can.

We mustered in the field, then went to tents. Our train departs within the next three days. No one is certain of the exact day or time yet.

Barry is in tears. Irene was unable to see him the past few nights. He talks of slipping out to find her and convince here of his love. I will sleep with one eye open, on guard to stop him, just in case.

La Panne, France: Tuesday, 13 November, 1917

Dear Mr. Quaite,

This morning after breakfast we marched to the train depot near the waterfront, past the broad beach at Dunkirk, and boarded. The cars were outfitted with slat beds for seats. We are packed in to the point that writing is difficult. Even moving about is awkward, as our full packs take up most of the floor.

Continuing – **Somewhere in France**
Wednesday, 14 November, 1917

We had hoped to head south to Paris. Instead we are pushing into Flanders. The train stops for no reason in the middle of nowhere, then starts up again without notice. We are not permitted to disembark. This makes private behavior a public spectacle.

Continuing – **Somewhere in Italy: Friday, 15 November, 1917**

Yesterday we were treated to the Riviera and the sky blue Mediterranean Sea. All along the route – Toulon, Nice – the train was met by villagers bringing food, wine and flowers. This continued until we passed through Savona. Still, no one was permitted on or off the train.

The station of Nice looks like a white palace. Most of the others to the north resemble giant conservatories. We had thought we would be routed through Switzerland, but the wisdom of the British Infantry prevailed again, finding the longest way to the objective.

At Genoa, where the station was completely dark and empty, we headed north between two mountain ranges. It is getting colder by the minute, but most of us are thankful the car windows are stuck open, bringing in fresh air to lessen the foul stink of us.

Continuing – **Somewhere in Italy: Sunday, 18 November, 1917**

Our concentration area is the town of Asola, which we reached late last night. Finally, we are off that train. CSM Tranter advised us we are to begin the march east at first light, with no rest. The Italians may not hold the Piave line and we are to cover 150 miles on foot without delay.

Pradelle, Italy: Monday, 19 November, 1917

We skirted the base of Parco Mincio outside of Asola. Good solid footing, flat valley land. The 90-lb packs are unwieldy, but dry, so the straps do not cut into shoulders. We are not met by villagers, yet they watch us from houses and hillsides.

Vallese, Italy: Wednesday, 21 November, 1917

Geography changing. Distant mountains, snow-capped. We remain
south of Verona. Very few of us falling out, though the ground now
inclines against us. Yesterday we passed through Isola Della Scala
where the 10th was headquartered. They are a full two days ahead of
us.

Albaredo, Italy: Thursday, 22 November, 1917

Crossed the Adige this afternoon and marched through the city. A
few cheers from windows, but no residents ventured out. The
prettiest town so far was Tombazosana, east of the river. SM Goulds
reports we have covered 67 miles.

Friola, Italy: Sunday, 25 November, 1917

Still heading north and east at a steady climb. The city of Soave is said
to be famous for a white wine, but we did not stop to try it. Instead,
we took the southern trail around Vincenza before swinging north to
Ospedaletto. The mountains are growing bigger. These are the Alps.
We crossed the Brenta river, swollen to flooding in some places. We
stopped east of Tezze Sul Brenta in a field of dying yellow. Real food,
including fresh fruit, makes this feel like a picnic, but most of us look
forward to sleep.
Another 45 miles covered.

Volpago del Montello, Italy:
Wednesday, 28 November, 1917

Hillocks tumble into the valleys from the Alps, with villages tucked
in the crevices like colorful bits of hard sweets. Much colder here.
After two full days of rest, we are freshened. Only 16 have fallen out.
We counted many more than that encamped along the road from the
10th, which came through yesterday. We have nearly caught them.

Somewhere in Italy: Saturday, 1 December, 1917

Dear Mr. Quaite,
We have reached the Piave and taken position at a big bend along
The Montello, opposite Casonetti. The Italian soldiers were grateful to
see us. They are anxious to take the fight to the Germans, who hold
solid defensive positions across the river.
Yesterday, we marched through a town named Bavaria. It was
startling to read that sign. Some thought we might have wandered in
enemy territory.

The nearest city is Nervesa, which has a tall tower, previously targeted by the German artillery. No direct hits to date.

The river is wide and fast, the current driving past small islands. We can see no activity in the trees on the other side, but are told Fritz conducts regular patrols there.

We have been staring at those same mountain peaks for over two weeks, watching them get closer. The Alps now look close enough to touch. Capt. Rodgers told us that the 11th had the fewest men fall out on the 152-mile march of all battalions. If we had not been so exhausted, we would have cheered.

Somewhere in Italy: Thursday, 6 December, 1917

Dear Mr. Quaite,

The Montello is wooded mostly with evergreens and oak and walks through it are fragrant. From the road that winds around it, the river is clearly visible for miles. Today, large chunks of ice rode the current, crashing against islands with such force they cartwheel.

We are told that the Italians are buoyed by our presence. The Piave Line is crucial to the protection of Venice, less than 30 miles to the south, where the river empties. There are occasional thuds of artillery in the distance, most to the south, beyond Nervesa.

Back on rations until the battalion is resupplied.

The Montello, Italy: Sunday, 9 December, 1917

Stragglers arriving. CSM Tranter processing them. Those who fell out during the march are to be given extra duties on sentry and latrine details.

Some flooding from up-river. Southern bank eroding as the current carves it up. The water is cold enough to numb fingers. Barry set up a sniper blind at wood's edge, but he and the other sharp-shooters have been instructed to fire only on uniformed enemy troops attempting to cross the river.

We go into Nervesa this week for supplies. Looking forward to that.

Somewhere in Italy: Friday, 14 December, 1917

Dear Mr. Quaite,

The city of Nervesa bustles with activity. The church tower beyond the center of town stands over a large courtyard, filled with uniformed men. CSM Tranter oversaw the loading of our supplies. Barry and I were permitted to remain behind and wait for any from the 11th who fell out during our march here. We are still missing 6.

In the very center of the city there is a park surrounding an old abbey made of white rock. Sant'Eustachio. It has been hit several times by artillery that fell short of the domed tower farther on. Children run through the rubble and climb the ragged edges of the walls. There are a few craters in the grass, some half filled with water, like reflecting ponds. Even in this condition, it offers quiet from the supply trolleys and the movement of our heavy guns over the streets.

There are Italian Alpine troops in the city. They wear broad-brimmed hats with a raven feather in the band, and their dark blue tunics have green cuffs! We thought they were part of a traveling theater troop when we first saw them.

Our posts are being sent, but we have yet to receive any letters or packages due to our repositioning. I hope this will be corrected by Christmastime.

The Montello, Italy: Thursday, 20 December, 1917

Half-moon coming on for the solstice tomorrow. My father's favorite day, being the shortest of the year and allowing him extra sleep. I think I now know how he feels. Nights here are cold and stark, but what little moon there is now reflects on the snowcapped peaks and the hard running river. We have nothing like this at home. I volunteer for night sentry to be closer to the water and the view. This allows me to miss morning muster and sleep until the sun is well up. A routine of ease, though Barry thinks me mad to take duty relegated to new recruits.

Somewhere in Italy: Monday, 31 December, 1917

Dear Mr. Quaite,

We spent Christmas Eve and Day in the evergreens. Fine dry weather until today. A light snow is falling. The air here is so clean. It smells of flowers, though none are in bloom. There is talk we may be billeted in town. Most of us hope we will remain in the trees.

A parade in the city is planned for Sunday. The Epiphany here is a more important occasion than Christmas itself. There is to be a band and a special wine, much like champagne, but sweeter – Prosecco. Barry and I plan to be among the first to try it. Our promotions to Corporal will become effective in April. We are to be paid as full Corporals starting in March. Everything is expensive here, except broccoli and pears. They taste good, but are hard on the stomach. Cabbage and onions are in everything here, especially the soup.

Our first post is scheduled to arrive this week. I hope to have letters from you and packages from my mother and Madge. I sent them small animals fashioned out of pine by wood carvers here. They are brightly painted. If I can find some in their natural state, I will post them to you to go with the ones from India you keep in your office.

The Montello, Italy: Saturday, 12 January, 1918

The coldest day yet. Barry thought he saw a child in the river. It turned out to be a young goat, carried down by the current and frozen solid.

Some shells fell into the river south of the city, blown off target by the stiff winds out of the mountains. No one understands why the Italians have yet to advance.

All stragglers finally reported in. CSM Tranter placed me in charge of the morning scheduling. I have more friends now than ever before, each asking for favors and light duty. Many of them will turn into enemies when I fail to oblige them.

Somewhere in Italy: Sunday, 20 January, 1918

Dear Mr. Quaite,

I received 6 of your letters and have read them each several times. I did not realize that the censors would blacken out so much of the detail in my letters. I will not be able to provide that information until I am back home.

Packages and non-letter post are being held at Asola due to the disruption in transit routes. We will not get them until we withdraw. Some are bored to the point of planning rogue raids across the river, which has now flooded the south bank, forcing us back up the slope. Rafts are being built. They cannot be used until the river is lower. The good news is that Fritz will also be unable to cross and threaten us. During the day, the river grumbles as it rushes by, but at night, it hisses. There is no explanation for this.

The Montello, Italy: Saturday, 26 January, 1918

Full moon. The ground is silver with frost. The Piave has been angry of late. There are at least two main currents. One follows the south bank, the other hugs the higher far bank and is much stronger there. Sgt. Jeffs threw a full pozzy tin toward the north bank and it sailed down river as fast as birds fly.

New talk that we will be sent back to Flanders. Much grumbling and a refusal to work by many. The raft building has stopped. OC has not put in an appearance to deal with to the rumors. This has made matters worse.

The Montello, Italy: Tuesday, 5 February, 1918

Barry confided he will go missing rather than return to Ypres. His feeling is shared by several in A Company.

SM Goulds ordered the raft building to resume. The busy work has offered some relief from the boredom.

A big snow hit yesterday. Relieved sentries looked like snowmen coming back in. Our gloves are no match for this weather.

Tomorrow we are to test fire our MLEs. They have not seen action in three months. There is concern the cold will have affected the ammunition, creating misfires. Sgt. Jeffs dismisses this and has offered to fire any man's rifle – for a day's pay each. So far, he has no takers.

Somewhere in Italy: Tuesday, 12 February, 1918

Dear Mr. Quaite,

Yesterday, Lt/Col. Corfe rejoined us and resumed command of the 11th. Thinner but still ram-rod straight, his arrival comforted all of us. He invited Barry and me to dinner last evening. Several others, including Major Jiminez, were present. The OC talked to us privately, believing we had saved his life at the Salient. Barry responded that we had both done as much for others in previous battles. He shook our hands and told us it was his privilege to command the 11th and his honor to serve alongside to two of us. We were left speechless. Later, drinking that sparkling wine made locally, the OC addressed rumors that we would be sent back to Flanders, joking that he expected the 11th to be relieved here by the end of the month and that the War Office would not have ordered a man so recently wounded back into action for any reason other than to lead our homecoming. He then read the New Year's Honours list, which cited him for a second bar to the D.S.O. and Major Jiminez for the M.C. Barry and I were listed for our D.C.M.s.

We are still thick-headed from too much wine and glory, now with visions of soon returning to England.

The Montello, Italy: Thursday, 14 February, 1918

Awaiting movement orders. Despite the OC's assurances, worry
persists and rumors of another stint in Ypres linger. There is
eagerness for action from the subalterns and recruits newly arrived.
Sgt. Jeffs thinks they are as daft as ducks, bent on suicide.

Rafts ready, though the river is still too high for safe travel. MLEs
tested. Ammunition not defective.

Boots polished for our dinner with the OC look out of place among
the rank-and-file. Even CSM Tranter noticed.

Somewhere in Italy: Sunday, 17 February, 1918

Dear Mr. Quaite,

Barry and I have been selected to trail a patrol to the north bank. It is
to be the first of several before we are officially relieved. Lt/Col. Corfe
approved it, with instructions to retreat at once if we encounter the
enemy. Sgt. Jeffs and Capt. Rodgers are selecting the crossing points,
calculating the current these past few days. They will take the main
group over. We will follow to protect the raft tie ups when the patrol
goes forward.

SM Goulds promised this will be the only patrol Barry and I would
be sent on. Since it is the first, SM believes we will have the element
of surprise, making this crossing less dangerous than those to follow.
We have not seen any sign of Fritz on the high bank, further
improving our confidence. There will be a half moon tomorrow, but
with low clouds coming off the mountains, we should be well
concealed.

There is now a train running in Treviso, a half-day's march south.
Once we are officially relieved, it will take us straight through to
Milan, well removed from this front. There is an opera theater there
that has not missed a performance since the war began! I would very
much like to see it and take in a show – if we are permitted off the
train this time.

BOOK THREE

SISTERS

14 JUNE, 1918

1

They moved small groups of them at night, the newest first. Fresh from the northern flank above the Brenta River, those Italian soldiers had the latest information the Germans wanted. Not Germans, according to the sharp-nosed Italian Corporal named Ezio. "Austriaci," he said. "More bad." Even their Hungarian allies feared the Austrians.

There were caves in the nearby mountains. Once there, prisoners never left. "The mountain eats them," Ezio said, translating what one of the others had overheard the guards laughing about.

With fewer men in the pen, rations decreased. After the first week, they were down to a single meal each day. Some sort of liquid, the color of rusty water, served in sets of cups everyone had to share. Those trying to sneak back in line for a second helping were taken out, stripped and flogged with wet canvas belts, left face-down until the blood began to dry and the welts swelled.

Reg couldn't shake the daily hunger headaches. His fingernails began clouding up. His skin hurt when scratched. Like the others, he ate new snow as it fell, huddled closed for the warmth of body heat. The second week, they took everyone's boots. Some now wore their soft caps on their feet, others pulled their trousers lower to cover what was left of their socks.

Crawling on knees replace walking. Movement in early morning, when the soil had lost all its warmth, became difficult for all, impossible for a few. Men urinated where they lay. Bowel movements no longer occurred. Groups of guards came in and took buttons and insignias, ripping them off rather than risk carrying sharp objects or knives in to do the job. Pieces of dirty, rotting uniforms came off with many of those buttons, leaving openings for freezing air to target brittle skin.

Late one afternoon, after the snows had stopped and the wind warmed, the guards led a lame horse into camp, shot it and butchered it, letting the blood stream into the pen. They cooked the meat over the open fires that they huddled around all day and night. The aroma of burning flesh made Reg sick. He vomited, but nothing came up. Eyes closed, he could hear them chewing: little satisfied grunts punctuating their swallows.

That Lieutenant Rommel had not been seen in camp again. No officers had been spotted until yesterday, when a column of heavy guns growled down the road toward the river. There had been more noise this morning: the tramp of boots on hard ground, the rumble of equipment rolling on carts.

"They strike," Ezio said. "Like Caporetto." When he hung his head, his whole body seemed to get soft. "We die here."

The others must have sensed that, too. They stopped looking through the wire at the guards, the mountains. They sipped cold broth in silence. Conversation stopped, but some lips still moved in prayer. The pen had never been this quiet. Even the guards noticed.

It felt as though the inside of his head was shriveling up. His ears throbbed with a constant drumbeat. He tried to sleep, but except for the moment he must have passed out, he couldn't get his mind to mirror the new silence. The cool ground was actually trembling – or maybe that was him, shivering. There were voices running together: Mr. Quaite barking above the clatter of a linotype, his father at the plow shouting at the old horse that never obeyed, his mother clattering pans in her kitchen, the boys from the sweeps caves yelling as they ran naked down to the water to clean up and cool off, Madge tapping the store window to point out that new dress, Barry laughing at his own jokes so hard that air filled his nose and made him snort.

Then it started. The big guns lit up the still-dark sky, booms coming from all sides, even from behind, with shells whizzing high overhead like birds on fire. Black Marias for sure. Distant explosions filling the narrow spaces between the thunder of the artillery. Now the guards were cheering, dancing around their fires. The ground was so alive with sound and shaking, it felt like riding on the water.

It didn't stop. The crumps began to hurt his chest. The more he hugged his body, the worse it got. He tried to stand. Dizzy, he sank to a knee. Some men covered their ears, curled into balls. Others cried out – more prayers, probably. Maybe profanity. It all sounded the same now. He could feel a scream building in his lungs. The cool air hurt too much to let out that fast. Like living inside a bass drum, all the noise made him nauseous. Was he fading into the rumble of the guns or being torn apart by it? Was that the sun coming up or was the castle on fire? Can a person drown in sound?

If he crawled to the wire, pulled himself up and found the strength to make it look as if he was trying to escape, maybe they would shoot. That would be better. He rolled onto his side, got to his knees.

It stopped.

The shock of that sudden silence crippled him. Toppling over, he gasped for breath. It hurt to blink. He felt his face tighten, straining as if about to break.

His tears surprised him.

2

They ate. Hard bread and warm broth, chunks of potatoes bobbing in it. Fresh water. A celebration, the guards said, of certain victory. The Arch Duke Josef himself had led the assault, taking Nervesa, capturing The Montello. The Piave River was theirs. The plain above Vicenza would be next. The Brenta would follow, then its valley. Surrounded on three sides, Venice would fall.

If the Austrians had marched through the flood plain to cross over into Nervesa, Gabby would be taken. Teresa and the girls would be found. Troops would occupy all structures still standing. Some might be warming themselves in front of the small hearth at Luigi's right now or eating fresh cheese under the slate roof at Teresa's, drinking from her well.

And what would be left of 11th? If they were still there, the bombardment would have pushed them up the western slope of The Montello. Lieut/Col Corfe would not sit there for long. He would not retreat. He had not come back from the dead to lead the entire battalion to its own destruction. Would he get to see the Arch Duke before it was over? Would Sgt. Jeffs have one more Mills bomb to throw before all of his wars caught up with him? Were those stacks of undeliverable letters CSM Tranter kept now kindling for Fritz's cook fires?

The potatoes would not stay down. The sound of 150 men throwing up, then picking through their vomit for those same chunks, chewing and swallowing them again, filled this afternoon of sun, some warmth and no wind.

All in all, it felt like a good day.

•

Ezio crumbled the pieces of potato in his fingers, and like a father bird feeding his young, sprinkled the crumbles into the mouth of his friend, the one who spoke German, Hungarian and French. The wheezing man could barely muster the strength to swallow. His uniform hid how much weight he had lost, but his ankles told the truth: bones stretching skin so tight, the grimy features looked like a skeleton lying on the dirt.

Aircraft engines droned out of the north. Everyone in the pen scanned the sky, but no one wanted to see which side those planes belonged to. They had to be German, and when the first bombs hit on the other side of the Piave, the sound of the final death blow caused

Reg and the others to stare at the dirt, their last reality, the only thing left that could not be taken from them.

When the aerial machine gun fire got closer, some of the prisoners cried, others ducked their heads under their arms. The guards watched the skies, mumbled to each other. The fat one began gathering up ration tins. The stocky Corporal checked his rifle, sighted down the long barrel at the prisoners in the corner nearest the road, then just as quickly lowered the weapon and went back to eating horsemeat.

Bombs kept exploding in the distance. Aircraft engines got closer, then farther away, their machine guns stinging the sky. Artillery shells screamed though the valley just beyond the first rise leading down to the river. A dreadful lullaby, rattling the air, the ground, his brain.

Ration tins clinked in a sack slung over a shoulder, turning the fat private into a grotesque Father Christmas, slinking away toward the old cemetery for his own private feast, the dying light swallowing him. Reg closed his eyes, unwilling to see any more of this. Curled up near the others, he struggled to fill his mind with images of Denny Bottom, *The Gazette* office, Madge, that first kiss on the walk home from Tunbridge Wells, the first time she had let him touch her breast – at the door to shed at the farm, when they were both sweaty from chasing each other across the north field – but he kept imagining Gabby, her back to him, staring out the tiny window, looking for that pesky jay she treated like a pet. The sound of her whisper drew him toward sleep and the warmed dirt.

●

Sun painted the others still sleeping. The guards had left their post. Their fire had gone out. No sign of their food stores. He fought dizziness, made it to the gate. Some sort of bolt lock held it shut. He took off his tunic, wrapped it around a strand of barbed wire, tried to pry it off the post. Two of the other prisoners came to help, using their uniforms the same way.

Then they saw them coming. Straight at them. A dozen of them zigzagging across the camp. Elves. Hats with feathers. Bits of green and gold on their arms. Ropes over their shoulders, grappling hooks, rifles. They darted through shadows, barely making a sound.

The two Italians at the wire began cheering, "L'Alpini!" over and over again, like a chant. Others in the pen stirred, joined the cheer, tried to stand. Those fast-moving elves reached the wire, cut the strands near the gate and ripped the wire free. They greeted the

99

prisoners with hugs. One of them brought in water. A few others began helping those who couldn't stand. Those who could were dancing now, their voices rising like song.

Reg put his tunic back on, stepped out of the pen. He got water at the barrel by the guard post. Through the commotion in the pen, he could make out Ezio, sobbing, his friend of the many languages motionless beside him. Reg found an empty tin, filled it with water, carried it back in, helped hold the makeshift cup to Ezio's mouth.

"L'Alpini," he said, taking a sip. "From the mountain. Safe now."

They were everywhere at once, checking teeth, eyes, ears, hair, fingers, feet. They handed out grain. And chocolate! It felt like Christmas Eve.

3

The two dozen who could still walk were led up the road , over a small hill and into the woods. It was slow-going, the rugged ground battling bootless feet. Beyond a narrow meadow, the three Alpine Rangers leading the group got everyone into a small depression, then covered them with branches. The spoke in quick bursts, like rifle fire. They pushed water and grain bags under the pine needles. Then they jogged back toward the castle.

"We stay," Ezio said. "They return."

Reg watched them get smaller. "How long?"

With a shrug, Ezio rolled onto his side. "No move. Stay."

Through the branches, Reg could make out part of the ancient road that ran across this little valley from the river, the same ground he had walked after being captured. Nothing moved down there. The scent of fresh-cut pine covered the stink of the men. Every time a few of them would start whispering, one of them shushed them. After a while, most were napping, sipping water, chewing the crumbly grain that tasted like old seed even a cow would refuse to eat. Those Alpine troops survived on this stuff. For weeks. Longer. No wonder Ezio and the others saw them as the best of the best.

It wasn't until dusk that he realized the guns and the bombs were getting closer. Aircraft engines roared over tree tops so fast he couldn't read their markings. Artillery seemed to be coming from the river now, that whizzing getting stronger as the shells pierced the dryness before striking the ground. If this kept up, everything would sweep over them, blowing up every tree, every rock, every living thing.

•

The creak of wagon wheels woke him up. Carts filled the road. Horses, small artillery guns, a swarm of men in uniform moving at different speeds, no longer a column, more like a scrum. Bombs started exploding again. Big shells kicked up clouds of dirt and debris down the valley.

Now aircraft engines. Machine guns strafing men and animals on the road. Unable to outrun the bullets, some turned to fire at the planes, using the carts as shields. But the planes kept circling like falcons, swooping in, relentless machine gun fire splintering the carts, shattering the soldiers, ripping the horses apart.

Every now and then, a stray bullet would strike the edge of the meadow a few yards from the shelter. None of the soldiers down there thought to climb the embankment to the woods. Instead, they fled up the road toward the castle or skidded further down the slope to the valley floor.

It all stopped as suddenly as it had erupted. The planes flew off, leaving the road quiet. Bombs and artillery shells kept falling in the near distance, but the only thing moving down there was a horse struggling to stand. It took the better part of an hour for it to die, its last snort soaked up by the wreckage.

He kept watching: a vulture on a perch. His scan flitting over each body, he looked for any sign of breathing, any finger movement. He started to crawl out from the branches.

Ezio grabbed his tunic. "Hungarians. They die a long time."

Reg kept moving. On this stomach, he made it across the opening and into the saplings and brambles on the slope down to the road. From here, he could see them clearly. What was left of them. The brains of a few were still leaking onto the ground. After what felt like a long time, he got to his knees, then stood. Then he started down the slope.

A dead soldier wrapped in brambles had his rifle still strapped to his shoulder. Reg freed the weapon, opened its bolt to make sure it was loaded. He checked for aircraft, then took baby steps between the bodies, looking for someone his size. He found him near one of the horses. Its side had been opened up by bullets almost as if a vet had stopped in the middle of surgery. What was oozing out was not recognizable. Some of it was green.

He struggled to unknot the top laces, loosened the rest, then yanked the boots off the dead soldier. They fit. He laced them tighter and started back between the bodies toward the slope.

Something grabbed his ankle. The shock made him stumble. He looked down his leg at the hand gripping his boot, the wide eyes of the soldier. "Segíts," that bloodied face said.

Reg aimed the rifle, put his finger on the trigger. He stopped. The sound of a gunshot might signal the enemy. He kicked free of the soldier's grip, crawled over bodies to a bayonet glinting in sunlight. He picked up that rifle and readied a lunge at the throat of the Hungarian with the outstretched arm. But that body wasn't moving anymore. Reg unlatched the bayonet, knelt to put the point against the man's Adam's apple, felt for a pulse. Shrapnel had punctured the man's cheek, turning it into lace. He withdrew the blade, stood, slung

102

a rifle over each shoulder, and made his way up the slope and back to the shelter.

The others stared at him in silence. He stabbed the bayonet into the ground, handed a rifle to Ezio. "We'll take turns. Guard duty. I'll go first."

Brittle fingers with big knuckles ran over the weapon. Ezio nodded, whispered to the others, who whispered back. He turned to Reg: "Boots for them?"

"Later," Reg said. "When it gets dark. I'll go down and get them."

When the others heard Ezio's translation, they nodded and smiled. "Campione," one of them said.

"Eroe," Ezio patted Reg on the shoulder. "You. Hero."

It made him laugh. "Thief's more like it. A scavenger."

The little man shrugged. A moment later, he was passing the rifle around. A new breeze, quiet through the evergreens, made the meadow grass dance. Reg braced the rifle at the edge of the shelter and settled in. So much daylight left, so much thunder creeping closer, so much doubt about what might come up that road.

•

They came from the other direction, the castle at their backs. Two Alpine Rangers dashed over the carnage, nudging bodies, long guns at the ready. They checked inside what was left of the carts, around and under the dead horses, even down the artillery barrels. They scanned the trees before scampering through the brambles on the downslope to the valley, thrashing through tall brush, then running back up to the road. One of them turned toward the castle and waved his hat.

Slowly, a band of villagers — all older men, at least 30 of them — walked toward the riddled corpses. They pried rifles from hardening fingers, picked through uniform pockets, tucked bayonets into their belts, pocketed ration tins, yanked boots off, tied the laces together, hung them around their necks. In the dusk, they looked like rats sneaking in to crawl over trash, hunting for morsels.

One of them was Luigi.

Reg tried to swallow. He climbed out from under the branches, stood. Both Alpine Rangers swung around, training their rifles on him. He raised his arms. "Luigi!"

The stooped over man squinted.

"You know this one?" Ezio poked through the pine branches. "How?"

Reg nodded, then shouted: "Luigi DaPonte!"

Ezio took the rifle from Reg and handed it behind him to the others now coming up out of the hiding place. One of the Alpine Rangers was already halfway up the slope. He was grinning. He said something to Ezio, then began helping the others to their feet.

"We are dead too he thinks," Ezio said, following Reg down the little hill.

At the line of brambles just off the road, Luigi could finally make him out. He dropped his rifle and the ration tin. "L'Inglese? È possibile?"

That hunched over body moved like a teenager. He reached Reg in the brambles, hugged him, kissed his cheeks, touched his face as if to make sure it was real.

"Ask him about Gabby," Reg said. "And Teresa. And the girls."

Luigi didn't wait for Ezio to finish the question. "Sono sicuri. Tutti."

"All safe." Ezio said. "How you know these?"

Four more Alpine Rangers ran down the road, barking orders. The villagers took what they could carry and climbed the slope toward the shelter. Grabbing the rifle and two tins of rations, Luigi led Reg back through the brambles, pushing him to move faster and talking to Ezio the whole time.

"In the trees, we walk." The frail soldier fought a cough. "The Hungarians run now."

"Why are we going toward the gunfire?" Reg said.

Ezio crossed one arm over the other, pointed in opposite directions:" "They go. We come."

The game trail through the evergreens was wide enough for single file, but the Alpine Rangers forced the group to trample light brush at the edges to quicken the hike into the safety of the denser wood. Then the pace slowed. Villagers passed out boots, helping the soldiers put them on, kept them moving. No one spoke. Giving his rifle to Reg, Luigi silenced the tins in his pocket, looped an arm through Reg's. Together, they moved down the narrow path as if heading down an aisle toward a church altar.

•

They stopped in the dark when the artillery guns quit firing. Bayonets opened ration tins, served as spoons. Most dug in with fingers. It was saltier than Maconochie and just as awful.

According to the villagers, the Arch Duke had taken the northern half of The Montello and all of Nervesa the day of the endless bombardment. After vicious fighting, he was driven back, his troops pinned against the river. Many drowned – thousands of them shot as they swam. Aircraft followed those who made it across, strafing, bombing. A slaughter.

The Italians flooded the river on purpose. Floating bridges were swept away. The Austro-Hungarian forces were split, most fleeing over the north ridge of the valley, near San Michele, the smaller segment crossing the Piave at the bridge south of Nervesa. The plan of the Alpine Rangers was to keep to the woods in between both retreating factions and work down from the north back toward Colfosco, allowing the pursuing Italians to clear the area in pursuit.

"Three day." Ezio eyed the tired ex-prisoners. "More if they fall."

"What about the others we left at the camp?"

"In castle, with the wine." Ezio's smile revealed bleeding gums. "Lucky, no?"

Reg sipped water from the goatskin. "If the river flooded, is your house still there?"

Weathered hands took the water bag. He shrugged. He told Ezio something about Gabby and Teresa.

"She goes to her sister. No river." He took a long swig, let out a sigh as if he had been holding his breath. "He say you save her. And him."

Luigi held out a hand. An identification disc dangled from his fingers. That thin piece of metal felt warm. Reg put it around his neck, tucked it under his gray shirt.

The two Italians exchanged fast words. Ezio smiled – "He say, thank you for life" – then kissed Reg on the cheek, patted his shoulder. "Amico."

A moment later, the Alpine Rangers had everyone up and moving again, cutting through the darkness, feeling their way tree to tree like hunters scouting prey, yet followed by heavy footsteps, a gaggle of coughs and wheezes, the clinks and clanks and the rattle of rifles against tinned rations and bayonets.

It sounded like hope.

4

The forest above San Daniele-tombola was canted on a foothill, with no level ground. Tree trunks acted like braces, preventing the weak from skidding down the slope. Below, the town stirred with villagers doing morning tasks. The war had passed by here without leaving a mark.

But it was not safe. Stragglers from the retreating army might find this place, use it to hide, plunder supplies, kill. The Alpine Rangers would go down there tonight. Once past the village, Reg and the others would have to make the rest of the journey south on their own.

A rutted road cut across a terrace. To stay in the cover of trees, the road had to be crossed. One of the Alpini went east, another west, scouting. Birds chirped, black ants scurried over pine needles and decaying leaves, but nothing else stirred until both Rangers strolled toward each other on the road. The other two Alpini led the group down out of the trees. Most skidded on their butts. A few tumbled sideways. It was a little miracle that none of the rifles discharged.

Using their ropes and grappling hooks, the Alpini rigged a line from the road to the plateau beneath it. Hand-over-hand, each member of the group went down, digging heels into the slippery soil to maintain balance. Luigi had no problem with the trip, but Ezio's lack of hand strength forced him to hug the rope, stopping his own progress and holding up the procession. By the time everyone had reached the landing area, most of the ex-prisoners were exhausted. The Alpini led them to a resting area at the edge of the plateau.

From here, while eating cold tinned stew, Reg could make out the big river, its water shimmering in sunlight. It was a long way down. One of the villagers said he had hunted up here as a boy, when wolves owned these woods. The smallest Alpini laughed at that, saying no one had seen a wolf in this area in 40 years. He used a twig to draw a map in the dirt, showing the way over the plateau down to Casonetti, a town they should stay clear of because the enemy army had staged operations out of it.

All four Alpine Rangers stood, formed a line shoulder-to-shoulder. In unison, they saluted the group. "Vai rapido e sicuro, e essere intelligenti." The small one grinned at the villager who had hunted here. "Come il lupo."

Then they turned and headed back to their ropes, climbing back up to the road. Reg couldn't remember any of them drinking any water or eating any food. The way they moved, they didn't seem human.

"They say go fast, safe," Ezio told him between swallows of stew. He tapped a temple with his index finger. "And smart. Like the wolf."

The ropes slithered through the trees like frightened snakes. Then nothing, just wind out of the mountains. The group surrounded the map in the dirt. There was discussion, then an argument, then disgust, anger, pointing fingers and snarls. Reg pulled Ezio aside.

"Ask Luigi if he knows the way."

Surprised, the old man nodded.

"Then let's go," Reg said. "You lead."

Drawing a deep breath, filling his lungs with pride, that stooped over body started a slow, steady trudge through the heart of the sloping forest. "Andiamo."

•

The plateau fell away into little valleys, some steeper than others, but none as treacherous as those above San Daniele-tombola. At the end of one crevice, where another began, he could smell them.

On the flood plain below, hundreds of bodies, possibly thousands, lay scattered as if placed there by an invisible current. Some still had helmets on, the metal shining. They had been out there for at least four days. Crows had found them. But not a villager in sight.

The stench got worse with each step of the descent. At the edge of Casonetti, where the road could be seen unwinding into a straight shot to the river, Reg could make out separate groups of bodies. Some had hardened in awkward poses: legs in the air, knees bent, backs folded in half. Down where the woods ended, he could make out individuals frozen in panic: hands grasping air, heads on almost backward, faces wearing tormented smiles. And birds – ravens, crows, jays – pecking at eyes, cheeks, everything still soft.

They waited at the lip of this gore until nightfall. The odor made some men vomit. Most tried to breathe through their mouths. No one could eat. Luigi rubbed pine needles in his fingers to break them up, releasing their scent. He drew air through those hard cupped hands, and soon all the others were doing the same thing.

There would be a big moon tonight, almost full. A group like this straggling over a broad plain would be easy to spot, easier to target. Less than a hour's walk to the river, then less than that to Colfosco and even less after that to climb the little swale to Teresa's, and it could all end here, out in the open, in the middle of all those bodies – from one lone machine gun or even a rifle in the hands of a sharp-shooter like Barry. He shuddered at the thought of taking a bullet so close to seeing Gabby again, of falling on top of those decomposing bodies, sinking into that foul ground, becoming part of all this rot: fresh food for birds.

He pulled back the bolt on the rifle – a straight pull, this bolt did not rotate as his MLE did – and took out the clip. Just five round-nose bullets. The silvered tips were lead, the cartridge body brass or copper. Taking the weapon apart to clean it risked his being unable to put it back together the proper way. He reloaded, slammed the bolt home.

Five rounds. Not enough for a poor shot like him. He broke up more pine needles, breathed in their aroma, and as the sun began sliding behind the mountains on the other side of the river, he convinced himself that there were no machine guns lying in wait down there.

•

There were wolves.

Packs of them, each staying to separate areas. They lapped water from puddles left by the receding river, ripped flesh off the bodies, played tug-of-war with the larger chunks. When they saw Reg and the others, they ran like scared cats, taking cover in the tree line. Some yelped as they got entangled in the barbed wire still standing.

They looked silvery, though some were tawny from the blood of their feasting. They were beautiful.

The brawny villager who used to hunt in these mountains remained silent. He smiled at the moonlight, relishing the muttering of his doubting friends.

•

The north bank was littered with bodies, washed up in clumps. A few of them looked as though they were still climbing out of the water.

Pieces of floating bridges – big rafts, really, put together like scaffolds – stood on edge like fence posts. Some of the splintered wood, hurled like spears by the current, had impaled fallen soldiers. Where the river had flooded, all the grass had been washed away. The dark soil was speckled with debris: bits of tent canvas, helmets, mess tins, cart panels, brown jugs, bottles, body parts.

One of the villagers snapped a necklace off a decaying body. He examined the gold chain, opened the locket. Inside: a soggy portrait of an unsmiling woman. Thin fingers pinched the picture, tossed it onto the body, pocketed the locket. The night breeze rustled the little photograph, inching it down the dead man's legs toward the hungry river.

They walked on. Trees on the eastern slope of The Montello still smoldered, smoke following the current south like a mirroring fog. New craters dotted the flood plain. Some held twisted bodies, misshapened equipment. Torch lights in Nervesa streaked out of buildings shattered by bombs and artillery. The water carried voices from the other side — Italian.

By the time they got up the road, Colfosco was already asleep. A handful of men with rifles and shotguns, all smoking cigarettes and drinking wine, sat on a low wall in front of a brick and stone three-story building. When they saw the gaggle of unifoms and villagers tromping toward them, they scattered, running into the building through the street level doorway.

Most of the villagers in the group said their goodbyes and headed in different directions. A few of the others guided the ex-prisoners into the old building, where those hiding inside sent up a cheer. Ezio hugged Luigi — "Stai attento. Sempre." — then Reg. Those slim lips trembled, but no words came out. He turned, struggled to reshoulder the rifle, and limped through a doorway framed by crumbling mortar and exposed stone and brick. After all he had been through, would this building fall in on him — all of them? Was there any safe place left?

"A casa," Luigi said, taking a narrow side street toward the eastern edge of town, where the land fell away to the river, then rose again in a gentle swelling of tiny hills, where she would be, waiting.

5

He wanted to clean up first, wash the stink off. With hand gestures, he got that across to the old man, who primed the hand pump. It groaned, but softly enough not to wake anyone inside.

They had taken the long way, walking up from the far side of the swale, staying clear of the old road to Susegana, just in case. From that angle, the house looked different. It sat on the rise, bigger and more solid: commanding. Hard moonlight bounced off the black slate roof. The ladder lay on its side, where he had left it. He rested his rifle against it.

The bucket filled with cold water. Reg stripped down. The tunic slipped off easily. The trousers didn't. Sores on his legs had scabbed into the wool. It felt as though his uniform refused to let go. Some of those sores tore open. Blood and puss oozed down his thighs, thin rivers dribbling nowhere.

The long gray shirt was the most difficult to get out of. The light flannel had stood up better than the wool. His shoulders and arms ached, his elbows burned as he wriggled free. He used the shirt as a wash rag, dousing it in the bucket.

He had not looked at his body since being captured. Ribs he had never noticed made his chest seem small now, almost caved in. His knees were ugly knobs – deformed growths. The muscles in his legs looked stringy, not muscles anymore but cords, like wire. He dabbed at the open sores, saw the blotches of black-and-blue on his arms, his legs, his stomach. Most of his body hair was gone. His testicles had shriveled. They hurt went he ran the wet cloth over them.

How bad would Ezio look? Or the others who had been in the pen for so much longer? How had any of them managed to stay alive or make that trek up and down the mountain trail? He felt ashamed for equating his condition with theirs.

Steadying himself against the pump shaft, he pried off his socks. He needed a sliver of slate to scrape wool from the sores on his soles. Those scabs didn't bleed. They left new skin, so pink it didn't look real. Running the wet shirttail between his toes, he cleared cobwebbed clumps of fungus that smelled like dead rats.

Luigi came back out with a shirt and a pair of pants. His own, not the clothes Reg had worn at the river house. With the flat of his hand, he wiped dampness from his skin.

And she was standing there, just outside the door, watching.

Her stare grew smaller as it ran over him until she couldn't look anymore. Eyes closed, she wobbled, sobbing. The old man caught her, but her arms and legs weren't working, her head slumped against Luigi's round shoulder, her hair in streaks over his chest. The faded blue nightgown he had never seen before had worn so thin that in spots her skin seemed to be leaking through.

Before he could get a foot into the second pantleg, Teresa came out, a white kerchief on her head. She gasped, crossed herself. Dark eyes stayed wide open, but got glassy. "Un morto che cammina."

"No," Luigi bent an elbow to make a muscle. "Lui è forte."

Reg pulled up the pants, held them there, reached for the dry shirt. Gabby climbed the old man's arm, steadied herself. She walked to Reg, kissed his cheeks, put her arms around him. He began crying so hard he lost his grip on the pants. Naked in moonlight, he held on. The warmth of her made him shiver.

Then she was backing away. Her sister was draping him with a blanket, bracing him as he stepped out of the pantlegs. With the old man holding him up from the other side, she guided him toward the door, each step a tiny dagger into the tender new skin of his soles, stabbing his heels, the balls of his feet.

He glanced at the cloudless sky, those shiny black tiles. "No rain," he said.

•

They didn't speak. They got the fire going to heat water and soup. The kerchief got ripped into strips. A bowl clattered on the table. A chair scraped against the wood floor. Somehow, the noise didn't wake up the two girls in the far room. Teresa pulled that door shut, careful to make no sound. He was glad the little ones wouldn't have to see him like this.

Teresa scrubbed – too hard – every inch of him, between his legs, his butt cheeks. She was softer with his privates, but not gentle. She seemed to resent the task yet enjoy the grime she was removing, as if everything coming into her house had to be clean, even people. The hot water stung at first, then made the open sores itch. She rubbed something thick and buttery on the sores of his soles. It felt cool. It looked like lard. She wrapped the strips of her kerchief around his feet, tied knots on top to hold them in place.

He wanted to tell her she should have been a nurse. "Odd socks," he said.

Those dark eyes glared. "Shh."

At the edge of the fireplace, unable to look at him, Gabby watched soup bubble in the pot. She had lost weight, too. Her feet looked boney.

The blanket felt scratchy. The soup tasted briny, though sweetened by carrots. Steam rising from the bowl tingled his face, making him realize he had forgotten what hot food was. While he sipped broth, Teresa dried his hair with a rag. Wet strands came off in her hands, covering her fingers like dirty spiderwebs. It made her quiver. She found scissors in a basket near the arm chair, began clipping the little beard on his chin.

"Domani." Luigi kept the bowl to his mouth and slurped his soup. "Lascialo dormire un po '."

They guided him across the room. Her bed – in the corner behind the dark drape, near the door to the girls' room. Teresa helped lower his head to the pillow, touched his forehead so softly it felt like a blessing, drew the curtain closed.

He could hear her clear the bowls, put the chair back. He could smell the soup, the fire, Gabby's scent on the pillow. The main room went dark. The old man began snoring. The two women rustled under the covers in the big bedroom. No sound of artillery, no machine gun fire, no bombs, no aircraft engines, no death coughs, no screams of horses – just his own breath against her pillow.

When he realized he had left the rifle out by the hand pump, he shifted his legs to get up and bring it inside. He stopped, snuggled under the blanket, then smiled: "Tomorrow."

6

At first he thought it was a downdraft from the chimney, something he knew only too well from windy mornings in the old house in Rusthall. But this didn't smell like wood burning. The smoke was sour with something else — maybe something in a pot, one of Gabby's awful stews. This smelled like guff and flesh on fire.

He gathered the blanket around his waist and pushed past the drape. Through the side window, smoke billowed near the ladder. If the flames reached the rifle he had left out there, that open bullet clip might explode.

Barefooted over the cool floorboards and the sun-warmed flat pathway stones, he found her near the well, stirring the fire with a long branch. Flames snapped at his uniform and boots lying on top of old pine logs.

Nearby, the two little girls — he couldn't remember their names — chased each other in a game like tag, paying no attention to the flames or the stink of filthy wool, the sweat-stained leather burning.

She must have felt him standing behind her, because she turned halfway, that long gnarled branch like a staff, challenging any comers. "Si potrebbe mai indossare questi ancora una volta."

The thick tunic collar shriveled under the heat. "It was na-poo anway."

"Se i tedeschi ritorno e lo trovano," her free hand sliced across her throat like a knife, "uccideranno tutti." The tip of that branch now pointed at the little girls racing around the well pump. "Anche le ragazze."

Something about Germans killing everyone, even the girls. He studied the flames, wishing he could have seen the new Corporal chevrons burn, the ones he never got to sew on. "It still smells awful"

"Senza di loro," she said, stirring what was left of the tunic, "non si può essere di nuovo un eroe."

Was she calling him a hero or telling him he was not one? "No Er-oh-eh," he said, pointing a thumb at his chest. "Not me."

Her stare softened. Those blues got lighter and she allowed a tiny smile.

Teresa came around the corner, his rifle in one hand and a small kerchief bundle in the other. The older girl snatched the big white knot as if it were a brass ring on a carousel and ran into the house, never breaking stride, the little one trying to catch up.

"Torna in casa." Those dark eyes nodded at the doorway. She set the rifle against the ladder. When he didn't move, she nudged him toward the house. "Adesso."

The girls were placing small tomatoes in a bowl on the table, polishing each one with the kerchief. The littlest one — Sancia! — smelled each one first.

"Tuo zio si avvicina." Their mother walked past the table and disappeared into the bedroom. The girls ran outside. He watched them go up the swale to meet the old man who lumbered toward the house, a rifle slung over a shoulder, a sack in his arms. The bigger girl took the sack and lugged it back inside.

Little hands found a loaf of round bread and a chunk of white cheese in the sack, placed them on a plate, stared at them like presents that could not be opened until their birthdays had finally arrived. Sancia climbed a chair to reach for the cheese. Her big sister batted her hand away.

The small one had her mother's shiny dark eyes. She wagged a finger at him. "Non mangiare."

An instant later, both of them were back outside, singing and dancing around the fire and the well pump. Teresa strode from the bedroom, arms full of clothes. She dumped the pile on a chair. "Vestirsi," she said, moving toward the doorway, where she stopped and glared at him. "Adesso!"

Whatever she said, she meant business. He started with the socks, carefully pulling them on over those makeshift bandages. He searched the pile for underwear, found none. The pantlegs didn't reach his ankles, but the waist fit. No need for a belt. The dark shirt fit, too, though the sleeve cuffs came up short of his wrists. He stepped into the slippers. So soft, they felt like another layer of skin.

Gathered around the flames, they saw him coming. The old man gasped, Gabby dropped the branch. Teresa's eyes flared, she crossed herself: " Sembra come il mio Carmine."

Both Luigi and Gabby were giggling now, pointing at the length of the trousers and sleeves. A few seconds later, Teresa was chuckling, too. These clothes must have been her husband's. The little girls kept staring at the dark leather slippers.

"He's shorter than me." Reg joined them at the fire. "But our feet are about the same size."

He picked up the branch — it looked like oak — and poked the flames. That pile of smoldering dead wool and foul leather resembled the remains of a Viking funeral now. It was impossible to see that uniform whole anymore. He handed the branch back to Gabby and sniffed a laugh: "Finest set of clothes I ever owned."

They studied him as though he had dropped out of a cloud, some strange bomb in human form sent down to confuse them, a burden to feed and clothe and nurse, the man who kept showing up at their door like an unexpected package from some faraway land, the colorful stamps all over it more interesting than what might be inside. He didn't belong here. And he didn't want to leave.

"I know you think I'm bats," he told them, "but I promise to behave myself." He pointed at Gabby — "As long as she doesn't cook anything" — then glanced at Teresa. "Ah-dess-oh."

They were all squinting now, even the girls. He curled his fingers into claws, raised his arms and started creeping toward the well pump. The little one screeched a laugh and began dodging his advance. The older one didn't catch on as quickly, but by the time he reached the pump handle, she was moving with her sister, scampering past the ladder, then darting toward the swale.

"No fair," he said. "You're too fast for me."

"Si gioca giochi ora? Pazzo!" The dark-haired woman shook her head and marched back into her house. "Ragazzino!"

"I didn't scare them," Reg said. "It was just a game."

"Suo marito, Carmine," the old man laid a heavy hand on Reg's shoulder, "non ha mai giocato i giochi dei bambini."

Huband, named Carmine. Babies. Nicoletta — that was the older one's name! He waved at the girls.

Gabby didn't look up from the fire. Her voice sounded sad, as though she was revealing some unfortunate secret: "Carmine non ha mai giocato nessun gioco."

This husband Carmine must be an odd one. Reg let out a sigh. "Sounds like he's a real kill joy." He bent his legs, making himself shorter, then forced a big frown. "Carmine?"

Luigi laughed so hard he almost toppled into the fire. Gabby stopped laughing long enough to help the old man sit on the ladder.

"Un pazzo? No. Un ragazzino, sì." A thick thumb tapped his chest. "Qui. Bene, bene."

"Bello," Gabby said.

When she smiled, he could feel his heart thumping under the new shirt, and summer sliding up those short pantlegs.

7

ometime last Fall – that had to be the last hot meal he had eaten that had actually tasted good. Maybe that grilled sandwich in Nervesa he had with Barry, stuffed with meat and cheese and a cream and tomato sauce.

Everything Teresa cooked was delicious. Her kitchen filled with the aroma of sweet and tangy herbs. She used a shallow pan for frying, a small pot for boiling and a large domed pot for baking – all going at the same time over a wood fire that she kept alive with branches Gabby and the girls brought in, sometimes several armfuls a day. This morning, her scrambled eggs had cheese and real crushed pepper in them. The old man usually preferred to suck his egg straight out of the shell, making a slurping sound loud enough to be a wake-up bugle. But not today. He savored each bite, closing his eyes as if chewing a memory: "Come tua madre ha fatto."

If her mother cooked like this, how was it that her other daughter never learned how? Sunlight glinted off her yellow hair. She ate like the little girls, face down over the plate, with such single-minded purpose, it looked as if they had not eaten in days. It made him smile.

Luigi kissed the tops of their heads and walked up the swale, rifle slung over his shoulder. He would be gone all day, spending most of it in the village, returning before sundown with food. The day he came back with flour, Teresa cried. She made bread in that big pot, gave the old man the first slice. She cried then, too.

"Delicious," Reg told her. "Bello."

Dark eyes blinked. She tapped her plate with her fork – her signal for the girls to clear the table. Small fingers made quick work of it, sliding the plates and utensils into a water bucket. They did not let Gabby help them, and when she went to stir the pot of boiling vegetables, they glanced at their mother, who jerked her head – another signal for the little ones to drag their aunt away before she could touch anything. The narrowing of those black eyes told him she understood that he knew what she was doing, but she would not smile back. Ever.

The mug of water had cooled. It had to be boiled. The first time he had tried to drink straight from the well pump, Teresa had thrown a stick at him. "I morti. E lupi."

The rotting bodies may have spoiled the water. The wolves, too. The girls were not allowed outside by themselves and never permitted to draw or carry water – that job belonged to Gabby, along with sweeping, scouring, mending. She took the cup of weak tea made from flowers that Nicoletta had given her, but what she really wanted was the bread and jam her big sister was getting ready.

"Ecco." Nicoletta set the plate in front of him. "Piatto."

He held up the fork. She picked up hers: "Forchetta." He touched the mug. "Tazza," she said, her voice fluttering with laughter. She pointed at the big bread knife in her mother's hand: "Coltello."

He repeated the words, then picked up a spoon. "What's this?"

"Cucchiaio."

"What?"

"Cucchiaino." Teresa said it like a teacher. She placed a large spoon next to the smaller one – " Cucchiaio" – then slid the small spoon next to to the big one: "Cucchiaino."

He couldn't say it without laughing: "Cookie - eye - *eeh* - noh." He studied it: "Spoon."

Sancia giggled with her mouth full of jam. Nicoletta and Teresa just smiled. Gabby stirred her tea. "Spoon," she said.

"That is precisely what it is," Reg told her. "A spoon."

More giggling, wider smiles. Then both girls darted from object to object – chair, table, pot, bowl, bed, broom, door, window, open, shut. The littlest one got under the table – "Sotto il tavolo" – at the same time the bigger one lifted his plate and set it back down – "Sul tavolo."

Shaking her head, Teresa carried her tea outside, the hard sun polishing her hair as she turned to scan the sloping meadow. Through the open doorway, she looked like a statue, her honed edges digging into the soft green of new grass.

"Fuori." Gabby nodded at her sister, then pointed to herself. "Dentro."

When he squinted and shrugged, Sancia took him by the hand, led him to the threshold – "fuori" – then back inside – "dentro." She nudged the soft leather on his foot with her toe: "Pantofole."

All the words, even the simplest, sounded so much sweeter in her language. At the table, he lifted a leg onto an empty chair – "pantofole. . .sulla. . .sedia" – then quickly slid it under the table – "pantofole. . .sotto. . .?"

"Il tavolo," Nicoletta slapped the table. "Tavolo. Tavolo."

Her little sister moved in close and whispered, "Tavolo."

117

He nodded, then pointed at himself: "Pazzo."

In the little silence, birdsong filtered through the doorway and even Teresa was smiling.

·

Like a teacher monitoring her class, she did chores while barking corrections from every corner of the house. Sometimes, her sharp tones came from out of nowhere, as though she could hear and see everything without needing to be the same room. It didn't bother her daughters, who must have been used to it, but it made Gabby sigh with disgust. It made him laugh.

Her last name was Cusato. The girls' father, Carmine, was a soldier – they showed him a photo of a small stern man in uniform, standing next to an arm chair that held only his military cap, soft and misshapen, with a short cloth brim in front, looking like a sad cushion someone had accidentally sat on, then tried to fluff up. He stood ramrod straight, like a colonel. His uniform said he was a private.

"I out rank him," Reg told them.

"Babbo," the taller girl said.

"Non parlare di tuo papà." Teresa ripped the picture frame from her daughter's hand and carried it back into the bedroom. " Sfortuna."

"Senza fortuna," Gabby said, biting off thread and knotting it on the patch she had sewn into the old man's shirt.

"Everyone has some luck." He stroked the little one's dark curls. "He'll be home soon. Qui, molto presto."

" Cos'è questo?" Sancia said, shaking the empty arm of the shirt.

"Shirt," he said. "Camicia."

"Molto bene." Those tiny lips formed a big smile. "Shirt!"

"*La* camicia." The disembodied shout sounded as if it came from a cave. Maybe she was in a closet in there. "Ottenere i rami per il fuoco. Adesso!"

Gabby folded the shirt, set the needle and thread back in the basket. In this dusty light, she looked young enough to be a school girl. The three of them went outside, stacked armfuls of branches, brought them back in and set them beside the hearth. No wolves again today. No sound of the big guns. Just wind, bending the ankle-high grass toward the river. Rusthall Commons wasn't this big. Or as quiet. He bundled branches against his chest.

Teresa seemed surprised to see him. She stared as his slippers, then began telling her daughters and her sister what to do next.

He wondered how to say Sergeant Major in Italian and whether he would ever have the courage to call her that to her face.

118

•

The bombed-out house up the road and to the north of the old man's place had wolf scat all around it. He kept the rifle at the ready as he picked through the splintered wood, the charred remains of furniture, careful to keep his balance, hoping not to stumble and fall and shoot himself, becoming more food for wolves and, at the end of the day, unrecognizable, identified only by the the disc dangling on his neck, and that might be ripped off by a souvenier hunter or washed away by the next flood or incinerated by the next Black Maria bombardment if the Germans ever came back.

From the gentle rise, he could make out the southern edge of Nervesa across the river and the long straight road up the valley toward Susegana. A house here would have a sunset over The Montello reflected in the current every night.

Near the far corner of the rubble, where old bricks lay in bits, as if sledged, weeds grew in bunches. The tallest ones smelled like licorise. Under the curved arm of what must have been a parlor chair, he found a small metal bowl, misshapen by the heat of the blast that leveled this place. It had its own odd beauty. Mr. Quaite would treat it as a prize and put it on his desk, probably invent a sad story about it to convince a businessman to take out an advertisement in *The Rusthall Gazette*, and another story, a happy one – a romance – to enthrall members of the Ladies Auxillary and get them to sponsor an article about their own event, which he would gladly write for free.

Reg dug for more, found only a singed painting: an unsaddled horse, brown with a black mane and tail, its rein held by a gloved hand. The rest of the groom had been burned away. He up rolled the canvas, tucked it under an arm and carefully stepped out of the wreckage, the little bowl in his pocket, the rifle above his head.

Where the grass was still not growing, river silt was drying out, no longer muddy and thick. The top crust crunched under foot now. At the old man's house, he looked for any sign of where her garden had stood, but found nothing, just a pattern of swirls in the soil where the water had tried to climb the last three feet or so to the cabin before falling back into the flood plain. That little house had probably withstood several lifetimes of floods, always threatened, but never touched by the river.

Inside, nothing had changed. Even that small black dress had been rehung on a hook over Gabby's bed. At the window, he studied the view, wondering if he saw what she saw, even a part of it. A new

119

tree trunk had sprouted out there. Except it had no leaves. When he reached it, he nudged it with the rifle. Not a tree. A pipe of some sort.

Not a pipe. A gun barrel.

Too wide to be a rifle barrel, so there would not be a dead soldier attached to it underneath all that river silt. With both hands, he began rocking it to work it free.

Luigi's shotgun was still in one piece. The wood stock was still solid. Cleaned up, it would still be something the old man might want, even if it could never fire again.

He started toward the road, arms and pockets loaded with found treasures.

•

The black river mud on the shotgun smelled of dead fish and soldiers, decomposing in summer heat. Caked mud like that would not come off with water, it would have to be chipped away. He placed the weapon barrel up behind the ladder, where the girls could not reach it.

Teresa had tonight's vegetables chopped on the table. He handed her the rolled up canvas. "For your house," he said, blurting out the Italian sentence he had practiced on the way back: "*Per la vostra casa.*"

She dried her hands on the long apron, unrolled the canvas. She covered her open mouth with a hand. He smiled and plunked the misshapen bowl on the table, next to the quartered onions.

Gabby must have heard the sound. She came out of the girls' room, broom in hand and the two little ones at her heels. Her sister took the broom, gave her the canvas. The smile disappeared as Gabby studied the horse. Her eyes widened: "Tesoro."

She steadied herself with a chair back, then sat, her fingers tracing the singed edge of the canvas where the holder of the reins would have stood. Now those sky blue eyes got wet. She touched the rim of the bowl as if testing to see if it was sharp. "You go to our house?"

"Sì," he said. "The little house and the one that got crumped – bombed – just up the knoll."

A tear rolled down her cheek. The girls stared at her, then hugged their mother's apron.

Teresa stroked their hair. "Il cavallo di suo marito."

"Your husband?"

She nodded toward Gabby. "Paolo."

"Pah-oh-low?"

"Ziccardi," Gabby said. "Capitano. Di cavalleria."

120

A cavalry officer. He inched closer to her. "Is he. . .?"

Teresa told the girls to put the vegetables in the pot, then took his elbow, led him toward the hearth. "Niente posta vieni qui." Now her eyes were tearing up. "No letter."

As if in a trance, Gabby was humming to herself, her stare fixed on that horse. And Teresa was gone, shutting the bedroom door. A moment later, she was shouting in there. It sounded as though she was cursing her husband Carmine because his name laced every sentence.

Her daughters pretended not to notice. They scooped chopped vegetables into a kettle. Sancia, standing on a chair to reach the table, signaled Reg to keep quiet, a finger to her lips.

"Carmine no need to go," Gabby said in her best English. "Vecchio — old." She glanced at the girls. "Due bambini." She took the little bowl to the mantel, turned it so that the side that had not melted out of shape faced the room. "Paolo need to go. Nessun permesso, capisce?"

How could she have a husband? How young had she been when she got married — 15? He tried to picture the man missing from the painting. Anyone who owned a sleek horse like that had to be rich. Probably handsome. Dashing. Every woman's dream. How does a lowly Corporal wearing someone else's clothes measure up to a cavalry officer? "How tall is he," Reg said, realizing too late that he was thinking outloud.

"Che cosa?"

The shouting in the bedroom stopped. She was crying in there now. The girls stared at each other.

Gabby stepped back to admire the bowl. "Argento," she said. "Di mia madre."

Her mother's silver bowl looked smaller on the mantel than it had looked in his hand. "Bella," he said.

She took his hand, squeezed his finger, kissed his cheek, leaving her new tear on his face. "Grazie."

Paolo would be tall. And strong. A master horseman. One of those people who walk into a room and make heads turn. Even when his image was burned away, he was there. Paolo was why she had kept staring out the window at the old man's house, searching the flood plain, waiting for this man, the man of her dreams — her husband — to come home. He shut his eyes, hoping to stop seeing it.

121

"Madonna mia!" The old man's voice boomed through the open window. He stormed into the house, holding the mud-caked shotgun over his head. "Guarda!"

Two steps later, he stopped, making sense of the quiet, the sound of crying behind the bedroom door. He slid the rifle off his shoulder, set it by the hearth, set the shotgun next to it. He saw the bowl on the mantel, squinted at Reg, then stepped to the table, kissed the girls on the top of their heads. He saw the canvas, stared at Gabby.

"I found your shotgun in the mud by your house," Reg said.

The words didn't register. But Luigi was smiling. He laid a warm open hand on Reg's cheek – "Bravo" – then grabbed the shotgun and started back outside. He stopped in the doorway, turned: "Grazie."

"I was going to clean it for you."

That big hand waved in the air. He sat on an upturned bucket, pulled a knife from a pocket and began scraping the mud off the shotgun barrel.

Reg stood there, feeling invisible, not even here – in some new no-man's land, everyone too busy to notice him. If he left now, if he stayed, nothing would change.

"How do you say 'nothing'?" he said.

"Nulla," Nicoletta told him.

"Niente," Sancia said.

Gabby had the canvas stretched in her hands again. "Zero."

So many ways to describe the same thing and, for once, it didn't sound better in Italian. He walked outside to watch the sunset and wait for the moon.

8

In the older section, the streets angled one way, then another, routed past buildings that predated the pavement. Towels and sheets dried on short balconies and window boxes. The smell of garlic roasting leaked out onto the alleys so narrow that bicycles could not pass each other. Here and there, a baby cried, a child shouted, but the buildings were otherwise silent.

The market stood in the square at the end of the street where Reg had last seen Ezio. Tables and carts lined the edge closest to the street – the road that led northeast to Susegana and the castle. A small group of women, their heads kerchiefed, had gathered at that end. They watched those testing and buying the vegetables, breads, cheeses and fruits. A smaller splinter group of young women, all bare headed and some younger than Gabby, stood nearby, looking at nothing.

At the opposite end of the square, by the steps of a burned-out building, the men smoked, drank wine, argued, told jokes. They saw Luigi approach, mumbled questions about the skinny man in slippers at his side. The introduction was more of an announcement. Reg caught a few words – *eroe*: hero, *l'inglese*: the Englishman, something about a rifle and a house – but the look on those craggy faces told the story: they grinned – some were almost toothless – and nodded, their eyes looking to the sky as if in prayer. Then they applauded. Each of them came to shake Reg's hand, their own coarse skin like sandpaper on his. A few patted him on the back. Every one of them was over 50.

The one they called *il capo del villaggio* – probably the mayor – wore frayed braces, bleached tan by years of sun. He guided Reg to the vendors, made sure he got a taste from each table and cart – all free. Some had umbrellas to shade the fruit and cheese from the sun, now almost directly overhead. Others used small boards or their hands to fan flies away. The baker kept his loaves under a sheet, only pulling back an edge for a customer. "Gli uccelli," he said, pointing at the blackbirds flitting on and off the steps. "Bastardi."

A short women in a dark dress pulled a reluctant teenager toward Luigi. The young girl looked like what Teresa might have at that age, only sweeter. And kinder. She kept glancing back over a shoulder at her friends. The old man introduced them to Reg, who offered both of them an apricot slice. The mother ate it in a single bite. Her daughter nibbled at the edges. After her mother elbowed her, the teen said, "Grazie."

Another mother and daughter approached. Another introduction. The first mother nudged her daughter closer to Reg. The other woman did the same with her daughter. They kept inching closer, backing him up against the lettuce cart. The man behind the lettuce yelled at the women and reached over to protect the small leafy heads. Reg squeezed out of the way: "Mi scusi."

The other young girls were craning for a better look now. Their mothers and aunts were talking to each other. Luigi pulled Reg by the sleeve toward them. "L'inglese. Mi amico. Re-ja"

In unison, their lips silently mouthed his name. They listened to the old man talk of Germans, heroes, rifles and the castle. With each new detail, the older women oohed and ahhed. The younger women stared at him, then at the ground, in a rhythm that made eye contact impossible.

The Mayor yanked Reg away and steered him back to the steps, handing him a cup of wine. "Stai attento. Le donne mangiano la tua anima."

Women eat your. . .soul?

Questions flew at him, each man in the group asking something different. Reg shook his head, shrugged. The men began gesturing: one aimed and fired an imaginary rifle, another pretended to bayonet an invisible foe, and The Mayor ran a finger across his own throat. They must have wanted war stories. Their sons and grandsons might still be out there fighting. Or lying dead in places they had never heard of, never expected to visit.

The wine tasted crisp. "Soave," The Mayor told him, handing him a chunk of pale yellow cheese. "Ecco formaggio asiago. Bellisimo, no?"

It was sharp and tangy. "Bellisimo, sì," Reg said and the men applauded.

Luigi was still talking to the older women, who used their hands when they answered him. A couple of them were pointing toward Reg. Their kerchiefs of different colors and dark dresses created a scene that looked like one of those impressionist paintings Barry had liked so much that he wanted his father to buy some for the hotel lobby. Maybe it was the way the sun hit the gray and brown buildings behind the women or how they all seemed cemented to each other so when one of them moved, they all moved − whatever it was, they looked as soft as that runny French cheese that smelled like dirty socks. In contrast, their daughters looked spindly, like leafless twigs.

"Non più tedeschi," The Mayor said, the wine bottle above his head. "Per sempre."

No more Germans. Forever. Reg drank the toast, passed his cup to the next man, who added, "Lo spero."

"I hope so, too," Reg told him.

And they were singing. A tune about a saint named Lucia. Two of them danced with each other, arms locked at the elbow. Hands began clapping to the slow beat. The mayor grabbed Reg by the elbow, twirled him in dance. Everyone laughed, even those young girls.

Luigi took a long swig from the cup, fed a chunk of Asiago into his mouth, handed Reg an empty sack. "Ha trovato il mio fucile," he said, slapping Reg on the back, then punching the air like a prize fighter. "Ho combattuto i tedeschi per esso."

Something about his shotgun and fighting Germans. Whatever it was, it impressed the men, who applauded again. More pats on the back as Luigi led the way to the vendors and began bargaining, using Reg to gain sympathy. The vendors shrugged, sighed, waved their hands, but the old man kept haggling until he got what he wanted.

Except from the olive seller. Tight-lipped, arms crossed, his sweaty bald head shook every time Luigi said anything or used fingers to quote a price. With an angry grunt, he led Reg out of the square to scattered applause and shouts of "Ciao!" from the men, smiles and waves from the women, quick secret glances from the teenage girls.

Down the road, past the crumbling building Ezio had disappeared into that first night, the old man kept mumbling curses about olives, spitting to punctuate his sentences, as if getting rid of a mouthful of sour fruit. He rubbed the rifle slung over his shoulder, suggesting he might go back and shoot the olive vendor for being so stubborn.

Reg laid the sack over a shoulder, put an arm on Luigi. "You make going to market an adventure. . . un'avventura."

Creases in those wrinkled cheeks deepened. The old man let out a short laugh, then went back to cursing the olive man and didn't stop until he started down the swale to house, where the girls ran toward him to see what miracles he had brought home this time.

•

They came down in pairs – a processional of mothers and daughters over the foot path, now the only aisle through knee-high grass. Arms full of pans and baskets, each covered by a white napkin,

125

the parade made its silent way toward the house. Three sets of them, like a small platoon. The young women – not one looked older than 16 – were all trying hard not to act like or walk like their mothers.

They saw him by the ladder, sorting pine nuts that had been drying in the late summer sun. They didn't see the old man until he stopped wiping down the long table behind the house and started up the swale to meet them. Dish towel in hand, Teresa caught him at the doorway. The sharpness of their words caused the train of women to stop in midstep.

Up from the river plain, Gabby led the two little girls toward the house. A soft breeze fluttered through her hair, made the hem of her faded dress dance. She studied the women, the argument at the door, the confused look on Reg's face, and she started laughing. With a wave, she welcomed the mothers and daughters to her sister's house.

The dish towel snapped like a whip. Teresa went back inside, shut the door. With a sigh that turned into a smile, Luigi walked toward the visiting women. The little girls ran to Reg.

"Who are they?" Nicoletta said.

He gave each of them some pine nuts. "Ask your uncle."

•

Nods. Smiles. Smells – smokey and sweet. The bounty they brought sat on the table. Benches got wiped down. Cups and a pitcher of water came out in the hands of Gabby and the little girls. Then the napkins came off the baskets and pans: bread and cheese in one, roasted garlic and onions in another, puff pastry dessert in the last one.

The old man sat Reg at the head of the table, in an arm chair. The reeds of its basket weave seat had frayed. Some had rotted out. He tested it, then sat, half hoping it would collapse so he could claim injury and get out of all this.

The mothers served. They spoke to Luigi, but not to each other. They overfilled Reg's plate – too much bread, a big chunk of that Asiago cheese, far too big a helping of garlic and onions, dotted with crinkled strips of red and white. And three round pastries, sweet cream leaking out their ends. He held the plate up to Gabby: "Help me eat all this."

She shook her head, nudged the little girls over to him. Sancia bit into a pastry smiling. The cream puff broke up in her tiny hand, but she caught the pieces on her fingers and tongue.

He pointed to those red and white strips, whispered to Nicoletta: "What's this?"

126

She shrugged her shoulders just like her uncle did.

"Radicchio," Luigi kissed his fingertips, flicked them toward the sky. "Treviso Rosso."

Reg gave a strip to Nicoletta, who tasted it – it was raw and crisp and made a snapping sound in her mouth – and she nodded. "È buono."

"My personal food tester," he said. No one at the table smiled. The strip was bitter, but when eaten with the sweet, soft garlic cloves and the sweeter browned onions, that raw vegetable added a sharpness. He smiled and the mother who had brought the dish smiled back.

He gave half of his cheese to Nicoletta and some bread to Sancia: "A mama. Adesso."

They scampered off toward the house, past the glare of the mother who had brought the cheese. He made a point of taking a bite and smiling at her. "Bella. Grazie."

She elbowed her daughter, who muttered, "Prego."

New plates got passed around. The women ate, their daughters nibbled. Standing behind the skinny girl with the black hair, Gabby puffed up her cheeks, nodded down at the girl's mother as if to say, *She will get fat, too.*

He hid his smile in more cheese.

In back of the short girl with curly brown hair, the one whose dress had a scooped front to show off her cleavage, Gabby mimicked her small bites.

He coughed a laugh, chewed it away with a piece of bread.

The other girl seated on the side nearest the ladder and the house was not eating, despite the urging of her mother. When offered water, she shook her head. With a conspiratorial glance at Reg, Gabby shook her head slowly, then handed the girl's plate to the old man, who dug in with both hands.

Through the back window, those dark eyes missed nothing. What her sister found amusing, Teresa found annoying. He could imagine her coming out with that old shotgun and blowing the baskets and pans off the table, reloading, then aiming at visitors she had not invited.

He squeezed his eyes shut to get rid of the image. When he opened them, Teresa was feeding cheese into a sour smile, as though plotting revenge. It made him shiver.

•

Diana, Rosalie, Beatrice. Left to right. Or was it Beatrice, Diana, Rosalie?

The short one with the big breasts had nibbled her way through a full plate. The quiet one who would not eat or drink kept sliding the plate of food back toward her mother, who kept nudging it back. The skinny one left half her food uneaten, but stared at it with the longing of a starving child.

He burped. It made the women grin. And Gabby laugh.

The afternoon breeze picked up, rustling kerchiefs and napkins. If the old man was right and the Germans were on the run now that the Italian Army had crossed the river south of here, then these young girls would have their pick of the soldiers who came home. Some of these teenagers might have been 11 or 12 when the war began – a few years older than Nicoletta was now. He couldn't imagine her at this table, in a scoop-neck dress, her mother at her side. Nicoletta would run away before allowing that to happen.

And the mothers, stranded in this small village, hiding in cellars and forests for so long, were now able to cling to a twinge of hope, yet frightened by it, by the uncertain reality headed their way, the inescapable tears – happy or sad – and the reunions that might occur for some, never for others. In Rusthall today, his own parents would be feeling the same thing. So would poor Madge. Only Mr. Quaite would keep himself busy enough to hold off those feelings.

Was it like this everywhere? How many of these perfectly horrible lunch parties were being held today? How may empty chairs lined dinner tables? How many little hands were clasped at bedsides, begging for miracles?

"More prayers than stars in the sky," he said, but no one at the table understood. Unable to look them in the eye, he sipped water. If he could find a bridge across the river, if any bridge still stood, he could make his way west over the same route that had brought him and the 11th here. These girls and their mothers would not stop or follow him. There might be a train. Back to France or Flanders? To autumn rain and sticky mud? In slippers? And trousers that didn't reach his ankles? With no money?

He sat back, watched Gabby clear the plates. Maybe her husband was already dead. Maybe none of the husbands and sons of Colfosco were coming home. Just old men and teenage girls, a whole village of them. How long had she been living with that same dread? Is that

128

what she saw each time she looked at him – a reminder of what might be lost?

He put a hand on hers to stop her from taking his plate. "Sit with us."

She shivered, then yanked her hand free, gathered the wide-eyed looks and gasps from all the women at the table, spun on a heel and hurried into the house.

The large woman stood first. She sneered as she scooped the remaining cream puffs into her basket, covered it and yanked her daughter from the bench, marching up the path to the swale. The others followed, shooting dark glances his way before turning the corner around the house.

The old man shrugged, wet a finger and picked crumbs up from the table, fed them into his mouth. "La crema . . . è troppo dolce, no?"

If the cream puff filling was too sweet, it was only because everything else wasn't.

9

They found him a room in the southern part of town, where the road up from river forked north toward the castle and the new front line, now beyond Conegliano, with the Germans in full retreat. A bed, a chair, two candles in wooden holders, a drafty window overloooking a street of flat stone squares.

They promised to send the old man in with food every day. The Mayor promised to check on him. They made Reg promise not to visit – either the house on the knoll or the cabin at the river. Teresa's decision. She was too strong-willed for her sister or the old man. If it had come to a vote, only hers would have counted.

By the third night, he realized she had been right to banish him. A young man – and a foreigner – living in the same house with two married women whose husbands were off fighting a war, and two little girls. The stuff of scandal.

He took walks through the tangle of streets. The men waved. Some stood at attention and saluted, as if he were a superior officer, not a lowly Corporal. He returned each salute with parade-ground snap. The women looked away or turned their backs. Their teenage daughters smiled and giggled, only to be scolded and forced inside, where they watched from doorways and windows until he had passed by. He had experienced similar treatment as a boy, dressed in dirty overalls, helping his father unload cabbages, potatoes and onions at hotels in Royal Tunbridge Wells, where the staff and guests valued the produce more than the people who grew it.

On the north slope out of town, in the crease of the foothhills, the goat man could see Reg coming for half a mile. His soft new cheese was velvety and sweet, the perfect companion to hard bread. His shirt and pants had not been laundered in weeks. The wiry man smelled almost as bad as his animals. That stomach-turning odor got easier to take from the upwind side, so Reg found diplomatic ways to position his own back to the Alps and keep the goat man on the valley side. From here, the village looked like those painted clay buildings in Christmas displays.

The notion of reading – a letter, a newspaper, a book – amazed the goat man. So did music. His father, also named Rodolfo, played a lute, but that instrument had been destroyed in the fire from the artillery shell that had flatened their cabin. Months ago, Rodolfo, Sr. had left to borrow tools from a cousin in Conegliano, but had not yet returned. The son missed the music as much as he did the companionship. He dared Reg to prove he knew how to read and write, then begged for lessons – in exchange for cheese.

Reg offered the use of the wash tub in the house in town, but the goat man was unwilling to leave his animals, especially with wolves around. He asked how many goats a rifle like the one Reg carried would cost.

"The wolves have lots of other meat to eat," Reg told him, trying to chase the image of the packs feasting on all those dead soldiers.

What was worse – the small empty room, silent day and night, or the stinky goat man struggling to understand Reg's limited Italian? The room was better, he decided. In that room, he could dream.

•

The Germans were finished. Pushed by the Italians toward Vittorio – the mayor called that city Ceneda – on the plain drained by the Piave and Livensa rivers, about 30 miles northeast of Colfosco. The advance was so fast now, the big guns could not keep pace. Nights now were filled with only the sound of the river and the wind through long grasses.

To celebrate, the town organized a feast. Cheese and bread, pastries, goat meat – Reg wondered if he had watched this animal grazing – and music that might drift into the foothills for Rodolfo, Jr. to hear.

From a corner facing the square, Reg watched old men dance with each other, women taste the food, teenage girls huddle as far away as their mothers would permit. As The Mayor tried to make a speech, Luigi led his neices and the two little girls into that puzzle of faces and shadows. The trumpet and clarinet kept playing. The Mayor gave up and the men and the women cheered his decision.

Rifle still slung over a shoulder, the old man offered a hand to one of the women. His friends whistled, applauded, laughed. They fell silent as the couple slid across the dirt, as spry as teenagers, smiling as they danced.

Gabby's stare wandered past the dancing couple. She saw him leaning against the building across the street. When she wriggled her fingers in a small wave, the little girls followed her gaze. Their eyes widened. They raced toward him, into his arms, pulled him back to the square.

"Mama!" Nicoletta said. "Lui non è morto!"

"Who told you I was dead?" Reg knew the answer before finishing the question.

131

Those black eyes squinting, Teresa turned and began sampling goat meat.

Sancia put her feet on top of his. Nicoletta took his free hand. He took tiny steps, more swaying than dancing. The men clapped. The women glowered. The teenager girls looked dazed. Gabby's face wore a velvety smile, one he had not seen before. When Teresa turned and saw her daughters dancing, her face softened, she stopped chewing. Whatever she was going to say got smothered by the applause the old man got when he cut in and took over dancing with the little girls.

Reg took slow backward steps, off the dirt, feeling the rounded and chipped shape of each cobblestone through the soft soles of the slippers. He took the first side street toward the foothills and didn't stop until he couldn't hear the music anymore.

Maybe the high valley with the goats was better than that tiny room. In that valley, he could breathe.

●

The goats scattered at the sound of the gunshot. Rodolfo, Jr. dropped flat in meadow grass, disappearing as if swallowed by color. Reg unshouldered his rifle, took cover behind a low rock outcropping, scanned the foothills and the path from the village. He saw the old man before a second shot cracked off the mountains.

Luigi straightened up, waved for Reg to come down to the path. Out of breath, he wiped his nose on his sleeve. "Teresa – è scamparsi."

"Missing?

One of those big hands found Reg's arm, squeezed. "Aiutaci."

"Of course I'll help." Reg re-slung the rifle over his shoulder. They started down toward town. The old man's words came out slow and he stopped between sentences to wipe away snot and sweat. A soldier from Susegana had come to the house the day after the celebration in town. He had news that Private Carmine Cusato had been killed in action somewhere on the Asiago plain. The bundle the soldier left with Teresa contained a handkerchief that she had embroidered and a photograph of her on her wedding day that her husband had carried with him. Blood had soiled the bottom edge of the picture, but the handkerchief was unstained.

As they skirted the village by the southern road, the old man slowed his pace, no longer getting the benefit of the downhill slope from the foothills. He was shuffling his feet, exhausted. There were bits of dry grass stuck in his hair. When had he last slept?

Teresa had fallen silent at first, sitting on her bed, staring at the photograph, her uncle said. The two girls knew enough to keep their distance. Gabby stayed outside so her sister would not hear her crying. The old man had gone into town for food – she liked *friggitello* as a child, he remembered, and he had looked everywhere for those sweet yellow-green peppers, but without luck – and when he got back, the black-haired woman had vanished. Gabby and the girls had searched until dark, all the way down to the river and back up into the evergreens.

That night – last night – was the longest Luigi could remember. Every sound awakened him. He lit the lantern a dozen times, carrying it outside to see if what he had heard was his niece coming home, only to discover it had just been the wind or a squirrel or rabbit. He worried that the wolves would find her before he did.

He had come into town this morning to enlist Reg in the search, but had found his room empty. One of his friends told him how the Englishman walked into the foothills every day, speaking to no one. The old man said he had not been on that path in years, since his argument with Rodolfo, Sr., who he described as a hermit.

Their disagreement had been over a kid for Easter, so long ago now the old man was not sure Gabby or Rodolfo's son – Secondo – had been born yet. Rodolfo had sold that young goat to another villager for a higher price than Luigi had agreed to pay. That was why the old man had shot in the air – to let the goat man know he was armed.

"He's not there," Reg told him. "Neither is his house. Just the son and the few goats the Germans didn't take."

"È morto?"

"In Conegliano."

Luigi shrugged, then pointed to a game trail through the evergreens. The shortcut brought them out below the house, on the last high ground before the flood plain. The girls ran to them the moment they saw them walking up. Their mother wasn't back yet and their aunt was cooking. It was the worst day yet.

Gabby didn't look tired, just overhelmed. Steam from the pot had dampened her hair, making it fall in wide strands, darker than her normal color. Some sort of soup to go with the hard cheese and bread on the table. She stopped to smile and say, "Grazie," before ladling the soup into bowls.

She must have learned something from watching her sister because this broth wasn't as terrible as he had expected. Even the girls

133

were surprised. He asked about Teresa's favorite childhood places, but Gabby didn't know – she had been too young to go with her sister and her sister had always been in too much of a hurry to take her along.

"Il fiume," the old man said, his mouth full of cheese. But he had checked the river bank near the small house the day before. No sign of her. No footprints. No crumbs or scraps.

She had taken no food, no shawl. The only thing missing from the house was the photograph in her bedroom of Carmine in uniform.

Gabby pulled him away from the table so the girls would not hear. She was worried about wolves. They had stopped howling. She wanted to go with Reg, but knew she had to stay with the little ones. Her uncle had shown her how to use the old shotgun, now cleaned and tested. Reg couldn't imagine her shooting it.

In the bedroom, he hunted for clues. She owned three dresses. An extra pair of shoes sat next to a polished pair that Carmine might have worn only for church, weddings or funerals. He had probably been married in those shoes. Nothing had been broken. Not even an overturned chair. The dark-haired fury had gone cold, like the autumn sun.

The old man was now asleep at the table, his chin on his chest, a piece of cheese still stuck in his fingers. The girls were clearing the table, quiet as hotel maids. Gabby stared out the back window where browning leaves littered the long table. Reg wanted to tell her he would find her sister, that she would be safe. Instead, he patted Sancia's head, hugged Nicoletta and walked out into the cool breeze.

He headed straight for the river, refusing to look back for fear they would see his tears.

•

No one had been down under the lip of the high bank for a long time. Or perhaps the river had washed away any sign of them during last winter's flood. Only the large rocks remained, rubbed smooth and rounded by the water. All the small pebbles he remembered had been sent downstream, eaten by the currents.

It was possible to walk along the river's edge all the way up to the bend where the Piave wrapped around The Montello. No sign of the old encampment, no cook fires smoking in the trees. He found the spot he and Barry had tied up the small raft, though he couldn't be certain. The river had reshaped the bank, gouging out yards of soil as it re-routed itself around the wide corner. It was quiet now, as if sleeping, the water gliding by, clear and cold, finally purifying itself.

Not far from the edge of the new bank, the barbed wire had been cut, the posts kicked down. Grasses wove their way through the tangle. Beyond, where the road ran north, the corner of the tower in Collalto stood out between branches in the woods. It looked like a black rook on a chess board, a good mile away.

He found a ridge in the steep bank, climbed to higher ground. Some of the dead still lay out in the sun. What wolves and scavenging village women had left amounted to little more than wool scraps, bones, bits of glinting metal too small or damaged to serve any use. Lots of footprints, some of them small enough to belong to children, and trails where heavy objects had been dragged off. The stench was gone, replaced by the heavy sweetness of wet grass and old rot. There were times when Denny Bottom smelled like this, after heavy downpours had turned the low spots into bogs, bringing sunken debris back up to the surface before a dry spell would cause it all to sink again, layered with things newly dead, like rabbits, even frogs, trapped in the quicksand of fresh mud.

She could be under there, swallowed by the softened soil, pulled down by the weight of dead soldiers. With a long branch, he jabbed the dirt, testing for quagmire. The sun was over the river already. It would drop behind The Montello in a few hours. Squatting at the edge of the bank, he stared down river, trying to visualize his own ride, first on the raft, then in the water. It wasn't the same river now. This river wasn't angry. He started walking south, toward Nervesa, watching sunlight stretch out on the current, shimmering fingers pulled by the gentle flow.

She might be in the evergreens behind her house. She might have come home. She wasn't here. He should have known better than to trust an old man's memory. What would a young girl have been doing playing down by the river? By herself? What parent would have allowed that?

The flood plain up to the old cabin, still smoothed by new silt, might hold sinkholes − those old shell craters might be unstable enough to consume anyone foolish enough to walk over them. Testing with the branch before each step, he scoured the flatland for footprints, crisscrossing the field, working his way from the river to the house. On the off-chance she had come here, he stepped inside, checked the little cellar under the bed. At the table, he stared out the window, reached for the chair.

There was no chair.

Not at the table or by the hearth or the sleeping nook. And there was no black dress hanging there. The rosary was gone, too.

From the doorway, he scanned the brown dirt. Not a single footprint or the track of a chair being dragged. Tall grasses had shot up at the back end of the little house. He watched the late breeze bend those green blades toward Venice. At the place an old dry-set stone wall had collapsed, he spotted trampled grass. Probably an animal – a small one, because that new trail was narrow.

He followed it back to the water. Old stone footings that once supported the Roman bridge that had given Luigi's family its name – DaPonte – were cohorts of the same footings that had split Reg's skull open just a few yards upstream. They stood on dry ground that was covered by mounds of those smooth, round pebbles, deposited here and nowhere else by a ruthless current, without memory or mercy.

Above the whisper of the river, he heard the mumbling. He readied the rifle, just in case, and inched his way down the bank. At the nearest footing, the one that still held part of an arch, he peered around the edge. The long black hair was darker than her dress.

Seated in the chair, facing the river, she rolled the rosary beads through her fingers, muttering something with each bead. Two photographs lay at her side, held down by stones. Her husband's face and her own looked up a her, witnesses to her prayers.

He set the rifle against the footing, walked to her, put his hands on her shoulders, felt her shudder before she leaned back into him, her head touching his stomach. He bent and kissed her hair, then knelt beside her, ran a hand through the pebbles as if they were his rosary beads.

"I thought I would die here, too," he told the river, convinced he was watching her murmured prayers ride the quiet current, taking the same route that had carried Barry and Capt. Rodgers to the Adriatic. "You have to come home. Your sister is cooking."

Her lips stopped moving. The hint of smile creased her cheek.

10

She had intended to walk into the river and let it do whatever it wanted to her. She had hoped that her mother's best dress – the one made the month her own husband had vanished and that she had worn every day for two years of mourning – would get heavy with water, make the struggle go faster. She showed him the thicket where she slept last night, where she tried to find her courage.

She had gone back to the house for the rosary. She took the chair to keep the dress from getting dirty. She had wanted to look as regal as her mother had in it. She wished she had remembered to bring her best shoes.

Sitting by the water, she had remembered the little girl who wandered through the remnants of the old bridge. Those weathered stones, she told him, had been her only true friends, her best playmates. They had refused to release her. She prayed for the strength to leave them.

Her steps squeaked in the grass, misted now as the light quickened. She hated her husband, she said. For enlisting when he didn't have to. He was married with one child and another on the way. The army would have let him stay. His pride wouldn't. She had hated Carmine from the day he left. She had hated him more on the day Sancia was born. She hated him now more than ever, for dying.

"Cusato." She said his last name, now her own, like a curse. "Orgogliosi. Tutta la sua famiglia."

He wanted to tell her that being proud was part of being a man, but he didn't want that fire to return in her until he got her back home. He slid the chair to the table, waited outside while she changed back into her own clothes and hung the black dress and rosary back where they belonged.

Carmine Cusato was really a coward, she told him, afraid of what the other men in the village would think of him if he didn't join the army. The things they would say about him, behind his back at first, then to his face as the war got closer, would be worse than the bullets that killed him. If he had been shot. He might have been blown up by the big guns. Or stabbed by the bayonets. The soldier who had brought the news didn't know how her husband had died or exactly where.

He was buried somewhere near Valdobbiadene in a mountain valley. She thought they should have buried him with the photograph of her he had carried. The dried blood on it was his final insult, staining his daughters' future. She had wanted to burn it — to destroy the woman in that white dress — but could not find matches or a flint at the little house.

She had wanted to smell his blood burn, she said.

•

After the hugging and kissing and the crying, she took the girls into her bedroom. They chattered at her. She didn't silence them.

From his seat at the table, the old man kept glancing at her, as if making sure she was still there. He said he had checked the old bridge footings. How could he have missed seeing her? Reg tried to explain the rabbit warren she had slept in, but his Italian wasn't good enough. Luigi cursed himself, his stupidity, his old age, his weak eyes. Reg pushed his own cup of wine across the table, watched a big hand lift it in a half-hearted toast. "Le donne mangiano la tua anima."

Maybe women did eat your soul. According to the goat man, every male in Colfosco, regardless of age, believed this to be true.

"Più minestra?" Gabby put a fresh bowl of soup in front of him, carried another into the bedroom. He waited for Teresa to tell her sister what the broth needed. Instead, she sat up and spooned it eagerly, smiling and nodding with each swallow. She saw Reg take a spoonful and she grinned: "Gabriela cucinato. Buona, sì?"

It did taste good. A few more spoonfuls, then he stood, slung his rifle over a shoulder. "Buona notte."

With a sigh, the old man put down his wine, walked to the door and hugged him. The girls ran to him, held onto his legs. Gabby wrapped some bread and cheese in a napkin, handed it to him, kissed his cheek, letting her lips linger on his skin, her breath warm the spot of her embrace.

Teresa was in the doorway to her bedroom: "Rimani qui."

Nicoletta squeezed his leg. "She says to stay."

"Stay," Sancia said, a little echo. "Here, with us."

A moment later, he was back at the table, the girls on his lap, Sancia digging into his bundle of bread and cheese, Nicoletta spooning up his soup, the old man drinking his wine, Gabby humming as she stirred broth in the pot and Teresa backing into her bedroom, closing the door gently. He smiled at the sounds surrounding him and at the thought of the moon waxing full as it began its slow climb over the river, glinting off those ancient stone footings and the hard secrets they held.

She dropped the water pail, ran to the back window, cowered against the wall, chewed on strands of blond hair: "Don't let them in."

Teresa squinted at her, then glanced out the kitchen window. Untying her apron, she stepped to the door.

"No!" Gabby's scream made the little girls stop chasing each other around the long table outside. "Lock the door!"

Three Italian soliders were coming down the swale. The tallest one was an officer, tapping his swagger stick against his palm as he walked.

Reg knelt to her, put an arm around her, felt her shiver. They were coming to tell her that her husband had been killed. He wanted to feel sorry for her, tell her it would be fine, wondering if he was ready to say that for her or for himself.

The more she snuggled into him, the worse he felt for hoping it would be the worst news, that Paolo would not be coming home, that his wife would be a widow, like her sister. He wanted to ask how long the mourning period had to last before she could remarry. Having that thought — feeling it course through his body with her in his arms, clutching him — soured his stomach.

"L'inglese." The officer's thin moustache barely moved when he spoke. " Dov'è?"

Teresa started to turn, but the officer didn't wait. He brushed past her, tapped that riding crop against his leg as he studied Reg, then motioned for him to stand.

Gabby refused to budge. Reg freed himself, stepped in front of her. "Is it her husband?" he said in his best Italian.

"Afraid not," the officer said. In English. A posh accent. From London. The same one the rich tourists used in the hotels in Royal Tunbridge Wells. "We've come for you."

•

There was no way past all three of them. No way to reach the rifle against the wall. And that riding crop had stopped moving. The two other soldiers came up to grab Reg by either arm. The Captain reached into Reg's shirt, pulled up the identification disc. "Reginald Olcutt, a Field Court Martial will be convened to consider the charge of desertion."

"What?"

"The penalty for which is death by firing squad." Slender fingers let go of the ID disc. "Where is your uniform?"

Reg shrugged. "Lost."

Those moustachoed lips formed the stale smile familiar to any hotel waiter or bellman at the spa, every porter or maid, cook or sweep, the smile that claimed superiority and offered a small coin as proof. "We'll have to find you another one, then," the Captain said.

They got him moving before Gabby could stand, before Teresa could speak or block the doorway, before the girls could round the corner of the house. Their voices chased him up the swale: "Re-ja!"

11

Nervesa was no longer the bustling small river city with open-air markets and brigades of soldiers. Only military personnel and transports were permitted to use the floating bridge that crossed the Piave a mile to the south. The car, a Fiat touring model with a convertible top that looked like a bonnet and only covered part of the rear seat, sputtered at low speed, as if the engine was gasping from the dust of so much rubble. Oversized wheels on wooden spokes guaranteed a rough slow ride all the way down to Treviso. Jumping out and making a run for it would mean getting shot in the back. Captain Tipple would enjoy using his sidearm to put the final bullet in the back of Reg's head.

The Field Hospital – a small stone building surrounded by a dozen or more gray tents – sounded like a stockyard from the wails and grunts of wounded men. Under guard, Reg sat on a bench that creaked each time he moved. Nurses and orderlies kept stopping to check his ID disc and write his name on a different sheet of paper. No one seemed certain what to do with him.

The British Army doctor started his examination at the feet and worked his way to the groove in Reg's skull. With each poke, the same question: "Any pain here?" The doctor smelled of sweat and rubbing alcohol. He trimmed the hair on top of Reg's head down to the skin for a better look at the scarring. Stiff fingers tapped the flesh there. An instant later, Reg was left alone again, only the shadows of the guards and their rifles against the tent walls to keep him company. Crawling under the rear of the tent would make him an easy target – the only man here in civilian clothes.

A skinny orderly limped into the tent carrying a plate of bread and cheese and a bundle of hospital blues under his arm. The cheese – dry, tasteless – made him thirsty. The blue uniform felt cold, but soft against his skin. No rank, no name sewn into the fabric. He pulled on the new gray socks, slid his feet back into Carmine's slippers just as the guards came back and ushered him out of the tent.

The same car took him and an angrier Capt. Tipple, who sat in the front passenger's seat this time, back north toward The Montello.

"They need to take pictures of your head," the Corporal said. "The machine is in Milan."

"His skull," the Captain said. "An X-ray. Damned waste of time. Invented by a damned German. Don't trust it."

Nearing Montebelluna, that riding crop got busy again, rapping the side edge of the windscreen. He turned toward the rear seat, smiled: "The X-ray will take less time than the train ride there. If you're breathing, you will be found fit to court martial. And shot."

The Corporal swallowed so hard it was audible.

Reg stared at the southern slope of The Montello, the evergreens dotted with color from turning leaves on oaks and beech trees, the soft blue sky. No way to reach those, nowhere left to run.

"Beautiful, isn't it," he said.

●

Civilians and Italian Army soldiers rode the train south. None were allowed to approach Reg. They ate cheese and fruit, talked about how the track out of Treviso needed repair and how it had been that way for months and why it was irritating to live within walking distance of a train station that no one could use. They talked about women, food, wine, their boots – everything but the war. Their sentences in Italian sounded like notes from a cello over the persistent drum beat of the wheels on the track.

In Padua – the sign at the station read, *Padova*, prompting the Captain to mutter, "Can't even spell Padua" – a different train, carrying fewer people, only some of them soldiers. They mistook Captain Tipple and the Corporal for one of their own and tried to start up a conversation. The Corporal struggled to explain in broken Italian before the Captain sighed, shook his head and said, "English! Inglese!" The soldiers lost their grins, shrank back to their seats, occasionally turning to look at Reg's blue outfit and wonder aloud if their own new uniforms would be that same color.

"We dress like Italians," the Corporal told him, "so the Germans wouldn't know we were here."

His name was Bill – Young Bill to his family because his grandfather was the real Bill – and he had broken his leg his first week at Aldershot, so he wound up behind a desk, first sorting forms, then filing them, then filling them out. The Captain picked him to come to Italy because identifying remains and setting up Field Courts Marital required dozens of different forms – "a damned nuisance" – and because no one would volunteer to work with an officer who grumbled all day and night.

Past Vicenza, en route to Verona, Reg studied the varying speed of the train, estimated how many steps it might take to reach the rear exit, visualized how to jump off and roll, then start running. How long could someone in blue hide?

142

"You were the talk of Susegana." The Corporal smelled of cigarettes and hair pomade. "The English soldier who saved the lives of villagers near the river."

"I don't remember saving anyone."

"Then why did the Germans take you prisoner?"

"I was in uniform," Reg said. "Couldn't escape."

Captain Tipple let out a little grunt. "No self-respecting solider surrenders."

The slippers felt even softer with the new socks. Reg ran a finger over the groove in his skull, ragged after the hair had been clipped close. It felt puffy yet hard at the same time, like pie crust riding on lumpy stew. Near the back end of the wound, the scarring pinched his scalp when he tried to brush away the normal length hair near it.

"A real whack on the bean," the Corporal said, glancing at the folder of papers, each with Reg's name on it. "How'd you get it?"

"A rock, I think."

"What happened to your tin hat?"

"The river?"

"Accounts for the memory loss, I suppose." Corporal Bill nodded and closed the folder. "I've seen worse, of course."

To him, victims of mustard gas were the most gruesome – "Burns holes through their uniforms." – their bodies blistered blue and green, tinged with a motley yellow. "You'd swear it was painted on."

No more trees out there now: flatland and gullies, none deep enough to hide in. Corporal Bill would not have to be an expert marksman to hit a target on this landscape.

Reg fought a smile. These were his countrymen, his comrades, yet he was imagining how to escape them. The world had turned upside down. "Inside out, really."

"What is?" the Corporal said.

The smile won: "What isn't?"

•

At dusk, the big lake west of Verona took on the color of worn slate. It ran north into a fold of mountains. The Alps looked bigger here, closer, filling the sky. How cold would that water be? If everything went numb, would freezing to death hurt?

Captain Tipple stepped out of the lavatory – a small room at the rear of the car that would have a hole in the floor for human waste to drop onto the tracks. A hole too small for a man to squeeze through, something Barry had complained about on the way out from France.

143

"It will be dark when we arrive," the Captain said. "If you try to run, I'll shoot you myself." He settled back into his seat. "Save the Army time and money, so be my guest."

Corporal Bill swallowed hard again, then leaned in close and whispered, "He means it."

•

The train station had a high roof of glass and girders, like Victoria Station. Starlight made it through the smooth arch. Milan stood quiet and dark. A Red Cross ambulance waited at the curb. Its rear doors were missing. "Scavenged for the front," the wide-faced driver said. "Hold on so you don't slide out."

The empty road leading away from the station fed into a cluster of streets that ran along a park, the opera house, the cathedral, its white spires poking the night sky. The ambulance made sharp turns through the city center, but those spires were always visible. The ride stopped in front of a big brown five-story cement building, with a balcony on the third floor, spanning a wide arch. A white flag with a red cross hung over it. Almost a full block long, with a fancy facade, especially around the windows on the third floor, it looked like a hotel.

Inside, it smelled of amonia but felt like a brothel, filled with women in white dresses scurrying past one another, their arms full of pots or charts or dirty linen. It could have been a silent ballet. It didn't seem real.

The ambulance driver reappeared from an office near the entrance and led the way up the stairs to the second floor. A small ward – a dozen beds, six against either long wall – stood off the darkened hallway. Reg got the second bed from the door, between a dark-haired man, hard asleep, whose crutches rested against the little table near his pillow and a balding man, whose snore sounded like a dying engine.

The mattress felt soft, the sheets cold. On his back, he could make out the intricate patterned squares in the ceiling. This might have been an expensive hotel before the war, the equal of any in Royal Tunbridge Wells. Or an apartment house for the wealthy. When the Corporal locked the ankle shackle to the bed rail, it felt like a prison, with tall Captain Tipple the smug warden whose solid boot steps echoed on the stairs and back up the hall.

"What if I have to use the watercloset?" Reg said.

Corporal Bill let out a long sigh. "Apologies."

The cheerful ambulance driver knelt and pulled a steel basin from under the bed. "Careful not to spill."

They left together, leaving only the sounds of sleeping soldiers and the grip of cold iron on his ankle.

12

A boyish broad face. A smile that might have been a sneer. Tough dark eyes that studied the shackle, the urine-filled basin on the floor, Reg's face. A wide hand held out in greeting. "Ernie," he said.

Reg rolled on a side, shook his hand. The grip was firm − too firm. The young soldier wasn't wearing hospital blues. He slept in graying underwear. Behind him, his uniform was draped over a chair. Not British. Not Italian.

Reading the chart hanging from Reg's bed, the dark-haired teenager started nodding. "A Brit! So, where'd you get yours, Reggie?"

American.

"I don't think the place had a name," Reg said.

"This is Italy. Every place as a name. Sometimes more than one." Those wide hands let go of the chart and fumbled with the crutches. He stood and patted his legs. "Got mine at Fossalta di Piave. Not even picking up the wounded. Delivering cigarettes and chocolates."

He swung a crutch over the basin on the floor, then moved to the chair and began putting on his uniform. Red Cross. Darker than the wool of the British Army. More pockets in the tunic, too.

Reg draped his legs over the edge of the bed, squinted at the newspaper on Ernie's mattress: *Il Popolo d'Italia.* The headline suggested that the Italian Army stood poised to capture the city of Vittorio.

The tall teen had his trousers on. He pushed the newspaper toward Reg's bed. "We've got the Huns trapped in Vittorio. Romans used to call it Cedeno − what I meant by more than one name for everywhere here."

"You read Italian?"

"Agnes reads it to me. That's three days old." He started buttoning his tunic. "It'll be over soon. We can all go home. Where's yours?"

Those printed words formed a jigsaw puzzle of the familiar and the strange. "I'm not sure anymore," Reg said.

"You shouldn't be out of bed." The lanky nurse set the crutches in a corner, out of Ernie's reach. "The doctor's making rounds."

A smile made that broad young face look even younger. "Say hello to Reggie."

146

She was staring at the basin of urine and the ankle shackle. She glanced at his chart. Her lips formed a sad frown. She adjusted the belt on her loose-fitting white dress, full of pleats and buttons down the front. Her little cap sat well back on her head of short brown hair. "I'm nurse von Kurowsky. We'll take good care of you, Reginald."

American.

Ernie was on the edge of his bed closest to the door, his body half-turned into the ward. He grinned at her, patted his mattress.

"Remove your uniform," she told him. "The doctor will want to examine your legs."

She scanned the other patients, some of whom were still sleeping, then she walked into the hall, where she became part of the parade of other nurses and orderlies.

The teenager began unbuttoning his tunic. "Reggie, I'm going to marry that woman."

•

The bed for the X-Ray machine was really a bench, hard and covered in leather that had been stained by blood and body fluids. He was glad he didn't have to lie down on it.

The machine looked like steel scaffolding in the shape of an upside down L. The doctor moved its high arm to different positions: first the top of the head, then the left side, then the back, then the top again. At each stop, he fiddled with dials on the boxy console, watched the needles jump on the gauges. If he heard the growling buzz the machine made, he didn't show it.

Captain Tipple was right. It took less than 10 minutes.

•

"I couldn't remember a thing about what happened to me for almost a month." Ernie stretched out to full length on the unmade bed sheets. When he laughed, it sounded like a cough. "They keep telling me I pulled two soldiers to safety and got hit by machine gun fire. They're even giving me a medal!" His grin puffed out his cheeks. "I couldn't walk. Or stand. My hand was useless from shrapnel. So tell me, how did I drag two soldiers out of the rubble after being nearly blown up by a mortar and shot by a machine gun?"

Reg shrugged. "But you remember how you did it now?"

"I pretend to." He stared at the ceiling as if watching a moving picture. "All I really remember is the pain. And the blood. Some of it was even mine. But mostly, the pain."

This office must have been a broom closet once. The doctor had to step into the hall to hold the X-Rays up to the sun pouring through the windows. His shoes creaked. His finger traced a ragged line, four inches long, on the top right of the skull. "It's knitting."

Captain Tipple had to bend for a closer look. "Then he's fit?"

Nurses moved past, glancing at the black and gray X-Rays, Reg's slippers, the shackle and chain that Corporal Bill held onto.

"There might be some bone fragments in there. We'd have to operate to be certain." The Canadian Army doctor stuck another X-Ray against the pane. "This side view shows the angle of the fracture."

That line in the skull was smoother in this X-Ray. It ran from above the temple toward the top of the head. It looked longer than in the first film.

"But he's fit to stand before a court martial," the Captain said.

Back in the office, the X-Rays slapped file folders stacked on the desk. It looked like CSM Tranter's desk gone beserk. "Hairline fractures can heal completely," the doctor said, "but this one is worth watching, because of its location." He tapped Reg's head at the groove in his skull. "Any pain?"

"Some soreness," Reg told him.

"Headaches?"

"At first. Not so much anymore."

"And memories. Any coming back to you?"

Reg looked away from the dark stare of the Captain. "Water. Stones. Artillery craters. German guards. Italian soldiers in the dirt of the pen by the castle. That village."

The doctor stepped back. "You run them together as if they happened on the same day. Any memories of home? Before the war? From childhood, perhaps?"

He wasn't sure how much to tell them. Would they arrest Gabby and Teresa or Luigi for taking care of him? He shrugged: "A horse. Chestnut."

A slender rusty water stain ran from the edge of the wall toward the corner. The doctor smiled. "Did you ride it?"

No one rode Walter. That horse pulled the plow. "I don't remember ever riding any horse."

The small doctor pulled out a cigarette, thought better of it when he couldn't find an ashtray among the folders cluttering his desk. He nodded at the ankle shackle. "Is that really necessary?"

Captain Tipple was holding up one of the X-Rays, squinting at it in the dim light. For once, his swagger stick stayed quiet at his side. "I don't see any fragments."

"He needs to be moved to the observation ward." The doctor reached for the film in the Captain's hand. "We'll be needing the beds in post-op."

The tall man let the film slip from his fingers back onto the pile. "Then discharge him."

Two nurses ran past the doorway toward cheers. The doctor squeezed past the Corporal, into the hall, stopping another group of nurses. One of them waved a newspaper: "It's over! The Austrians surrendered!"

He carried the paper back into his office, scanned it. Reg could make out a headline: 20,000 prisoners captured at Vittorio. His legs felt weak. He braced himself against the side of the desk. Corporal Bill helped him into the doctor's chair.

That riding crop began beating the air along the Captain's pantleg. "What's it say?"

"They've set an Armistice. For next week." The doctor opened to a different page, then lowered the newspaper, sat on his desk, knocking over a stack of files and the X-Rays. He didn't seem to notice. "It's true," he told the open doorway. "It's actually over."

13

Ernie told his story as if it were one long sentence, all the details slamming into each other. Nurse Agnes did her best to keep up with him, translating for the pudgy man in the gray suit, whose pencil moved furiously over his pad.

The American teen blew smoke rings as he talked. The long drive out of Schio to the Piave Delta in ambulance Number 4, a new Fiat with roll-down canvas side curtains and a complete tool kit – perhaps the only one in all of Italy – in a box on the running board. The dugout where Italian soldiers huddled in that half-sleep everyone experiences at the front, a dull daze that switches off at the crack of a rifle or the song of a Whiz-Bang. Their faces when they saw the chocolate bars, the grit on their hands when they reached for them, the explosion that destroyed the dugout, blowing the legs off two of them, filling his own legs with shrapnel. The coughing that came as a relief because even though he could no longer hear anything, he could feel that cough in his chest, proving he was still alive. The dust and smoke he crawled out to, the ground spitting dirt at him – those must have been the machine gun bullets – and the sight of Number 4, still in perfect condition, sitting in the street like a monument.

The newspaper man asked questions. He knew that area. He had been injured near there himself. He still had sharpnel in him – "Quarantaquattro" – 44 pieces. The hospital they sent him to was also in Milan.

"Reggie here got his up the river, near Nervesa." Strands of black hair had been plastered back with pomade, making Ernie's broad forehead look even bigger. "He can't remember a thing. Not even his own name."

Large round eyes opened wider. The balding man stuck out his chin and nodded as if he understood something deep and secret. He put down his pencil, offered his small hand. "Piacere."

Those slender fingers felt hot from all that writing. They went back to scribbling the moment Ernie started up again, detailing his three operations, how he could now walk with a cane, but used the crutches when he got tired and his eyes betrayed him. Those weak eyes were the reason the American Army wouldn't take him. Driving ambulances was his only way into this war.

The interview stopped when an Italian General stepped inside the ward. His entourage consisted of a Lieutenant, who looked lost, and a stoop-shouldered sergeant, who opened the lid of the thin leather box. Before Ernie could stand, the skinny General pinned the medal on the Red Cross tunic draped over the chair back. The Lieutenant read from a scroll – something about a Cross of War. The old sergeant set the box and the scroll on the bed. A man with a bulky camera ran in, too late for the presentation. His boss, the editor, barked at him, told him to photograph the medal on the uniform. He had to wait until the three Italian soldiers had walked back into the hall.

As if stunned, Ernie put out his cigarette. "That was it?"

"They're busy." Nurse Agnes patted his knee. "And you're not Italian."

The newspaper editor shoved the photographer through the doorway. "Sempre tardi."

"He's always late." She stood and pulled the tunic off the chair. "It's a beautiful medal. The Silver Cross."

Big hands held up the uniform. Those dark eyes squinted to focus on the medal dangling above the woolen pocket.

Nurse Agnes joined the newpaper man in the hallway. They spoke softly. Arms folded, she made him look as if he was fidgeting, his hands punching the air with each phrase.

"He's too young to be an editor," Reg said.

"The editor I had at *The Star* was 80."

"*The Star*?"

Ernie turned the tunic to show off the medal. "Kansas City daily paper."

"You wrote for a newspaper? In Kansas?"

"It's in Missouri. Freelance." He put on the tunic, buttoned it. "Let's go make the rounds."

Reg jiggled the shackle chain.

The tall teen sighed. On crutches, he made his way around the bed. With his nurse on one side and the balding editor on the other, he started down the hallway, those crutches tapping the floor like drum sticks.

If a fire broke out, if a bomb hit the building, no one would think of unlocking the ankle shackle. The bed, the sheets warm from his body, the metal basin at his feet, these would be the last things he would see before the smoke choked him.

Better than a trench, he told himself. *Better than mud.*

He fell back against the pillow, laughing.

She was wearing a cape. "Where is Ernest?"

"Showing off his new medal."

Her smile came on slowly. "He is a hero."

"He's in love with you."

"So are twenty others here." Nurse Agnes set a copy of the Italian newspaper on Ernie's bed. "He's so young."

"He talks about taking you home. To an oak park."

"He's only 19." She glanced at Reg's chart. "Any headaches?"

He shook his head.

"That newspaper editor wants to interview you." She hung the chart back onto its hook at the foot of the bed, examined the shackle on his ankle. "No bruising. That's good." That slow smile again, broadening her cheeks. "Doctor Ainsworth thinks an interview might be good for you. A way to jog your memory."

He shrugged. "Why the cape?"

"We're supposed to be going to a celebration. Near the race track at San Siro."

"And we are!" Ernie walked in using only a cane. "I've been looking all over for you."

She let out a quiet laugh and flicked the dangling silver medal. "We all know what you were doing."

"Met your Captain Tipple." He plopped beside Reg, jostling the mattress, threw an arm around his shoulder. "You crack your skull open and he can't wait to shoot you. Don't worry. Doc's on your side." He squeezed a quick hug, grinned at Nurse Agnes. "Ready?"

She squinted at him, but couldn't hold back a smile. "Where are your crutches?

"Roof." He wobbled, but the cane steadied him. "This will be fine."

"If you stumble – "

"You'll catch me," he said.

"You could reinjure your legs."

Ernie straightened up, started toward the hall. "More time here with you then."

She glanced at Reg. "I'll tell him yes? About the interview? I'll translate."

He nodded. "Have a good time. And – don't catch him."

"I heard that!" The tall teen's voice rumbled in from the hall. "Come on, Agnes. Try to keep up with a cripple."

She took a step, then stopped and turned back toward his bed. "I'm ten years older than he is."

Before he could speak, she was moving, her cape swishing against her uniform. She didn't look that old. Going on 30? Did Ernie know? Would he care?

The front page of the newspaper carried a headline about the Armistice. All ones – 11th hour of the 11th day of the 11th month. He realized he wasn't sure of today's date. Was it the 5th – the day the paper came out?

Inside, a story with a photo of a medal on a tunic and another of a driverless Red Cross ambulance. "Ernesto Hemingway, di Parco Quercia, America," the article began. That pudgy editor used a lot of words. Mr. Quaite would not be impressed.

●

He spoke Italian, German, French and English. His high forehead accentuated his chin. He wasn't a small man – except when he stood next to Ernie – and he wasn't pudgy – that was all bone and muscle. He had tiny, delicate hands and the way he held the pencil over the pad seemed catlike, ready to pounce.

He had also been wounded, over a year ago in the Isonzo section of the 400-mile Italian front, in a valley between the Julian Alps and the Adriatic Sea, when a mortar accidentally exploded during a training mission. Four of his fellow soldiers were killed. He, too, felt lucky to be alive.

And he himself had been accused of desertion – 15 years ago, when he left Italy to work at a newspaper in Switzerland. He was even convicted – *in absentia* – and returned under a general amnesty for thousands just like him to spend two years in the Italian Army.

He had written books, had been the youngest newspaper editor in Italy when he took over *Avanti!*, the official publication of the Socialist Party, and boosted its circulation five-fold. Now, as head of *Il Popolo d'Italia*, he was finally his own boss.

He believed in *Risorgimento* – the unification of all Italians, even those in Austro-Hungarian territory – and saw this War of Nations as the means to achieve it. Force, he now understood, was necessary, a complete reversal of his early days as a pacifist.

His mother was a school teacher, his father a blacksmith. He no longer shared his mother's devotion to the church or his father's dedication to a menial trade. He valued education and art. He would, he was certain, be a poet one day.

He wanted Reg to know all of this because he felt an empathy with the Englishman. Like Ernie, he had also experienced memory loss after being wounded. Even now, some parts of the event remained a mystery to him. But the pain of the shrapnel he still carried was real everyday.

It was like watching a stage play, where the lead actor walks on to deliver a long soliloqy that captivates the audience. Nurse Agnes and Ernie were spellbound by the balding man's growling voice that could suddenly turn from a whisper to an exploding shout. All Reg could focus on were his lips, the way they turned out and down in a pout when he made a point he was especially proud of. It made his chin look sharp, his face longer.

"We now start." Those slender fingers poised pencil to pad. "Your name?"

Reg started to pull his ID disc from under his pajama top, but Nurse Agnes had his chart at the ready. "Reginald Olcutt," she said.

It got worse from there.

•

Mr. Kipling's mongoose saved him.

At first, Reg pretended to be confused. The newspaper man simplified his questions. How could anyone not remember his boyhood home, his army battalion, the villagers who nursed him back to health?

Rikki-Tikki-Tavi distracted the snake, then reacted to its strike before it could recoil to strike again. Reg distracted them by offering answers to questions not asked. He described details of walls, paths, pebbles along the river. He remembered broken cribs and burned houses, charred dolls, shattered plates. He asked the editor why the smell of goats in a mountain meadow would make him think of plum jam, which he wasn't certain he cared for. He asked Ernie if he had ever smelled horse flesh roasting on a spit or if he had ever seen men starve. He asked Nurse Agnes if she had seen what Corporal Bill had: the discolored bodies of soldiers exposed to mustard gas.

He claimed he was trying to make sense of the jumble of images, smells and sounds filling his head. There were women – some old, some very young – at a table outside, eating lunch, smiling, and he didn't understand why they terrified him.

From the long pauses that followed each of his comments, he knew it was working. He could protect all those he cared about in Colfosco. Who would punish anyone who had helped a lost, confused soldier? He could have memories, he decided, but no connection between any of them.

When their eyes began to focus on the walls and floor and not him, he tugged on the chain of the ankle shackle. "Where am I supposed to run off to?"

Nurse Agnes put her hand on his. Ernie hung his head and sighed. The newspaper man narrowed his stare, arched his head back slightly, then began nodding. "So," he said, "you are still in the river."

Reg smiled. "I thought this was a hospital."

The loudest laugh came from Ernie.

•

One hour and a dull headache later, they took photographs. Every snap included the editor, who preferred to be called by his last name only – Mussolini. Benito, he said, made him sound like a little boy. His father had picked that name out of his admiration for a Mexican socialist, Benito Juarez. Standing next to Mussolini was like brushing against a tree trunk. He was solid, immovable, and his handmade brown suit made him look like a sturdy oak.

"A real patriot," Ernie said after the editor and his photographer had left.

"Full of himself," Nurse Anges told him.

"With a right to be." An open palm brushed black hair off that wide forehead. "Educated, literate, soldier – a philosopher, too. A real man."

Reg stretched out on the bed, covered his face with an arm. Mr. Quaite would probably agree. He might even hire Mussolini to take over *The Rusthall Gazette*.

The thought of that made him swallow a laugh. The young editor, king of Milan, would never settle for anything as small or rural as Rusthall. What must it be like to work for someone like him? Could he be satisfied with the work of anyone but himself?

"Like my father," Reg said. "A tyrant."

But neither Ernie or his nurse were there to hear him. They were holding hands in the hallway, smiling into each other's eyes. Older men married younger women all the time. Gabby and Teresa had. It might be the same for older women and younger men. Maybe those two could be happy together.

He shut his eyes, hoping to see her, her light hair catching sunlight in her garden. Instead he saw Walter, the bulky chestnut, shivering each time his father whipped a haunch with a green branch, the plow digging deeper from his weight, the dark crumbly soil

155

roiling up the furrow. All that for new potatoes the swells in Royal Tunbridge Wells would eat in hotel dining rooms, never caring or understanding they were eating the sweat of a man who hated his horse, his life – and his son, the boy who would rather play with words than dirt, who was no real help on the farm, just another mouth to feed.

He wondered if Mussolini's father-the-smithy had ever felt the same way.

"Sunday." The lanky teen fell onto the bed, making it creak. "I ask her to marry me Sunday."

14

The roof offered a view of the cathedral and downtown Milan. Nurses ate lunch up here. Corporal Bill hoped to meet the short dark-haired one who reminded him of a girl he went to school with — Emmy. He unlocked the shackle. "Walk around," he said. "Maybe in her direction?"

Reg scratched his ankle. "Won't you get in trouble for this?"

"Captain can't hold you over anymore." Graying hairs grew in his nostrils. "The end of the war means the end of all Field Courts Martial."

"What happens now?"

"Keep walking," the Corporal said. "Almost there." He found his best smile and began speaking louder. "I can't file any form that isn't legal. I take the responsibilities of my position quite seriously." He doffed his cap. "Ladies. A little chill in the air up here today."

The three nurses made little noises of agreement.

Reg sat on the wall ledge, looked up at the short dark-haired nurse. "Your name wouldn't be Emmy, would it?"

She cocked her head to the side. "Victoria."

He nudged the Corporal.

"So, British then?" Corporal Bill touched his cap brim again. "I'm William. This is Reg."

"We know who he is." She was looking at his slippers, but smiling. "He's the talk of Milan." Cool mountain wind scattered some napkins. She sat next to him. "Haven't you haven't seen the paper? You look nicer in person."

The tall nurse with mayonaisse on the side of her mouth nodded. "Younger, too."

"Much younger," the older nurse said, taking another bite of her sandwich.

He stood. "I'd like to go down and read the paper."

"So go." Corporal Bill slid next to the dark-haired nurse. "I'll be down later."

He pointed at the shackle bunched up in the Corporal's hand. "What about that?"

"I told you," the Corporal said. "I can't hold you over for any legal proceeding that is no longer authorized."

"I can just — leave?"

"You're still restricted to the hospital, of course." Corporal Bill was using his official voice, the one he probably learned from his Captain Tipple. "But, yes. You may return to your ward."

His legs felt wobbly. He turned and started for the door to the stairs.

"Bye, Reg." Victoria gave him a little wave. "Nice to meet you."

The voices of the other nurses ran toward him, but all he heard was that wind and the sound of the door blowing shut behind him.

•

It was all about the newspaper editor.

Even Nurse Agnes was surprised. Some of the sentences she read made her stop in mid-translation. Written as a memoir of his own struggles in war and the wounds he had sustained, Mussolini had used Reg's confusion to lay out an heroic tale – his own.

The head wound Reg suffered from was a blessing, the article said, blocking the horrible images of war, images Mussolini could not forget, would never forget, images of death and destruction beyond description, images he shared with his countrymen, especially his comrades-in-arms.

The detainment of this Englishman was criminal. This was a man separated in battle from his unit, exactly as Mussolini had been ripped from his unit by the explosion that should have killed him, the event that steeled his resolve to serve his country even after he stopped wearing his uniform. He carried those 44 pieces of shrapnel as reminders of that resolve, and every time he sat down at his editor's desk to write a story, he dedicated himself to the glory of Italy and its people. He would, his article said, never write anything critical of an Italian, even though some of his former colleagues might have said and written unflattering things about him. He would model himself after the wounded Englishman and remain detached from the frenzy. Calm, resolute, he would use all his skills as a writer to promote a new country where all Italians could share the same future.

The big photograph showed the balding editor smiling, his arm on Reg's shoulder. Two smaller photographs captured Mussolini asking questions and writing on his note pad. Nurse Agnes was in one of those. Ernie wasn't in any of them.

"He writes like a florist." Leaning on his cane, the tall teen struggled into the hall. "And why didn't he interview me in English?"

She watched Ernie leave. "I think he's jealous."

"At least his article was about him," Reg said.

"How could it be about you?" She slapped the page with the back of her hand. "You aren't sure about anything that happened to you."

He lowered his stare, nodded.

She touched his hand. "Sorry. I didn't mean – " Clearing her throat, she translated the last paragraph:

"I hope for an Italy no longer divided by provinces and dialects. Where we are from will matter less than where we are going. I see a country free of the biases and limitations of our past, as newly innocent as one Reginald Olcutt – The Englishman who forgot his own name."

The newspaper made a rustling sound in her lap. Not bothering to fold it, she left it on the bed, then stood,, kissed the top of his head. "I'm happy you're not a prisoner anymore."

Her footsteps got softer in the hall. Those photographs stared back at him. The editor's grin stopped looking smug and satisfied. It began to look silly, like those grinning barkers in checkered suits outside tents in the traveling circuses that came twice a year to Rusthall Commons to put on a show that was never worth the price of a ticket.

There would be the sliver of a moon tonight. The roof would be quiet, the city even quieter. If he started up the stairs now, he would have the best seat in the house.

•

Chaos. Ambulance sirens. Squealing tires. Shouts from stretcher bearers. Directions shouted by nurses and doctors. Moans and cries from the wounded. There must have been 200 of them.

"Only those who could travel," Corporal Bill said. "We've got thousands still at field hospitals."

"I thought it was over."

"This is what over looks like." He peered over the roof ledge. "She's not going to have time for dinner."

"Are they all from Vittorio?"

The Corporal nodded. "Vickie says they're moving everybody to make room. You'll be reassigned."

The Armistice was a day away. Some of those wounded soldiers might not live to see it.

"Where?"

Corporal Bill blew cigarette smoke at the moon. "Does it matter?"

Reg let out a little laugh. "You call her Vickie now?"

It was as if the long-nosed soldier had smiled for the first time. "She's a plum, isn't she." He drew in a deep breath. "Let's talk a walk. Over to the opera house and back."

"I thought I was restricted to the hospital."

"You are." That droopy smile again and a glance down at the flurry of nurses in white and all those bloody bandages. "Something tells me you won't be missed."

•

His black shoes had been shined to a military polish. The collar of his white shirt looked bright against his ruddy skin. The red tie, its knot slightly lopsided, stood out against his blue woolen suit. Black fedora in hand, he grinned the moment he saw Reg and started across the lobby.

"Re-ja," he said, pressing a hand flat against his own chest. "Ezio!"

Ezio?

Strong arms gripped his. "Ezio. Your friend."

Ezio.

Reg hugged him, felt those dry lips kiss each cheek. "I wouldn't have recognized you."

"I eat." He locked his arm through Reg's and led him back across the lobby to a small woman in a tiny black hat with a veil. Three children stood with her, each in their Sunday best. "Mia moglie − my wife. Ilba."

He didn't know whether to offer his hand. She didn't give him the chance. She took a small white box from the taller boy. "Charlotte di mele, alla Milanese."

It felt heavy. It smelled of lemon and sugar. He untied the string, opened the lid: a little round pie, golden brown crust.

"The apple pie," Ezio said. "With the sultana." He kissed his fingers. "Perfetto."

He could smell the apples. "Grazie, Ilba."

She was smiling, but her eyes were tearing up. He smiled at each of her children as she introduced them. The thin 12 year-old looked like a healthy version of the gaunt Ezio back in the prison pen at the castle. The 10 year-old girl was a smaller version of her mother, down to the little hat. The youngest, a boy with scraped knees, watched the stretchers move by, the uniformed bearers chased by nurses and doctors.

"She − we − say for them, thanks to you." Ezio beamed at his family. "Taste!"

Sweetened juice of baked apples and raisins leaked down his chin. The soft crust tasted of lemons. "Perfetto," he said.

He offered the pie to the children, but after seeing their mother shake her head, each of them declined to take a bite. "Solo per te," she said.

"Only for you," Ezio told him. "You come for Natale, we make the feast. With the panetonne."

Another bite, bigger than the first. Tourists in Tunbridge Wells would marvel at this apple pie. "How did you find me?"

He pulled a copy of the newspaper from inside his suit jacket, opened to the photograph of Reg and the editor. "I see and tell them, this is he. You. My friend."

The more Ezio talked, the sadder he got. Born in Milan, educated here, married here, employed here – he taught poetry and language at the university – he was home now, with his children, his wife, his job, his city. It was a life he never thought he would get to live again, a prospect his wife must have shared because she was dabbing at her tears now. But she smiled when her husband recounted the kindness of the Englishman in the prison pen who shared his food, the escape he was a part of, the long trek he had helped lead through forests and down to Colfosco.

"I keep the rifle," Ezio said. "When they finish here with you, come to live with us. We make you strong, for when you go to England."

Reg stared at his slippers, grateful they didn't have to see him in that ankle shackle. He wanted to tell them that he didn't know if they would ever be finished with him or if he would ever return to Rusthall. He thought of telling them about the short walk he took two days ago – his first real glimpse of the city – led by Corporal Bill to the statue of King Vittorio Emmanuel II on horseback, who seemed to be riding straight toward the arched entry doors of that many-spired cathedral despite flocks of pigeons crowding the base of the monument, cooing on top of elaborate figures adorning the pedestal – lions and and eagles, the raised arms of the countrymen the king had united. Ezio's Milan would be more interesting – the perfect place to plan a way back to Gabby.

He finished the tiny pie in two more bites, licked his lips, imagined eating meal after meal at Ezio's table, all the new and exquisite tastes.

"Squisito," he said.

Only a handful of patients were awake when the bells struck 11. Hospital staff was too busy to do anything more than pause, then go back to the hectic business of keeping the wounded alive. The Armistice came in on snores and moans and the long silence that followed the final clang of the cathedral bell.

Ernie pulled a silver flask from his pocket, took a swig, then offered it to Reg. "Grappa. Take your head right off."

"Might be an improvement." It smelled like perfume but tasted like brandy, his father's favorite. It made him cough. "Too strong for me."

"Made from grape skins. Just the skins. Ingenious." The silver cross on his tunic looked even shinier. So many fingers had touched it, adding a patina to the metal. "First snow's overdue. They'll have to move some of the wounded back inside. We'll be shoved out." Those dark eyes shut. "She said no."

Reg took the flask, pretended to sip more Grappa. "Sorry."

The tall teenager let out a laugh and fell back on the bed. "I'll just keep asking her."

Love was relentless. Worse than war. Love was never over. Horrible and beautiful at the same time.

With the smile on that young face, those eyes closed, the dark-haired American in the next bed might have been in a casket, laid out in his finest uniform, medals and all, peaceful at last. "I'll wear her down. She'll come around."

Love was hopeless.

"A fine plan," Reg said.

•

The tunic was new. Two chevrons on the sleeves: full Corporal. It felt heavier than he remembered. New grey shirt, socks, briefs, even boots. And a soft cap, but without the Royal West Kent emblem.

"Still working on your owed pay." Corporal Bill checked his list against the items spread out on the bed. "Captain says you won't be entitled to it." A wink. "He's not the one who submits the forms."

"Which part of the hospital are they moving me to?"

The long-nosed man had been shaving twice a day for over a week and his skin looked red from the razor. He had had his hair trimmed. With all that pomade, it looked like a dark shiny skull cap. He had even been polishing his boots. Nurse Vickie was getting the full treatment. "Having trouble finding new puttees, but I threw in a set of mine."

162

The leg wrappings stretched across the bed like long, dingy bandages. For an instant, he couldn't remember how to get them started.

"Why isn't he ready?" Captain Tipple struck the bed rail with his swagger stick "Did you read him his orders?"

Boney fingers fumbled with papers in the big yellow envelope. "Just about to, sir."

The riding crop went under an armpit. "Corporal Olcutt, you are being transferred to stand before a General Court Martial on the charge of desertion." He scanned the uniform pieces. "Get this man dressed and shackled for transport."

He stormed out, the swager stick beating his trouser leg.

"I thought they couldn't do that," Reg said.

Corporal Bill stepped to the doorway, peered down the hall to make sure the tall officer had gone. "This isn't a Field Court Martial. They can convene a General Court Martial any time."

The uniform bits looks like those diagrams in the training manuals. He stood, unbuttoned the top of the hospital blues.

"I couldn't talk him out of it." The form the Corporal held out was a jumble of words in boxes. "No room for you here anymore. But I did get you a cushy spot. New convalescent house, in Tunbridge Wells." He tried his best smile, the new one he had found while courting his nurse. "You're going home."

BOOK FOUR

BLIGHTY

27 NOVEMBER, 1918

1

It was the wrong place.

After all the fits and stops and broken train cars, the ruptured rails, the camps of tents set up in the rubble of once vibrant villages, all the waiting women searching for a familiar face among men in uniform moving through bad-smelling streets, that Channel crossing over a sea so angry it had turned black in the middle of the day and made turning back impossible, the unswept coal dust and litter that had turned South Eastern Station from the grand entrance of a town royal into yet another place to escape from – after all that, General Hospital on Grosvenor Road had no room for him.

"He's assigned to Calverley Lodge," the waiting room clerk said, tapping a section of the travel orders. "Short walk."

It would have been short, but not in new boots. So heavy they made his shins ache, this pair squeaked, turning him into the unquiet Dormouse that announced its unwanted presence with every step, each creak of the sole calling attention to the shackle that hobbled his ankle. He longed for Carmine Cusato's slippers, the feel of rounded cobblestones and new grass underfoot.

Down Upper Grosvenor back toward the train station, he made the dark streets noisy. Without the shackle, it would be a short run to Wellington Rocks off Langton Road and all the good hiding places in those trees. From there, an uphill trot into Denny Bottom, where a person could disappear for days in the nooks near the Sweep's Caves and the slopes falling away from Toad Rock.

Not in this weather. Not without a mackintosh. The scratchy blanket they had given him barely kept the wind out. The cold got through at every opening. It made the uniform trousers feel stiff. The sleet coming in would make it worse. Some traces of rotten snow near Crescent Road promised a brutal winter, the kind of weather his father cursed.

Did his parents know he was back? And alive?

The old stone mansion had a portico of white columns facing the street. Behind it, the darkness of Calverley Grounds caught night wind in its evergreens and sheltered fields. Madge dreamt of a house in the South Ward, near the shops on Camden Road.

Did she know?

"He doesn't belong here." The tall nurse checked Reg's name off her list. "The shell-shocked and gassed go to Bidborough Court."

167

Sergeant Dickson smiled. "It's two in the morning. We've been traveling straight on for six days."

"He should be at Bidborough."

"Yet he is here, as his orders require him to be." His warden's cough sounded deeper than it had just a few days ago, when the French countryside was drenched in winter rain, turning much of it into the slop Reg had hoped to forget. "He requires a lockable room. And not at ground level."

It was hard to tell if they were arguing or flirting. Neither one of them seemed fit for their jobs. The Sergeant had been a stone mason before the war. A Fritz machine gun in Flanders had taken that trade from him. Prisoner escort was all that was left to him, he had said when he took charge of Reg in Lyon, where Capt. Tipple and Corporal Bill had made the transfer, though the glare the tall captain wore said he wanted to stay with this prisoner through to the firing squad.

And the night nurse wasn't actually a nurse, just a local woman someone had handed a uniform. Sent to this Volunteer Auxiliary Hospital, she probably lived near enough to walk home, which might be empty if her husband was still serving. Or dead. Or he might be one of the patients here, among the brain-rattled men this war had created.

The stocky Sergeant was talking about the field stone used to build this mansion. He knew the tools used to cut that stone and, from the color and facing, guessed the location of the quarry it had come from – Maidstone. Fascinated, the VAD nurse found a room in the attic space above the third floor. It held a cot, and its small window – too small for a person to fit through – overlooked the rear garden.

They left Reg there. It felt every bit as cold as his tiny room on the farm. Even in the dark, he could see his own breath. The canvas of the cot smelled musty. Someone might have died on it. So tired – almost as exhausted as he had been in the prisoner pen by the castle – but it no longer mattered. He pulled the blanket over his head, listened to the wind – his wind, the same one that had sung him to sleep over all those years. The shivering would stop, he knew, in less than an hour. Without a moon, dreams would come fast.

•

The man in the doorway was standing in a puddle made by his dripping overcoat and umbrella. He took off his wool cap. His face was wet, too. Mr. Quaite looked heavier. Maybe it was from all the layers of clothes he was wearing.

"I had to make sure it was really you," he said, his soft voice cracking like new frost. "Welcome home, lad."

Sgt. Dickson stepped over the puddle, grabbed the knob and began pulling the door shut. "You've had your look in. No visitors 'til staff authorizes it."

"I'll be by later this afternoon." Mr. Quaite's voice got softer behind the door. His wet shoes slapped the hallway floor, then the stairs, then nothing.

Reg got off the bed, slid a toe into the puddle at the door to make sure it was real. Cold rain trickled down the small window pane. Out there in the sopping gloom, home was crying.

●

The little editor didn't come back that afternoon. Or the next. Only doctors came in. One of them had seen the X-Rays from Milan and asked about headaches. Another asked if Reg knew where he was and why he was shackled. A third doctor used a tongue depressor to examine his throat and mouth, a penlight to look up his nose and into his ears, a stethoscope to listen to his heart and lungs. The last doctor just sat on the stool he had found in the corner and waited for Reg to speak. When he didn't, that doctor scribbled something on a pad and left.

Tripe for lunch. Tea with supper: tripe-flavored soup, with bread. It wasn't until he lay down for the night that he realized he had only been allowed to use a spoon − nothing with a sharp point.

Cucchiaio. Cucchiaino. The words made him smile and, for an instant, he swore he could smell her river.

●

"They have a reasonable case, unless you can remember what actually happened." The Major smoked too much. Ash from his cigarettes dusted the papers in his folders, his uniform, the floor. "Our only defense is your head injury and your being taken prisoner." The papers got shoved back into a brown attaché pouch. "If we could verify that. How did you escape?"

"Italians. Alpine troops."

"How do you know that?"

"That's who they said they were." Reg twisted the ankle shackle to stop the itching. "And their uniforms."

169

"Good. Very good." The sharp-nosed officer stood. Still jotting on his notepad, he tucked the pouch under an arm. "We'll get that horse galloping."

He left the door open and headed for the stairs, then stopped and came back to shut it. "Sorry. Regulations."

The room felt bigger with the door closed. The roof timbers showed through the patches of missing plaster. This might have been servants' quarters. The view out the window would not have changed much: hedges trimmed around a stone patio, and beyond those hedges, a broad expanse of parkland, dotted with evergreens. Formal, stately, Calverley Grounds looked like the opposite of Rusthall Common. Did anyone picnic here in summer? Was it permitted?

He used the stem of the spoon to slip under the shackle and scratch his ankle. The rusty iron band popped open. The spoon slipped out of his fingers. He kept staring at his naked skin, the discolored strip the iron had covered, the blistering rash near the inside ankle bone.

He picked up the spoon, put it on the tray next to the bowl that had held lunch − tripe again − and got dressed. The uniform felt heavier from the humidity. Tray in hand, he opened the door and walked down the hall, taking the rear stairs to the ground floor. The doctor who had examined his nose and mouth had one foot on a bench, using his thigh as a desk to write on a chart.

"Where would I find the kitchen?" Reg said.

Without looking up from his work, the doctor pointed at the rear corridor. Reg carried the tray in that direction, drawn by the faint clinking and clanking of pots and pans and the rush of voices. He set the tray on a rolling cart filled with bins of plates and cups outside the double doors. Steam was leaking through those doors. At the end of the corridor he found a wide door to the garden. From a barrel by the coat rack, he picked an umbrella.

The rain felt warmer than he had expected. Past the end of the terrace wall and at a gap in the low hedge, he walked onto Calverley Grounds. The pebble road running through it curled around a muddy pitch and led to a broad street: Mount Pleasant Road. The train station, a block away, would be the first place Sgt. Dickson would check. Reg headed north, in the opposite direction, turning left onto Crescent Road. From here it was only a half mile to Wellington Rocks, less than 10 minutes on foot, even in the rain. He quickened his pace.

Across from the Trinity Theater, The Lenton Hotel looked small by this town's standard, but it had two uniformed porters standing at the front doors. They watched a waterfall off the roof spatter the entry stones. They nodded at Reg and opened the doors.

The lobby stood empty, except for a silver-haired woman in a beaded dress who sat hands folded in a leather chair, studying the landscape paintings on the front wall. A slender man in a black suit and tie stepped to her, a luggage tag in his hand. "We've located your case, Lady Wheaton," he said. "I'll have it cleaned and sent up directly."

"Cleaned? What on earth for?"

He held out the stained tag. "Apparently it slipped off the motor car into the mud."

"Carelessness." She stood, smoothed out her dress. "I'll expect the hotel to pay for any damages."

"I'll inform the manager myself."

"Thank you, Yorke."

He watched the beads on that dress shimmer as she waddled toward the main stairway off the front desk. When she had climbed to the first landing, he snapped his fingers twice, summoning a bellman in a dark blue uniform that matched the carpeted stairs. The luggage tag changed hands. "Get this up to the Lenton Suite," he said. "And not trace of mud on it anywhere."

Before the young bellman could turn to leave, long fingers stopped him by straightening his round cap. Another finger snap and the bellman was on the move.

"May I assist you, Corporal?" Barry's father didn't look anything like his son. "Visiting one of our guests?"

Reg shook his head. "The rain. Always wanted to see this lobby."

"Lovely, isn't it." He nudged Reg off the carpet onto the slate floor, took the umbrella and plunged it into an empty brass stand. "Feel at home to walk through. But not up the stairs – house rules. My son was a Corporal, in the Queen's Own."

"Yorke!" A growl shot through the lobby. "My office."

Touching his brow with a finger in a mock salute, Barry's dad turned and strode toward the front desk, slipping behind it and disappearing into a side office. That narrow door slapped shut.

The sound of the rain, muffled by the thick walls, made the summer and autumn landscapes in the paintings seem out of place. Those French impressionists painted rain: rain on streets, on flowers, on ponds and lakes. Barry was right: they belonged on these walls.

Reg grabbed the umbrella handle, stepped over the wet patch on the slate – the amber light from the sconces made it look like blood – and headed back out into the storm.

2

Rain tumbled down Inner London Road, then funneled onto Castle. It felt like walking alongside rapids. A lorry rumbled by. Without traffic, the center of Rusthall would be less than five minutes away from Calverley Lodge. He took a soggy game trail through the short woods. Wellington Rocks, darkened to charcoal from the weather, lay as a giant low mound of smooth, slippery boulders, far too dangerous to climb when this slick.

The balloonist Mr. Quaite had interviewed years ago claimed the rock formation resembled a tortoise when viewed from above. He had strayed off course, compounding his error by misjudging the afternoon wind, which swirled in this little hollow, making kite flying a challenge. Depositing his basket and passengers in the clearing beside the rocks, the balloonist had walked directly to The Beacon, a half-mile off through Happy Valley, and ordered lunch: *A pint and a cheese sandwich, with onion and mustard,* the article had noted in Mr. Quaite's standard style of using detail to convince readers the account was true. Able to finish that lunch before the authorities located him. the balloonist was never seen again. His balloon was taken away before nightfall, but that wicker basket remained overturned on the short grass for weeks – a favorite new toy for local boys before squirrels took it over.

Reg followed the foot path along Neville Park. Where it curved north toward Langton Road, he took the climb of Neville Ridge, cutting through the trees and setting foot in Rusthall for the first time in such a long time that, for a moment, he wanted to stay under the oak limbs for fear that nothing would be the same.

St. Paul's had not changed. Gray stone, rooked bell tower, massive gothic arches in front and taller slender ones with stained glass lining the sides. Too far from the farm to walk to in Sunday best, coming here had always meant a special occasion – baptisms, christenings, weddings, funerals. He tried the front door, then took the walk past the side graveyard, where old stones stood like drenched mourners. The rear door was unlocked.

The back foyer smelled of disinfective. The iron gate across the entrance to the tower steps wore a shiny new padlock. The main hall, dark from lack of sunlight, had filled with damp air. He walked away from the altar, keeping to the corridor made of a row of stone arches that separated the center pews from the side walls. There would be no one in the choir loft – the perfect place to rest and dry off.

The woman in a tan wool coat stood outside the anteroom. Next to her, a shirt-sleeved man with a mop watched rain drip from the roof into a stew pot. Startled, the woman stepped behind the man: "How did you get in?"

"The door was open," Reg said.

She shoved the man – "Go lock it" – then thought better of it and grabbed the mop handle to stop him. "No, stay here, with me." Squinting, she studied his uniform. "Not Belgian, are you?"

"One of ours." Air whistled through the man's missing teeth. "Full Corporal."

She let go of the mop handle. "Go get the vicar."

The man rolled down his sleeves, set his mop against the wall and stepped into the anteroom.

"Tile must have fallen off," Reg said, wondering what kind of special equipment a slater would need to stay safe on the step pitch of this roof. Had it rained in Colfosco? Did Teresa's roof stand up to it?

"They're everywhere now." The woman eyed the pot. It would take hours to fill at this rate. "All dumped on us like so much refuse." Her smile looked brittle. "The Belgians, you see. Why we keep our doors locked."

A young man in his 30's, wearing an undershirt and mud-splattered work pants, followed the shirt-sleeved man out to the front foyer. He spotted Reg and strode over, his hand outstretched. "Come to help us with the roof, Corporal?"

"He's not Belgian," the woman said.

"I can see that, Mrs. Stather." The real vicar, Reverend Walrond, must have died. It was the only way he would have ever left this church. "We have services today at our secondary parish hall, on High St. Easier for most in town."

"And safer." Mrs. Stather wore that tight smile again. "You may escort me there, Corporal."

"What brought you to us?" the young minister said.

"The rain. A place to dry off."

"All right to leave mop?" The man had his shirtsleeves rolled back up. "Like my tea now."

"Fine, Robert." The reverend adjusted the stew pot so the drops fell dead center. "Pour a cup for the Corporal. Help chase the chill."

"I should be going," Reg said.

The woman started toward the anteroom. "I can be ready in two shakes."

"Actually, I'll be heading toward The Beacon."

She stopped. "You're in hospital there?"

"The Beacon," he said. "The hotel?"

In the silence, Robert picked up his mop, held it across this chest like a weapon. "Nurse's hostel now. Tents for wounded on the grounds."

"Wounded Belgians," the woman said. "The overflow from the Girls School."

"Must be 200 up there now." The man with the mop was nodding. "Least 50 over at The Beacon. Soldiers not allowed in with nurses."

The young minister tried a small smile. He touched Reg's arm. "Have you been wounded?"

"I'm fine now," Reg said.

"But you're in hospital?" The minister's fingernails were grimy with mud. "Here? In Rusthall?"

Shaking his head, Reg took a step back. "Thanks for the offer of tea, but – "

"He may not be right in the head." Mrs. Stather was half-hiding behind the man with the mop. "Most of them aren't." She caught the hard look the young minister shot at her. "Well, it's true enough. The gas, you see."

"And the shell shock," Robert said.

"Please, both of you." The new vicar steered Reg to a pew. "The Corporal and I are going to speak with each other. In private."

The woman's sniff sounded angry. The sigh of the man with the mop had a little growl in it. They disappeared into the anteroom.

"I don't have anything to say," Reg said.

Leaning back, his head arching slightly over the rear of pew bench, the young minister drew a long breath. "Neither do I, Corporal. I just wanted to be free of them."

They shared a laugh. Dark roof timbers curved to match the steep roof, ending at stone footings on the inside of the stone arches. The rain was still out there, but it made no sound in here.

"As beautiful as it is," the vicar said, "the garden is more beautiful still." He rubbed the mud on his trousers. "I should have been a farmer. Did you know you can lay hot coals down and plant in frost?"

His garden must be a small patch. Not enough coals in all of Rusthall to warm a farm field. "Grave diggers do that."

"Same purpose, different intention."

Another laugh.

"If you're in trouble," the minister told those graceful roof timbers, "we can help. We all of us need help now and again."

"I wasn't wounded. Not really." Reg looked at the cream-colored mud on those work pants. "Our mud is so much lighter."

"Lighter?"

"Than Flanders. France. Italy."

Those trousers shifted in the pew. "You saw action there?"

Reg nodded. "Captured. Escaped."

"Well done."

"You're the vicar?"

"Too young, you'd say?" He stretched out his legs. "I'm only temporary. Rochester Diocese will be filling the position. Parishioners still tell me about the Reverend Walrond, and he's been dead for years."

Even from this far away, the altar looked regal, backed by all those carved scenes, each set in a pointed arch. The old vicar had come to the farm before Reg was born. His mother had described it as if it had been a royal visit. Reverend Walrond matched the grandeur of his cathedral, she never failed to say, prompting his father to respond, "Aye, hard as stone, that one." Had they met this temporary replacement? If the young vicar showed up in these trousers, he would never be allowed inside his mother's kitchen.

Something clattered outside. Then a thumping on the front door. Mrs. Stather ran from the anteroom, skidding on the mopped floor, and unlocked the main door. Wind, rain and three soldiers came in. One of them was Sgt. Dickson.

"What's the meaning of this?" The young minister was on his feet. "Mrs. Stather, what have you done?"

"This one's gone missing." The Sergeant took off his cap. "From Calverley Lodge VAD. On your feet, Corporal."

"He's welcome here," the minister said.

"He's under arrest," the Sergeant told him. "About to be court martialed."

Reg shook the minister's hand, then stepped to the Sergeant. "The shackle fell apart."

"Saw that." Sergeant Dickson gestured for the other two soldiers, both privates, to take Reg by either arm. "Thanks for holding him here, sir."

"He wasn't being held. We were talking. About his travails."

176

"Travails." Mrs. Stather said it as if biting the word. "Thank goodness for the telephone."

The soldiers ushered him toward a black sedan. The rain had turned to little more than a drizzle. It felt warmer out here than in the church.

"They say they speak French." Mrs. Sather's voice followed him outside. "But they don't. That's how you can tell."

Sergeant Dickson cocked his head. "Sorry – what?"

"That they're Belgian," she said.

He blinked, shook his head to clear it, then put his cap back on and touched its brim. "Good day."

The three of them stood in the giant hollow arch of the doorway – the young minister looking sad enough to cry, Mrs. Stather squinting in anger, Robert clutching the mop and knowingly nodding his head.

The car smelled of wet wool. The door shut.

"Odd trio that," the Sergeant said. "You're well out of there." He tapped the back of the front seat. "Drive on."

•

The black sedan took Langton Road past Calverley Lodge, where the street changed names to Crescent. A left onto Calverley Road and the car stopped at the corner, where Sgt. Dickson stepped out. He grabbed a handful of Reg's sleeve and led him toward the white columns of Town Hall.

"Look at those stone blocks," the barrel-chested man said. "Couldn't build anything similar today. Take four men per stone."

"Why are we here?"

The Sergeant brushed rain from his tunic. "The jail."

3

Inside, the foyer and halls were dark. They walked by an open door to a large room with a horseshoe-shaped table framed by high-back chairs all around. It looked like something that belonged in one of Queen Victoria's palaces. Another hall led to the Police station.

"Everything in one place," the Sergeant said. "Courts, Fire, City Council, Police."

It was even darker back here. The jail smelled of tobacco. At a door marked *Police Court Missionary*, those oversized knuckles rapped the wood. The man who opened that door must have just finished lunch: mustard stained the lower edge of his moustache.

"Customer for you," Sgt. Dickson said.

A small desk with nothing on it sat in the corner. On a side table, a plate of crumbs was balanced on top of file folders. The chairs in here were uncushioned, nothing like the fancy ones in that big front room. The mustachioed man let out a long sigh, then led the way to the cells.

The first row of iron bars reminded Reg of a dungeon. The odor of liquor and cigars hung in the air. Small barred windows kept most of the light outside. The cell door needed oil. The floor needed sweeping.

"Only one escape." The Police Court Missionary helped Reg into the cell. "And I found him – Sidney Dunn, back in Ought-Nine. April, it was. Squeezed through somehow."

The bars were less than a half-foot apart. Sidney Dunn must have been a skeleton of a man.

"Dreadful down here," the Sergeant said.

"Worse at Aldershot." Licking his moustache, tasting that mustard, the official stepped out of the cell, stared at Reg. "You don't want to be in either place, son. And you don't want me chasing you down."

Sgt. Dickson pulled Reg out of the cell, swung the noisy door shut. "Thank Mister Camforth for the tour of his facility."

Reg nodded. "What was he arrested for?"

"Who – Sidney Dunn?" Mr. Camforth chuckled. "Stripping lead off a roof in Ferndale. Planned to haul it off and sell it. Knocked himself unconscious in the process." He walked back to his office, opened the door. "If you decide to have him arrested, Sergeant, bring me the paperwork."

The wood door slapped shut. Sturdy fingers steered Reg away from the cells. "Wanted you to see the direction you're headed," Sgt. Dickson said. "Spent time at Aldershot. Hated it. Hard town. They shunned us in uniform. Don't want to go back there. So, I'll have your word you'll stay put." He led the way past the room with the fancy chairs. "We'll lock you in, but no more escapes – understood?"

The portico of those massive white columns held off the cold drizzle that was puddling the street. The fresh air smelled sweet from dank and rotting leaves.

Opening the umbrella, the Sergeant nudged him into the weather. "If I have to take you to Aldershot, you'll be bound head to foot and stowed in luggage car."

Instead of turning back toward Calverley Lodge, they walked up to Camden Road. Just beyond the tan awning of Chalkin's the Outfitter and The Prince of Wales pub next to it, a banner had been strung across the street, running from the brick front of the Friendly Societies' Hall to the steepled roof above Waters, the draper shop, at the corner of Garden Street. With a bower of still-green leaves below it and two Union Jacks standing up on top, the banner read, *To Our Victorious Army.*

"Wanted you to see this," the Sergeant said. "You've an MM and a DCM in your file. If they'd ask me, I'd say you were no deserter. You've been gazetted, and that counts for something with me." He steered Reg under Chalkin's awning. Rain made the stenciled letters on it stand out: *The Old Firm.* "I've a pension coming. Next summer. Took a small house up Varney St. Doing all the stone re-work myself." His stare hardened. "Can't risk losing that, son. You'll not cost me my last years."

Throwing an arm on Reg's shoulder, the old stone mason gave him a short squeeze that passed as a hug. "All I need now is a handsome woman to keep company with," he said. "She wouldn't have to be all that handsome."

They shared a laugh, the light rain sliding off the slick umbrella skin. "I'd like to see your house," Reg said.

"That you will, lad. When it's presentable."

They followed Monsoon Road back down to Mount Pleasant. At the corner of Crescent, Reg could make out The Lenton's gables shedding the rain. Barry's father might be off duty, enjoying hotel tea in the kitchen. How many rainy afternoons had he shared with his son in that hotel? How did the rain feel to him now?

"I didn't mind Aldershot," Reg said.

The Sergeant stopped short. "Good sign you remembering that. But if you fancy that town, your head wound must be worse than anyone thought."

The rest of the short way back to Calverley Lodge held no more words, just the drumming of drizzle on the umbrella, the slap of boots on wet pavement: a late autumn symphony in the South Ward, so much louder than soft rain on the grasses of Rusthall. He hadn't realized he missed that, and wondered if he would ever hear it again.

•

"How did you know to go there? To St. Paul's." The balding doctor listened to his heart and lungs with a stethoscope. "It's so off the beaten path."

"Followed my instincts," Reg told him.

"And you remember Aldershot now?"

"The barracks. There was a park in the middle of the city. With fruit trees."

"This is excellent news." The doctor dug into his bag, but didn't find what he was hunting for. "Stand up and start jogging in place. Knees up high now."

After a minute of stationary running, Reg was told to do deep knee bend squats. Then more jogging. Then another listen to the heart and lungs, the metal disc of the stethoscope not so cold on his skin this time.

"With all you've been through, you're remarkably fit." The doctor found his tube of tongue depressors, pulled one out and, eyes widening, stuck it in Reg's mouth. "The malnutrition as a prisoner alone should have done you in." He wiped the piece of flat wood on his sleeve, put it back into the tube. "Someone has taken excellent care of you."

He wanted to tell the doctor about the worst soup in the world and the woman who made it. And that creamy goat cheese, the tang of the Asiago, the crispness of that white wine.

"Cream puffs," he said, seeing the white goo leak out of little Sancia's mouth. "Not our cream. Sweet cheese."

Rubbing his scalp, the doctor waited for Reg to keep talking. When he didn't, the doctor shoved the tube back into his bag and stepped to the door. "Dizzy?"

Reg shook his head.

"Any head pain?"

Another head shake.

The doctor opened the door. "I'll notify your barrister. Congratulations. You're fit to stand trial."

Sgt. Dickson stopped talking to the short nurse holding a tray of cups and saucers. He took Reg by the elbow. "Not to worry. The Major's up in Lewisham. Won't hear of this until tomorrow at the earliest. Take him days to get back down." He squeezed Reg's arm. "You're no priority to him."

"That won't make a difference."

"Time, lad. Time might make the difference." He started Reg up the stairs. "There's talk of no more executions. Not much stomach for it now the war's over." At the door to his small room, those strong fingers gripped Reg by the shoulder. "Mind me. And have faith."

The door lock clicked. The moon would not come back for a week, just in time to greet the sharp-nosed officer down from Lewisham. Until then, Calverley Grounds would stand dark, waiting for snow.

•

"It's news!" Mr. Quaite's shout ran under the door. "Was there an escape?"

"Can't be up here, sir." The Sergeant's tone was calmer. "There'll be no information but from his appointed, Major Richardson."

"Where is he?"

"Up Lewisham."

"What is he doing there?"

"Lives there, I expect." There was a smile in Sgt. Dickson's voice now. "Be coming down in due course."

"Well, may I interview the prisoner?"

"No, sir."

"Can his mother see him?"

"His mother? Is she here?"

"In Rusthall." From the sound of flesh on bone, Mr. Quaite must have slapped his own forehead with his palm, something he did when words began to fail him. "I could bring her within the hour."

"Need a doctor's authorization for that, sir."

The knob of the door rattled. Mr. Quaite must have tried to open it. "I'll be back, Reg!"

"You know the lad?"

"That I do. And he's no deserter."

After what felt like a long silence, he could hear them on the stairs, talking normally, no longer arguing. He imagined them becoming friends now. They might even take a pint together. But not in town. Mr. Quaite never drank in Royal Tunbridge Wells – "Or any place royal," he liked to say. In reality, he couldn't stand for the high prices. A pint here cost more than three at The White Hart in Rusthall. "Robbers," the editor would be telling the stone mason, who would probably agree.

How long would it take for them to walk to The White Hart – 15 minutes? How long might they stay there? How much information would Mr. Quaite be able to squeeze out of the Sergeant before calling it an afternoon? The overcoated editor would then slog up the hill to his three-room cottage, the uniformed old soldier striding in the other direction for another bash at his stonework on Varney St.

That image made Reg smile. Then he remembered dinner would be brought up in less than two hours. With the window nailed shut, the smell of tripe would linger in the tiny room past nightfall. The bittersweet taste would remain on his tongue until tea at supper.

A key in the lock startled him. The door opened a crack. A young VAD nurse glanced inside, set a small book on the floor. The door shut as quickly as it had opened. The lock clicked.

The book was green. A sketch of a ship, it's sails billowing on the sea, stood on the cover below the gold-lettered title, *The Day's Work*, and above the author's name: *Rudyard Kipling*.

Inside, short stories, more than a dozen of them. On the bed, he paged through, almost afraid to begin reading. With only a few hours of daylight left before the room went dark, he found a spot just below the window, ran a hand over the smooth leather cover, wiped the tear dribbling down his cheek, and opened to the last story, *The Brushwood Boy*.

•

"You've a visitor." Picking the little book off Reg's chest, Sgt. Dickson turned the slender volume in his fingers, then dropped it on the bed and waited in the doorway for Reg to put on his uniform. "You'll take breakfast downstairs today."

The hallway felt cold. The weather had changed. The stairs, still damp from the rain-filled air, creaked underfoot. The dry wind had arrived. Snow and winter would be right behind it.

"I don't have anything new to tell the Major," Reg said. "Can't I just go back to the room and read?"

182

The Sergeant steered him away from the kitchen and into a side parlor. On a lilac-colored settee, in her Sunday best – black dress, wool overcoat, that button hat – his mother put a gloved hand to her mouth as soon as she saw him. That hand and her lips trembled: "Reggie."

4

The horsehair padding of the settee made a crunching noise when he sat next to her. She pulled off a glove, touched his cheek. "Doctor says you may not remember me."

If he had passed her on the street, he might not have recognized her. Out of her gray housedress and smock, buttoned to the neck, sleeves rolled up to the elbow, wiping her hands on a yellowing apron or that white hood cap she always wore to keep her hair out of the food, she looked like a different person. He kissed her fingers. "The moment I saw you, I knew – Mum."

Her cry came from deep in her gut. Tears flooded her eyes. She drew him close, hugged him. She smelled of cinnamon: her special breakfast scones would be waiting on the table with butter and sugar.

He turned to the sound of someone else sobbing. Sgt. Dickson used a sleeve to dab his eyes. When he saw Reg looking at him, the barrel-chested man cleared his throat and stepped into the hall. "Doctor! We've a breakthrough here!"

""We thought. . ." She tugged a lace handkerchief from her sleeve. "We were so proud." Her sigh had a flutter in it. "Now they say you may be shot. How can that be?"

"It's coming back to him." The Sergeant ushered the bird-faced doctor into the room. "He knows her."

Squinting over the wire rims of his spectacles, the doctor stopped in the doorway. "Is this true?"

His mother squeezed his hand. "Knew me straight off. And you said it might be the gas."

"Or his head wound." The doctor was on top of Reg now, fingers pushing hair out of the way for a better look at the scalp. "Healed nicely, though."

She took Reg's face in both hands, bent him down to see that wound for herself. A fingertip traced the groove back to front, then she pushed his head farther down to look at the back crown. "Fell off Toad Rock once. Nine, he was. Up and about next morning."

That had been Digger's fault. Three years older and well on his way to being the bully of Denny Bottom, that tow-headed boy relished shoving his playmates off any hill or rock. Sitting up straight, Reg ran a hand through his hair, stared at the black stockings showing at her ankle, the black shoes laced up, nothing like the scuffed up brown pair she wore around her kitchen. "You didn't have to dress up for me," he said.

"For town is why."

"You didn't walk in this cold."

"Your Sergeant drove me down in his motor." She shot a small smile toward the doorway, which was all it took to start the old stone mason tearing up again. "I thought we'd slide into the Common, he went so fast."

"Safe as pudding," Sgt. Dickson told her. "We'll go slower on the way back."

"So you say." She glanced at the doctor. "Can he come with? Home?"

In the silence, the doctor pried his glasses free, studied the brown carpet.

The Sergeant drew a deep breath: "He's in custody, ma'am. Confined to hospital."

Her chin lowered. Breath whistled out of her.

"Actually, it might help." Staring at the clouds through the window, the doctor was nodding to himself. "Might jog his memory. You could use the shackle if needed."

The word made her twinge. She looked up at the Sergeant the same way she looked at the altar in St. Paul's, in silent pleading.

"Shackle's worthless," Sgt. Dickson said. "A relic from the Crusades."

"Then accompany him." The doctor was on his feet and heading toward the hall. "He needs to see familiar surroundings. Rusthall, isn't it?"

She nodded, then squeezed his fingers. He didn't need to look at her to know she was smiling.

"I've his word he'll not try to escape," the Sergeant said. "Good enough for me."

"While the weather holds, then." Just into the hall and fitting his spectacles back on, the doctor turned back toward the settee. "Tea, ma'am?"

"I'm not bothered," she said, taking the doctor's nod. "Won't it be wonderful to ride home together."

A raspy whimper seeped out of Sgt. Dickson. He wasn't trying to stop his tears anymore. He turned away, almost bumping into a young nurse. She guided him to a bench across from the doorway, sat next to him and stroked his sleeve.

"That one shouldn't be in charge of machinery," his mother said. "A danger."

She leaned in close, as if to kiss him goodnight, and whispered. "A walk might do us both good."

•

He wasn't there, of course. No sense clanging the bell to call him in. That would simply anger him. She wouldn't risk walking out to find him and interrupt his workday, even if he was napping in the shade before getting back to the task at hand.

"If he had known, he would have been certain to be here." She eyed her apron and smock on hooks near the back door as if debating whether to tie them on over her best dress, then glanced out the kitchen window at the empty field. "Hops. For ale? Rascals to harvest, he says."

"These scones," Sgt. Dickson said with his mouth full, his head bowed over a plate at the table. "Brilliant."

Reg sat in his old place at the table, his back to the pantry. "Where did he plant those?"

"New acreage." Her hair was matted down from that little hat. "Leased from the Krieslers." She set another place for tea. "Terrible that influenza. Had to burn all their clothing and bedding."

His father had never cared for old man Kriesler. In Spring, the two of them would plow in sight of one another, neither willing to quit until the other had surrendered to hunger or the dying light. "Massive appetite, Mr. Kriesler had," Reg said.

"He fancied my scones, as well."

The Sergeant's hand hovered over another scone, then pulled back. "Best I've had. Shouldn't spoil supper, though."

Someone in a leather hat with a droopy wide brim walked past the window. The back door opened. The worker stepped out of boots, walked into the kitchen in stocking feet. When the hat came off, long hair fell onto narrow shoulders. The girl looked surprised to see anyone else in here.

"Mrs. O, you've company?"

"My son." She took the girl by the elbow, led her to the table. "And his . . . soldier friend. This is Verna."

They stood, nodded at her, watched for her sit at the new place setting, in his father's chair. She took her tea with milk, no sugar.

"You've taken in a boarder?" Reg said.

"Heavens no." His mother checked the jam bowl to make sure enough remained. "She's from the government."

Sgt. Dickson squinted at her, then at Reg. With a shrug, he grabbed the scone he had been eyeing, began buttering it.

"Women's Land Army," the girl said. "Doing our bit."

"A Godsend, your father calls her." She slid the butter closer to the girl. "No days off for this one."

The sweet taste of sugared cinnamon got mixed with the over-steeped tea. "He pays you?"

When the girl laughed, her hair bounced around the straps of her overalls. "Room and board. The WWAC pays my wages."

"What's that?" the Sergeant said, his stare on the last scone, the one he knew he could not reach for.

"Women's War Agricultural Committee." Verna took big bites. Jam trickled down her chin. "Give me a kit and eighteen shillings."

His mother scanned the cold field out the window. "Eighteen, is it?"

"A week."

Reg added sugar to the tea. "Where do they put you up? Barn?"

She pointed to the planked door just beyond the kitchen, the small space that had served as his bedroom for his entire life. "Comfortable. Good light."

His mother was trying to keep her stare focused outside, but her eyes betrayed her. She glanced in his direction, but could not look at him. "Cold in barn."

"You look lovely, Mrs. O," the girl said. "The Mister should see you as you are."

Any day now, snow would cover that back field. There would be no point looking for signs of life out there then.

"How's Walter?" Reg said.

"The old horse?" She took the last scone, making the Sergeant sigh. "Sold off."

No one would buy that horse, not to work a field. A glue factory special.

"How do you work the place then?"

"Tractor, of course."

He straightened up in the chair. "Tractor?"

"You saw fighting?" she said. "First hand-like?"

"Gazetted, this one is," Sgt. Dickson said, mourning the last bite of scone, butter and jam now going into her mouth. "Twice."

"Tell our Reg about the hops." His mother took the empty plates to the sink. "And the rash."

187

"They have these hooked hairs," Verna said. "Nasty if you work them without gloves."

"Why did he sell Walter?"

The girl shrugged. "Didn't earn his keep, I'd guess."

He wouldn't have come in even if he had known his son was waiting in the kitchen. He would stay out there, doing whatever had to be done with the hops until the work was finished or he got hungry enough to stop. Reg couldn't imagine him on a tractor. He wondered if Walter felt glad to leave here, out of reach of the sapling branch whip, out of the stall in the barn that didn't get mucked out often enough.

"What do you do with the hops?" Reg said.

"Dry them and send them off. Government buys all he can grow." She finished her tea, stood and carried her cup to the sink. "We're burning the cut vines now."

From the back, she looked like a boy, the gray overalls hanging on her slender frame. At the door, she put on her hat and stepped into her boots. "Pleased to have met you both."

And she was gone. A solitary gray figure crossing the empty field, taking the short cut through the copse of firs to Kriesler's. A whisper of smoke, the same color as the new storm clouds, floated over those pointed tree tops. In 10 minutes, she'd be back at his side. She would tell him about the men in the kitchen, how one of them was his own son. And still he would not come in.

"We should go," Reg said. "More weather on the way."

The Sergeant pushed back from the table, wet his finger, picked up crumbs, fed them to his grin. "I envy the man who gets your cooking, Mrs. Olcutt."

She smiled, but her heart wasn't in it. She watched the gray girl disappear in the evergreen branches.

Reg kissed her on the cheek − "Be back when I can" − and stepped into the new breeze. The car engine started on the first crank. The seats rattled. Tires crunched stones in the trolley path until they reached Broomfield Rd. His mother would already be out of that dress and shoes and back into the comfort of her house dress and her empty kitchen.

"Sad about the horse?" Sgt. Dickson said.

The first rain drops hit the windscreen just north of where Coach Road met Langton. Reg turned in the seat for a final glimpse. None of Rusthall was visible in the thickening mist back there.

"In a better place," he said.

5

He couldn't remember what he didn't know.

All of this felt new. On past his trips here, he had never had time to walk around and appreciate Royal Tunbridge Wells. Even if there had been time, there would have been no sense to it: everything here was too expensive.

Along Camden Road from Calverley, long lines, mostly made up of women, snaked around the barrows of venders, all of whom were men. Ticker the Grocer and Fletcher's Butcher Shop had the worst of it − or the best of it if measured by commerce. Shorter lines still ran out of shops and into the street at Rogers Confectionery and The Leather Shop, run by Alfred Badcock, who had once made a harness collar for Walter. Did that thin man with the orange-stained fingers know the old horse was gone? Did anyone need horse collars anymore?

"Madness." Sgt. Dickson steered Reg around the barrow of winter melons. "Been like this for two years. They water the milk, you know. Even whiskey. A disgrace."

It got quieter on Varney Street. As they approached Market Road, Reg began pointing to stone houses and asking, "That one yours?"

The Sergeant shook his head each time. He stopped at the Varney Street Hostel. "Communal kitchen now," he said. "Wives and children of servicemen mostly. Tragic."

The sound of a brass band floated up Market Road from Golding St. The Salvation Army was out marching in front of their brick Citadel. The tune was unrecognizable, like the sloppy voices of drunken soldiers in brothels.

They took a shortcut to The Five Ways, where stalls and barrows of everything from food to trinkets lined the short blocks up toward General Hospital.

"Found an old stone shaper here," Sgt. Dickson said. "Fell apart on me."

Afternoon wind quickened through the buildings. It felt stronger on Upper Grosvenor Road, where the Rescue and Preservation Association Shelter had been turned into a home for young women. "Fallen women we called them in my day," the Sergeant said. "Betrayed women they call them now. Better, I suppose." He started walking faster. "Best not to dawdle. They've had enough of us − khaki fever."

"Wasn't that way over there," Reg told him.

"Not in the bars and brothels you and the rest of our boys frequented." The Sergeant turned toward The High Street. "Different story in our cities and towns." He studied the angled bridge at Vale Road, built of red brick like the nearby South Eastern Station, but papered over with advertisements and hand bills. "Bombs and bullets aren't only what destroy lives. Lust, you see."

The square tower of Christ Church shadowed the street. The clock at Payne's Jeweler jutted straight out from the second story like a round fist at the end of a slender arm. "What about love?" Reg said.

"Not familiar." Sgt. Dickson took the walkway in front of S. Rutley & Sons Ladies Tailor and its neighbor, a hat and umbrella manufacturer. Both stores stood empty of customers. Opposite, a conveyer belt growled behind the tall wall of Medway Coal Company. "We'll take a pint before heading back."

They crossed to the South Eastern Hotel and Restaurant. It looked more like an old barn than a hotel. No tourist for the spa waters would ever stay here. The Sergeant slowed as they passed the storefront of Nevill's Bakery, his stare taking in the pastries and cakes on display. He seemed torn between the ale waiting for him one door down and the desserts within reach.

At the counter, a pudgy young man took paper money from the till. His girlfriend came out from the room behind the counter, saw him pocket the money and planted a smiling kiss on his cheek.

Madge looked happy. And in love.

Her head turned toward the front window. Before he could meet her stare, Reg took the Sergeant by the sleeve and pulled him toward the hotel. As they reached the door, he began laughing.

"Something funny then?" Sgt. Dickson said.

"Love," Reg told him. "Lethal as a Jack Johnson."

With a shrug, the Sergeant strode into the lobby toward the bar. "Stewed rabbit tonight at the VAD. Don't want to miss that." He held up two fingers, signaling the bartender. "And just what might you know about love?"

Reg drew a long breath to quiet his laugh. "Not familiar."

●

Christmas decorations had been put up in most of the shops along High St. in Rusthall. A light snow had dusted the rooftops, but no trace of it remained on the roads. *The Gazette* office near Hill View Road, opposite the Post Office, was locked. The handwritten sign in the door window read, *Out of Town. Regrets − A.Q., Ed.*

190

"Expected him back by now," Sgt. Dickson said. "Gone to Lewisham and London, tracking down your Colonel Corfe."

That new linotype machine must be in the back room, near the double doors – the only way to bring anything that large inside.

"Your Colonel's testimony will prove vital." The Sergeant cupped his hands to the glass. "Looks like a stationer's."

"He keeps it neat to impress advertisers," Reg said.

"And you worked here?"

"There was a desk in the corner where I'd leave my copy."

"A writer then?"

"Reporter," Reg said. "Small things. Football matches, cricket."

"Sports! What I read first!"

"And crop prices," Reg told him. "All the easy things."

The Sergeant smiled as if he knew a secret. "No wonder he cares for you then. Spending time and money on your behalf." He started shaking his head. "A good thing, too. Your barrister's a fool, if you ask me. All book learning. Sell you down the river if push came to shove."

The Iron Monger's, which shared the same roof as *The Gazette* office, stood empty. There were no queues anywhere on this High Street. An old lorry from Pratt's Dairy rumbled back toward Royal Tunbridge Wells, the only thing moving between the Post Office and the Girls School, now a VAD annex. Tents dotted its lawn. Nurses in black cloaks over their white uniforms carried supplies in and out of the tents. Near the main entrance, a long line of women with baskets waited to see the wounded.

"All the scum and riff-raff of Europe." A man in a great coat and bowler hat led his wife up to the railing next to the Sergeant. "Not what either of you fought for, I'll wager."

"When the wind changes," his wife said, "you don't need to see those Belgians to know they're there."

Some of the men in those tents might have been in Pop, at the same bar the men in the 11th got drunk in. Barry would have known them on sight.

One of the women stepped out of the queue. The hem of her dress was ripped. She carried her basket to the railing, pulled back the cloth, revealing home-baked pastries. Sgt. Dickson took one with a chocolate drizzle. Reg chose what he hoped was a cream puff. When the Sergeant offered a coin, the woman shook her head and offered the basket to the husband and wife at the rail. Both took a

191

pastry. With a curtsy, the Belgian woman pulled the cloth over her basket and walked back to her spot in line.

Licking his fingers, the Sergeant swallowed the last of his pastry. "Lovely that."

The cream puff wasn't as sweet as those in Colfosco. Sancia would still eat all she could have gotten her little fingers on. He trained his smile on the man's wool muffler, the small purple flowers pinned to the woman's coat. Each of them took small bites, trying to identify the unfamiliar taste.

"It smelled worse in the trenches," Reg told them. "We smelled worse."

They stopped in mid-bite.

Touching the brim of his cap, he headed back down High Street. "The White Hart will have something to wash that taste away."

"But I like the taste of chocolate," the Sergeant said.

"Is there anything you won't eat?"

"Have to ponder that." The sugar must have kicked in. Those thick legs were striding now, in a hurry to try the local ale. "Ever tell you the time we ate rat in India?"

•

The jam sandwich was too messy to eat with his tunic on. He stripped down to the gray shirt, sat at the end of the cot, half bent over to avoid any drips or crumbs staining his trousers. Someone knocked on his door.

The young ginger nurse smiled in the doorway, but stepped back when she noticed he was in his undershirt. "You've a visitor. She's – impatient."

He started to hand her the sandwich, but thought better of it and left it on the side table, put on his tunic, following her down the stairs.

On the same settee where his mother had sat, Madge was dabbing her eyes with a lace handkerchief. Spotting him, she ran into his arms. She smelled of vanilla. Stepping back, she adjusted her hat. "Your last Christmas present to me."

It had a feather sticking out of it and little black dots suspended in mesh fashioned into a veil.

"Very nice," he said.

She pulled him toward the settee. "I thought I was seeing things. At the bakery? Three days ago? I was sure you were dead. I ran out to find you, but the street was empty. I almost fainted. So straight to your mother I went and she told me about this place. I would have come yesterday, but – are you really being tried for desertion?"

It sounded as if she had said all that on a single breath. He nodded.

She inched away toward the window. "Did you?"

He moved to the chair. The ginger nurse was watching from the bench in the hall. "Don't know what else I could have done," he said. "Behind enemy lines, woozy from a head wound, then captured and escaped, but no way across the river back to the battalion."

"How dreadful," she said. "And you couldn't write?"

He sighed, sapped of the energy to explain it to her. "Your new beau – "

"I thought you were dead!" She cried into the lace. "I would never. . . He's the owner's son. Harvey."

"Any relation to Lady Nevill?"

She shook her head. "But very successful, the bakery."

Harvey didn't look like a baker – more like someone who liked to eat baked goods. "Strange hours then," he said. "Up nights, sleep the day away."

"He doesn't bake. He would, of course, but he's better suited to the business side." She glanced at a tall nurse now sitting next to the ginger one in the hall. "Do they serve tea here?"

"It's a hospital."

With a nod, she sobbed again. "I was devastated when we realized you were killed. Tried to busy myself. Worked at Central Laundry and Mending."

"Really?"

Another nod. "It was horrid. The clothes were alive with pests."

"Trouser rabbits, we called them."

She drew a long breath – "Had to take a sheep bath after each shift" – then shivered at the memory: "I had to quit. After getting my badge for Voluntary War Work." This deep breath seemed to steady her. "Then, I went over to the mending side, but" – she held up a hand, removed the brown glove, wriggled her stubby fingers: "It's not my fault. I was born with short fingers. Isn't that true?"

There was a third nurse on the bench now, all of them looking in. He nodded.

"And I couldn't be a munitionette," Madge said. "No munitions factory in Royal Tunbridge Wells, is there?" She leaned forward, whispered, "Plus, so many of the girls got TNT poisoning." Staring at the window facing the back garden, she sighed. "I did very much like their dusters and head caps though."

Would she have put a feather in that cap, too? "Are you happy? With. . .him?"

"Harvey?" She nodded rapidly, but began crying into her handkerchief again. "I thought to become a VAD assistant" – she glared at the nurses in the hall – "but one must pass the St. John's Ambulance Exam. And you know how I tense up on examinations."

He took both of her hands in his – one gloved, one all flesh cold with goose bumps. He wanted to thank her for finding someone else, for freeing him of having to live up to her expectations, of having to live in Royal Tunbridge Wells, to share a miserable life with her. "You did nothing wrong," he said.

"I know, but. . ." More tears. Her whole body was shaking.

"Can I meet him?" Reg said.

"Harvey? Oh, I don't think – he doesn't know much about. . .us." She had stopped crying. "Could we find a place for a bite?"

"I can't leave," he told her, feeling grateful for that for the first time. "They have me under guard."

She glared at the five nurses now assembled by the bench in the hall. With a sniff, Madge stood. "It took all my courage to come here."

"I'm glad you did," he said.

She nodded, put the lace to her nose and mouth, pressed her eyes shut. "I don't think I can come back."

"Of course. No need."

Straightening her shoulders, she offered her hand. Before he could take it, she lunged forward and kissed him on the lips. "Oh, Reg, I did love you so."

And she was marching out of the parlor, ignoring the nurses and striding up the hall toward the front lobby.

Three of the nurses walked off in different directions. The ginger nurse stepped into the parlor. "You two were betrothed?"

"Three years."

She might have been Irish, or possibly from up north near York. "I wouldn't think her your type."

"I have a type?"

With a little laugh, the nurse nodded. "And she's the furthest from it."

He grinned, held out his hand. "Reg Olcutt. Would you agree to evaluate all my future girlfriends, Miss – ?"

"Now you're making fun of me."

194

"Of myself," he said. "I realize now I have questionable taste in women. And hats."

She covered her laugh with a pale hand, then gestured toward the hall. "It's Bridgette. Bridgette Connelly. I would have fetched you both tea."

He walked toward the back staircase. "Love's a trap, isn't it. The more you struggle, the tighter the iron jaws get."

"You were kind to her." She adjusted her cap, a white boat on a red sea of hair. "It was – romantic. We all thought so."

The now-familiar climb to his small room felt like going somewhere safe. "There's always hoping, I guess."

6

They were marching toward Town Hall, hundreds of them, despite the gusting winds that swept cold rain over them. One of them carried a bouquet of red, white and green.

"Suffragettes," Sgt. Dickson said. "Their first Polling Day – well, the first one they'll be voting in."

The Rusthall Gazette front page carried a photograph of Amelia Scott and her sister, Louisa, of the Poor Law Guardian. They were encouraging all women over the age of 30 to turn out to the polls. They could not have known that on this gloomy Thursday, miserable weather would stand as one final price women would have to pay for the right to vote.

They didn't seem to notice the wind or the drizzle. His mother would not be in that gaggle. He wondered if the day might come when she would find the courage to defy her husband and walk down to High Street in her Sunday best to cast her vote.

"Think I'll stroll down myself," the Sergeant said. The glint in his eye would serve as a warning to all those women, and his uniform would not be enough to overcome their disdain for a man who would use Polling Day as an excuse for chatting them up.

"But the weather," Reg said, too late for the stocky man to hear. Heavy footsteps echoed in the hallway, then down the staircase. Turning away from the little window, Reg sat on the edge of the cot, began unlacing his boots. A shadow flitted across the doorway. By the time he had his foot out of the second boot, that shadow returned. A small broad-faced man stood in a puddle of rain water dripping from his clothes.

"As I live and breathe," the man said, "I never thought I'd see you again."

When he removed his wool cap, his rain-soaked face caught the light from the hallway windows. Sgt. Jeffs wriggled out of his great coat and stepped into the room. One jacket sleeve hung empty at his side. With his remaining arm, he hugged Reg.

He smelled musty. Pulling the stool toward the cot, he smiled. "You look fine."

Reg reached down to put on his boots. "How did you get up here?"

"Don't bother with those." His shoe nudged the boots farther under the cot. "I'm up in Bidborough VAD. Mansion, it is. Bidborough Court. You learn how to evade the enemy – Nurses."

Reg tried, but couldn't stop staring at that empty sleeve.

"Artery shattered." The round little man flicked fingers at the dead sleeve to start it swinging. "Fitted me with a wood arm. Makes me feel like a marionette."

"How did it – "

"On our raid. No sooner did I hurl a Mills over the wire, they shot me twice. Didn't pass out until we rafted back." He patted his jacket as if searching for something. "Lost all but two. That new recruit got me out." His stare narrowed. "Yorke?"

"The river took him," Reg said. "Captain, too."

Sgt. Jeffs nodded. "What we thought. Bloody stupid. Worse, I had to stay in hospital when the battalion left for home. You know we disbanded. In March. A Sunday, it was."

"So, there's no more Eleventh?"

"Or Tenth." He leaned back in the chair, stared at his empty sleeve. "I still feel it tingling, like it wants scratching. Doctors say that's to be expected." He let out a small laugh. "Daft as ducks."

"I can't believe you braved this weather," Reg said. "How did you know I was here?"

"Your friend, Mr. Quaite. Come to visit me." His pudgy face went sour. "Only one I've had. Except for the Adjutant. Had to make an X on the forms. Wish it had been my left arm." He patted his pockets again. "This business with going lost – can't be true, can it?"

"By the time I regained my strength, I was captured."

Sgt. Jeffs nodded. "Astonishing you survived. And in one piece." He must have seen how uncomfortable Reg was because he inched the stool closer. "What I come to tell you is, I'll vouch for you. And to give you this."

From a low jacket pocket, he pulled out a small tin, set it on the cot. Tickler's jam. Strawberry.

For an instant, Reg was too surprised to touch it. He picked it up. "How – ?"

"Never you mind that." He was his old smiling self again. "Sorry I've no rum to wash it down."

"We can't eat it," Reg said.

"You're right there. It's just for you. Consider it a Boxing Day gift in advance."

Turning the cold tin in his hand, Reg let out a long sigh. "Never strawberry."

"Never say never's what I say." He tapped Reg's knee. "You eat every last drop of that, Olcutt. No sharing it with the nurses, either."

An order. He felt like saluting, then realized the one-armed man could not return the salute. "Finest gift I could have."

Sgt. Jeffs leaned forward and stood. "Best be going back. They toss a fit when I miss physical therapy. Image that — for a bloody arm I don't have! Whole world's gone daft."

Reg darted ahead of him, picked up the water-heavy great coat, helped him into it and buttoned it at the collar: "Let me put my boots on and walk you down."

"Best they don't know I was up here." He headed toward the staircase, then stopped and turned. "Belated congratulations on your promotion to Corporal. Proud of you."

He made no sound going down the stairs. Except for the small puddle in the doorway, it was as if he had not even been here. The tail of his great coat fluttered when he turned at the landing.

Standing at attention, Reg threw a salute down the stairs. Then he walked back to his room, sat beside the tin of strawberry jam. Barry would have had it open by now, digging in with his fingers. With a little laugh, Reg stretched out on the cot, set the tin on his chest, watched it move up and down with each breath, almost as though it was alive, too.

•

In the parlor doorway, Mr. Quaite wore his best gray suit and a broad grin. He took Reg's hand, pulled him closer. "At last," the editor said. "Let me look at you."

"Went to *The Gazette*," Reg said. "But you were up in London."

"Had my fill of trains and buses." His eyes were beginning to tear up. "I've a special present for you this Boxing Day."

"But I don't have anything for you."

"You're here. That's enough." He steered him into the parlor. "How's the head?"

"Still there."

The man standing at the window, studying the rear garden and its view of Calverley Grounds, looked like an old soldier. For an instant, Reg took him for Col. Corfe. But he wasn't tall enough and those shoulders were far too narrow, that hair too thin and what was left of it graying. When he turned, a dark moustache and wire-rimmed eye glasses framed his face. His black eyebrows made him look as if he had been sketched in charcoal. With a sliver of a smile, he took a step, stretched out a hand.

"Reg," Mr. Quaite said, "Mister Rudyard Kipling."

"Call me Kip."The famous writer already had Reg's hand in his. "Honored to meet you, son."

•

All of this had been unimaginable yesterday, which had felt more like an ordinary Tuesday than Christmas. Alone, without the usual bustle of VAD aides, nurses and doctors, Reg had found it oddly comforting – an island of personal peace.

He had thought of visiting his mother, and Sgt. Dickson had been eager for the full holiday dinner he might have taken at her table, but that would have meant sitting across from his father, enduring the criticisms, the sharp silences. He could have dropped in on Mr. Quaite, but had not been certain the editor would be in Rusthall, since he often spent holidays with his sister near London. So Reg had wandered in the back garden, still damp from recent rains.

Since the Sergeant had spent the day at his home – if that stone house actually did exist on Varney Street – Reg had taken dinner in the kitchen with the cooks and staff, all older women who doted on him and kept offering extra helpings. And he had slept. All in all, it had been one of the most relaxing and pleasant Christmases he could remember. Perhaps he was meant to be alone, like Mr. Quaite, who had never married.

It would have been different in Colfosco: the two little girls opening treats, the feast Teresa would be serving, how there would be nothing for Gabby to do or be permitted to do, except keep company with Luigi, who no doubt would slip away at some point to visit friends in town. The images made Reg feel connected to the blond-haired woman he still dreamt of. Neither of them had anyone or anything of their own.

Unless her husband had come home from the war.

Would he be in one piece? Had he been gassed? Did he suffer from shell shock? Was he anything like the man who had left for the war?

Or had he been killed in action? Buried in some unmarked grave too far for anyone from the river town to visit? Or left out on the battlefield to suffer the indignities of animals, birds, scavenging villagers?

Trying to visualize the cavalry officer, Reg instead saw Rodolfo, Sr. trudging back to his goats – or what was left of that flock – and to his son, hoping to hear a lute fill the darkness with the promise of a new house, a new beginning.

The flood of these reflections made today even more astonishing: Rudyard Kipling in the parlor, smiling, taking tea, making small talk with Mr. Quaite. It felt like sitting in the cinema, watching the moving pictures. And to hear Kip – *Kip!* – talk about Reg's diary entries and letters home from the front, admiring the details. "Being specific is the only path to reaching the universal," the great writer had said, causing Reg to shiver with excitement.

When told that Reg had carried the pocket copy of *The Jungle Book* with him into battle and had read stories from it to soldiers in the 11th, Mr. Kipling had been so touched that his voice failed him. He had simply put a hand on Reg's forearm to squeeze a thank you.

Near dusk, and anxious to catch the train south to his estate in Burwash, Mr. Kipling told Reg, "We should talk about your future."

"Not certain I'll have one."

That moustache didn't move when he smiled. "As a writer."

Watching Kip walk toward the front lobby, Mr. Quaite found his umbrella, overcoat and muffler. "He'll try to contact your Colonel Corfe himself. It will turn out for you, lad. Have faith."

Not something I've ever had, Reg had wanted to tell him. Instead: a handshake, no words of goodbye.

Now, in the moonless dark, he watched snow hit the roof tiles and immediately melt, like tears, and he decided that this had been the best Christmas and Boxing Day ever.

7

Acourt martial would be convened, sometime in February or March. The Major assigned as Reg's barrister was convinced there would be a conviction on the charge of desertion. General Routine Order 585, in force since the beginning of 1915, required the assumption of guilt unless and until *sufficient evidence* could be provided to prove innocence.

"Exactly inside-out," Mr. Quaite said. "We have to get another advocate appointed. This bloody idiot is only prepared to argue against execution."

Sgt. Dickson rapped his knuckles on the tea table. "Five minutes with him is all I ask."

"Ill with the Influenza." The little editor sighed into his cup and handed Reg a note. "Army's not in a rush to go into a sick man's house to retrieve his records."

In a flowing hand, the note from Mr. Kipling read:

> *The absurdity of this offends me. To prove*
> *something did <u>not</u> happen is nonsensical. It requires*
> *an eye witness to the invisible. We cannot withstand*
> *more incompetence from our government officials.*

"Kip had some harsh words for Sir Charles Hardinge," Mr. Quaite said, "in his poem, *Mesopotamia*. I expect he'll press this with the Prime Minister."

The editor and the Sergeant continued bantering about what options Reg might have had, stuck behind enemy lines with a head injury, then captured, only to escape malnourished and weak and be taken in and protected by villagers. It felt as if they were discussing someone else. The New Year had come and gone, but the past still ran the calendar. There was no escaping it.

"The Major might die then," Sgt. Dickson said. "The Influenza takes a good many."

Mr. Quaite nodded. "An epidemic. They say tens of thousands will perish before it's through."

They were both smiling, as though the thought of the dead cigarette-smoking officer would be a good outcome.

"They're only following regulations," Reg said.

"Don't be quick to forgive them." *The Gazette* editor rubbed a chill from his arm. "They're the ones who should be on trial."

The ginger nurse Bridgette walked in with a tray and began placing the cups and saucers on it. From a pocket in her white dress, she pulled out a note, handed it to Reg. Without smiling, she watched him open it.

The printed letters were not from his mother's hand. The girl must have written it: *Father ill. Come home.*

He handed it to the Sergeant, who jammed the last of the biscuits into his mouth, drained his cup and stood, giving the little note to Mr. Quaite. "Bring him frontside. We'll drive out, the three of us."

The editor left the note on the tray, gathered his hat, muffler and coat, looked around for his umbrella. "This weather's to blame."

"So sorry." The ginger nurse touched Reg's hand. "I hope he'll improve."

He couldn't tell her that improvement was not one of the old man's goals. Or that any kind of sickness, even the Influenza, might bring him down: he had the constitution of a feral cat. It had to be some sort of accident – a fire, a fall, that tractor. Putting on his cap, Reg nodded at her, then followed the shuffle of Mr. Quaite toward the snow blowing past the windows in the main lobby. With luck, he thought, the car and its worn tires would not make the climb out of Rusthall to the farm.

•

Not sick.

He had been running the tractor inside the shed, to warm up the engine before taking it out to till before the first frost. The fumes had made him dizzy. The government paid-for girl farm hand had found him.

"I thought – his heart," Verna said. "My own Da had two attacks."

The old man was sitting in his chair in the front room, a wool blanket up to his neck and almost covering his new slippers. A wood fire burned in the fireplace. The coal bucket had been newly filled with kindling.

"Clear some land?" Reg said.

"I'm fine." Those dull eyes blinked. "No need for you to be here."

The sofa he had not been allowed to sit on as a boy felt lumpy. "We walked behind the tanks. Terrible stink. And the noise – "

"Best thing I ever did." He had lost a little hair and gained a few pounds. "Tried for years to convince the bank to stand behind a loan. They can't get enough of my business now."

"When did you sell off Walter?"

"I never." He was rubbing his arms under the blanket. "Had offers, from the workhouse to the butcher. Give him to the Frasiers, I decided. Hard times for them now."

For the first time since he was a little boy, he felt like hugging his father. "That was kind."

"Sensible is all. Never high on those Frasiers, but −" He groaned when he changed positions in his chair. "Government buying everything we can grow the last three years. No telling what will happen now. War's been good for us."

The girl added a log to the fire. "I can show him the tractor."

"Don't let him on it." He squinted at Reg. "Tell me straight out − you didn't walk away from your duty, did you?" He sat up, leaned forward. "Because if you did, I couldn't live with the disgrace."

He imagined thrusting a bayonet into that pot belly, gutting him, sticking a live Mills bomb inside him and blowing him to bits.

"Mr. Quaite believes him innocent," Sergeant Dickson said from the kitchen doorway.

"Of course he would."

The Sergeant clasped his hands behind his back, rocked on his heels. "And Mr. Rudyard Kipling."

The aging farmer cocked his head to the side, raised an eyebrow.

Reg stood. "The only thing I'm guilty of is surviving." He reached out to put hand on his father's shoulder, but saw that body recoil under the blanket. "Happy you're not ill," he said and he walked past the Sergeant into the kitchen.

A small box sat on the table. At first, he thought it might be a Boxing Day gift.

"We kept your things safe." His mother stirred the pot on her cooker with a long slotted spoon. "For you to take." She turned to smile. "You'll stay for dinner?"

The Sergeant moved toward the pot, sniffed the air. "Beef, is it?"

"Stew is all," she told him. "Potatoes and carrots, for flavor."

"We can't," Reg said, and before the Sergeant could start arguing, he walked out into the snow and got into the car.

•

The Frasier house needed paint. And a new post for the one rotting at the eave of the porch. The frail man who opened the front door looked half asleep.

"I've come to see Digger," Reg said. "And our old horse."

Steadying himself against the door jam, Mr. Frasier looked him up and down. "Turned out fine, Reg. A man now." He stared into the falling snow. "Your Walter's in barn. Can't miss him."

"Could you let Digger know I'm here, sir?"

He was studying his stocking feet now, each sock a different shade of gray. "Our boy fell in Flanders. Going on two years now. Buried there, they said."

Unable to speak, Reg stared past the man in the frayed flannel shirt and down the hallway he had scampered through a thousand times, chasing or chased by that tow head, the same one who mastered the rock climbs all the way down to the Common, always the fastest, the strongest of any of them.

"Your father's done well," Mr. Frasier said. "Fine head for business." He spotted the Sergeant behind the wheel of the black car. "Will you and your driver be coming in?"

"I'll just look in on Walter, if I may."

He flicked a boney hand toward the little barn. "Hasp's rusting out. Mind it doesn't fall off."

"Sorry to disturb you. Regards to your wife."

With a smile and a small nod, the frail man closed the door.

●

The Sergeant braked to slow the car down the steepest length of Coach Road. "Remembered you, did he?"

"He ate the carrot," Reg told him. Walter had actually looked better than the last time he had seen him. The horse was probably not seeing much time in front of the plow, not if Mr. Frasier was working the land himself. Good pasture and feed had put some weight on his sagging frame. "He seems to like his new home."

"It all works out, lad. What I've been trying to tell you."

At the bottom of the box: a small tin of chocolates. Reg traced a finger over the image of King Edward VII on the left side of the lid. Handed out on Empire Day, just six weeks after Tunbridge Wells was allowed to use the "royal" appellation in 1909, the tin and its contents had been a surprise treasure.

"I was eleven." Reg pried the lid off. One shiny lead soldier, its paint flaking off, lay on a bed of scrap linen. "Tommy this and Tommy that."

"Beg pardon?"

"Mr. Kipling. His poem, *Tommy Atkins*."

"Oh, aye. Famous that."

The lid clicked back in place. He set the tin back in the box.

"Keepsakes, then," the Sergeant said. "Memories make a room cozier."

His boyhood sat on his lap, but nothing in that box was worth holding onto. The car turned onto Langston Road, passing Denny Bottom. "At night, we'd watch owls hunt voles and mice. Digger swore he saw one get a grass snake once. We never believed him."

"Sorry about your friend." Thick stone mason fingers steered the car through the storm of white. Ahead, the lights of Royal Tunbridge Wells created a yellow haze. "Going to be late for supper."

He was probably still angry at having to leave that beef stew, but at least he had stopped grumbling about it.

"Even the Reverend called him Digger," Reg said. "His name was John."

•

"Brilliant." Mr. Kipling turned the lead soldier in his fingers. "For its directness, Sergeant."

"He said it, sir. Not I."

The heaviness of that little soldier made a thud when it hit the linen lining the tin. Those slender fingers replaced the lid, tapping it shut at a corner. "The only thing he's guilty of – is surviving."

"I don't see your point, Kip." Mr. Quaite had his sleeves rolled up as he dug through the box. "What's the legal significance?"

"Not legal." The moustache didn't move much when he smiled, but his eyes got smaller. "He stands accused of a deliberate act. We agree. Except that, his deliberate act is survival." He held up a finger: "So that he could rejoin his unit."

Outside, a heavy wind bent evergreen branches. More snow on the way, a blizzard if driven by that wind. Reg tapped the pane, so cold against his fingertip. "They won't accept that."

"They'll have to." The famous writer paced behind the settee. "No choice in the matter. None!"

"Beg pardon, sir," Sergeant Dickson said, "but it's the army we're up against. They've their own logic."

"Which is why" – Kip slapped the top of the settee – "we get one of their own to advance our notion."

"Corfe," the little editor said.

Nodding, Mr. Kipling stepped to the window, watched the wind. "Jot down what you recall, after your head wound. I'll arrange for the Colonel to confirm every action you took was to survive." He squeezed Reg's upper arm. "And I'll persuade that delusional incompetent Viscount Hardinge of Penshurst to certify it."

205

"Is that possible?" Reg said. "Actually?"

The breath leaving Kip's nose seemed to be the true force moving those fir branches in the back garden. "With honorable men, like your Colonel, only what is real and true can be accepted. To idiot diplomats and politicians, like Hardinge, the convenient is always possible."

Mr. Quaite cleared his throat. "The man hates you, Kip."

"Precisely why he'll be keen to see me." Those slender fingers reached out for the Sergeant, shook his hand. "Brilliant."

With a shrug, the little editor followed the famous writer out of the parlor. Sergeant Dickson sat on the settee as if unable to stand anymore. He nudged the box on the table. "No one's ever called me that before. Especially not someone like him."

"You think he can succeed?"

"Not to concern yourself, Reg-lad." His soft laughter filled the room with something close to music. "It's only your life at stake."

No matter how hard he tried, the words weren't right. Neither was the rhythm or the sound of them.

"You don't want Kip to see this." Mr. Quaite dropped the pages onto the low table. "Put down movements, locations, people. Nothing lovely. Make it like your diary."

That little book had come back with his other possessions – mostly clothes and spare Hussies and 4x2s – when the 11th left Italy. The Adjutant's office had delivered the single package, marked *Effects*: *L/C R. Olcutt, R.W. Kent R,* to the farm. Reg's mother had asked Mr. Quaite to take it. She couldn't look at it. His father didn't want it taking up space in the government girl's room.

The little editor must not have been sleeping well. Dark circles under his eyes made the rest of his face paler. When he moved out of the sunlight running in from the window to the rear garden, he looked like a corpse.

"The information is more important than the words used to convey it," he said. "We have to know what happened. Those facts will make your case at court martial." He coughed into his hand, checked his pocket watch. "New issue to put out. Back tomorrow or the next day." He hardened his stare. "Have something for me. Something factual."

For the first time Reg could remember, Mr. Quaite had left him in anger. That sheaf of pages littering the table had been four days of effort. Halfway through every sentence, his mind had wandered to Gabby. Even when she played no role in what he was trying to describe, he wound up focused on her. It felt like a sickness.

Restacking the pages into a neat pile, he stood and walked toward the rear staircase, determined not to disappoint the little editor again.

•

Whatever had flown into the slanted window above his cot, it had been big enough to crack the pane but not heavy enough to shatter it. The wind might have hurled a piece of bark or branch into the glass. The next thing to hit it, even a small bird, would let the outside in.

He pushed the metal frame cot from under the window. Light from a half moon highlighted the dust outline of where the cot had stood. His foot prints had been stamped into that rectangle of dust, making it look as if someone had walked over a freshly dug grave.

With his back against the cold wall, he rolled the pencil back and forth between his finger and thumb, stared at the blank paper. He could refer to Gabby only as "the younger sister." Teresa could become simply "the older sister," Luigi merely "the uncle." After all, being unable to speak Italian, who could expect him to remember names? Sancia and Nicoletta didn't have to be mentioned at all. The Piave and the towns of Colfosco and Susegana needed no disguise. He laughed at himself, realizing he couldn't actually remember if the castle was called San Sebastian or San Salvatore.

Time didn't make sense in all of this. How long had he been at the small river house? In the prisoner camp? On the mountain trails? At Teresa's? Anywhere? The safest approach would be to claim he had stayed mostly with the goat man in the foothills. No one would go looking for Rudolfo, Jr. And because no bridge had been left standing, could anyone fault him for being unable to cross the river to rejoin the 11th at The Montello?

With those moonlit footprints aimed straight at him, he grinned and put pencil to paper.

•

The Gazette office felt smaller than he remembered. And colder. The Sergeant kept inching closer to the old coal stove.

Mr. Quaite tried to muffle his cough with a handkerchief. He was smiling because Mr. Kipling was nodding as the read the pages. Finally, he took off his glasses, rubbed his eyes at the bridge of his nose. "You don't recall their names?"

Reg shrugged. "None of them spoke English."

"We should name them." He tapped a page with his pencil, then jotted notes in the margin. "Two young women nursing a wounded soldier. Fine story." He flipped through the pages to find what he was looking for. "Goats – excellent. But you'll want to describe them. The smell, the noise, that sort of thing."

"Would the court martial care about that, Kip?" Mr. Quaite said.

"Not for them, Andy." That pencil was moving across the top of the first page. "We have enough here for them. But for the story – we need to flesh that out."

"Story?" Reg said.

Long fingers offered the pages back. In printed letters, a title had been added to the first page: *The River of Two Women.*

208

"We can work on it at Bateman's," Mr. Kipling said. "For the present, this should be transcribed for the Adjutant. And a copy for me to bring up to Penshurst."

Taking the pages, Mr. Quaite started toward the back bay, then stopped. "What am I thinking? Reg, time you learned copy." He quieted his hacking with a throaty growl. "To run the shop, you must know copy."

"Have that cough looked at." The famous writer had his glasses back on. "How long will the transcription take?"

"The better part of an hour." Ink smudged fingers flipped through the pages as if counting them. "Two if Reg does it."

Mr. Kipling was already up and slipping an arm into his gray overcoat. "Sergeant, care to join me for lunch?"

"An honor, sir."

"You haven't seen him eat," Reg said. "He's – enthusiastic."

Those dark eyes widened behind the wire rims. "Humor would also be a good thing to add to your story." He opened the door to High Street. "Good work. Mind Andy now. I'm told he had a decent teacher once."

"A thousand years ago," Mr. Quaite said.

Kip stepped out into the bluster and sleet. "Longer than that, I believe."

The door shut. Head down against the wind, the stout body of Sgt. Dickson moved past the office window, leaving a view of the empty winter street.

"Bateman's," Mr. Quaite said. "That will be something to remember."

Reg looked up from the sheaf of papers. "You've never been?"

"When Kip took the place, it had no working indoor plumbing. With his travel schedule, and the loss of his boy, I suppose there was never an appropriate time for a visit." He was sweating. With the handkerchief close to his mouth to catch the next cough, he smiled, his round face seeming to swell. "Until now."

•

It was The Influenza.

"Caught it traveling north," the Sergeant said. "Visiting your appointed barrister, no doubt." He shifted into low gear for better traction up High Street. "General Hospital wouldn't take him. Sent south to Isolation Hospital on Benhall Mill Road."

"That's nearly out of town," Reg said.

209

Once reserved for Scarlet Fever and Plague victims, that hospital now served as a catch-all for patients with every communicable disease. Despite public denials by the Medical Officer of Health, stories of people going in with one disease and dying of another were commonplace.

"Say what you will," the Sergeant said, "but it's a far sight better than the Dislingbury in Capel. You'd sooner be drawn and quartered than sent there."

Reg rolled down the window just enough to let fresh air clear the fog on the windscreen. "We can drive down after we see to the office."

"In this weather?" He steered toward the shoulder of the street, braked to slow the car to a stop. "House for the sick and the dead. Seen enough of both." He glanced at the white building. "Won't let you in to see him at any rate."

"You're afraid. You think you'll catch it, too."

The Sergeant jerked his head toward the building. "Be quick about it. I'll keep motor running. Don't want to get stuck up here in this stuff."

The front door of *The Gazette* office was locked. Reg ran around the corner to the rear doors. *Locked.* The bay doors to the Iron Monger's had been braced open. Heat from the smelter leaked out. He hurried back to the waiting car.

"I told you he would have seen to it." The Sergeant let the car creep forward before he found low gear. "Risking life and limb on these streets."

"It's everything he owns." Reg drew a breath to calm his anger. "It was good of you to make the drive."

"Haven't you realized it yet, lad? I'm a saint."

They shared a small laugh as the car made a U-turn back toward Calverley Lodge. Approaching the hill where Lower Green Road fed in from the north, the Sergeant was still smiling. "Walked all this way to hospital, through sleet, high fever and all. A man with a constitution like that will walk out of hospital under his own strength. Mark my words."

"I worry about him," Reg said. "Even when we were in trenches, I worried he would be working too hard. He's all alone."

Sergeant Dickson kept his focus on the blurry windscreen, tapped the brake downhill. "Not anymore, is he."

•

The letter from the Adjutant's Office in Lewisham was actually a notice:

Major C.F. Richardson is no longer available to serve as legal counsel. Pending a new appointment, convening of the General Court Martial referenced herein will be delayed until further notice. All custody and travel restrictions pertain indefinitely.

The Sergeant took back the letter and placed in a file folder. "More waiting then. I'll relay this to Mr. Kipling." He put the folder under an arm and started for the rear stairs. "He'll get to the bottom of it."

The empty hall filled with the faint sound of bitter wind. At least the weather had eased. The streets would be clear enough to make the walk down to the Isolation Hospital, but there was no point to that: the ginger VAD nurse had checked with her superior and learned that visitors were not permitted at the Benhall Mill Road facility. Worse, if Reg did manage to get inside, he would have to remain there. "Quarantine means quarantine," Bridgette had told him. "You'd put us all at risk. And there's no telling what you'd come down with in that place."

Stripped down to his gray shirt, he sat on the cot, wondering how long it would take for that glass window pane to give out and for sky to fall in.

•

"He succumbed to the Influenza." Mr. Kipling's slight smile seemed out of place. "They found him a day or two after he had died."

Bright sunlight angled through the back garden window, landing on the set of folders on the low table. The top folder, marked *Maj. C.F. Richardson, Adj.*, was filled with handwritten notes, indecipherable.

"I've persuaded the Adjutant's Office to postpone another appointment until I've met with Sir Charles," Kip said. "The man is being deliberately difficult. I'll carry these files up to Penshurst and leave them in his study, if need be."

Reg couldn't stop staring at the folders. "What if Mr. Quaite dies?"

"I'm told he's stable." The thin writer sat next to him on the settee. "Improving possibly."

"They have the same disease."

"Different men," Kip said.

"What I told the lad myself." The Sergeant poured himself more tea. "Massive constitution on that one. Massive."

Mr. Kipling's grin did not last long. "Still awaiting a reply from Colonel Corfe."

"But – if Mr. Quaite dies – "

"You'll take over *The Gazette*," Kip said, "merely sooner than expected. It's what he wants."

"And if I'm execu – unable?"

The tweed suit made a rustling sound when he stood. "Sergeant, bring the car up. We have business to attend to. Cheer the Corporal up."

•

Tents dotted the grounds near The Beacon. At the top of the 101 steps leading down to St. Paul's, Mr. Kipling turned back toward the car. "I'd like to see the famous Toad Rock instead. If that's on our way."

The Sergeant looked confused. "Have map in car."

"No need." Reg walked to the car, opened the door. "Just up Bull's Hollow."

•

The car crept past Lion Rock, where a black cat with white paws walked over the back of the reclined figure of the king of the jungle weathered in sandstone. A quick turn put Elephant Rock and Parson's Nose in view.

"Each one is named," Reg said. "Left here." He pointed to a formation of slabs rising 15 feet. "Fireman's Ladder."

The Sergeant kept squinting. "Don't see that."

"That's Table Rock," Reg told him.

The Sergeant rolled down the window, shook his head.

"Park here." He tapped the dashboard. "That's Toad."

From the edge of Harmony Street, it looked more like a hunched over man, but from the clearing, the side view explained why this was the most famous rock in all of Kent. Perched on a pedestal of ever smaller slabs, the huge squatting figure stood over 11 meters high.

Mr. Kipling moved in for a closer look. "And safe to climb, you say?"

"We clambered all over it," Reg said. "The village is always threatening to put up a proper fence."

"Then we should take advantage of the present opportunity." Kip turned sideways to follow Reg through a broken section of iron fence, then looked for a foothold at the wide base of the pedestal. "Any trick to it?"

"Not recommended, sir," Sgt. Dickson said. "Slick from weather, those rocks."

"Easier from here." Reg stepped toward the back of the pedestal, put his boot on top of the first slab. "Move forward as you climb. Like this."

In six quick steps, he had reached the top of the pedestal, his head against the belly of the great toad. Mr. Kipling took the same route, accepting a pull up the last two steps, then ran his hand over the smooth stone of the toad's haunch.

"You can sit here," Reg said, lowering himself to the ledge between the top two slabs of the pedestal. That stiff pinkie popped against his weight. He clenched his fist, opened it: that little finger worked now. He kept bending it to make sure. "Better view from the other side, but a more difficult climb."

"This is fine." Kip took care in sitting, his legs quivering under the strain. He drew a deep breath of Winter. "What a boyhood you must have had."

He didn't want to tell the famous writer than none of his friends bothered with Toad Rock most of the year, when tourists picnicked in the clearing and jammed the road with their cars and trolleys. Hordes of them stayed at the inn nearby. By day, their voices carried down to Happy Valley and at night, their clamor scattered the owls. "Best in late Autumn and winter," he said. "It becomes itself then."

Those dark eyes behind the wire rimmed glasses narrowed to focus on him. The corner of that moustache inched up. "Finding things as they are – truly are – is the secret. You have that already."

"Not stuck there, are you?" Sgt. Dickson said, his hands cupped to his mouth. "Need help getting down?"

"Impatient, your keeper," Kip said.

"He's hungry."

Sharing a laugh, they inched down, one slab at a time, with Reg steadying the thin writer by holding him by the arm, guiding him to the landing.

"I hope I'm not being a royal pain, Sergeant," Kip said, dusting off the seat of his overcoat, "but I could do with a bite to eat."

"No, sir. I mean, yes, sir." Sgt. Dickson cleared his throat and started down to the car. "Of course, sir. Next stop, The White Hart."

•

The next stop was Bishop's Head, then Dog's Head, then Little Toad, the Ship and Loaf Rock behind it. Each time the car parked, even for an instant, the stone mason's thick fingers drummed the steering wheel. Once back on Rusthall Road, and knowing the route to the pub, that barrel chest filled with air, exhaled through a grin that said, *at last*. He turned halfway toward the rear seat. "Won't be another minute or so, sir."

His mind on menu choices, he never noticed the smile passing between Reg and Kip.

9

They went in the front, because the big doors at the rear tended to stick in icy weather or after a long rain when the wood swelled. Mail pushed through the slot lay on the floor. None of it looked important.

Mr. Kipling inspected the calendar on the desk blotter, full of annotations by the little editor. "Could you put the paper out by yourself?"

Reg shook his head.

"Anyone who might help you?" Kip said.

"He did it all. Alone."

The Sergeant had pushed through the swinging door to the back bay, but stopped in mid-step, as if something lurking there had frightened him.

The linotype machine looked like a large black insect. It took up half of the bay. A stool sat in front of a keyboard at what must have been the front. The narrow base of the machine had four feet – more like fins. A large wheel stuck out of one side of what had to be an engine, with wires and hoses attached.

"Mistook it for a monster in the dark." Sgt. Dickson bent for a better view of the underside. "Must make a racket."

Running a finger over the keyboard, Kip let out a long breath. "Beyond me," he said. "Don't suppose you know how to operate it."

"It wasn't here before," Reg told him. "He bought it used after I'd gone off."

The thin writer strode back to the front office, picked up a piece of scrap paper from the desk. Back at the linotype, he jotted jotted down the manufacturer's name and the model number. Offering the paper to Reg, he said, "Look them up, phone them. Learn how this works."

"It's too big a job," Reg said.

"Make the paper small," Mr. Kipling told him. "Keep all the adverts. A few stories. The Sergeant will help you."

"Beg pardon, sir, but I'm not a literary man. Not in the least."

"With the driving," Kip said. "Get him around to collect the information. All his readers care about is their names spelled correctly." When he narrowed his stare, those bushy dark eyebrows dominated his face. He looked as fierce as that linotype machine. "Find the last issue. Contact all the advertisers. Advise them of the situation. Ask for their forbearance. No – demand it." He put a hand on Reg's shoulder. "I'll see to getting you some help from *The Observer* in Hastings. You can do this. You must."

Reg nodded, but felt certain he would fail. How did Mr. Quaite pay for supplies? How many paper boys delivered *The Gazette*? Were the pages printed on the old letterpress in the corner? Would the experts from Hastings laugh at this set up?

"Wee pail here," Sgt. Dickson said. "Some sort of metal drippings in it." He pulled his head out of the underside of the linotype. "You don't suppose it melts itself."

"Hot lead," Kip told him. "How the type is set."

"It catches fire, then?" The Sergeant scanned the bay. "In this space?"

"Inside the workings." Those big eyebrows knitted together as he inspected the dross pot. "Somehow."

Gazette office set on fire by Corporal awaiting court martial. The perfect headline.

"No fear, lad." The Sergeant patted him on the back. "You've come through worse."

The terror creeping through him felt different than combat. He had been trained for that, and if a Whiz Bang or Flying Pig hit nearby, all would be over in a second. That linotype machine promised a slow death. The letterpress, an even slower one.

He spotted a cot standing upright behind the swinging door. How often had Mr. Quaite slept here on that dilapidated canvas relic, pulled out to the front room to get close to the old coal stove? The space between the front door and the back bay double doors might have felt like a prison on those nights.

"No wonder he's alone," Reg said.

The Sergeant turned back into the room. "Come again?"

Shaking his head, Reg walked to the desk, sat in Mr. Quaite's straight back chair, the only piece of furniture from his mother's house that his sister had permitted him to take. The arms felt sticky from sweat, ink and grime. He studied the notes on the calendar. "This may take some time," he said. "Better drive Mr. Kipling to the station."

Kip was smiling. "That's the spirit. I'll send word on the help from down south."

The Sergeant held the door open. He started to follow the thin man outside, but stopped long enough to ask, "You'll remain here. No scurrying about."

He felt the cold rush inside. "No place to go."

The door shut. No bell. There had been a bell on the top rail, triggered at the casing. It had made a dull *ding* – sad, as if apologizing – and by the greening of its copper and brass, it might have been older than the building itself. He could make out the outline of where that bell had been attached to the door: a scar no one else would be likely to notice.

Williams' Stationer and Library on Mount Ephraim would be the first business to contact. If Mr. Williams or his wife were still alive, they would remember the boy who stacked cartons for no pay, just for the right to read a new book in the storeroom. He circled the name written on the calendar, then moved to the next scribble: *Pratt's Dairy.* The old St. Peter's neighborhood would not have changed. Another circle.

By the time the Sergeant returned, dusk had settled in and most of the names on the calendar had been circled and transferred to a list, including addresses from the book in the side drawer of the desk.

"Been busy, I see." Sgt. Dickson put his hands on the front of the desk and leaned in to look at the calendar. "No place to go, he says. Hah! *The Gazette* pays for the petrol, certainly."

The cash box in the bottom desk drawer had a few pound notes, plus coin. Reg slid it across the blotter. "Take what you think is necessary."

"I couldn't. We'll tally it by the week." He watched the cash box go back across the desk, the drawer shut. "Lock it, shouldn't you?"

Reg sat up, stretching his back and arms against the chair. "When I started here, he never even used to lock the office. Nothing worth nicking."

"Five quid in there, at least."

Opening the bottom drawer again, he pulled out the cash box, shoved it back at the Sergeant. "Take it. You are now the official Paymaster of *The Rusthall Gazette.* Congratulations."

The gunmetal box looked tiny in those hands. "Am I to take orders from you now?"

"Directions," Reg said. "You give the orders, I give the directions." He pocketed his list of names and addresses, pushed the chair into the hollow of the desk. "We begin tomorrow. At no pay."

"Story of my life, lad." He opened the front door. "There would be a meal allowance, of course."

"You'll have to discuss that with the Paymaster."

"But – that's me."

Locking the door, Reg turned toward the car and didn't stop laughing until the motor started.

•

The main story would be about the government girl brought in to help at the farm. Details about her background, her experience, her impression of Rusthall, of farm work, of what is was like to be doing her bit for England in the Women's Land Army.

"Harder than I thought," she told him. "And longer days. Rest on Sunday – unless the weather's up."

The food was good and plentiful. She had true affection for his father and mother. "Decent people doing honest work," she said. "Never a cross word from your mother."

He knew exactly what she meant by not including his father, who had no doubt scolded her for the simplest errors – this from a man who bungled his way with every tool he had ever owned, and had the scars to prove it.

Her only request was to change her name. "For the story," she said. "I've always hated it. People always making fun of it. Verna. No one else in the world with that name."

"What would you like me to call you?"

"Elizabeth?"

"Done."

"And the last name as well. Make it – no, no last name."

"Just Elizabeth?"

She nodded. There was a smudge of dirt on the side of her nose. "And say I'm from nearby. Not Yorkshire."

He scribbled that note. "You'll be the feature. The only other article will deal with our footballers and the new season."

"Needs her sleep." His father tapped out his pipe against the door jam. Bits of charred tobacco that he would not be sweeping up fell at his feet. "Shouldn't be buggered with questions."

She stood, flashed a smile and went into her room – his room – and gently closed the door.

"Never needs reminding, that one." The old man rebuttoned his ragged cardigan, stretched now by his growing gut, and moved back to his chair by the fire. "Tell her once and it's fixed up here." He tapped a finger against his temple. "A Godsend."

Folding his notes and pocketing his pencil, Reg stepped into the kitchen, where the Sergeant was at the table, sopping the last drop of gravy from his plate with a chunk of bread. He looked disappointed when he realized it was time to leave. "Certain you've got what you came for?"

Nodding, Reg rubbed his mother's arm, still warm from the cooker and pot of stew bubbling on it.

"It's a fine thing you're doing for Mr. Quaite," she said, whispering to be sure her husband would not hear. She touched his sleeve. "You won't bring Mr. Kipling here. I'd faint. And there's no telling what your father might go on about."

"That gentleman can fend for himself," Sgt. Dickson said. "Taken a shine to your boy, he has. A compliment to you to be sure." He was wearing his full-stomach smile. "And if he ever tasted your stew, you might never see the back of him."

She laughed, but covered it with her hand to silence it. She waved to both of them as they went out the back door.

"Thank you," Reg said, opening the driver's door for the Sergeant. "That was good of you."

"Meant every word, lad."

"I can't remember the last time I saw her laugh."

That strong jaw softened. "Now you've shot me in the heart." He glanced at the glow from the kitchen window. "House without laughter's never a true home."

Reg walked around the front of the car toward the passenger's side. "Story of my life."

10

They walked in as if they owned the shop. The oldest, clearly the man in charge and the only one wearing a necktie, scanned the front office, then told the skinny man in the black slicker, "Must be in the back. See to it."

Even dry, that slicker made a scraping noise when he moved. Wriggling out of it, he hung it off a knob of the double doors, pulled the stool up to the linotype machine.

"Copy ready?" The young man with his black hair slicked back with pomade stopped at the desk. "Typed, I hope."

Reg held out the pages he had typed out, offered his hand. "Olcutt. Reg."

The young man took the pages and started reading as he walked into the back bay.

"Clarkson." The senior staffer shook Reg's hand. "Martin. Managing Editor, *Hastings Observer*. Didn't expect a Corporal to be in charge." He studied the uniform for a moment. "Stock kept back there as well?"

Reg nodded and followed him through the swinging door.

"This is good," the young man said, handing the copy to his boss. "Interesting."

Clarkson pushed it away. "Just copy edit." He smiled at the big black linotype machine. "I know this model. Solid as they come." He patted the shoulder of the man on the stool. "Warren, show him how it works." An instant later, he was at the rolls of paper and cans of ink near the letterpress. "Bloody hell," he said, running a hand over the cast iron press. "A Wharfedale. Stop-cylinder, traveling bed." He squatted to inspect the gears on the underside. "Beautiful. We use rotary presses now, but this workhorse takes me back."

He turned the big flywheel using the hand knob. The machine clattered as it came to life. With the traveling bed exposed, he inspected *The Gazette* banner and advertisement lead forms locked in place on the front page. "Set up for the next edition."

Next, he turned the small roller sitting like an awning above the big cylinder and tested the tautness of the leather bands connecting that small roller to an even smaller one. "Paper feed. Lads, this can do two thousand impressions per hour. More if he runs it off a motor." His finger traced the first part of the embossed lettering along the main frame: *The Wharfedale W. Dawson & Sons Makers Otley*. Smiling,

Clarkson waved Reg to his side. "Your Mr. Quaite has set it up for hand operation. Allows him to go at his own speed. Hand-inked as well. I envy you."

"Copy's ready." The young man pulled off his eye glasses. "Only two corrections" His index finger pointed to copy marks he had made, fixing punctuation. "Very clean." He clipped the sheets to the linotype machine so that Warren could read them, then stepped to the Wharfedale and began inspecting the clamps on the forms. "A flat bed?"

"The rotary is much faster," his boss said. "But the impression from this Wharfedale is nothing short of beautiful." He turned toward the young man. "Leave the clamps locked, Teddy. We'll build the new forms at size."

"Are you sure it works, sir?" Teddy said.

Chuckling, his boss pulled open a wide drawer near the paper rolls, drew out the last issue of *The Gazette*, held it up. "And this is just the proof."

It had been deliberately under-inked to show the imperfections in the lead type. Still, the page was readable.

"We lose something with progress." Mr. Clarkson slid the proof back in the drawer, closed it slowly, as if it were a burial vault. "All right, Warren. It's your show now."

With a nod, Warren cracked his knuckles, then pushed a lever at the front of the linotype. With his left hand hovering over the first two columns on the keyboard, he began punching keys, his right hand darting over all the other columns. Occasionally, he stopped to push a lever under the keyboard. Teddy dragged a low table to the machine, which spat out lines of lead, still hot. He used tongs to set the lines into a small empty form, about the size of two columns.

Heat from the hot type and the linotype machine motor and lead pot began to make the bay feel cozy. Mr. Clarkson shed his overcoat. "Won't be long."

"Not sure I understand any of this," Reg told him.

"Excellent. Then you can learn the proper way." He patted Reg on the shoulder. "We'll get your issue out, then guide you through the next one. Make a real newspaper man out of you" − he winked − "in a year or two."

•

"He grumbled the entire train ride up." Warren watched his boss check the proofs. "I've never seen him happy like this."

"Must be glad to be out from under the Chief," Teddy said, adding in a whisper, "Our editor couldn't find his way out of a crate if you left the top off."

His colleague snorted a laugh. "Telling anyone who'll listen that he and the great Rudyard Kipling are now personal friends." He shook his head, lowered his voice. "Promised an exclusive interview, a visit to Bateman's and signed copy of the next book. Morocco-bound, no less."

"Teddy!" Clarkson laid out the proof sheets on the composing table that had been covered with two pieces of cardboard. "Press proof."

The young man put on his eye glasses as he stood. "Bring a straight edge," he told Reg. "We go line to line."

•

It took longer to proof the pages than to set the letterpress up for printing. It had to be oiled, the rollers inked – Clarkson used a putty knife to scoop the ink solid from the can – and the paper roll got laid over the leather webbing of the top feeder. Everything they had done in two hours would take Reg all day to accomplish – after he had learned to use the linotype keyboard, and if there were no problems. It would be another full day to print the 3,000 copies. Then the folding, the bundling – done by the paper boys, but not without supervision.

No wonder he slept all day Fridays. On that day, when *The Gazette* got delivered, Mr. Quaite could not be reached.

The clatter of the letterpress refocused Reg's attention. He watched his words come to life.

•

The Sergeant dug into his eel pie, watching the six paper boys fold and bundle the new issue. "Do we pay them from the coin box?"

"They pay you," Reg told him. "Collect very week from subscribers. Twice weekly from store stacks. You collect from the advertisers." He set a copy under the cash box. "Drive that down to the Isolation Hospital so Mr. Quaite can see it."

His mouth full of the last of the jellied eels, the Sergeant tried to protest, but all that came out was a muffled grunt.

"You don't have to go inside the wards," Reg said. "Drop it off at the waiting room for him."

The swallow sounded like a burp. "First light tomorrow."

"Tonight," Reg said. "He needs to be the first to see it."

Glancing through the window at the darkening sky, the Sergeant got up from his chair, wiped his mouth with the napkin tucked under his shirtfront. He picked up the cash box and the paper. "It's a good thing I like you, lad, or I might resign my position."

"You can't. Neither can I." Reg opened the door for him, felt the cold drift in. The paper boys instinctively spread their hands and arms out to prevent the copies from scattering in wind. "We're all lumped together in this."

"Back in trenches." The Sergeant couldn't stop his smile. "Very well, Corporal. But don't let those rascals into my sweets."

"If you can," Reg said, "find out how he is."

The paper boys watched the broad shouldered man move up the street, out of sight. The smallest one got to his knees. "Sweets, sir?"

"Hard candy. Desk. Top drawer, left," Reg said. "Leave some for him."

As they scurried to the desk, he walked through the swinging door, pulled the stool to the linotype keyboard. Without turning the motor on, he ran his fingers over the keys, as if composing the first lines of his feature story:

> *Newly 18, Elizabeth arrived from Mayfield expecting to learn farming. Instead, she learned she was part of the war effort – the part that made soldiers and sailors on the home front happiest: growing hops for beer and ale.*

●

There was too much to master. The linotype posed a degree of complexity far beyond any piece of military or farm hardware Reg had handled. Most of it was automatic, but only if the right keys and levers were depressed in the proper order. Added to that, the lead mixture that the line was cast in – *the slug* – had to be in precise ratio of lead, tin and a metal he had never heard of before. If not, a *squirt* could result. That was the reason for that pail – *the hell bucket*, because molten lead often ate through the pail bottom as if "going to hell."

Too-fast key strokes could produce transpositions, spoiling a slug. It was then faster to fill the ruined line with nonsense letters from the first two columns – *the run down* – and cast it, then start the line all over again.

The only thing Reg felt he understood was that no oiling of the magazines was permitted. Oil mixed with dust to create grime that jammed the mechanisms.

The letterpress was simpler. The putty knife had to slice through the skin of the ink forming in the cans. Small dabs allowed the rollers to ink themselves uniformly. The traveling bed needed oiling before and after every use – in over 16 places. The forms had to be unclamped, but the adverts and banner and masthead were left in place. All the other slugs were removed, de-inked in alcohol, dried, ready to be melted down again.

Rotary presses, he learned, like those employed by *The Hastings Observer*, used curved forms locked onto the cylinders. It took four men to run them. Mr. Quaite had put out an eight-page paper every Friday for nearly 30 years all by himself.

"Like God," Clarkson said. "He's more a relic than that old Wharfedale."

"No way to talk about a man in hospital," the Sergeant told him.

"He meant it as a compliment," Reg said. "He admires Mr. Quaite."

Nodding, Clarkson tightened his tie knot, put on his overcoat. "We'll return Thursday next. Have your copy ready by noon. And the machines in proper condition. And the paper roll in place." He opened the door to the darkness. "Four pages again. Write to the space open. Start tomorrow. Deadlines have a way of sneaking up on you."

The slicker over his arm, Warren followed him outside. Teddy patted down his slicked black hair and stopped in the doorway. "If things should not work out for Mr. Quaite," he said in a quiet voice, "I'd be pleased to leave Hastings – lend a hand."

"They'll work out," the Sergeant told him.

"I hope so, for his sake," Teddy said, staring at the scuffs on his brown shoes. "I've been in copy four years. No hope of writing for *The Observer*. Or moving up."

Reg stepped to him, shook his hand. "Don't miss your train. We'll talk more next week."

"Not in front of them." He glanced up the street at his two colleagues. "Solely between us?"

Reg nodded, watched him quicken his stride to catch up to the others.

"Relic," Sgt. Dickson said. "I could have poled him." He yanked open a desk drawer. "Those rascals have decimated my sweets!"

The door clicked shut. "They're boys," Reg told him. "*The Gazette* will buy you more."

"See to that, I will." He sat in the editor's chair, unwrapped a candy. The crackle of the paper made him smile. "When I finish a line of stone, get it just right, I feel the way you must now, having put that paper out."

"I'm exhausted," Reg said.

The Sergeant fed the candy ball into his laugh. "Another twenty years of this, lad, and you'll be a relic like the rest of us. Something to look forward to."

11

Less chilly here." The Sergeant set his duffle on a bench at Etchingham and studied the stone block station house as the southeastern train for Hastings pulled out. "Sussex has the finest weather."

Just 30 minutes by rail south of Royal Tunbridge Wells, the landscape was open, like parkland. Four automobiles sat in front of the station house. One of them was a black Rolls Royce. A middle-aged woman stepped out from behind the wheel wearing a heavy tweed coat and dark leather gloves. She waved.

"Can't be for us, can it?" Sgt. Dickson said. "A lady driver?"

She opened a rear door, then quickly slipped back into the driver's seat and shut that door. Mr. Kipling sat near the far window, facing forward. "Morning," he said. "Don't let the cold in."

The leather bench seat felt like a small bed, only softer. The walnut paneling glistened with dark swirls. The engine didn't cause the vehicle the shudder and it didn't make half the noise of the Sergeant's sedan. The driver steered the big car in a small semicircle, then took a narrow road south.

"Is she competent?" Sgt. Dickson said.

"Dolly is competent at everything," Kip told him. "My assistant. Essential." He tapped the top of the front seat. "Miss Ponton, Sergeant Dickson and Corporal Olcutt."

She glanced back and nodded, then fixed her attention on the turn onto High St., getting the Rolls up to speed.

"A bit fast," Sgt. Dickson said.

Kip cleaned his eyeglasses with a handkerchief. Without them, his eyebrows looked bushier. "Always feels that way in the rear."

"Red roofs." The Sergeant bent low for a better look, not realizing that he was crowding Mr. Kipling. "Tile of some sort?"

"Weald clay," Kip told him.

"More brown than red," the driver said.

Straightening up, the Sergeant grimaced as they passed a sign marked *Burwash*. "Not long now, I imagine."

"Less than four miles." Dolly must have been smiling: her voice sounded too sweet. "Few up and about in the village at this hour."

"Fortunate," Sgt. Dickson said, adding in a whisper, "Wouldn't want to run anyone down at this speed."

A man in a horse cart was the only person out in Burwash. He doffed his cap as the Rolls drove by. The dark dray horse never flinched.

When she turned left onto a lane barely wider than a single track, she slowed the car. Relieved, the Sergeant watched oaks and poplars at the sides of the road give way to broad expanses of meadows.

"Had this graded in," Mr. Kipling said. "A bit of engineering. Not a tree disturbed."

"Oak," Reg said. "Must be grand in spring."

"The Sussex weed," Kip told him. "They grow everywhere."

"How much land," Sgt. Dickson said, "if you don't mind my asking, sir?"

"More than we need."

"Three hundred and thirty acres," Dolly said. "The best part of Burwash."

The great writer bent forward toward Reg. "I prefer to think of it as part of Witherhurst."

The road widened after a jog left. Through bare winter branches, a stack of six chimneys stood out against the morning sky. The house stood bordered by a tall hedge. The drive gates − twins of iron, hinged off stone pillars that were each capped by balls of mortar − hung open. The Rolls stopped at the walk. Kip opened his door and headed up the stones, paralleling the house front. With the car motor off, the breeze rustled through the back meadow. In the distance: the sound of running water.

Blocks of gray and yellowed stone rose three stories. All the corners were thickly mortared. A round ball, similar to those at the drive gate pillars, sat atop each of the front peaks − the smaller one rising from the centered front entry patio, the larger one at the south end.

"Sandstone." The Sergeant was backing up onto the lawn to take in the full face of the house. "And well-windowed."

"Jacobean." Mr. Kipling stepped to the tall front door. Above the outside arch, *1634 AD* had been chiseled into an oval. "Tea shortly."

The Sergeant had nearly reached the front walk gate, a more slender version of the pillared drive gates. "Mind me remaining out here for a bit?"

"Of course."

The door opened without a sound. Inside, dark squares of hardwood paneled the walls, with two oval mirrors set in winged gold frames hanging near the beamed ceiling. The floor looked like a

227

checkerboard laid out by a drunk, light and dark squares of burnished wood in inconsistent patterns leading to a gloomy oak staircase, its single handrail sitting on spindled balusters. A large map dominated the walk up: *Norman Sussex*. Probably older than this manor house.

Tucking his cap under an arm, Reg followed the flap of Kip's overcoat to the head of the stairs and into a room off the landing. Early sun streamed through a large set of windows bracketed by bookshelves. A smaller window stood to one side, over a low table holding books and a typewriter, near a stretched out polar bear skin lying on a rug in front of the fireplace. All the area rugs were red and patterned − from India? − and overlapping each another. Hardly any of the plank floor was visible.

Kip removed a stack of books from a side chair, placing them on the window seat under the big window, already jammed with everything from books to carved figurines. He sat at his desk in the straight back chair that whined under his weight. At one knee, a large waste bin overflowing with crumpled paper. At the other, a world globe in a footed frame. There was another globe sitting on a black walnut night table near the full wall of bookshelves. Next to it, a footstool piled high with more books.

But his desk was the most cluttered thing in here. Books stacked at each end, an ink-stained blotter in the center, with hand carved paperweights holding down nothing, an ashtray empty of ashes holding a pipe beside a letter opener that must have once been a small Hindu sword, lying with its point facing the big window. A small open-top box in the center of the desk held note paper. Where things had been recently moved, their outline remained in dust.

Kip nodded toward an electric box by the small window. "Turn that switch."

Hanging from sturdy dark beams in the plastered ceiling, bulbs in the overhead chandelier came on. The room was little changed by the additional light.

"We run off a hydro turbine at the old mill," Kip said. "We'll see that tomorrow. Tricky bit of engineering. Reliable, basically."

The books nearest Reg included a thick novel by Mark Twain, so roughed up it looked ready to fall apart, a book on architecture, two Bibles, another title on religion, a slim volume of essays by a J.S. Mill and a collection of poems with scraps of yellowed paper growing out of it as book marks.

How did he find anything in here? And how did he manage to sit in these chairs without ruining his spine? The seats were set as diamonds, not squares, in the frame, so that the rear point formed the foundation for the backrest. Reg's chair had two carved lyres supporting the gracefully curved arms. It felt like sitting on a ridge.

"A man in uniform is poking around outside." The woman stood in the open doorway. "He's touching our walls!"

Reg got to his feet, knocking his cap to the floor.

She saw him and gasped. "For a moment," she said, "I thought – "

"That would be Sergeant Dickson," Kip told her. "The lad's. . . escort." He extended his arm toward the door. "My wife, Carrie. Corporal Reg Olcutt."

"He's a stone mason," Reg said. "By trade."

She took a small step into the study, nodded. "You're the letter writer."

He nodded.

Taking the measure of his uniform and age, the way his hair lay flat, she folded her arms across her wide front. The dark blue dress had a shine to it. Her sapphire earrings sparkled. She must have been up for hours already. "Tea in the lounge. Ten minutes."

Her footsteps beat the stairs. Kip squinted at the now empty doorway. He drew a pencil from a jam-packed holder on the desk, jotted something on a small piece of scrap paper, folded it, stuffed it into a jacket pocket. "She can see everything from her study," he was saying as he wrote. "Over the front door. Never misses the slightest intrusion."

•

Smaller than his study, the lounge had a bigger fire place and the same dark wood paneling as the front hall. A long rectangular couch faced the fire plate, backed by a heavy low table with twin drawers, their faces carved with a geometric pattern. The tea table, set with three chairs in front of the window, held a porcelain tea service and a plate of scones.

"Not much mortar, except at the corners, of course." The Sergeant added sugar to his cup, stirred it vigorously. "I'd be proud of this work." He swallowed a hot sip. "But it's no Jacob Bean, sir. Pure sandstone, it is."

Hiding a smile, Mr. Kipling nodded. "If you like, we can visit the oldest iron forge in Sussex in the morning. The Sheriff once ordered 30,000 horse shoes from it. In 1235."

"He never." Crumbles of scone and a dab of plum jam stuck to the Sergeant's lip. "The vines, sir. They'll need trimming. To keep the stone faces from pitting."

"Is that what that yellow is from?" Reg said.

"Lichen," Kip told him.

"Aye." The Sergeant turned the half-eaten scone in his fingers as if deciding how many bites were left. "Sandstone holds the water hard. Lichen love that."

"When they die," Kip said, "they leave a stain."

"Seen it thick as geese droppings on granite, I have," Sgt. Dickson said. "Chisel'em off's the only way. Worse than barnacles."

His pronounced chin thrown back, Mr. Kipling stared at Reg's plate, the scone untouched. "You're not eating?"

"I'm surprised I'm breathing," Reg said. "This is all — a wonder."

A broad smile made that chin look longer, those eyebrows heavier. "I feel the same way. Every day."

•

The bedroom had no bed. Instead, two tables had been set against a wall. Heaped with items, the tables resembled a sundries inventory. Slim fingers picked a pocket-sized book from the clutter, handed it to Reg. His *Jungle Book*, some of the war mud still caked on its edge.

"Andy sent it to me," Kip said. "Along with these."

In an open satchel on the floor: Reg's diaries, letters and a stack of clippings from *The Rusthall Gazette*.

Those fingers now held two full size books. Both volumes of *The Jungle Books*. "I hope you might be willing to exchange yours for these. I took the liberty of inscribing them."

"You want this?" Reg said. "It's nearly ruined."

"It traveled over the same terrain as my son did. This was his room."

Reg handed him the tiny book. "We heard he got crump — had been killed."

"At Loos. Before you enlisted." Tenderly, he set the fragile little pocket book next to a leather-covered box of medals and a pile of old school pads. "That smear of mud might have been something Jack trudged through a few years before you did." He cleared his throat. "They never found him."

The dull look in his eyes said that part of him believed some of his boy might be mixed into that mud and that by holding onto that tiny book was now the only way he could hold his child. Reg wanted to tell him how horrible it was slogging through that muck, but it couldn't have been more horrible than losing a son. He read the inscription on the frontispiece of the first *Jungle Book*:

Tuesday, 4 March, 1919 Bateman's
For Reg Olcutt, on the occasion of his first visit. With gratitude.

And signed. He fumbled the book, catching it before it hit the table. In the process, he toppled the pile of school pads. He began re-stacking them.

"Copy books," he said, grinning. "How we hated them."

For an instant, he was back at his school bench, copying line after line to get the handwriting just so. Old-fashion sayings – things no one ever used anymore – copied over and over.

He flipped to a page. In flowing script: *Good nature like a bee, collects honey from every herb,* with a poorer hand copying the letters five times below; then more perfect script as a new heading – *Ill nature, like a spider, sucks poison from the flowers* – and more failed attempts at perfection below it. Reg laughed. "These are a lot like the army. Imprecision masquerading as perfection. Deadly."

Those bushy eyebrows and the jut of his large chin made his features look set in stone. Mr. Quaite got that look sometimes, when he was writing in his head. Finally, Kip re-straightened the stack of copybooks. His mouth opened, but no words came out.

The second *Jungle Book* was inscribed the same as the first.

"These are magnificent," Reg said, rubbing the morocco leather, running a finger over the Nobel Laureate's personal bookmark in gold leaf: an elephant head with a Hindu swastika above its trunk, set in circle.

"He wrote those for you." Carrie stood just inside the doorway. "For your generation. Our Jack's generation." She glared at her husband. Then her face softened. "Have you shown him the hill?"

"Not yet."

"It's best glimpsed in full sun," she said.

He led Reg past her and down the hall to another room. This one held a bed and a view of the back pasture. A stream glistened in the light.

"The River Dudwell," Kip told him. "This is yours for the night. The Sergeant is two doors down."

Reg left the *Jungle Books* on a nightstand, followed the slim man back up the hall, past the now-closed door to Jack's room. Near the staircase, the woman in blue shut another door behind her. It was marked, *Private*.

They took a side lawn toward the back of the house, where the Sergeant was rubbing the stones at knee level, tasting the residue on his fingers. Kip pointed toward a clearing on a small rise, running from a ribbon of trees toward a small forest. "Pook's Hill," he said.

Puck of Pook's Hill.

"It's an actual place then?" Reg said.

Kip smiled. "I hope so."

"You've salt in the footing rows." The Sergeant offered his fingers for tasting. "Good sign. Water's draining out."

"Pook's Hill," Reg told him. "Full of magic and fairies."

"Don't be believing in them, lad." With a glance at Mr. Kipling, the Sergeant lowered his voice to a whisper. "Of course, they are there."

Staring at the western sky, Kip let out a stream of laughter. Finally, he cleared his throat and caught his breath. "I hear them at night. Might just be the Guernseys."

"Cows, have you?"

"Prize winners," Kip said. "At the Tonbridge Wells Cattle Show."

"You don't say. You've a bull then."

"And piggeries." A long finger flicked something out of an eye behind the spectacles. "And Red Short Horns. Poultry as well."

"I'd have never taken you for a farmer," Sgt. Dickson said. "Meaning no offense, sir."

That long chin out, eyebrows raised, Kip laughed again. "You're good for the soul, Sergeant." He turned and started back toward the front of the house. "Roast beef tonight."

Sniffing the air, the Sergeant grinned at Reg – "This is living" – then scurried after his host, intent on being first to the dinner table.

Pook's Hill held its color. Wind whispered through the sunlight and dead leaves. What must it have been like to grow up here? What must it be like now, living here with those memories of a son who never came home? Was it like this almost 300 years ago, when this house was built?

He wondered if he could ever muster the courage to ask those questions.

•

"Love at first sight," Kip said. "For each of us. We bought it that day."

The dining room table, longer and wider than the one in the lounge, had its dark top set in a lighter colored frame, making it look like a door lying flat in a simple jamb. It was accompanied by the least comfortable chairs in the house. The low seats confounded the Sergeant, who couldn't find a place for his elbows.

"Stanley writes he'll visit before Easter." Carrie cut a piece of beef on her plate, but she was looking at Reg. "Mr. Baldwin is Kip's cousin."

He must have been someone important. Reg nodded.

"What part of England might you hail from, ma'am," Sgt. Dickson said, "if I might ask."

"America," she told him.

He stopped in mid-bite, lowered his fork.

"New England," Kip said. "We lived there."

"Naulahka," she said. "Lovely pine and warm cherry. Tiffany lamps. Not anything like this."

"My big green ship." Kip dabbed his moustache with a napkin. "I wrote *The Seven Seas* there."

"And *Captains Courageous*," she said. "And the *Barrack-Room Ballads*." She glanced at Reg. "*Gunga Din*?"

"*Mandalay*." Kip said it as though he thought that was the superior story. "What energy we had then. All of us."

"All those letters from the children who loved *The Jungle Books*." She was watching the Sergeant eat. "He wrote those there, too."

"Why did you leave?" Reg said.

"The weather," Kip told him between bites of roasted potato. "The people."

"My brother." She slid the bowl of potatoes toward the Sergeant. "Please. Before they go cold."

Stabbing one with his fork, the Sergeant looked for a space on his plate to squeeze in the potato. "Have you called hospital to see if Andy's up and about yet?"

"He won't have a telephone in the house," Carrie said.

"Interruptive," Kip said. "It rings and one reactively feels compelled to answer it." He spooned horseradish from a small bowl. "Lord Hardinge will be discussing your matter with Lloyd George."

The Sergeant had a mix of beef and potato in his mouth. "The Prime Minister?"

"I'm surprised Hardinge received you," Carrie said.

"I found him sitting for a portrait." Kip had that napkin working over his moustache again. "When I told him I respected his repeated attempts to resign, he mistook it as a compliment." Those eyebrows angled down. "I was expressing surprise that, for once in his career, he had actually tried to do the right thing."

"And they go and give him a lifetime appointment," his wife said. "Your father and mother would have never tolerated that man."

"My father might have found some locals to set him afire," Kip said. "Mother would have brought the petrol."

The Sergeant started stomping his foot, laughing so hard he seemed to be choking. He washed it all down with ale. "Petrol. Capital."

"They met in Staffordshire," Carrie said. "At Rudyard Lake."

Rudyard.

"Could have been far worse," Kip said. "A nearby town is called Leek."

This time, the Sergeant roared. Bits of potato spewed from his mouth. He caught most of them in his palm. Tears flooded his eyes. He shook his head, still laughing – "Never in my life" – and held up his glass of ale – "To the rarest of men" – then sipped his toast and went back to his beef, chuckling as he chewed.

Sharing a smile with his wife, Kip slathered horseradish over his food and set to work with his knife.

•

He couldn't remember a better night's sleep. The sun had already climbed to roof level by the time he headed down the steep stairs. The table in the lounge had been cleared except for a plate of crumbs and a nearly empty jam jar. The Sergeant sat in a corner of the big couch, his head slumped to his chest, dozing.

"You missed breakfast." Carrie wore green today. She placed a serving fork on the plate. The noise startled the Sergeant, who groaned as he struggled to get to his feet. "We'll have an early lunch," she said, eyeing the barrel-chested man. "I'm sure no one will object."

That dress made a swishing sound as she walked out to the hall. She had left the plate and big fork behind.

"Eggs and bacon," Sgt. Dickson said. "Scrambled. In butter."

Mr. Kipling rapped the door jamb with a walking stick. Blackthorn, smoothed and varnished. He started buttoning his canvas and leather field coat. "Let's walk."

Cheeks stung by cold air, Reg followed the leader south, down a single track made narrower by the remains of unruly brambles at the sides. They looked like curved bare bones.

A stout timbered bridge crossed the river near a mill pond the size of a tiny lake. The breeze here blew stronger, colder.

"Dates to 1196." Kip aimed his stick at the white clapboard mill house. "Though the first recorded mention of it came in the 18th century."

"Then how do you know," Reg said, "about the earlier date?"

The calf-length oiled leather boots quickened their pace. "Research."

"Aye," Sgt. Dickson said. "And the structure tells its own tale."

Kip shot a smile at him. "Precisely."

The raceway ran from the river – the only straight line in the landscape. An iron hydro turbine spun at the side of the mill, but the old wood cogs and gears that once turned the grist mechanism were still visible under the building. The roof, covered with tiles faded brown and dotted with moss, sagged at the end near the chimney – like Walter's back.

A block stone wall, overgrown with vines, partitioned an access area. Its iron gate had not been opened for a long time: vines curled around the top hinge and seemed to tie the latch shut. The front door stood outside that gated portion. Nothing about the two-story building made sense.

Bleached wood floors, a narrow stairway, mill stones encased in wood stacked near a window. Where the driveshaft came through the floor, a small wood hopper stood to the side. Kip used his stick to ring the little bell attached to a leather strap on the hopper lid.

"The original fire warning system," he said. "An empty hopper meant the mill stones would grind against each other, throwing sparks."

He nudged the bell again, smiled at its dull ping. It sounded like the sister of that annoying bell Mr. Quaite had removed from the door of *The Gazette* office. "The corn was the only thing keeping the stones apart during grinding. The miller used this as a reminder to refill the hopper." He bent to get close to the bell – "Couldn't bear to discard it" – then straightened up and scanned the old tools and parts lying everywhere – "Any of it."

Outside, the Sergeant scanned the tree tops. "Can't make out the power line."

"Under the pond." Kip headed toward another foot bridge. "Special cable. We lived an entire year by candle light."

Reg stayed to the center board of the little bridge, wondering why no one had installed handrails. "Mr. Quaite said there were no bathrooms."

"Nor running water." His eyebrows knitted together when he squinted, but he was actually smiling. "A project. Even yet."

The path widened, leading to a small cottage. Miss Ponton walked out carrying a plate: toast and jam. "You had your breakfast," she said, keeping it out of the Sergeant's reach.

Reg took all three pieces, eating one before the solid-boned woman made it back inside her a small house that looked as old as the mill.

"Taught our Elsie and Jack," Mr. Kipling said. "Math and English."

Behind that low roof, off the trail, a newer little house stood surrounded by small bare trees. "New cottage," Kip told them. "Dairymaid and gardener live there. Married." He turned toward the back pasture — "She'll be down with the cows" — then turned in a lazy circle, eyeing the brambles and fallen limbs — "No telling where her mate might be."

At an iron gate, recently oiled because it made no sound when Kip opened it, Reg handed the last piece of toast to the Sergeant, who checked over his shoulder to be sure Miss Ponton couldn't see him before devouring it in three bites.

Half the distance of a football pitch later, by a strange gnarled tree — "Wriggly nut," Kip called it — they made a sharp right turn to another foot bridge that crossed a ditch. A large oak grew at the bank, leaning as if it hoped to fall back into the spot where it had begun. Just out of the shadow of that oak, a sundial had *It's Later Than You Think* molded into its face.

"I like to walk guests by here," Kip said, "in the hope they'll take the hint."

"We're taking the afternoon train back." Reg touched the cold iron letters. "I have to be ready for *The Observer* staff tomorrow."

"Not meant for you." With the tip of his stick, Mr. Kipling pushed moss off the side of the pedestal. "Have your stories in hand?"

Reg nodded. "I'm to set the type for the first time on my own."

"A natural," Sgt. Dickson said. "The lads from Hastings say so."

Walking faster, Kip moved down the trail, sure of every step, like an officer leading a squad. "Forge may not appear like much. History there though, for the finding."

•

It didn't look like anything more than a rubble of overgrown stones and a scattering of hand tools, some rusted so thin they lay like brown lace among the winter brush. The whole area resembled the rubbish slide in Happy Valley, before Rusthall cleaned it out.

There was no possibility that 30,000 horseshoes came from here.

•

The way back followed a new route, but met the old trail near the sundial. As they approached the new cottage, the anger in Carrie's voice reached them. She was standing just up from Miss Ponton's house, shouting something about a Captain at an old man in dirt-spattered trousers and a wool overshirt that had faded from red to pink. He cupped a hand to his ear.

Exasperated, Carrie marched toward her husband. "Captain got into the garden again. He needs to be tethered."

He watched her storm back toward the house, refusing to glance at the old man. "One of our drays likes to roll around to get free of his harness," Kip said. "A sense of humor. More than our cowman can handle."

The old man slid the frayed wool cap off his head, revealing an expanse of sunburned skin. "C'p'n wid Bl'k'br'd so now."

Nodding, Mr. Kipling walked on. The cowman stood as straight as he could, attempting to come to attention as the Sergeant passed him. Reg half-expected the old man to salute. Instead, he plopped his hat back in place and ambled toward the mill house.

"You understood that?" Sgt. Dickson said.

"Captain's with his stable mate, Blackbird." Kip was staring at the back of his wife, the tall stack of six chimneys visible in the distance above her head. "He's deaf, or nearly so. Dolly's the only one who can truly make sense of him."

"Got a stern talking to, he did." The Sergeant was staring at Carrie now, too. "Wouldn't want to be on the wrong side of your missus. No offense, sir."

Mr. Kipling tried to conceal his smile, but that moustache betrayed him. "My own Sergeant Major." He winked at Reg. "Don't mention I said that."

12

The inside of Chalkin's smelled like a wash line of drying flannel. Field jackets, similar to the one Mr. Kipling wore at Bateman's, hung on a wood rod in a front corner. Boots and walking shoes lined the platform of the main window, shaded by that long awning, its lettering – *The Old Firm* – wearing thin from weather.

"He'll have these." The Sergeant handed a piece of note paper to the small clerk, then opened a pocket of his tunic to reveal a wad of folded money. "A gift from Mr. Rudyard Kipling."

"You don't say." Smiling, the clerk studied Reg, touched his arms, patted down his shoulders. A quick glance at the list written on the paper and he waddled away, toward cubbyholes full of folded shirts.

"His missus wants you out of uniform for next visit," Sgt. Dickson said. "Proper fit out of walking wear you're to have. Suits to come later, when he takes you up to London."

"Expensive here," Reg told him. "How much did he give you?"

"Didn't count it, lad." The wide man tapped the bulge in his high pocket. "Over thirty quid. If there's anything left over, I'm to choose a few things for myself – to change into down there." He glanced at the wall clock. "Find me next door when you've finished." At the door to Camden Road, he made a stern face. "Take your time."

Next door would be The Prince of Wales, with brown ale on draught and a bar menu superior to the one at The White Hart.

"I've taken the liberty of rearranging the list." The short clerk held underwear in his outstretched arms. "Might we start with these?"

•

The trousers took four days to start to feel comfortable enough to sit in. The short boots still pinched his feet, especially when he wore the heavy new wool socks. But he couldn't stop looking at himself – in street windows, hospital mirrors, the dressing mirror in the water closet at *The Gazette* office, where Mr. Quaite had primped before meeting with advertisers and patrons. The reflection puzzled him. It looked like the man he never expected to be, yet there he stood.

"A proper country gentleman, your boss is." The Sergeant doled out hard sweets to paperboys sitting cross-legged in the front office. "But remember, I'm the one with the treats." He set paper five-pound notes on the desk, at least six of them. "And the one who collects for the adverts. Forty quid there. Your compensation."

"Put it in the cash box," Reg told him. "You're not wearing your new mufti?"

"Businessmen respond best to a man in uniform, I've discovered. Authority and all that."

"Scared you'll shoot them if they don't pay up," a dark-haired paperboy said.

Amid the giggles of the others, the Sergeant sat on the floor, began folding papers. "A long time since I shot anyone, lads. Now, that one there" − he jerked his head at the desk − "he's killed more Germans than you and me ever saw."

The smallest paperboy stopped in mid-fold. "That actually true, sir?"

Pretending not to hear him, Reg stood and walked into the back bay. Next to the Wharfedale, Teddy was using the composing desk to read the letters Miss Ponton had sent up on Mr. Kipling's behalf.

"These will make a good article." He had stopped pomading his hair. It was lighter colored now, a charred brown, no longer black. "You should sit with Sir Bromhead. Get his legal strategy."

Reg moved the copy editor's jacket and sat on the cot. "We don't do stories about ourselves."

"News." Teddy held up the letter from Colonel Corfe. "This supports your character. And valor!" His fingers darted to another note, the one from Sir Charles Hardinge. "A request for the charges to be removed!" The last letter he picked up was four pages thick, written in the bold hand of a retired colonial legal officer. "A portfolio filled with examples of unwarranted courts martial."

Those short arms were now reaching for the society paper, the back issue with Lady Annette Amelia Matthews, then newly the second wife of Sir Bromhead Matthews and one of the most prominent women in West Kent, proudly stating that her husband had never lost at trial. "She knows Sarah Grand!"

The Irish novelist, celebrated for *The Heavenly Twins*, lived in town and led rallies for the Suffragettes. Mr. Quaite admired her prose. He especially liked her characterization of the "New Woman."

"And Sarah Grand," Teddy was saying, "knows Bernard Shaw!" He fell back into the chair, banging an elbow on the bed of the letterpress. Grimacing, he slapped the desk. "You have the best story *The Gazette* could ever hope for. And you're at its center! You must write it."

In the silence back here, the rustle of papers being folded in the front office mixed with molars cracking hard candy. Teddy ran a

239

hand through his hair. "Reg, ask yourself – what would your Mr. Quaite do?"

Stretching out on the cot, Reg studied the long water stain in the plaster above the linotype machine. "You write it then."

"Me?"

"We'll give you a byline," Reg said. "Special to *The Gazette*."

It felt like a mistake the moment he heard himself say it. Mr. Quaite had never taken credit on any article. "Readers know who writes the paper," he had said whenever asked about it. "Put nothing unnecessary on the page."

"But you know these people." Teddy was on his feet now, coming around the composing desk. "You're familiar with the particulars."

Reg shut his eyes. "Interview them. All of them. Get quotes."

"I'd have to stay locally," Teddy said.

"The cot's yours," Reg told him. "Sergeant will give you a key. And meal money. Have the copy ready by Tuesday next. And proofed."

Teddy's feet shuffled back toward the Wharfedale. "I've never had a byline."

That rust-colored stain ran like a river toward the wall. "Neither have I."

•

There was no room left on his cot. Diaries and clippings from *The Gazette* based on his letters covered every inch. Only the pillow had been saved from the litter.

Under the cracked little window, Reg leaned against the cold wall. Spring was still a rumor whispered in frozen rain. Winter kept holding on. Even the stars seemed to realize that, their light hardened by icy night wind.

"May I?" The ginger nurse poked her head past the door she must have just opened. "I knocked, but. . ."

Leaving the door wide open, she set a letter on top of the two *Jungle Books* on the little table. "Sergeant said to give you this." She spotted the papers covering the bed. "Is that how it's done? Writing, I mean."

He shrugged. "Don't know where to start. Kip – Mr. Kipling – told me to let the facts order the story." He stared at those stars again. "Too many of them."

Bridgette was touching his uniform, hanging off hooks on the back of the door. "I could take this to launder. Up Grosvenor Road."

"Not certain I'll wear it soon," he said.

240

"For the court martial, though." She pulled his military boots from the corner. "These could do with a shine."

"Whatever you think best," he told her.

She pulled the tunic, trousers and gray shirt off the hooks, draped them over an arm. "Twenty *p* should cover all of it."

"The Sergeant will pay you." He glanced at the bed, sighed. "Difficult to read those. They seem to be written by someone else."

"Because you've already lived it." She switched the heavy clothes to her other arm. "None of you boys ever talks about what happened up there. You want to get on it with things. Get back to living."

He smiled at her. Holding that uniform, she could have been mistaken for his girlfriend. "Check the pockets before bagging."

"Wouldn't I be a fool if I didn't," she said. "Dinner in an hour. Sergeant's already down there."

"Of course he is. Thank you, Bridgette."

She backed into the hall and closed the door so quietly, he couldn't be sure she had ever been there. But the uniform was gone. The shine of the painted door tossed light back at him.

He rolled onto his knees, pulled the week-old issue of *The Gazette* from the satchel at the head of the cot. Nothing about the paper looked different from when Mr. Quaite put it out. Adverts and announcements made up the front page. Most of the two inside pages carried the news about his case, with Mr. Kipling, Lord Penshurst, Sir Bromhead Matthews figuring throughout. It was as if Theodore Dalbert, second under-copy editor of *The Hastings Observer*, were some famous author, spinning a Dickensian tale about a farm boy caught up among social and political giants. Still, the old Wharfedale had made the words look good.

He filed the paper back into Mr. Kipling's satchel, then stood. The new *Gazette* issue, out yesterday, carried his story about the new fence around Toad Rock, the old one having rusted out in so many places, anyone, even an aging writer, could wriggle through to sit on the base and pedestal. The article ran with an old photo, taken back when fewer tourists bothered with Rusthall and there had been no need for a fence. Had space permitted, he could have made that the real story.

In stocking feet, he stepped to the night table, picked up the letter. Inside, an accounting of back pay owing to him from February 19, 1918: four columns of numbers, some listed for L/Cpl, some for Cpl, totaling £4, 12s. A typed note at the bottom of the page:

> *An undetermined amount will be added for the period 12 March through final discharge.*

"Four pounds twelve." He laughed at the numbers: over a year's salary, worth less than Verna received each month for work at the farm. He carried the second page to the light near the bed to make out the handwriting:

> *The decision whether to abandon charges will be conveyed tomorrow. Expect we will prevail. B-Matthews, KG, OBE.*

The longer he stared at the script, the harder it became to read. Then he realized his hand had been shaking. So were his legs. Those thick wool socks were making his feet sweat. His throat felt dry and the groove in his skull began to throb. He dropped the pages on top of everything else on the cot. Combined, they looked like some strange work of art − a jumble of yellowing print, stained diary entries, snapshots murky from inking. Dizzy, he shoved part of the mess toward the middle of the cot to make room to sit.

He wanted to turn off the light, hide in darkness, sleep. He squeezed his foot into a new low boot and began getting ready to go down and face dinner.

•

The notice came before noon. It was not the one he had expected.

Delivered by an errand boy who, by the redness of his face and the cold wafting off his thin jacket, must have bicycled nonstop up from Benhall Mill Road. The note, dated today, 18 March, was addressed to *Acting Editor, Rusthall Gazette*:

> *Patient, Mr. A. Quaite, Rusthall, released from Isolation Hospital to family 0915 this date.*

Short enough to resemble a paragraph the little editor himself might have written, it left out details about his condition. Reading it over, it was unclear whether Mr. Quaite or just his body had been sent home in the care of his sister. Reg ran out to High Street, looked for the Sergeant's black sedan. He tried to chase down the errand boy, who already had his bicycle up to speed and pointed toward Royal Tunbridge Wells. Cold wind stinging his cheeks, Reg pulled up after half a block and marched back to the newspaper office.

Warm air leaked out of the Iron Monger's next door. Old Mr. Furston had left his front door ajar again. Reg stepped in, found the big man in his back bay, working something in his smelter. "Could I ask a favor?"

With forearms so thick it looked as though he had no wrists, the slump-shouldered giant set down his tongs, pulled off his heavy gloves and squinted. He walked to a small roll top desk in a far corner. The cubbyholes of that desk were jam-packed with slips of paper, some so old they had begun to turn brown. He glanced at a copy of *The Gazette* spread open on the desk, tapped the page. "This'd be you. William's boy?"

"Reg," he said. "I need to get to hospital."

"Feeling poorly?"

"To check on Mr. Quaite."

His head, wild with scraggly hair that might not have been washed in a fortnight, began to nod. "Wondered why Andy hadn't come in lately." He smiled. "Brings me tea."

"He was down in Isolation Hospital," Reg said. "Could you drive me?"

A wide hand scattered loose papers on the desk, found a key, tossed it to Reg. "Out back. You can drive a lorry, I trust."

"Yes, sir."

"Crank her first," the iron monger said. "Stubborn in this weather." He leaned a shoulder against one of the heavy doors to the rear platform. The cold raced in.

"Very warm in here," Reg said.

Another nod of that large head. "You get used to it."

"I'll return it straightaway." Reg stopped halfway through the door. "Forgot. I have to lock up *The Gazette* office."

He squeezed past the big man. That apron smelled of burnt leather.

"Made him custom door handles and hinges." Mr. Furston dragged the door shut. "Took a year to pay me. That would be near twenty years back." He let out a soft laugh. "Said the tea and conversation were for the interest I never charged him." He pulled his gloves back on. A moment later, he had the black tongs up and aimed at the smelter: "Mind you leave it where you found it."

•

The nurse in the side office pushed the notice back. "And what would be your confusion?"

"Is he still alive?"

She cocked her head. "We release living patients to their families. The dead go to the coroner." She ripped the notice from his fingers, jabbed at the typewritten sentence – "Released to his family" – and shoved the paper back into his hand.

243

"Was it his sister?" Reg said.

"We do not discuss our patients." She narrowed her stare, inched closer. "How did you come by that notice?"

"You sent it to my office. I edit *The Rusthall Gazette* — until he returns to work."

She stepped to her door. "Then you would know where to find him. Good day."

Walking out into the drizzle, he started laughing. Going from one cranky old biddy to another. The rusting, smelly lorry felt like the safer choice.

And Mr. Quaite was alive.

13

The small square house had been built for a gatekeeper more than 200 years ago, back when a Norman manor house dominated the parcel near Ashley Park. The fence and gate were both long gone. Up a wide road that had once been a narrow carriage trail, the big house had been replaced by three Victorians, one painted lemon yellow and each decorated with ornate accents. "The Ugly Sisters," Mr. Quaite called them when forced to look at them as he walked home on Manor Road.

Reg parked the lorry near the front path. The black iron entry plate featured a sprawling spiral pattern that resembled a spider web. The big strap hinges had that same pattern set in their centers. The broad oak door looked like the entrance to a castle. He knocked.

The thickness of that door muffled the sound inside the house, so he stepped back in surprise when the latch clicked. A matronly woman, her hair graying, stood in the doorway. Her charcoal gray dress looked new. She had the little editor's same broad face. The redness around her eyes said she had been crying.

"I'm Reg," he said. "His – assistant."

"Oh, my, yes." Her smile faded: she had just glimpsed the old lorry near the front walk. For an instant, she looked ready to run away. She opened the door wide and threw her arms around him. "He'll be so glad to see you."

She felt bony and brittle. He was afraid to squeeze her back.

"Drew! Look who's come to visit!"

Drew?

Propped up by embroidered pillows on his big padded arm chair, his slippered feet on a low stool, Mr. Quaite looked worn out. He raised an arm as if considering trying to stand. Reg rushed to him, took his hand, made certain he stayed seated. A prisoner of that chair now, the little editor didn't struggle.

"No uniform?" He fingered the wet canvas of the field coat. "Like Kip's."

Even his voice sounded tired. Pulling up a side chair, Reg saw close up how much weight his mentor had lost. "He paid for it," Reg told him. "All of it."

That balding head nodded. "Generous to a fault."

"He wants you to recuperate at Bateman's."

"Oh, my." His sister carried a tea service to the table. "Wouldn't that be grand."

Mr. Quaite waved the thought away. "Finally home and you want to ship me off."

She smiled. "I was hoping to accompany you."

He gripped Reg's forearm – "You'll tell me about it. In fine detail." – then glanced at her backside. "Did I tell you he went broke on his honeymoon? Bank failure. Had to start over again."

"Oh, my. How awful for his bride." She stepped to the chair, fluffed the pillows. One of them had an antlered deer embroidered on it. "I've read your war dispatches. My, what terror you endured. Our Drew was filled with worry." She laid a soft hand on Reg's shoulder. "You're the son he never had."

"Andrea, don't embarrass the lad." He squinted at Reg. "A byline?"

Clearing his throat, fidgeting in the chair, Reg stared at the plank floor. "He's up from *The Observer*. And I didn't want people to think I was writing about myself."

A gurgled laugh crept out of the little man like a slow bug. "Well done."

Those loose fingers managed another wave, this one aimed at his sister. "My case, please." He waited for her to walk into the bedroom. "Page three, your first issue. Misspelling of accommodate: double *c*, double *m*."

She set the leather case beside the big chair, then stepped toward the kitchen where a kettle had begun to whistle. Mr. Quaite reached for the case, but didn't have the strength to shift his weight. Reg picked it up. A short arm stopped him. "Review it later. Page three. Make a note so as not to repeat it." Studying Reg, he allowed himself a small grin. "Thank you."

"I thought the linotype composer would blow up on me," Reg said. "And the Wharfedale. What a brute."

"We should get combat wages." His laugh made him cough. "This Theodore – how much help did he need?"

"None, really," Reg told him. "Teddy knows his way around the machines as well."

"Excellent. You'll need an assistant. For a while." He used both arms to push himself back against the pillows. "Now, tell me about Bateman's. Omit nothing."

"Let the dear boy have his tea, Drew."

"He's been in trenches." He winked. "I'd wager he can manage tea and descriptive conversation simultaneously." The old Mr. Quaite was still in there. He narrowed his gaze. "No detail too small now."

•

After the first hour, it began to feel as though he was reading a bedtime story to a sick child. Eyelids fluttered. The little editor would nod off, then snap awake. About the time Reg got to the part about the deaf cowman, Mr. Quaite had fallen asleep.

Brushing crumbs off the invalid's chest, his sister covered him with a red and black crocheted throw with fringe on all edges, something her brother would have never allowed anywhere near him. She put a finger to her lips, gestured for Reg to follow her to the entry foyer. Rain pelted the roof. It sounded like hail.

"You've done him a world of good," she said.

"He's lucky to have you to look after him."

"Such a dear." She touched his cheek, then drew him to the door. "Be certain this is the life you want. This village, *The Gazette*. Don't do it for him."

Stunned, he searched for a polite way to tell her she was completely batty.

"He worries about that," she said. "He has for a number of years."

Those skinny fingers gripped his arm with vice-like strength. "Be like Mr. Kipling. Out in the world." She glanced over a shoulder toward the sleeping bundle in the big chair. "He would have if he could."

"Why didn't he then?"

"Broken heart. His – the love of his life. . ." She stared at the black strap hinges, her eyes were getting wet. "It wasn't possible. Not in Lewisham." She blinked. "All the rest was pure stubbornness." A weak smile betrayed her pain. "You must have asked yourself why he never married. So smart. So kind."

He put a hand against the cold oak, bracing himself. He tried to swallow.

"You're a lot like him," she said. "Have you a girlfriend?"

He nodded, then shook his head. "Engaged. Was."

"Well, you take your time," she told him. "You'll know when the right one appears. I did. The day I met my husband, rest his soul, I nearly fainted."

She hugged him and held on. For a moment, he imagined his arms were around Gabby and the rain was hitting the slate roof at her sister's house.

247

Opening the door, she peered at the lorry and the water running off its loading bed. "Is that banger safe?"

"If it starts." He turned up the collar of his coat, prepared to race to the truck. "If not, it's not far to walk."

He bent, kissed her cheek, then ran into the rain.

•

The notice on the desk at *The Gazette* office had been placed perfectly centered on the blotter and propped up by the squirrel paperweight. He reached for it.

The pounding on the rear door stopped him. He hurried into the back bay, struggled to open one of the big doors that the rain had swollen tight to the jamb.

"Heard you arrive." Mr. Funston didn't seem to notice the rain. He looked as though he enjoyed it. "She didn't disappoint?"

Reg dug the key out of a pocket. "Come in, please."

"Wet." A big hand took the key. "He's well, then?"

"Tired, but on the mend."

That giant head nodded – "Night to you then" – and started toward the open doors to his shop.

"I saw your work. The hinges and door plate?"

Another nod. "East Sussex iron. Best that ever were." He stopped in his doorway, smelled the fresh rain, smiled. "Last a hundred lifetimes."

"It's beautiful," Reg told him.

"Might be I should've charged him more, then." His shadow played on the wall near the smelter. Then the sound of a chair creaking. Then nothing – only rain attacking the old lorry, splashing out of the building's downspouts.

That rain felt warmer now. Spring might actually be coming on.

"Shut it, will you?"

Teddy had pulled the blanket over his head. His stocking feet hung over the edge of the cot.

"Sorry. Forgot about. . ." Reg dragged the door shut, latched it. "Night."

"Letter for you. On desk." He pulled his knees up. "No heat back here. How does he stand it?"

Another question Reg would never be able to answer. He walked back to the hat rack in the front office, took off his field coat, dried his hands on his shirt. In Mr. Quaite's chair, he stared at the envelope on the desk – a new one from *B-Matthews, KG, OBE* – and waited for his body to stop shaking.

248

•

The Sergeant brought a date. Two of them. The night nurse – Ruth, from Lamberhurst Down, who wore her white uniform because she would not have time to change for her shift later on – and Bridgette, dressed in tweed and a collared green blouse that matched her eyes.

"Celebration requires company," Sgt. Dickson said. "The ginger one volunteered to be yours."

Then he introduced both women to the paperboys. Most of them held plates of treats, courtesy of advertisers, a few of whom were standing together by the far wall.

"Where's Lamberhurst?" the smallest boy said.

"Southeast of Bell's Yew Green," Ruth told him. "And Lamberhurst Down is below that."

Those dark eyes narrowed, an eyebrow arched in suspicion. "Not having us on, are you?"

She laughed and stopped the Sergeant before he could swat the boy, who was now focused on the ginger nurse. Reg led her to the composing table that functioned as the bar in the back bay. "Short glass for the Sergeant and Ruth," he said, handing them to her. "Come back for yours."

Smiling, she passed Teddy in the open door way to the front room. "Who's that?" he said.

"Bridgette," Reg told him. "Nurse at Calverley Lodge VAD."

Smoothing down his hair, the copy editor from Hastings picked up a pint in each hand and went looking for the red head.

"My dad lets me have ale." The small paperboy studied the glasses on the table. "Just a taste?"

Reg shook his head.

"The ginger bird," the boy said. "She yours?"

"How old are you?"

"I'll be service age – in five years."

"So, you're thirteen," Reg said. Taking the boy's nod, he put an arm on his shoulder. "And you drink ale." Another nod, more forceful than the first. "And you like older women."

"Who doesn't?" the boy said.

He turned the boy toward the front room, squared up his shoulders and gave him a gentle shove. "Go get her, sport."

The boy lost his confident step when he saw the Sergeant blocking his path. He squeezed by the big man, who was holding up two pieces of paper. "Time for the official announcements," he said.

Reg followed him, stopping by the desk, now a serving table for sweets and nuts − bits and bats, the boys called them. The room got quiet. The Sergeant opened a letter:

"This concerns the owner and editor of this newspaper, Mr. Andrew J. Quaite. We are happy to announce his release from hospital."

As soon as the applause died down, he held up a broad hand. "Recovering at his home," Sgt. Dickson said. "Expected to return to us shortly."

He waved the other letter during this round of hand clapping. "And here we have the news of the day. Of the year!" He glanced at Reg. "Corporal Olcutt, front and center."

"The notice says I'm no longer in the Army, Sergeant."

"Now you've ruined my speech!" Slapping his leg with the hand holding the notice, the Sergeant drained his short glass. "Corporal − er, Mister Olcutt − has been discharged from the 11th Battalion, The Queen's Own Royal West Kent Regiment, British Army. All formerly pending matters now concluded."

Amid a failed attempt at Hip-Hip-Hooray, the small paperboy, left Bridgette, took steps toward Reg. "What's it mean?"

"No court martial," Reg told him.

"No court martial!" The Sergeant's loudest voice shot through the crowd. "Our own Reg, twice decorated and gazetted, returned to us − with honor!"

The applause sounded even louder than the Sergeant. Reg held up both hands, but the old stone mason was waving another piece of paper now − smaller and gray. "This telegram," he said, "marries the two causes we celebrate tonight."

"Marries?" The small paper boy nudged Teddy out of the way and looked up at Bridgette. "Daft as a duck."

This time, the Sergeant was able to reach the boy, slapping the telegram against that head of dark hair. Straightening his tunic, he held the telegram out to Reg. "If you would read it to us."

Reg shook his head. "Teddy wrote the story. Let him read it."

With a shrug, Sgt. Dickson gave the telegram to the copy editor.

"Congratulations," Teddy said, reading the type. "Bring A.Q. to Bateman's when able to travel. Return from France next month. Then London, you and I, for talks with publisher. Celebrate. Kip."

Those big hands led the applause. "That'd be Mister Rudyard Kipling himself." He smiled at Ruth from Lamberhurst Down. "Likes us to call him Kip, he does."

"Would you like to see it?" Teddy said, offering the telegram to Bridgette. "He won the Nobel Prize."

The little paperboy snatched the small gray square of paper and led the ginger nurse toward the front window. "We can read it together," he said.

Staring at the meat pie Reg handed him, Teddy let out a long breath. "I think she smiled at me," he said.

He didn't want to tell him that she smiled at everyone. Smiling was part of her job. Putting people at ease, especially those who had seen the worst of it, was what she had been trained to do.

"Wouldn't surprise me," Reg told him, "if she fancied you."

Fumbling the pie, the copy editor stood taller. "I should talk to her then?"

"I would, were I you." Reg took back the pie. "No time like the present."

He watched Teddy walk toward her. Smiling, Reg took the pie and a pint outside. The air along High Street felt warm enough to walk in for the first time this year. He stepped through the open door to the iron monger's, found Mr. Funston dozing in a chair at the roll top desk. Setting the pie and the ale on the seat of the iron chair against the wall, Reg notice a spiral pattern in the chair back similar to the ones at Mr. Quaite's. This design had snakes intertwining to form the back rest.

It wouldn't be long before the little editor could share tea back here again. Reg could see him sitting in that chair. It made him smile.

The voices leaking out of *The Gazette* office sounded like those he had listened to as a boy on the steps outside Trinity Theater, where his father had left him for hours on nights he and Walter delivered crops to fancy hotel restaurants. The farmer always returned, always with whiskey on his breath and complaints about the poor price he had received. Tonight, for the first time, High Street sounded happy.

He shut his eyes, breathed the sound in.

The faint tang of the Piave startled him. It had to be coming off that old smelter. Or the sweat soaked apron and work clothes the iron monger wore. He wondered what the flood plain looked like now, after a new ice melt. He wondered if she still walked down to the river, if that ever reminded her of him, if she saw him when she closed her eyes.

"I 'd fire him." The little paperboy had sidled up to the low curb. "When it comes to women, that Teddy's an utter fool." He blew a smoke ring from a cigar stub he must have found on the street.

"Doesn't play football either. Did you realize that when you put him on staff?"

"I didn't put him on," Reg said. "He was given to us."

Those big dark eyes hardened. "Let's give him back."

He felt the laugh start in his gut. It tasted treacle sweet.

14

She wore dark khaki. Her tunic had large front pockets, closed with flaps, and a diamond-shaped pin insignia on her left lapel. The wide belt did little to alter the straight line of her uniform, all the way down to her ankle-length skirt and the mud guards covering the front of her shoes. "I need to know your intentions," she said, "about returning here."

For a moment, he was afraid she might strike him with her swagger stick or pull off one of her dark leather gauntleted gloves and swat him across the face. He thought about running out the kitchen door and hiding in the barn, the way he did when he was 11 years old. "I'm only here for dinner," he told her.

"About reassuming your role here." Her hat, worn at a jaunty angle with the front brim snapped down, hid piled-up dark hair. She looked familiar. "Well?"

Verna was watching from the door to his room — her room now. His father leaned forward in his chair, straining to hear better. His mother stopped seasoning whatever was in the small pot.

Studying the three diamonds running across the woman's tunic above the small left breast pocket, the Sergeant removed his cap. "Captain?"

"Commandant," she said.

"Mrs. Silcock runs the Women's Land Army here," Verna told him. "And the Volunteer Reserve."

"Mayor's wife," his father said. "Good man."

"Thank you, Mister Olcutt," she said. "I'll relay your sentiments. But James has been out of office for six years now." She inched closer to Reg, looking over his field jacket and boots. "You don't strike me as a man of agriculture."

"He's not." His father was up now, standing next to Verna, pulling her out of the doorway. "This one is."

That small gloved hand offered a sheaf of papers. "Notices and forms. Read and fill out. Make your decision by Friday next." She started toward the front door, the one no one ever used, then stopped and turned. "I'm happy for your safe return to us, Corporal."

The grunt came from his father. "Should be my decision," he said, watching her march outside to a waiting car. Then he shut the door and sat in his chair, stared at the far wall. "I can pay, Verna. Part-time, but real pay."

"They're to reassign me, sir. It's the law." She glanced at Reg. "Unless your son is – unavailable."

The forms and notices of the Women's Land Army were more complicated than those of his regiment. That's didn't seem possible. He took them to the kitchen table, began reading.

"My right hand, she is," his father was saying. "Never sick a day."

The Sergeant held up a proof of the latest issue of *The Gazette* so Reg's mother could see it while she cooked. "Complete account of his being exonerated. There's talk of a parade. Present the lad his medals at long last."

"Would have to wait 'til after Easter." His mother tasted the broth, added salt. "Comes a bit late this year."

"Might want to wait for after May Day then," Sgt. Dickson said. "Better weather."

"An expert on our weather now, are you?" His father's voice flew in like a wild bird. "The boy's not worked a day here since he enlisted. And before that, well, I wouldn't call what he did working."

The Sergeant's broad hand tightened into a fist. He shut his eyes, exhaled, relaxed his fingers. "Your Reg is presently the editor of *The Rusthall Gazette*. Until Andy – Mr. Quaite – returns."

"How is he?" his mother said. "Better?"

There was a section on the WLA forms dealing with pregnancy.

"He needs rest," Reg told her.

"Won't have that man in my house," his father said.

The Sergeant leaned in close Reg's mother, got a whiff of the aromas from the pots. "Invited down to Bateman's, Andy is. With your son. Personal guests of Mr. Kipling."

She wanted to say something, but knew better than to voice it. She smiled by pursing her lips.

"I liked what you wrote." Verna stood next to him. "About me – um, Elizabeth."

"And how are things in Mayfield?" Reg said.

Grinning, she put a hand on the table, bent close to his ear. "I want to stay on. Please. Going back home would be – difficult."

Mrs. Silcock was one of those women at the head of parade on Polling Day. In the blur of the rain that day, he had mistaken her and the others for police officers.

"Put ideas in her head." At the doorway to the kitchen, his father pulled his trousers up by the braces. "Fancy words. And we all know what that leads to."

"I like farming." Verna straightened up. "It's like gardening on a grand scale. And you're outside, where you can move about."

"The government will stop paying you – him," Reg said. "You'd be working for room and board."

"Said I'd pay her." His father moved into the kitchen, then inched back when the Sergeant took a step to block him. "Out of my own pocket. Part-time wages, I said."

"That would be fine," Verna said, "for now."

"He moves back, where do we put you?" his father said. "Barn, I suppose."

Reg checked a box on the form. "And a share of the proceeds."

"Don't follow," his father said.

"Room, board, wages and a share of the profits." He glanced at Verna. "Sound fair?"

She looked too surprised to swallow.

"And you'll be where?" his father said.

"In town," Reg told him.

"And take your meals – where?"

Reg signed the form. "You'll have only one mouth to feed."

His mother's head had drooped. She had stopped stirring the pot. She dabbed her face with her apron. "Madge dropped by," she said, keeping her back to the table. "Said you promised to take her to the Pantiles on your return."

He didn't know how to tell her about the baker's son. He folded the form, handed it to Verna. "See that your Commandant gets this."

"Making the proper choice." Sgt. Dickson set a heavy hand on Reg's shoulder. "It's your own life you have to live."

"Coming to Sunday dinner," his mother said. "I think the girl has come to her senses." She turned toward him, a soft smile on her lips. "Bakers keep the worst hours. Nearly as bad as farmers."

His father looked up from the forms he had pretended to be reading without his spectacles. "Kept a roof over your head."

"You knew?" Reg said.

That tight-lipped smile grew. She turned back to the cooker. "You'll find a room in Rusthall?"

"I'll speak to our clients myself," Sgt. Dickson said. "Very high on your son, they are." He stepped toward the cooker. "Give you hand with anything, Missus?"

"Serving shortly." She shook her head, let out a quick laugh. "Never in my life have I seen a man with your appetite."

"No one has," Reg told her.

His father's short grunt wasn't as loud as it usually would have been. He must have been pleased. Carefully, he re-folded the form and gave it back to Verna. "You'll see Mrs. Silcock gets this tomorrow. First thing."

"I thought we were going out to test for thawing?" she said.

"Can wait 'til midday." He lumbered back into the front room. The sound he made sitting in his chair was the same one he used to make after a holiday dinner: a satisfied plop, all the pent-up air running out of him. "Best settle that straight off. Before there's any change of mind."

Reg studied his mother's broad back as she craned from pot to pot, stirring, tasting, adjusting the seasoning. The window near the cooker had been blurred by a winter of hard weather. Through it, a half moon was rising over the tree line. He could have been 11 years old again, in the same chair – his chair, at the same table, breathing in the same smells.

Only his dreams had changed.

•

The Frasier barn needed paint. Even in the dark, he could see that. The inside needed tidying up. Rats had nested in a feed bin. And Walter's stall needed mucking out. He found a shovel against a wall, moved the wheel barrow into place and set to work.

The old horse paid no attention. Breath gurgled as it escaped its nostrils. It needed a good head wash. But its hooves looked fine. No splitting, no fungus. Except for fly bites, his hide looked to be in good shape. Mr. Frasier must have currycombed him this week. The dark chestnut short hair still had little rivers in where the comb had been pulled through. The cream-colored mane was a different story: a tangle of loose hay, dead insects, dirt knots.

He wheeled the manure outside, cleaned off his boots and hands with water from the pump. A squirrel or field mouse had left acorns in the pail inside the barn door. He took the water back to Walter, used a torn part of the harness pad to wet down that big head, scrub crust from the nostrils. If the horse remembered him, it didn't show it. It stood there, accepting the attention the same way it had always accepted the whip.

"It was me," Reg said. "Nearly killed you." The football he used to kicked around in the barn all those years ago, after being told repeatedly not to, must have knocked over an oil lamp. The hay had gone up in flames when his father tapped out his pipe, burning his own arm and leg as he led Walter outside. Reg used his fingers to untangle the mane. "Never thought you'd run back to your stall."

His mother had blamed the fire on vagrants and his father was only too happy to accept that, happy enough to take his rifle on a hunt for the culprits. In reality, that weeklong trip had been an excuse to test pubs as far away as Chiddingstone Hoath and Coleman's Hatch.

"I've been a poor son," he told the horse. "Not much better as a friend. Certainly not to you."

Held at an angle, the curry comb got through the top of the mane. He wet the tangles to allow his fingers to go deeper.

"The war spared you," he said. "He'd never have bought the tractor if not for the new crops on those government contracts. You'd still be pulling that plow until one of you dropped."

He could finally get the comb through all the hair in the mane. It looked stringy, but when it dried, it would fluff up again. He fed the horse a small mealy apple and two carrots taken from his mother's root cellar. Walter chewed them slowly, those yellowed teeth dulled by age.

"You're the one I'll miss." Reg nuzzled that sharp-boned head, listened to the clean breaths the big horse was taking now. The sound made him smile. "As terrible as it was, I think the war might have saved us both."

•

She had a dustpan in her hand, looking for a place to dump it out. She found one near the edge of a low bush, covered in burlap. "I can't get the rear door open."

He stepped inside, went straight through the kitchen to the boot locker and the back entrance. The old wood had blistered and swollen from too many winters without paint. No East Sussex iron hinges or door plates here. "We'd need a chisel. Or a pry bar."

"I don't suppose he has either of those." She put the broom and the dust pan in the closet. "He's resting now."

The standing clock in the hall read 10:15. Its walnut case made it stand out against the cream-colored walls.

"Breakfast was always his favorite meal," his sister said. "Such an early riser, even as a boy. So much energy." She dried her hands with a tan dish towel. "He'll get that back, won't he?"

Reg shifted the satchel to his other hand. "Could I look in on him?"

257

"Don't wake him. He's much improved. He even thought of coming down to the office later this week."

He carried her hope through the living room and down the short hall to the open bedroom door. On his back, his blue pajamas made the small man look like all those soldiers in hospitals. His chest rose and fell with long breaths. Someone had combed what was left of his hair. His eyelids fluttered, then stopped. The gray suit he wore to the office had been laid out on a chair near the closet. His sister must have chosen the red and blue striped tie. Probably a gift from her some Christmas or birthday ago, something that had been hanging in that closet untouched for years.

From a deep coat pocket, Reg drew the note he had penned last night in *The Gazette* office, at the editor's desk, in the editor's chair. Writing it, he had imagined watching Mr. Quaite read words Reg knew he could not say out loud without tearing up:

Monday, March 31, 1919

Dear Mr. Quaite,

I knew before I enlisted, and I know now even more so, that I could not repay your kindnesses to me should I live to 90. It troubles my heart to be leaving you and The Gazette at a time when you both might need me most. I would not fault you for seeing me as a deserter after all. I can only hope your disappointment in me will not be so great that you forget it is your example I am following – yours and Mr. Kipling's – to find a life that renews me each day.

The Gazette will be overseen by Teddy until your return. He will make a better assistant than I could ever have hoped to be.

I am leaving the clippings and letters in the satchel for you. Re-examining those experiences is not something I can face at present. May I suggest that you undertake writing the story, under the same guidance Mr. Kipling has promised me? I hope that the publisher will reward you for it. My true hope is that the writing will keep me in your present a bit longer.

With gratitude, admiration and love,

Reg – the son you always had.

He leaned the envelope against the small brass lamp on the nightstand and backed out of the room. He set the satchel beside the big chair, where Mr. Quaite would be certain to see it, then started for the front door.

"I put the kettle on." She had replaced her smock with an apron. "Could you stay for lunch? He'll be up and about by then."

"He can return the satchel to Mr. Kipling when he visits Bateman's," Reg said. "You must go with him."

"I'm not invited."

"Of course you are," he told her. "And kiss him for me?"

"Who? Drew? Or Mr. Kipling?"

He let out a small laugh. "Both."

"Oh, my. That moustache."

Another quiet laugh. He stepped to her, kissed her cheek. Before she could ask him to stay longer, he yanked the front door open, its heavy oak swinging smoothly on those strong hinges, and walked down the front path to Manor Road, forcing himself not to turn back for a last look.

•

He wrote down the address, handed it to Teddy. "Check on him every morning. His sister's name is Andrea." He watched the copy editor scratch his head. "Keep him updated. Follow his instructions."

"I don't quite understand," Teddy said.

"Give notice at *The Observer*," Reg told him. "You're Acting Editor here now."

"What about you?"

"I'm − on assignment." Reg sat at the desk, pulled out a fresh piece of note paper. "Get out to that interview at Pratt's Dairy."

"They're expecting you."

"Test the milk," Reg told him. "Certify they're not watering it. Tell them, this will make their customers trust them. More revenue. That sort of thing."

Pulling on his overcoat, Teddy opened the door to High Street. "We'll discuss this in full when I get back."

"You'll be brilliant." Reg leaned back in the chair. "Now go."

The door slapped shut. How many times had Mr. Quaite sat here and heard that sound? Picking up the pen, he began writing:

Monday, March 31, 1919

Rusthall

Dear Mr. Kipling,

I hope this finds you, Mrs. Kipling and all at Bateman's well. I regret that I will not be able to see you before leaving. Your generosity and encouragement have meant the world to me, but as I explained to Mr. Quaite, I find myself unable to delve back into my experiences at the front for fear of reliving them. I hope you will agree to assist Mr. Quaite with the writing of a book he is far better suited to pen than I am.

259

You have been instrumental in giving me back my life. I have come to the realization that living that life, as you did at my age traveling through India and elsewhere, is my only true option. I know you will understand.

Sincerely yours, Reg Olcutt

He blotted the ink, folded the note, slipped it into an envelope addressed to *Mr. J. Rudyard Kipling, Bateman's, Burwash, East Sussex.* Five orange one-pence stamps sat in the top drawer. He separated one, affixed it to the envelope, the profile of King George V facing Mr. Kipling's name. He left the note in the late post bin for pick up before supper.

The Spring breeze rolling up High Street made men hold their hats in place as they passed by the office window. A good day for kites. He started grinning before he reached the door.

•

The game trail had lost all its snow, but the thaw had yet to turn it into mud. Things unseen scattered in the scrub brush as he made his way through Denny Bottom, feeling the tumbling slope of the land in his feet, leaning back against the hill to hold his balance. Racing down this valley, he had careened into trees and bushes too many times to count, getting scolded by his mother for soiling his clothes, slapped by his father for ripping a shirt or muddying a good pair of shoes.

He stayed in the trees along Rusthall Road, then crossed Langton Road into the Common, keeping under the rise of Mt. Ephraim all the way to the Lower Common and Crescent Road in Royal Tunbridge Wells. The entry hall of Calverley Lodge stood empty. The Sergeant was not in the dining area or in the kitchen. Reg took an early dinner in the corner where the cooks ate. Ham with apples and red potatoes today.

His laundered uniform had been laid out on his cot. He folded it, placed it back in the laundry bag, boots and all. He pulled the string, closing the sack. *The Jungle Books* and *The Day's Work* went on the bottom of the smooth leather valise from Chalkin's, meant to serve on his visits to Bateman's. The extra shirts, trousers, underwear and socks piled in next. With the hand towel by the water pitcher, he cleaned his new boots. Then he recounted his paper money − £92, all from *The Gazette* − and the 8s and a 6d Tanner in pocket coins.

With a glance at the darkening sky through the cracked window, he carried the laundry bag and valise down the back stairs in search of Sergeant Dickson.

●

The night nurse Ruth walked in smiling. "We were just discussing you."

"Is he outside?" Reg said.

"At home." She took off her cloak, hung it on a wall peg. "He'll be dozing – big meal, roasted lamb – but happy for a visit."

"He never showed me which house on Varney Street is his."

"Varney Street?" She squinted. "He's one block up, on Basinghall Lane." The look on his face must have flustered her. "Near the end, at the rubble by Victoria Road?"

He tightened his grip on the laundry bag, angry at the stone mason for misleading him. He plopped the bag on the high desk – "Give him this" – and turned to leave. He stopped after the third step. "May I have pen and paper?"

She pulled the laundry bag off the desk, set out a blank sheet of paper and a pencil. While she opened the sack and examined its contents, he scribbled a note:

Dear Sgt. Dickson,

Please see that a soldier in need gets my uniform. Look after Mr. Quaite and pay visits to my mother as well. You are still The Gazette Paymaster.

Sincerely, Reg

He handed her the note. "Leave that in the bag for him, please."

Frowning, she opened the note. Her free hand grabbed the edge of the desk to hold her steady. "You should go to him. If this is all he receives – "

"I told you I've no idea where he lives."

"He's not proud of his circumstances," she told him. "I had to follow him home and barge through the door or he'd never have shown me the inside." She slid the note back toward him. "Don't leave him with only this. It will break his heart."

He could see the wetness in her eyes. He opened the note, added a postscript:

P.S.: Ask Ruth and she will say yes.

He handed it to her. Reading, she nodded, tears starting down her cheeks. From around his neck, he freed the leather strand holding his ID disc. He set it on the desk, picked up the valise and hurried outside before she could catch up to him.

•

The bellboy at the Lenton knew exactly where to find his boss – in a makeshift office, hollowed out in the luggage room off the lobby. Mr. Yorke shot to his feet as soon as he saw the well-dressed intruder, mistaking him for a hotel guest. "At your service, sir!"

Reg held out his hand. "I was with Barry when he died."

The slender fingers went lifeless. Mr. Yorke fell back into his chair. How many years had he spent back here, stuffed in among other people's wardrobes, breathing in their perfume and cologne? It felt like a good place to hide – his own trench, just this side of a no man's land of leather bags.

"He was shot," Reg said. "Our Captain as well. Carried down river."

"February." Barry's father removed his reading glasses, pinched the bridge of his nose. "The nineteenth, they said."

"He was dead before he fell," Reg told him. A lie. "He felt no pain."

"A Tuesday." His voice was just a whisper now. "We had it circled on our event calendar. A special dinner party for Miss Sarah Grand. Such finery that night." He searched Reg's face for some answer he knew he would never get. "I couldn't wait to tell the boy about it. To give him reason to keep going. Purpose."

"It could as easily have been me." Reg wanted to pick him up and give him something – someone – to hold on to. "Our best marksman. Our best man. The finest pal I ever had."

"Lady Emson arriving!" The bell boy smoothed his tunic. "Six bags."

Nodding, Mr. Yorke stood, straightened his tie, offered his hand. "Good of you to come by."

"Reg," he said, feeling a stronger return grip now. "Olcutt. Corporal. Queen's Own 11th."

The expression on that gaunt face must have been his professional one. Not quite a smile, there was no feeling in it. He turned sideways to escape his cubicle, then walked out to the lobby.

"Don't let the manager find you back here," the bell man said. "Sack the lot of us."

Lady Emson had difficulty walking. Her girth dwarfed Barry's father, who struggled to keep her steady. They looked like two drunkards dancing, an odd couple of lovers stumbling toward the terrace overlooking the garden.

Outside, the bell boy carried armfuls of matching white luggage under the careful gaze of the chauffeur, who looked as though he disapproved of his employer's choice of lodging. He tipped his cap when Reg walked by.

On a different night, under a smaller moon, Reg might have knocked that cap off and flung it into the trees. He quickened his pace, forcing him to silence the coins in his pocket.

·

He was certain he needed to travel south, to Hastings, then east.

The Station Master frowned, one his silver-colored eyebrows raised in contempt. "Nearly caused me to spoil a ticket." He readied his pen again. "You're to change in Tonbridge, take the straight-line east from there."

"That's north," Reg said.

"You don't say." Checking a timetable at his elbow, he jotted a number on a new line of the ticket. "Change at Ashford, south to Dover."

"The straight-line?"

"Straight as your nose." More numbers on more lines. "Through Paddock Wood, Marden, Headcorn. Best track in all of Kent."

The ticket felt warm from those cigarette stained fingers. Reg took it and his change to a slat bench at trackside. Someone had left a half-eaten sandwich under the bench. It smelled of mustard and relish. Opening the tin Sgt. Jeffs had given him, he breathed in the aroma of strawberries, dug in with his fingers, savoring the sugared fruit.

If Tickler's strawberry jam truly existed, then anything might be possible.

There would be maps all along the way, he decided. And someone would speak English. With more money than he imagined he would ever hold in a single billfold, he would find his way back to her and the river.

The northbound to Tonbridge would arrive by the time he had emptied the jam tin.

He didn't mind waiting.

BOOK FIVE

THE OLD MAN
AT HIS RIVER

3 MAY, 1919

1

Daisies. Fields of them.

He couldn't look at them without seeing Barry playing that idiotic game, tearing off one petal at a time and changing the rhyme from *She loves me, she loves me not* to *She loves me, she loves me lots*. The image stuck in his head night and day now, from that first night on the ferry to Dunkirk and the short train ride back to La Panne, where the new tenant had said Mrs. Lawson had dropped dead in her parlor chair and her collie Rufus had been so protective of her body, the dog had to be destroyed.

He saw flowers blooming from the train south of Brussels and Mons, Ghent and Maubeuge, red ones in rutted pastures that might have been recent battlefields, in villages and cities down to Sedan, and yellow ones along the Meuse, through Haute-Marne to Dijon, off the banks of the Saone and down to Lyon. The more stops he had to make, the more trains he had to wait for, the more odd jobs he had to find to make his money last, flowers tinged a landscape he remembered as filth and mud.

In tunnels, like the short one near the bed of the L'Arc and the long one out of Saint-Antoine into Italy, he welcomed the rock walls where nothing grew. By the time he crossed the Po past Asti, only £11 remained in his pocket and he couldn't risk stopping in Milan to search out Ezio. The closer he got to the end of the line – Brescia, Lake Garda, Verona – the stronger the images of Barry's fortune-telling game became, the louder his ghost voice grew, twisting now into a maniac's chant. Reg felt as though he was carrying his own insane asylum around in his head.

The track north from Treviso ended in Spresiano. Work on a bridge across the Piave had not begun. It took almost two hours to walk up to the river. Along the inland route up to Nervesa, gardens had been replanted, blackened trees had come back into leaf. The teenager at the boat steps just short of town said he could take Reg across the quiet river for 10 lire. The stubby bow of his small boat pointed at the floodplain on the other bank and the little house where Luigi lived. Up the river, a steady stream of smoke followed the water south.

"La distrutta." The skinny teen jabbed a thumb over his shoulder. "Come la mia casa."

Someone was burning the remains of the bombed-out house where he had found the painting of the horse. He took it as a good sign. He reached into a pocket for the bills he had exchanged in Milan. "Luigi," he said, pointing finger at his eye, then across the river to the little house. "Have you seen him?"

"DaPonte? Il vecchio?"

Reg nodded his head, began counting the Italian money.

The long fingers stopped him. "Non è necessario. Entra."

The boy might have missed being called up into uniform by a year or two. He might never know how lucky he had been. He waited for Reg to sit on the board spanning the broad bow, then shoved the boat into the water. A moment later he was rowing, his back to the opposite shore and his arms pulling on the oars. Stronger than he looked, he cut through the current. He whirled the boat around with three quick oar strokes, crouched and leapt off, yanking the craft onto the pebbled beach of the long island.

Helping Reg out, the teen glanced up the island. "Le rocce lì." His hand made a hump in the air. "Camminare su di loro."

The rocks he was pointing to were from the old bridge, settling downstream after the final shellings of Nervesa and the floodplain. The boy saw Reg digging into his pocket again, but he pivoted on a heel and shoved off the island, bounding onto his seat and working the oars, pulling for the other shore, pausing just long enough to nod his farewell.

The sight of that beat-up little boat making its way through the soft Spring current brought suprise tears to Reg's eyes. He turned to keep them hidden. Midway across the slippery stones, he couldn't stop the tears or the mewling cry leaking out of him.

Winter had undercut the high bank, turning it into an overhanging cliff. He had to walk downstream toward the southern tip of the island before finding a way up and out. The settling smoke stung his eyes and nostrils. It felt like being back at the front, only this time, he could simply walk out of it, valise in hand instead of a rifle, into clear fresh air and sunlight.

Patches of new grass, spongy when stepped on, dotted the plain to the little house. A new hasp and padlock held the old door shut. He started up the path toward Teresa's, then realized that the old man would probably be tending the fire up river. In the place Gabby's garden once stood, Reg found the pockmarked wheel hub that had served as a bird bath for her blue jay. Small green stalks grew out of it. He broke one off, breathed in the scent of licorice. Following the

268

gentle slope above the flood plain, he walked toward the smoke, his mind flooded by memories he didn't know he had – of approaches made on burning buildings in Flanders, where Germans hid or lay in wait.

Rather than scamper over the rock outcroppings blocking his way or risk the soggy ground below, he hiked around them, up to a path that ran down toward the bombed-out house. If anyone had used this trail recently, they had been on foot. No hoof prints, no manure. *Another good sign: cavalry officers owned horses.*

Through the smoke, he could make out someone moving a long pole, stirring the fire or moving new rubble into it. He quickened his pace, cupped a hand to his mouth: "Luigi!"

That long pole kept moving. The old man must have gone hard of hearing. He grinned at the prospect of a surprise attack.

She came out of the up-river edge of the smoke cloud, her hair tied back with a dark ribbon, making the free end flutter like the tail of a horse. Her dress was sky blue. New. And loose on her frame. She carried a plate of bread and cheese.

He dropped the valise. "Gabby!"

The plate slipped out of her fingers. Before it hit the ground she was moving toward him, her arms out.

He hurried down to her. Her arms felt heavy on him, her body wider than his. She kissed his cheeks, wiped away her tears and his. "Re-ja," she said, burying her face into his chest.

A tall man carried that long pole out of the smoke. Its tip was smoldering. "Che succede?"

"È lui." She turned toward the man, profiling her swollen stomach. "Re-ja! Qui!"

The man's glare disappeared. He gasped. Dropping the pole, he ran straight up the path. Unable to move, Reg readied himself to be tackled. Instead, strong arms scooped him up and twirled him in a fast circle, then planted him facing the river and kissed his cheeks. Through tears that ran through ash sticking to his sweat, the tall man squeezed Reg's shoulder: "La mano di Dio vi porta di nuovo a noi."

It wasn't the hand of God that had brought him back. It was a small newspaper and a smaller dream. He studied the two of them, both blond and blue-eyed. Their baby would be beautiful. It would look like them. In that moment, Barry's chant vanished, as if the smiling joker had been shot dead a second time.

Something turned in his gut. A foul taste rose in the back of his throat. He wanted to scream, but couldn't let the breath out of his

269

lungs. Sure he would pass out from the pressure building in his chest and brain, and already planning a route back to England, Reg held out his hand:

"Welcome home, Paolo. Piacere."

●

The table behind the house had been newly varnished. It glistened in spots where sunlight got through the leafy shade. From his chair near the well pump, he could make out a full garden on the far side of the house. In addition to good looks and an athlete's build, Paolo also had a green thumb. The ex-cavalry officer kissed his wife's belly when she set a plate of sliced tomatoes in front of him.

Next to him, Nicoletta wore his field jacket. She rubbed the dark suede, then the light canvas, over and over. Sancia had moved her stool to his other hip. Wanting cream puffs, she saw only bread and jam. "Nessun bignè," she said, pouting.

"I'll get some for us in town," he told her.

Luigi nodded, but he wasn't smiling. "È colpa mia. Perdonarmi?"

"They would have found me sooner or later." Reg squeezed the old man's hand. "It's not you fault."

"La sua bocca fa il guaio." Teresa slid a plate of cheese just out of her uncle's reach. "Sempre."

She blamed Luigi's big mouth for bringing the British soldiers to the house. Maybe everyone did. Even Luigi. Especially Luigi.

"He thinks you die." Paolo cocked a finger and made the sound of a gun firing. "But here! You sit!"

"Non ho fame." A thick hand patted Reg's shoulder. "Scusa."

Watching the old man walk away, Paolo tapped his temple with his knuckles. "Senile."

Luigi didn't seem senile, just sad.

At her husband's side, Gabby turned her chair just enough to avoid looking at Reg. She held a hand to her face, hiding her unwashed hair.

"Scarpe nuove." Teresa sat next to her oldest daughter. "Caro, no?"

"Very expensive," he said. "But I didn't pay for the boots." He took the wine she poured. It glinted like bubbling golden water. "They took Carmine's slippers. Mi dispiace."

Her shrug told him she understood enough. "Benvenuto a casa."

"Il nostro eroe." Paolo has his wine glass raised above his head. "Ti saluto."

It was the same wine from the feast in the village. He tried to smile, but knew he had made a mistake coming all this way. And now he didn't have enough money left to escape. By quick calculations, he estimated he wouldn't get past Verona before he'd have to find work. "I might never get back," he said.

"Che?" Teresa offered the plate she had made for him: tomatoes, soft and hard cheese, bread. "Va bene?"

"Molto bene," he said. "Grazie."

That simple word made Gabby turn and glance down the table. Her mouth softened, her eyes looked glassy. She studied the plate of food in front of him, then looked away, feeding a piece of cheese to her lips and hiding behind that hand again.

High wind stretched the clouds thin above the foothills – a taffy pull across the sky – but down here in the swale, the air was heavy and still. Stifling. The scent of fresh flowers hung close to him. Then he realized that Teresa must be wearing perfume.

He bolted out of the chair and ran, hoping to make the treeline before he threw up.

•

He knew just enough Italian to be confused.

Listening to the ex-cavalry officer talk, words flying at him like rapid-fired bullets, Reg began to understand why Gabby was always so quiet. No one, not even The Mayor, could keep up with Paolo.

Something about rebuilding his house. Having to wait for the winter river to recede. Having to burn corpses, the refuse of battle, the shattered remains of the building itself. Some great plan to turn the flood plain into a vineyard.

It was Luigi's turn to tap his temple. "Sognatore."

"No!" Paolo slapped the table, rattling wine glasses. "No dream." He smiled at Reg. "You help? *Insieme*. With me?"

The dark-haired woman nodded at the roof, touched his finger and, leaning close to Nicoletta, whispered something to her in Italian.

The young girl nodded. She had grown at least two inches. "Inside no rain."

Another table slap, harder than the first. Plates jumped this time. "Bravo!" Paolo said. "Allora è deciso."

From the arguing voices that came from every side of the table, it didn't sound as though anything had been decided. The old man waved away Paolo's words, telling him there was good work in town, for good pay. Teresa spat a mocking laugh, asking her uncle if he thought there was no good work here. Gabby kept silent and began clearing the table. Her ankles looked swollen. When she caught him staring at them, she hurried into the house, Nicoletta running to keep up.

"Dove si vive?" the old man shot back.

Paolo shrugged. "La vostre casa fiume."

"No," Teresa told him. "Qui."

He didn't want to live at the little house at the river and he didn't want to live here. "I can live in town," he said. "In Colfosco."

Those dark eyes glared at him. The word "Qui" – *Here* – slipping past her teeth sounded like an order.

The new argument got so loud, Sancia hugged Reg as if too frightened to watch the snarling faces. Paolo had padlocked the river house to keep squatters out. Teresa kept repeating that the little house had no water and that the river was still unsafe to drink.

"Fai bollire l'acqua," Luigi said, wheezing. "Come sempre."

Reg couldn't see himself hauling water up the flood plain, then boiling it, waiting for it to cool, bottling it – the way it had been for hundreds – thousands – of years here. Compared to that, a village job felt more sensible.

"Lo pagherò!" Standing to his full height, Paolo punched the table with a fist, then stared at Reg. "I pay. You. Sì?"

Before he could respond, Teresa had his hand and was tugging him toward the house. Sancia hung on as if growing out of his hip like a tumor. Her mother pried her free once inside the front room and stepped to the first bedroom, tapped the door: "Gabriella e Paolo qui." In the corner, she rustled the dark drape that hid the space where he had slept. "Il vecchio qui." At to her bedroom, she swung the door open. "Le mie figlie – Nicoletta, Sancia – e me."

Gabby came out of her bedroom with Nicoletta. They wore puzzled looks, almost as if they didn't recognize this version of the dark-haired woman, who was now at the rear wall of windows pointing at Reg – "E voi" – then at the floor – "Qui."

That low table running the length of the windows wasn't wide enough to sleep on. "There's no bed," he said.

Teresa squinted at her older daughter, looking for help.

"Nessun letto, Mama."

Both hands swatted the air as if pushing back an attacker. "Paolo ne comprerà uno."

"Zio Paolo buys." As the words came out, she realized what it meant – "You stay!" – and she began jumping up and down, pulling her sister into a dance.

"Pazze." Luigi sat at the table. "Ma in Colfosco – "

Teresa let out a shriek. The girls stopped dancing. The old man threw up his hands in surrender. Paolo laughed and put an arm around Gabby, rubbed her belly. "Rej-a è un buon nome," he said. "Per il bambino."

"No," Reg said. "Not after me. Name him Luigi."

"Sfortuna." Sad old eyes stared out the kitchen window at the light blue sky. "Ma grazie."

Why would his name be bad luck?

"Then Vittorio," Reg said. "For the victory."

Paolo shook his head. "Come il re?"

"The king?" Nicoletta said, shaking her head, slower than her uncle. "No."

"Uberto," Gabby said. "Per mio padre."

"Nostro padre," Teresa told her, nudging the girl who now came up to her waist.

The old man coughed a laugh. "L'uomo invisibile."

The invisible man? The remark made the room fall silent. No one moved.

"Your father." Reg smiled at Gabby. "Perfect."

"Perfetto!" Paolo clapped, then bent to that swollen belly and kissed it. "Ciao, Uberto."

"What if it's a girl?" Reg said.

After Nicoletta translated, her mother waved a finger. "Non possibile. I segni sono chiari."

"The signs," Nicoletta said. "She knows."

"Maria," Gabby said. She pulled away from her husband, backed into the bedroom, glanced at her sister – "Per nostra mama" – and shut the door.

Paolo laughed and drained his glass of wine. "Madonna."

"Tutte pazze." Luigi hitched up his pants and walked outside, stealing a chunk of cheese on the way.

Swirling the new pour of wine in his glass, Paolo held it up to the window. "L'uva Glera. Il nostro futuro."

The Glera grape might be the big man's future, but Reg knew his own prospects were paper and ink, cast iron and lead, 1,000 miles away. He wondered if any of it would still be there for him when he got back.

2

The slat bed had come from the basement of the crumbling building the Alpini had hid in. It smelled of mold. One look at it – one whiff of it – convinced Teresa she would not allow it inside her house.

It took two days for The Mayor to send over another bed. This one came from the house of The Mayor's mistress. Teresa understood what that meant: The Mayor and his wife could never be invited for dinner. And that seemed to please her. She beat the mattress with a broom handle before letting it inside.

It might have been those two nights on the floor, but this was the most comfortable bed Reg had ever slept in, despite flitting images of The Mayor and his mistress having sex in it. Which one of those village women would agree to sleep with that pompous man? Maybe any of them whose husbands did not return. Maybe all of them.

He caught even shorter glimpses of Gabby these days. Up later than everyone else, she spent most of her day resting in her bedroom. She no longer took meals with the rest of the family. On his way out to work with Paolo, he could hear her sobbing behind her door.

•

The bombed out house had been built over 100 years ago by a great grandfather who died the week the roof went up.

"I think this in war." Paolo kept the fire going. "Build for yourself, you die. Build for your children, you live."

He knew exactly what his winery would look like – a giant Z for Ziccardi in the tile roof that even people across the river in Nervesa could see – and how many kegs and vats the cellar would hold, how many bottles the line could produce every day. His son would work there. His grandson, great grandson. They would pass a portrait of him in the entry hall each morning they came to work, each night when they left. Long after anyone could remember who the handsome man in that painting was, he would be alive in the walls he had helped erect, the business he had created, the Prosecco wine he had perfected, his blood cursing though the generations he had sired.

The long days of June filled with handcarts of ash. Every drop of it had to be saved, to be used in the vineyard. Reg stopped counting the hauls up the trail off the flood plain, covering the ash before dark with old sheets, weighting them down with rocks. He smelled like cigars, requiring him to strip, rinse off and change clothes before dinner. Paolo had given him work clothes that Teresa had altered, but his new boots were taking a beating. Each dusty step felt like an insult to Mr. Kipling.

The new house would be built on a foundation raised two feet above the footings of the old place. A berm would be built on the high bank with earth from a channel dug parallel to the river. Weeks of hand digging had to be finished before winter, when the ground would no longer be workable, and to handle the early Spring floods.

"A horse would help," Reg said.

The ex-cavalry officer nodded. "Tesoro non era un cavallo da aratro."

His horse, the one in the painting, was not for pulling a plow or a wagon. It was for galloping. It had been at full gallop when the bullets had struck it. At least its last seconds had been at top speed and full of life. "Non ha mai mosso," Paolo had said. "Stop move."

"A cavalry officer without a horse," Reg said. "How did you survive?"

"New horse," Paolo told him.

"How?"

Those broad shoulders shrugged, his lips pursed. "No ask."

There was probably never a doubt that Paolo would survive the battles. Nothing seemed to worry him, no challenge frightened him. He was used to winning. Had Reg met him before the war, even for a few minutes, he would have realized that the big man would be returning to his bride and the life he had laid out in such detail. Nothing could stop him.

"In Victa" Reg said, seeing the motto of the Queen's Own on a cap he no longer owned.

"Invincibile." Paolo thumped his chest. "You, me – *insieme*. Together."

Reg shoveled more ash, knowing that the big man didn't need help from anyone to make his dream come true, a dream he was living at this very moment. No wonder Gabby had said yes. Compared to her husband, everyone else seemed second-rate.

"You go little house." He pointed the long pole at Luigi's place down river. "Make good. Together."

"It's Luigi's," Reg said.

That head of blonde hair, dirty with flecks of ash, shook. "Mine."

The story took a long time to tell because it was full of apologies. The old man's sister had sold it to Paolo's father after her husband disappeared. She and Luigi would be permitted to live there until

275

they died. It was not something the elder Ziccardi had wanted to do, but he had felt obligated, because all the land on the flood plain had once belonged to the DaPonte family.

"Dig water," he was saying. "Pump. Make perfetto. I see Gabriella there" – he nodded toward the little house – "first time."

Me, too.

Another story, this one savored over warm wine and cheese, up wind of the smoke. She was four, he was 14 and in love with a girl in Colfosco – Amelia. Ten years later, he spotted Gabby in town. Struck by her beauty, he followed her home and couldn't believe it when she walked inside the little house. She had been living in the house nearest to his, invisible, secret. He brought her flowers the next day, little white ones that grew among weeds, hand-picked from the river bank. They married that winter.

"She was 14?" Reg said, having to flash five fingers twice, then holding up four.

He flashed five fingers three times. "Quindici."

By then her mother had died and her sister had married. She had been stuck in that little house with her uncle. And the war had come. Less than three months after the wedding, and less than six month before Reg had climbed out of that bomb crater, Paolo had finally been forced into service, something he had been able to bribe his way out of for almost four years.

"Scrivo poesie," he said. "Poema, for Gabriella. Ogni giorno."

A poem, every day. He must have loved her. The warmth Reg felt in his chest came as a surprise. He was glad she was loved. And by such a man. She would be fine. She would have children, flowers, poetry.

"Nessuna posta," he said. "No mail. Is war."

The Germans had pushed the Italians back across the Piave by then. There would have been no hope of getting a letter – or a poem – back to the other side.

"Basta." He pulled folded money from a pocket, counted out five bills and waved them like a rag for Reg to take. "Luigi, you, Colfosco."

Something about dinner in town and how The Mayor would be happier to dine with Reg than with Paolo. That story would have to wait for another afternoon, because the big man fell silent on the walk back to Teresa's, stopping only once to pick a handful of red poppies, tying the stems with a ribbon of long grass as he led the way home.

The Mayor's mistress had the finest home in the village. Two floors of dark furniture covered in colorful fabric. Paintings in ornate frames filled the papered walls. She wore yellow, setting off her black hair. Much younger than her lover, she moved like a ballerina. When she saw Luigi, she ran to him, kissed his cheeks, held him close. One hand holding a bottle of Soave, the other a bouquet of cut flowers, he gestured toward Reg. "Re-ja. L'inglese."

She nodded and stepped aside to let him enter. "Piacere."

Unsure if he should offer his hand, he made a small bow.

"L'eroe!" The Mayor waddled down the stairs, slipping his arms through his suspenders. "Bravo! Dov'è Paolo?"

With a shrug, the old man began talking as he walked through the foyer, that white marble making him look as if he were crossing river ice.

The long table in the dining room had a candelabra in the center. Three red candles, slender, tall. Reg stayed in the open doorway to allow the others to sit, then took the open chair opposite the hostess. Behind her, above the small vase she had put the flowers in, one of the paintings on the wall depicted a stately looking horse standing in front of split rail fence. All the other paintings were landscapes. He recognized the location of one of them: The Montello rising from the river, as viewed from the opposite shore, close to where the bombed out house stood. He couldn't stop looking at it.

"Bello, no?" She was smiling at him. "Il cuore ricorda."

He nodded − *the heart remembers* − and raised his glass to her. "Grazie. For the bed. Il letto?"

She flicked her fingers as if shooing a fly. "Di nulla."

"Amelia," The Mayor said. "Il cibo."

She rang the little bell beside her plate. A maid carried a silver tray from the kitchen. The aroma of roasted meat filled the room. The maid lowered the tray to her employer, who glanced at the dish and nodded in approval.

That horse in that painting. That view of The Montello. *Amelia.*

No wonder Paolo didn't want to be here seated opposite his old flame. No wonder The Mayor was pleased to see Reg in his place. No wonder Amelia was doing her best to hide her disappointment.

The two men at both ends of the table had to raise their voices to hear each other. That made Amelia smile. She raised her glass of Soave to Reg.

The goat meat tasted sweet.

Too much food, too much wine. Still, he realized the old man was walking in the wrong direction. When Reg tried to stop him, Luigi yanked his sleeve free and took a narrow alley to the back door of a stone house that faced the main square: "Andare a casa. Questa è la mia casa."

"Isn't this The Mayor's house?" Reg said.

A finger went to the old man's lips, then knuckles of that big hand rapped the door. "Torna a casa. Subito."

Reg thought of grabbing him and pulling him away before he made a fool of himself. The door opened. A middle-aged woman in a rose-colored housecoat stood in the doorway. She pulled the garment closed at the neck when she saw Reg. But she was smiling.

With a wink, the old man stepped inside. Gently, The Mayor's wife shut the door.

Off and on, Reg laughed all the way back to Teresa's.

•

They came from Susegana and Casonetti and as far away as Conegliano. Some even braved the boat trip across the summer Piave in their Sunday best. The few young men who had returned safely from the war – two of them still in uniform – all looked like strangers, as if they no longer belonged among the teenage girls, their mothers and grandmothers, their fathers and uncles.

At the far edge of the gathering, Rudolfo, Jr. stood next to an old man strumming a sad tune on a small lute. The frail priest from Susegana needed a chair to get through the ceremony and an umbrella to shade him from the July sun. The polished wood coffin holding Luigi DaPonte bounced light back toward the unseen river.

The Mayor's tribute had to compete with the sobbing of his wife, whose broad-brimmed black hat and full veil made her look like the most important person here. Two other older women were also crying, but quietly, almost as if grateful they had lived to see this day, when the man who had left them for another finally stopped belonging to anyone.

Stone-faced, Teresa stood with an arm on each of her dazed daughters. Beside her, Gabby rested her head against Paolo and studied the grass. Her belly stretched the fabric of her dark dress, its bottom hem covering her ankles. She didn't notice the hard gaze of Amelia, but Paolo did. He met that glare with a dry smile.

For the final blessing, the priest stood. His wobbly legs made him stagger, as if he might fall face-first into the open grave, saved at the last minute by a sudden burst of energy. Crossing himself, he fell back into the chair and let out a long sigh.

One by one, the congregation moved past him, then past Teresa and Gabby, stopping just long enough to nod or touch an elbow, pat the head of one of the little girls, shake Paolo's hand. No one spoke. They ambled down the road like a half-starved herd, headed toward the main square where a food and wine would be waiting.

Only Rudolfo and his father stood their ground. When the family withdrew, the old goat man made his way down to the gravesite, sat in the grass beside the coffin and began playing a new song – a sweeter one.

"I thought he and Luigi were angry with each other," Reg said.

Young Rudolfo nodded, but didn't speak. He brought Reg to his father. "Questo è l'inglese."

Still seated, the lute player finished his tune. Deep wrinkles lined his face, browned by sun and age spots. In a mellow voice rivaling the sound of his instrument, he spoke slowly, as if searching for words, possibly inventing some of them. It gave Reg the chance to understand his unembellished Italian:

"Anger ends in the ground. You were good to my son. Come someday. We have cheese for you. And a goat."

Without waiting for an answer, he went back to his lute, knicked-up fingers plucking strings to a faster beat, the rhythm of a dance. The music made him smile.

"Celebrate the dead," his son said, turning from the coffin and leading the way back toward the feast.

Chel-leh-brar-eh i morti. Even death sounded sweeter here.

3

He didn't ask. He grabbed the old shotgun leaning against the bed in the drape-covered alcove, pocketed the shot − small iron balls − he found in a bag tucked in the old man's best shoes, a pair Reg had never seen him wear.

"Attenti," Paolo said. "Esplode tra le mani."

The blunderbuss did look as if it might explode in his hands. But the flintlock had been recently cleaned. The pouch of gunpowder felt dry. The ram rod had been poorly restraightened, but it would do the job. He hoisted the heavy weapon over a shoulder and walked toward town, just as Luigi must have a half century or more ago.

Reg imagined himself a youthful version of the old man as he climbed the foothill road through the north end of the village. Where the road steppened into a trail, he used the shotgun as a walking stick, for balance. Rudolfo, Sr. saw him coming from half a mile away, but did not move out the shade of an unfinished shed roof.

His crooked fingers caressed the gun barrel. "We hunted," he said in Italian. "Together. He never killed anything."

Reg refused to accept the shotgun back. "For the wolves."

The lute player rested the long weapon across his lap, then took the gunpowder and shot. "Nessun lupi questi giorni."

No wolves these days? Reg had seen them. So had the younger goat man. But there was no point in arguing. The shotgun wasn't for wolves. It was for the memories of two friends who hunted together, back when there were wolves and game birds.

The air going in and out of the old goat man's lungs made a whistling sound. He might have been working on his new shed for months. Tools lay scattered by the stack of planks near a corner. Rudolfo, Jr. would be out tending the goats, or milking them or making cheese. The tiny house might never get finished.

Reg draped his jacket over the empty chair inside the door. He tossed three long planks up on the roof, climbed the ladder, hammer in one hand, a small saw in the other. With luck, he would have the boards nailed down and ready to slate before he got hungry.

•

The young black goat tried to stop and eat grasses and flowers all the way down the foothill path. In Colfosco, it strained against its tether trying to reach kitchen scraps left out for garden compost. It had to be pulled through the small stretch of scrub woodland along the road to the river, wanting to nibble on wild berries.

The two girls screamed when the saw the animal coming down the swale to the house. Frightened by the sound, the goat backed up and lowered its head. The bag of cheese was too heavy for Nicoletta to carry. He tied the tether to a young evergreen to give the goat a patch of long grass to eat and far enough away from the house to prevent it from fouling the footpath.

Teresa opened the bag, saw all the cheese. Her eyes widened, then got even bigger when she spotted the goat.

"For the baby," he said.

Her grunt sounded like a growl. She took the bag of cheese into the house, kicking the door shut behind her.

Sancia kept staring at the goat. "Sembra mamma."

It did look like Teresa, rooting through the high grass to get down to the new green shoots, angry that it had to work so hard for so little.

The laugh came out of him like a cough. He hugged the little girl to his side. "It needs water."

"I do." Nicoletta scampered toward the garden to find a bucket to fill, with her sister running after her.

He promised himself he would take the girls for a walk on the day their uncle slaughtered the goat.

•

"Tre volte," Teresa said, rocking the baby she had to slap three times to get him to take his first breath. Hairless, scrawny, a face full of wrinkles, Uberto looked like a tiny old man, swaddled in cloth.

Gabby lay in the bed, her nightshirt drenched in sweat, too exhaused to move the wet strands of hair off her face or cover the outline of her breasts and nipples. Bloody rags sat on the floor near her feet. Watching her sister cuddle and quiet the newborn, the new mother looked relieved to have finally expelled the baby and in no hurry to take him back.

The father had missed it all. He didn't come home for lunch and made it clear he was upset that Reg had, when there was so much work to be done on the new house. Out of sorts for the past few days, Paolo might have discovered something to be afraid of for the first time in his life – becoming a father.

"Bello," Reg said from the bedroom doorway. "Brava."

Gabby offered a weak smile. "Forte."

The baby boy was loud, causing Sancia to cover her ears and follow Nicoletta, taking water up the swale to the goat. Teresa shooed Reg out of the bedroom threshold – "Vai fuori" – and shut the door. Alone in the main room, he sat at the table, a beam of sunlight running through a window and warming the plate of soft cheese and crusty bread. The churning in his stomach brought a taste of bile to the back of his throat. The hot August breeze made him feel out of breath and light-headed. He smelled his own sweat, the bitter odor of ash on his clothes. Teresa had been right to order him out of the house in these clothes. He took the plate outside, needing to be closer to the river, where the air would be cooler.

What was worse – having a child with Madge or never being a father? Those were his only options now. If he could find a spot on the high bank where tall grass would hide him from the ex-cavalry officer's view, there was a chance he might actually be able to keep his lunch down. If not, the river would take his vomit downstream. His sadness, too.

•

With the sun already down and a full moon rising, the water from the pump felt colder than usual. He rinsed off the grime of the workday in the garden, where the water would do the tomatoes and peppers some good. Pulling on his pants, he heard the sobbing.

Dark hair shining in the soft light, Teresa sat at the table, her back to the house, her head in her hands.

"Is the baby all right?" he said.

She looked up, nodded. "Il mio cuore lo vuole ancora qui."

"I miss him, too." He sat beside her, facing the windows that framed where he slept. "But he lived a full life. Over 80 years."

She squinted, shook her head as if rattling something inside it. "Carmine," she said. "Niente più bambini per me."

No more babies.

So few of the men from the village had survived the war and most, probably all of them, would choose a younger woman, one who had never been married, one without children.

"I know how that feels." He touched her hand. "I'll never be a father."

Most of her wail got stuck in her throat. She pulled away and marched down the trail toward the copse of evergreens. Even when the high grass began to swallow her, he could still hear her crying. If she tried to hurt herself again, who would look after the new baby? The girls?

282

He found her in a puddle of moonlight, pulling her fingers through a bed of pine needles. "Your girls are beautiful," he told her. "They need you."

"Non sono più una donna," she told the brown straws in her hand. "Solo una strega."

"You're no old crone," he said. "And of course you're still a woman." He turned her face to his. "E bella."

Something sparkled in those dark eyes – moonlight? – and made them open wider. She held his palm to her cheek, then kissed it, then pulled it down her neck to her breast. Watching his face, she must have seen his surprise. "Mostrami."

Frozen in shock, he couldn't show her. He stared at his hand, not believing where it rested. Her breast was softer than Madge's. The nipple felt harder. He wanted to tell her she was making a mistake. But she was smiling, even though a tear still dribbled down her cheek. And her kiss was soft on his lips, and wet. Her breath felt warm. He pulled back for air, gasped.

And she was on top of him. Her fingers squeezing his shoulders, his arms, his chest. Her lips pressed hard on his, her breath quickened. The whimper behind her teeth reminded him of the sound soldiers made when shot, just before they hit the ground.

The moment he realized he didn't want to resist, he never had a chance.

•

"Ho sognato questo," she said. "Di voi."

It saddened him to hear that she had dreamt of him. He couldn't tell her that he had never dreamt of her. And now she was going on about watching him wash up at the well each night, how seeing his wet skin glisten made her body ache, how she was afraid he would never want her, because she knew she was too old for him. "So che non sono la vostra prima scelta."

She was right: she wasn't his first choice. Not even his second.

"I have no choice now," he said.

"Non è vero," she said. "Sono qui – Here is me."

4

S now in sunlight. In the middle of September.

Teresa watched white flakes fall outside her kitchen window. "Tramontana."

"No," Paolo told her without looking up from the building diagrams on the table. "Il Borasco."

It didn't matter to Gabby if the surprise squall had flown in on the high mountain wind or down along the river from the east. She carried the baby outside, danced with him, her head back to catch snowflakes on her cheeks and forehead. It felt good to see her smiling again. The two girls joined her, grabbing handfuls of her sun dress and following her dance steps.

The black-haired woman studied him, her eyelids heavy, regret weighing down her skin. In that stare, he felt all the nights he had collapsed on the bed under the back window, too exhausted from manual labor for conversation. Or sex. Like her, he wondered why his energy had disappeared. Before the war, he could put in a full day of chores at the farm, then run down to *The Gazette* office and help the little editor until well after dark, then race back up the hill for supper and still have the stamina to read, write, stargaze. Now, he craved sleep, wanting to hide inside it.

That must be what Teresa was sensing. He was hiding from her. The cold wind rushing through the doorway made him shiver.

"È buono per l'uva." Paolo wet the tip of a pencil with his tongue, began sketching on the diagrams. "Più dolce."

How could snow be good for grapes – for anything that grew? That pencil roughed in bigger timbers for the roof supports. One of those might come crashing down, crushing the ex-cavalry officer. Ashamed of owning that thought, Reg nibbled at his lower lip. Only a truly horrible person would wish that fate on someone.

"Fuori." Teresa waved a dish rag at him, as if creating a new wind to blow him outside. The smell of raw onion came off that wet rag. "Ballare con le bambine."

Seeing him dance with her daughters might improve her mood. And make her forgive him, if only for the afternoon. He stepped out into the wind. Not snow. Too wet for that. Slush, melting the instant it landed on anything.

And before he could reach the dancers, it stopped. The girls groaned. Gabby laughed − "La sua prima neve. . .his first?" − jostling the baby as she carried him back toward the house.

He couldn't remember his first snow, but he did know that his mother would not have taken him out in it. He watched the new mother walk inside. Her shape had returned, the swelling in her ankles had disappeared. That old dress clung to her, tighter than it had been before she she got pregnant, more revealing.

At the kitchen window, Teresa held her eyes shut and lowered her head.

I am a truly horrible person.

Sancia scooped up snow that turned to water in her fingers. "È morto."

"Snow doesn't die." He picked her up, twirled her. "It melts."

Her cold wet hands gripped his neck. "Mmmelt."

He set her down. The kitchen window stood empty now. Inside. Gabby had the baby on the bed, toweling it off. Paolo squinted at the diagrams on the table, muttering to himself. The door to the main bedroom had been shut. The girls opened it. Teresa was facing the closet, arms across her chest, hugging herself. He couldn't see her face.

He grabbed his jacket, stepped out into the remains of that cold wind. It got stronger near the top of the swale and the bare ground the goat had grazed. Tethered in new pasture near the stand of evergreens, it was now eating the last of summer grass near the spot he and Teresa first had sex, devouring every piece of evidence, every trace. A title for a story flashed in his mind − *The Eraser Goat* − knowing he would never write it.

There would be wine in town, and men in the square he could share it with without having to say a word. For the first time, he thought he knew how Luigi must have felt: escape offered more than hope. It promised solace.

•

She wanted to know about the bed − Was it to his liking? − and about the baby. And Paolo.

"I asked my father," Amelia said, crossing herself, "to buy him that horse − Tesoro. My first mistake. He refused to ride to town, fearing someone would try to steal it. So he walked. Always." She raised a hand from the balcony rail, pointed toward the main square. "That's where he saw her − Gabriella − by a cabbage cart. She had nothing of her own. A no one."

"Your second mistake?" Reg said.

Amelia shook her head. "My last one."

He followed her into the main room, where two glasses of white wine stood on a silver tray. "Why The Mayor?"

Grinning, she handed him a glass. "I fill him with desire. Like Paolo used to have for me." She sipped the Soave. "Even old men have fire." Her dark gray dress had lace ruffles at the neck and sleeve cuffs. "And the war took so many. Some who came back, they are no longer the same." She blinked at him. "You are the lucky one."

Looking around at all her finery, he didn't feel lucky. "We both lost," he said, "in love."

"Your English woman?"

He couldn't tell her the truth. Knowing that he meant Gabby would only intensify her old wounds. He nodded.

She rested her hand on his sleeve. "The pain leaves the body, but not the heart. Never."

Two newspapers sat on the round table by the chair at the window. One of them, from Venice, carried a front page story about the Treaty of Versailles, signed more than three months ago. News from outside the village seemed unnecessary these days, because it changed nothing. He wondered how Mr. Kipling would react if he found out Reg hadn't read anything all summer, not even a story from *The Jungle Books*. The scolding Mr. Quaite would have given him made him wince.

"I'm so glad you crossed my path today." At her low desk, she wrote a note. "Take this to the bank in Susegana. My uncle will keep your money safe." The cream-colored paper smelled like her – flowers and lemon. "Paolo keeps his accounts there. It's good he pays you."

He wanted another glass of wine, more conversation. "Why didn't you speak English to me at that dinner?"

"I wasn't sure I liked you then."

Her bed, the one she shared with The Mayor, would be even more comfortable than the one she had sent to Teresa's. Another glass of wine and Reg might have asked to see it, to plop down on it, test it out. He drained his glass. "It snowed today."

"Not here," she told him. "River snow. Il Borasco."

"Good for grapes," he said.

She laughed. "You remind me of him."

"Paolo is everything I'm not," he said.

"I meant Luigi." She led him to the foyer. "He blesses you still. Visit his grave. Find his spirit. Then we can talk again."

The tall door didn't make a sound when it opened or closed. The taste of sour mountain grass hung in the dusk. He strolled through the square, stopping to look back at her balcony. Empty, it caught the glow of her lamps, darkened by the red wallpaper up there. She reminded him of those fortune tellers who showed up every summer at the baths in Royal Tunbridge Wells to read palms. They sold the future. He wasn't sure he wanted to know his.

He stopped at the cemetary, but didn't try to find Luigi's grave. The cool air was enough to clear his head. He walked down to the old man's house at the river, watched the sliver of a moon paint a thin band of light on the water. When the new house was finished, it would be visible from here, surrounded by grape vines. This might be one of the last evenings of an unspoiled panorama.

He laughed at the flood plain. Ravaged by heavy artillery, reclaimed by the river, now holding on to the last shred of ground cover before the first frost, this spot was anything but unspoiled.

Night birds fluttered in trees along the road back to Teresa's. They might have been bats. He took the side path toward the trees, watched the goat curl up on pine needles and sleep. When the lamp in the main room went out, he walked to the house, crept inside.

He pulled the bag of money from the mattress, put Amelia's note in with the bills, then stuffed it back into its hiding place. Undressing in the dark at the window, he studied clouds beginning to hide what was left of the little moon. Stretched out on the bed, eyes shut, he envisioned that dark red wallpaper, the color of blood, wondering why he would remind a beautiful woman of an old man.

•

The hand shaking him pinched his shoulder. He rolled toward the window, hoping she would let him sleep and not wake the whole house by sliding in to arouse him.

"A Conegliano," Paolo was whispering. "Avanti."

Reg rubbed an eye with his knuckles. "Now?"

A hard hand dug under the mattress, yanked out the bag of money, set it on Reg's chest. "You take."

The ex-cavalry officer bundled up Reg's clothes and boots, carried them outside, grabbing the rifle by the sling on his way through the door.

It felt warmer at predawn than it had last night. Reg dressed near the garden. "Why?"

"Trattore," Paolo said. "Tractor. We buy. This day."

Reg stopped stepping into a boot. "With my money?"

The broad-shouldered man let out a soft laugh, nudged the bag of money with his foot. "No more for bed. For bank."

If Paolo knew about where the money bag was kept, so did Teresa.

"Is it safe to leave them here?" Reg said. "Unguarded?"

"They no know we go." Paolo was grinning. "Solo la capra. Just goat know."

•

The sun was already up when they reached the castle outside of Susegana. The sight of those old stone walls made him shiver. An overturned artillery gun sat off the side of the road, the wheels of its caisson facing the sky, untouched for over a year. Some thin vine had woven its way through the spokes and over the breech.

The town still slept. Near the bank, Reg dug into the money bag, waved the note. "Aren't we going inside?"

Paolo stopped, glanced at the piece of paper. His eyes narrowed: he recognized that handwriting. Crumpling the note in his fingers, he flung it to the ground – "La banca nel Conegliano" – then spat at the building and began marching up the street, rifle slung across his back.

Back toward the river, the castle turret stood out against the pale sky. "San Salvatore," Reg said, finally remembering its name.

" Sì. Che un vigneto farebbe, non è vero?"

It would, of course, make an impressive winery. But if the castle was in Paolo's plans, Reg wanted no part of it. Just standing in its shadow felt like a death sentence. The emaciated faces of soldiers, the stench of their wasting away, would haunt him from beyond those walls. He shouldered the sack of money and quickened his pace to catch up.

•

Even over a good road, the walk took almost four hours, including a stop for breakfast – sweet bread and hard-boiled eggs, dusty with lint from the big man's pockets – in a clearing where a cast iron stove now served as home to squirrels.

Along the way, Paolo rambled on about the city up the way. Railroad tracks would run from Treviso to Conegliano as soon as the new bridge over the Piave was built. Shipping and banking would be easier from there. The bypassed towns – Nervesa, Susegana, Colfosco – would never recover. A different kind of war, he called it.

"The paper," he said. "She writes. Amelia."

Reg moved the money bag to his other shoulder. "If we had a horse, we'd have been there and back by now."

The big man stayed quiet for almost a mile. Horses were like women, he told the red flowers in a roadside field. When you lose one you love, you're never the same.

The sack of money felt heavier. Reg nodded.

That hard hand slapped his back. "You buy our food," Paolo said. "I buy our tractor."

•

He withdrew more money than Reg had in the bag. Before leaving the bank, Paolo decided it would be easier, and save another long walk, to pay Reg in advance — through the end of the year — and handed him three months wages.

Pocketing some of the new money, Reg added the rest to what he had already deposited "I never had an actual bank account," he told the clerk, who rocked his head side to side while pouting — the same expression Luigi wore when he heard something that neither surprised nor interested him.

The ex-cavalry officer was already on the move, heading toward the agricultural center south of the city. The manager of the equipment barn was waiting out front, next to a dull gray tractor with metal studs welded to its rear iron wheels. The drive belt looked like something off the old Wharfedale press. The front wheel had wood spokes. In yellow letters running down the side of the radiator: *Landini*. It didn't look safe.

The pudgy man climbed up on the tractor and got the engine started. Smiling, he waved at Paolo.

Holding his fingertips flat to his own throat, moving them back and forth, Paolo signaled for the engine to be shut off. He stepped into the barn, the manager scrambling down to follow him. At the long desk inside, surrounded by machines in various stages of assembly, some so skeletal they looked like the demented weapons of torture, the papers got signed, the money changed hands. When the ex-cavalry officer walked out into sunlight, he patted the tractor engine, then led the way toward the city.

"Are we walking back?" Reg said.

The big man shook his head and pretended to steer a car.

Reg stopped. "Not on the tractor!"

Slowing down just long enough to narrow his gaze, Paolo started laughing. He didn't stop until they reached the little restaurant near the city square.

"She puts the eye to you." He leaned back and popped the wedge of cheese into his mouth, point a finger to his eye. "I see."

"No," Reg told him. "Not true. Non è vero."

The wine glass looked small in his hand – a hand that, made into a fist, could easily break a man's jaw. Reg readied himself to jump away from the table and start running.

" Teresa." Paolo wagged a finger. "Fuoco in lei."

His relief hearing that nameand not Gabby's didn't last long. He felt suddenly insignifcant, like the goat. The future winery owner had not even noticed the way Reg felt about the woman who had just borne him a son. But Paolo was right. There was fire in Teresa. How had her husband dealt with all that energy? Had he been a fool to leave her for war, or was he simply looking for a rest?

"What do you know about grapes," Reg said.

With a shrug, he started to explain in English, then waved away those words and spoke in his native tongue, turning it into a song sung slowly enough for a child to understand: "The Glera grape has been grown here since before the Romans. It belongs here. Like my family." Turning his glass of wine, he studyied its sunny color. "Where something belongs, it thrives." He picked up the glass, smiled. "Like you."

5

If he shut his eyes, the drone of the Landini, the clatter of its spiked rear wheels, sent him into *The Gazette*'s back bay, with the linotype humming and spitting out hot lead, the Wharfedale clacking with each pass over the flatbed. It was cooler here, and the river was down, making the bridge building go faster to the east, at Priula. But the new house had fallen behind schedule.

Materials remained in short supply. Labor was nonexistant. Paolo had taken to hiring old men from Casonetti and the foothills. The long days of heavy lifting and shoveling wasn't worth the money to these men, and money didn't buy much since everything was scarce. Rudolfo, Sr. had to stand guard all night now, making sure no one stole a goat. His son slept in the cheese house − a lean-to shed that reeked of the too-sweet residue of the curds − a long knife within reach in case a hungry stranger, displaced by war, caught the scent and tried to take a free meal.

Even Gabby had security duty: garden sentry, shooing rabbits, squirrels and birds, and on the lookout for those same wandering strangers who would think twice about confronting a woman with a rifle, guarding her infant, her garden, her home.

"Colfosco," Paolo said. "Means − with mist."

Fog rose over the high bank as if growing out of the river. It would lay like a blanket over the vines. If they ever got around to planting any. Reg had stopped asking when the cuttings would arrive for the first planting.

Walking the flood channel, the ex-cavalry officer nodded his approval with each step. "Gabriella sees too," he said. "How her sister watches you. How you play with her girls."

"She said that?"

"She says, Teresa is not for you."

"Too old?"

"Too hard." Paolo laughed. "When we move here, be careful. She will want another baby. A boy. To match her sister." He accepted a hand and climbed out of the channel. "*Oila e acqua*. Oil and water, those two."

Slate for the roof, now stacked near the lumber, had come down river on a small barge. It would take the two of them over a month to get the tiles up and in place. Winter would live inside the house house before anyone could.

"We need more help," Reg told him.

"We need a miracle." Paolo dusted off his work pants, then grinned. "And you need a body guard."

•

They didn't get more help. They got a miracle.

The two brothers from Valdobbiadene, up river where the Alps began, insisted on setting the cuttings up for rooting themselves – "to make sure they grow," they said. They finished that same afternoon, laying 500 cuttings in boxes filled with a mix of dirt they had brought with them in bags and the native flood plain soil. They oriented the boxes – 25 of them – north to south to make sure the sun stayed longer on the width of the cuttings, warming them through winter.

"Everyday, wet the dirt," the older brother said.

The younger one nodded. "And keep them covered in dirt."

Somehow, those cuttings would develop roots in the cold season. The brothers would come back and plant them in the spring: "And don't disturb them!"

They would not take any money. "Only if they root," the younger brother said.

"And bud after planting," the other one told them.

Then they were gone, like river fog evaporating in late morning.

"They saved us two weeks," Reg said. "And you still have money for extra hands."

Paolo watched Reg nail the first course of roof tiles. "Amelia's cousins. You see her for me. Thank her." He took the hammer, set a tile and nailed it, took Reg's nod of approval. "But not while The Mayor is there." Another tile, another nail, another swing of the hammer. He held up two fingers. "Maybe two bodyguards for you."

His laugh sailed down the river.

•

Even from a distance, her body glistened. Wet with the river, she cradled the baby to her chest, swaying with it, dancing to the tune she hummed. Her son's hair was growing in, slightly darker than hers. Seeing her naked body for the first time, Reg felt ashamed to be spying on her. But he couldn't look away.

She moved her breast to the infant's lips. She stopped humming. Her smile grew.

Reg yanked the tether to get the goat moving. Its startled wail made her search for the source of the sound. Pretending not to notice, he turned and pulled the goat away from the river.

292

The animal had put on weight, and its legs had grown stronger. Moving it to new grazing felt like a tug of war. Once past the edge of the evergreens, he could see the girls filling a basket in the garden. Near the pump, their mother rinsed her hair, shook water out of it. She heard the goat, squinted at the trees. When she spotted him, she pulled the straps of her dress off her shoulders, let the dark brown garment fall to her feet. Stepping out of it, she began washing her body with a small cloth, her stare fixed on him the whole time.

Her breasts were smaller than her sister's, but her skin looked just as smooth. From this far away, she didn't look like the same woman who had given herself to him in the pine shade. She looked new.

The goat started running, pulling the tether so hard it dragged Reg off his feet. He stopped his slide by digging his heels into the soil. Back on his feet, he couldn't see the well or the garden anymore. He let the animal lead him to the little meadow in the shadow of the trees, where sun had not yet dried out the grass or the tiny white flowers fighting the green blades for space. He tied the tether to a fallen log. It would take this goat less than a week to destroy all the pasture it could reach. No place here was safe from this eating machine.

With a naked woman at the river and another at the house, no place here was safe, period.

•

It had to be the wine.

"Why avoid her?" Amelia finished her dessert fritter with a large bite. "Are you – damaged? From the war?"

He shook his head and refilled his glass. "Not there. No."

"Something is wrong with her? Her body? The face?"

Trails of Soave slid down the side of the carafe. "I don't know why I even mentioned it," he said.

She stood, wiped her fingers with her napkin. "I know why."

And she was gone, leaving him in the big room with the wine and his half-eaten apple fritter. And the flowers Paolo had given him money to buy. For a moment, Reg wondered if he was even here. Would she figure out who he had been talking about? Would she tell The Mayor? Paolo? Anyone?

Idiot.

She walked back in carrying a large framed photograph. "The entire village," she said. "This year. At the Epiphany."

He blinked to clear his vision. "Where's that?"

"The Twelfth Day," she told him, "when the Magi found the baby Jesus."

The carved wood frame felt sticky. He wiped his fingers and the frame with his napkin, squinted at the people in the photograph.

"What do you see?" she said.

Gabby was smiling at the end of the front row, with her husband, still in uniform, beaming at her side. Stonefaced, Teresa stood with a hand on the shoulder of each of her daughters. Luigi was looking skyward, as if tracking a bird. In the center, The Mayor, surrounded by some of the young women who had come to lunch that day, with their mothers. The back row, where Amelia stood, was made up of the old men who had fed him wine and cheese.

"And what do you not see?" Amelia said.

"Rudolfo," Reg told her. "And his father."

"The goat man? No. The young men." She stepped around to look at the faces with him. "Fourteen from our village. The war dead." Her finger ran across the young women. "You have your choice of any of them. In other villages as well."

"I don't know any of them," he said. "And I work all day, at the river."

"There are jobs in town."

It was getting hard to breathe. "They're counting on me."

"You mean, Paolo is depending on you."

The girls enjoyed playing with him, teaching him Italian, learning English. Teresa fed him, lusted for him. Gabby had her hands full with the baby and her husband. Paolo was the only one who truly needed him.

Amelia tapped the face of Luigi in the photograph. "He lost his wife as a young man. Threw away the rest of his life mourning her. Then he took care of his sister and her daughers when that husband ran off." She sat in her chair, sipped wine. "After she died, he raised the girls. The only father they really had. He couldn't choose his family. You can."

So much sadness in the old man's eyes. So much wonder and mischief, too. "How did she die?"

"His sister walked into the river." Amelia studied how the white wine caught the dim light in here. "She left her dress on the bank."

He closed his eyes, saw Teresa in that same black dress, contemplating that same fate. "And his wife?"

"In child birth," Amelia said. "The baby, too. A boy."

He could feel his eyes well up and hoped no tear would roll down his cheek, because he would be powerless to wipe it away.

"Free yourself of the DaPonte curse," Amelia told him. "I will introduce you to our young women. Do this for Luigi. He wanted only the best for you." She was smiling now. "You should sleep here tonight."

He fumbled his glass, managing to steady it on the table next to his plate. "Work tomorrow. I can't."

Her laugh sounded far away. "Stubborn. So much like him."

He didn't want to be like Luigi. He didn't want to be cursed. And he didn't want to be here, searching a photograph for the faces of those stolen by war. In so many battles, 14 men had fallen in seconds, but the 11th Battalion carried on. Here, those 14 lost souls were the future that this village would now never know. He propped the frame against a table leg.

She pulled his glass away, rang a little bell at the edge of her arm chair. "Let's get some real food in you. For your walk back."

•

What would a London publisher's office look like? Men wearing spectacles and striped school or regimental ties. What would a real suit look like on him – the charcoal gray Mr. Kipling favored? And dress shoes, not boots? What would it be like to be thought of as an intellectual?

He would fool no one in London. No university, only a Rusthall education. No matter how much he read, he could never overcome that in the eyes of those who would determine his future as a writer.

It had been merely a dream all along, since his first day learning how to conduct an interview, following Mr. Quaite around in the cold blowing down High Street, being willing to take notes on a door step, never asking to be allowed inside, where it might be warm.

"Sogno." Nicoletta rested her head on a pillow her hands made. "Dream."

He nodded, pointed to the low sun. "Window – finestra."

From the table where she was cutting garden greens, Teresa had been watching and listening, sometimes mouthing the words. In that brown dress, she blended into the wood. The table seemed to grow out of her waist. In another hour, the sky would darken, and she might disappear completely.

The door opened too fast for the little hands to stop it from banging into the wall, knocking the rifle to the floor. Sancia's smile turned into a gasp. She stared at the weapon as if waiting for it to fire a bullet. But she held on to the small paper sack. "Caramella! Sweets!"

Paolo picked up the rifle, set it back against the wall, then ushered his wife and son into the bedroom, shutting the door. Nicoletta raced outside with her sister, chasing the white sack.

The rhythm of the knife on the chopping board, the final minutes of the day highlighting her black hair, turned her into a portrait by one of those French painters Barry liked so much. She had spent years at that table, with a lifetime in the same spot ahead of her. She didn't need him. She had her girls and the garden. They would never leave her.

New wind scattered leaves toward the river. Where would it blow him? That wind convinced him that only she could save him from all those young faces in the photograph – girls still, all of them – and their mothers. And from that town, where the houses huddled closer than the old men at the dried up fountain in the square. And from whatever manual labor he might wind up doing for the rest of his life. And from the children he would be forced to have to keep everyone happy.

And she could save him from the prospect of leaving, going back to England, surrendering to all of them, even Madge. And from the pleased scowl his father would always be wearing each time he caught sight of the son he might have already disinherited – his final insult.

He couldn't remember the last time Gabby had smiled at him. Or even looked at him. He couldn't remember the last time he had dreamt about her. She moved like a ghost through his days, the baby either in her arms or by her side, the pair of them lost in themselves, as unaware of their surroundings as shell-shocked soldiers wandering battlefields or hospital wards. Visible, occupying space, alive, yet not truly there – unreachable.

He stepped to the table, stopped the knife with his hand on Teresa's. She would not look up from the vegetables.

"I should have – I'm sorry." He struggled to explain in Italian, stringing excuses together, all of them with "troppo" in them – working too hard, too tired, too full of aches and pains. Too stupid.

She let go of the knife, silenced his lips with her fingers. They smelled of sour greens. "Dream," she said.

And she kissed him.

6

It was her secret place. Not even the girls knew about it. Especially not the girls, because down here, sweet things lined wood shelves: jars and covered bowls held jam, fruit preserves. Not even her husband Carmine had ever been here, because if he knew where she stored the vinegared peppers, he would have eaten them all in a single sitting.

Dark and cool, the dugout hid under a wooden cover, close enough to the well to be mistaken for a pump repair access. The ladder extending straight down had five steps. The room opened under the house, almost directly beneath his bed. An oil lamp sat on the block table that must also have been used to wax the lids of the jars. Clumps of hardened gray wax spackled the wood surface, drizzled down the sides.

Only Luigi had known about this place. He had removed a boulder from the building site and had slept here, underground, while digging the well.

"Now you," she said. "With me. *Insieme.*"

Together.

Had the war come to this house, she would have hidden down here with the girls. The blanket she brought down with her didn't cushion the lumpy floor. Remembering she had forgotten the pillow, she stepped toward the ladder, but he stopped her, pulled her to him.

That made her smile. And that smile, this cool place, was enough.

•

The land above the flood plain, where the winery would be built, once belonged to the DaPonte family, too. It offered a view to the north of the big bend in the river and The Montello on the opposite shore. Somewhere down there, Teresa's mother had disappeared. If it had happened at this time of the year, the hard-running current would have swallowed her in seconds. The icy coldness of the water would have done the rest.

Taking it all in, including the roof of the new house glinting in winter sun, Paolo sketched the layout of the vines running down to join those he would plant on the fertile soil closer to the Piave. From 500 cuttings, his plans called for planting 10,000 vines over the next five years.

"Il primo vino in tre anni," he said. "Three year."

No winery, no equipment, no rooted cuttings, nothing planted, an unfinished house, yet the satisfied look on his face said he could already taste that Prosecco. He started the tractor, aimed it at the new house and began plowing the centerline as a marker for the other rows of vines. Clumps of dead grass split and rolled up on the sides of the furrow. The ex-cavalry officer looked comfortable in the seat of the Landini, as if leading a battle charge.

Reg hammered the first stake in the corner of the plot where the winery would stand. Standing among the dead weeds, the building seemed impossibly big. Where would the stone and lumber come from? How many hands would it take to erect a structure of this size? Did that work force even exist? How much would it all cost?

Little dreams felt safer. His gaze fell on the tiny house downstream, all that was left of the DaPonte holdings. Paolo would probably tear it down and plant on top of it, stealing the last memory – his way of freeing his wife and son from Luigi's curse.

Farther south, the column footings for the new railroad bridge stuck through the swelling river like fence posts. By this time next year, trains would be crossing. The connection to Treviso would be the first step joining the north valley to Venice, just as the Romans had 1500 years before. By comparison, the new empire – Ziccardi Vineyards – encompassing most of what could be seen from this spot and probably smaller than the combined lands his father now farmed back in West Kent – would, on a map of the region, look equal to Denny Bottom.

Maybe it was a little dream after all.

He carried a new stake to the far corner marker, hammered it home.

•

River snow felt different. Wetter, heavier. It turned to slush in sun and ice at night. It flowed everywhere, between roof tile seams, inside window casings and door jambs, even key holes, freezing in the dark and splitting the metal. Just trying to nail siding in place was difficult now: the wetness had softened the joists and studs, warped the planks. Nothing wanted to stay in place here.

Less than a kilometer away, the snow at Teresa's was actual snow. Fluffy, light. None of it got inside, not even into the dugout cellar.

"Terreno bagnato," Paolo said. "La muffa. Un pericolo. La cenere aiuta."

No longer struggling to translate each word, Reg understood the meaning: wet soil brought the danger of mildew to the vines, but the ash would help prevent that. For the first time, he didn't resent all those cartloads of burnt lumber.

Teresa refilled his soup bowl, gave him another piece of bread, then brought the pot to her sister. "Di più?"

Nodding, the blond-haired woman jostled the baby in her lap, but she was looking at Reg. "E 'più grasso ora."

And he was fatter now. His trousers felt tight at the waist. He stopped chewing the bread.

"E più forte," the black-haired woman said, flashing that little smile again. "Strong?"

"Fortunato," Paolo said. "With the luck" – he gave his son's cheek a tender pinch – "like me, no?"

The sisters exchanged a grin. Some peace must have fallen over them, like the snow. They were partners under this roof, no longer staying out of each other's way. Gabby took the girls for walks during the day, giving her sister time to rest. Teresa sometimes burped the baby, changed its diapers and always did all the laundry, even Reg's clothes now, which she folded and left on his bed like presents from an invisible hand.

The sound of eating came back into the room – spoons in bowls, soup in mouths, swallows. The girls were the noisiest, slurping hot broth, gulping goat's milk cooled by frost. When Teresa returned to her seat at the table, she crossed herself again, though she had done it at least three times during this meal already. Maybe that was a signal, too, that she knew what would happen after her daughters had fallen asleep, where she would lead him through the cold, what heat she would make with her body.

He dunked the piece of bread into the broth. "Lucky – yes," he said.

•

"In Venice." Amelia tore one of the honey-dipped balls from a stack that looked like a Christmas pyramid. "With my cousin."

The Mayor let out a sigh. "The entire war – I feared you would never come back," he said in Italian. His eyes got glassy. "But you did. For me."

Her smile turned up a corner of her mouth. She fed the little pastry ball past her lips, let it begin to dissolve on her tongue. Eyes shut, she savored the taste, like bliss. "He had a boat," she said. "With a motor. We were always ready to escape."

What did she see in the balding man with bad teeth, a double chin and a paunch to match? Who would leave Venice for Colfosco?

"There are three holiday parties you must come to," she said. "All our young women will be there."

The honey and the buttery pastry went down easily. Reg tore another ball off the stack. "I can't."

"You must," she said.

The Mayor was squinting at them. "Piacere, in Italiano."

"I'm – involved," Reg told her.

She lowered her hand, left a little ball on her plate, wiped her fingers with a napkin. "Who?"

"Teresa."

"La strega?" The Mayor laughed. "Lei ti mangerà."

She wasn't a witch and she wouldn't eat him. Still, it felt like a good thing that everyone seemed to fear her.

"This is not possible." Amelia stood. "You will stop it."

"I was thinking about making it official." He turned to The Mayor: "Volete eseguire la cerimonia?"

"Quale cerimonia?" His eyes widened. "Matrimonio? No! Sì?
He nodded.

"Here, only a priest marries us." She wore that lopsided smile again. "No priest will marry her to you."

Something in her tone told him not to argue. Paolo would find a priest. Paolo would make everything possible.

"Not even Paolo can make that happen." She saw the surprise on his face, knowing she had read his mind. Carrying that smug smile back to her plate, she picked up the little ball, popped it into her mouth. "Keep her. As a mistress. A young wife – someone your age – might be grateful for that."

That warped view of marriage didn't sound strange coming from her. He glanced at the balding man using his wet napkin to scrub honey off his shirt front. She had not come back for this man. She had left Venice for Paolo.

"She needs me," Reg said.

Amelia's eyelids got heavy. She nodded. "She's a DaPonte. They need everything. Always."

"He'll never leave her." He tore two balls from the stack. "You have to know that."

Glaring at him, she clenched the napkin in her lap. "You don't know what I know."

"Her daughters need me," he told her.

Her laugh sounded like a sniff. "More DaPonte women to curse foolish men. Do not be one of them."

The balls − *struffoli* − crunched in his mouth. "Even foolish men need a home."

•

She was right. No priest would perform the marriage. Unless he became a Catholic. And that could take months, even years. And that would alert the authorities, who could deport him. Becoming an Italian citizen would involve a long, complicated process, with no guarantees.

"Allora − no do." Paolo tightened the last screw in the upper door hinge. "Finito!"

Just in time. There was snow in the clouds swirling off the mountains and threatening to cross the river. The door slapped shut with a sturdy thud. The ex-cavalry officer threw a heavy arm over Reg's shoulder, hugged him, then opened the door and stepped into his new house.

"Chiedetele − ask her, yes?" He drew in a long breath, let out a satified sigh. "*Ma* − but, no do."

"Won't people talk?"

"Certo. Sempre." Paolo pulled him into the foyer. "La pace qui."

There was peace here, in this house empty of everything, waiting to be filled with furniture and children. And people would talk, always. And the scent of new snow blew through the open doorway.

•

They called her La Befana. She came from the mountains, in the deep night, wrapped in snow, frost and the north wind, leaving sweets for good children, a stick for the bad ones. And she carried a broom to clean the house − and to thump any child who might spot her.

Not so different from Father Christmas, though this Christmas witch wore tattered shoes and a black shawl and she arrived on the eve of the Epiphany, the twelfth day after the birth of the baby Jesus, when the three Wise Men arrived at the manger with their gifts.

And La Befana liked wine, not the sweet milk children in England left out.

Most children in England, that is. Reg's father had no use for the Victorian version of Father Christmas who brought gifts to children. That character was either German − Saint Nicholas − or American − Santa Claus − and no foreigner received a welcome in Reg's boyhood home. The spirit visiting the farm in Rusthall on Christmas Eve was one who enjoyed feasts with adults and had no time for children. William Olcutt had styled Father Christmas in his own image.

"We can't let that happen here," Reg said, tracing a finger down the valley between her breasts, breathing in the smell of an open jar of brandied peaches – their feast in the secret cellar. "The girls deserve the best holiday."

"You buy the food, their shoes," she said. "You can ask Paolo for money for sweets and presents."

He grinned. "I have enough for that."

"You spoil them," Teresa said, but she was smiling up at him. "They will never want to leave."

"Home is the place you never leave," he told her. "You take it with you."

She threw an arm over her eyes, took a long breath. Shifting onto her side, she touched his cheek. "They should know the story. The three kings. To teach their children."

He nodded, admiring the simple folktale, the kind Mr. Kipling would have woven into something magical. In legend, La Befana allowed the three Wise Men to stay the night in her home, the cleanest in the village. They asked her to join them on their journey, but she had cleaning to do. After they left, she had a change of heart and went looking for them and the baby Jesus, never finding either, so from then to now, she kept wandering, searching for the infant.

She slid her hand back to her chest. "You will not leave?"

"No place to go."

"England?"

"Too far," he said.

"Colfosco?"

"Too close."

Her short laugh died in the space between them. "Venezia, Milano, Genova, Roma – "

He quieted her lips with a kiss, then rolled onto his back, stared at the stout timbers spanning the small cellar roof. "You'll be excommunicated."

"I will be a woman again." She sat up, ran her fingers through her tangled black hair. "Yours."

He chewed the last small peach slice, sipped the brandied syrup. "I think I'm drunk."

"Ubriaco in amore?" she said.

Drunk in love? This didn't feel like love. It felt like peace. There was no way to tell her that without hurting her.

302

He drained the jar, swallowing the sweetness and the glow of her skin in candlelight. He could be those ceiling logs. He could hold up this house, raise her daughters, make a future. "I already have my Christmas gift," he said, drawing her closer. "Here."

The way her body shuddered, the wetness of her tears on his neck, convinced him La Befana was real.

7

He had most gifts wrapped by Boxing Day, storing them in the cold cellar until the full moon on the Eve of the Epiphany. The slick white paper had come from the butcher in Susegana, whose supplies remained limited and his sales so brisk he frequently sold out within an hour of opening his shop. The twine had come from the melon man, whose stand and shed stood at the side of a lonely stretch of the river road to Casonetti. Brown and coarse, that twine tied up fish netting filled with winter melons, ready to be carted to markets from Valdobbiadene to Conegliano.

The girls would get sweets and money for shoes. The baby would get a mobile Reg had made from pine cones and bits of shiny metal dug up in the flood plain channel, held together by that fuzzy twine. Paolo and Gabby would get the goat, considered a pet by the girls, but too strong and unruly for them to play with anymore. His bed had already been carted over to the new house. The alcove off the girls' bedroom served as his sleeping quarters now, just as it had served Luigi in his last nights. From there it was 14 steps − he had counted them and could make the walk in total darkness − to Teresa's bed, warmed by her body.

He found jars for canning in the makeshift depot at Ponte Della Priula, where the new railroad bridge, still without tracks, spanned the Piave. He wrapped the jars for Teresa, reliving their lovemaking in the dugout cellar with each knot of twine.

The goat man and his father got Carmine Cosato's clothes and his shiny black shoes − unwrapped and with Teresa's blessing. It took less than three days for those shirts and trousers to look as though they had been worn by both men for years, full of dust and the smell of manure. The shoes were never seen again, perhaps eaten by the always hungry herd.

For The Mayor and Amelia, he wrapped up some of the goat cheese Rudolfo, Sr. had given him in return for the clothes. The Mayor didn't wait for January 6th − he opened the package as soon as it hit his hands. His balding head bobbed side to side, the corners of his mouth turned down, his shoulders slumped. He must have been hoping for Asiago cheese. Already in Venice with her cousin for the holidays, Amelia's perfume still infused the cushions in the front room, where her depressed lover left the cheese on a table and trudged out into the cold wind racing through the square, on his way to his own home and his wife, and the melancholy of a man orphaned by Father Christmas.

Reg couldn't walk through the village these days without middle-aged women asking him to help fix something in their houses: a leaky roof, a broken window, a swollen door, a rotting stair, a stuck well pump handle. Their daughters offered smiles and food, which he took back to the girls, especially the cream puffs little Sancia loved. He began to treat those walks into Colfosco as his personal collection route, no different from the paperboys who delivered *The Rusthall Gazette*, except this pay was better – and tastier.

He left the gifts on the kitchen table, names in block letters on each one. On the morning of The Epiphany, the girls awkened him by tearing open the wrapped candy. He pulled back the alcove curtain, smiled at how they stuffed their mouths full.

"Too much," Teresa said, both to her daughters and to him. But she didn't try to stop them. She retied the neck of her sleeping gown. "Thank you for the new jars."

He got off the bed built into the recess, felt the cold on his feet. "You saw them?"

"Two days ago," she said, stepping to him, kissing his cheek. "I have your gift" – she jerked her head toward her bedroom – "in there."

"But they're awake," he told her.

She had his hand and was pulling him to the doorway. On his side of her bed, nearest the closet, a pair of dark brown slippers sat on the red blanket. They were the same soft-stitched style as the pair he had lost – somewhere in Italy.

"Where did you get the money for – ?" He knew before finishing the sentence that Paolo had paid for the slippers. "He already gave me a bonus payment."

"It makes him happy," she said. "Like you, with the girls. With me." Her lips were wet on his neck. "Show them. It was their idea."

As soon as he stepped into the main room, the girls spotted the slippers. Nicoletta clapped her hands. Sancia ran into his arms. He carried her back to the table, let her feed him a hard candy the size of a rifle shell.

She giggled as she watched him rattle that sweet bullet around in his mouth, clicking off his teeth.

Her sister put a new piece in his hand: "La Befana likes you, too."

The baby crawled over the hardwood — a tiny white bear cub struggling across a dark meadow. At the hearth, Teresa kept an eye on the infant and on Gabby, who stirred the stew, her first family dinner in her new house. Outside, the girls tried to play with the tethered goat, but the animal kept shying from them, bleating its annoyance.

The river ran fast below the high bank. Watching it through the window, Paolo sipped wine. "The flood comes next month. We'll see how our work holds up."

From here, the hand-dug channel paralelling the north shore didn't look wide or deep enough to take all the Piave might give it. The floodplain might disappear under water if the snow melt was substantial. The cuttings would not survive that. The vines those cuttings might produce would wash away in future floods.

"So much depends on a ditch," Reg said.

It made Paolo laugh and clink his glass to the one in his guest's hand. "You worry like a new mother." His glass made an arc across the flood plain, as if toasting all of it. "Venturi. From Reggio Emilla."

"Tastes like Soave," Reg said, sipping the white wine.

This laugh was loud enough to make the woman turn from the stew pot. "Giovanni Venturi," the ex-cavalry officer said. "His formula. The water in our narrow channel moves faster than the river. No flooding. Downstream?" — he shrugged his shoulders — "But not here." He drained his glass. "We eat now."

He had not finished refilling his glass and taking his seat at the head of the table when the girls scampered in and the baby got scooped up in his aunt's arms and Gabby began ladling stew into new glazed bowls, decorated with hand-painted flowers of blue and green.

"The priest is back in La Parrocchia," Teresa said, balancing the child in her lap and inhaling the aroma of the stew. "He might remain this time."

"He's of no use to us," Paolo told her. "Even when he's here, he's running away."

The girls watched their mother blow on her spoon, taste the chunky liquid. She nodded, then handed the baby back to Gabby. The sound of spoons on bowls and of lips slurping hot stew made the table come alive.

Outside, the goat got quiet, enjoying being left with the river. A story would have to be created to explain its disappearance: it might

306

have chewed through its tether, run away, in search of new spring grass, in a meadow where it would be safe from hunters and wolves. The girls would believe that. And they would believe the meat they would be eating at the Easter feast had come from the butcher in Susegana.

"How do you know about Venturi?" Reg said.

The big man squinted. "Galileo, da Vinci — we use the genius of science everyday here. It's in our nature, as Italians." He was smiling now. "Our winery will be show that."

The potato chunks in the stew were frim, yet tender. The peas were still sweet. The carrots, too. The fish pieces melted on his tongue.

"More?" Gabby was beaming as she took his empty plate to the pot, the baby dozing against her shoulder. With her hair tied in back, she looked like the teenager she still was.

He glanced at the dark-haired woman across the table. "Your recipe?"

"Our mother's," she said, stopping to glance toward the river. "Stufato di pesce d'inverno. Trota marmorata"

Winter fish stew. Marble trout.

His refilled bowl wobbled when she set it down in front of him, making those lumps of fish appear to swim among the vegetables. It almost looked too beautiful to eat.

Almost. He dug in.

•

Venturi knew his stuff. The Piave crested the second week in March, spilling over the cut in the high bank where the channel started. The first flow crawled through the deep ditch, never getting halfway up the eight-foot high sides before dribbling out the far end near the remains of the Roman bridge, then back into its source. Within minutes, the water began to roil, churning the channel soil, taking on a darker color. Soon, the stream was speeding at three times the rate of the river, sloshing out only when debris made it into the ditch. With a long pole, Reg dislodged the items — pieces of tree trunks, pots, bits of clothing and broken furniture — and kept the channel clear.

Using left over lumber, Paolo tried to fashion a grate at the head of the ditch, but the surge of the water swept it out of his grasp. "Cement and stone," he said, watching the torrent. "And another channel. This summer."

The water made a gurgling growl as it exploded through the narrow ditch. "Sounds angry," Reg told him.

"The Piave, she hates us now." Paolo picked up a long pole and went downstream to help keep the flow free of clogs. "Never get too close." He tested the footing near his new position. "She will love us again when we feed her to the vines." He seemed surprised by his grin. "Come le donne."

Like women.

If the Piave truly was a woman, then no man – not even the great Venturi – stood a chance.

•

Down where the cuttings lay, below the frost line, the earth had sucked in enough river water to keep the soil damp. Roots, like tiny twisted threds, held on to the moisture. The two brothers from Valdobbiadene handled the pencil-length vines as if they were infants, gently placing them on a sheet of burlap – one by one. All but six of the 500 had rooted.

The older brother shrugged and shook his head. "What did we do wrong?"

"A bad cut." The younger one put his nose to the failed cuttings, sniffed them. "Too dry."

Reg climbed up on the first step of the tractor. "Why are they disappointed?"

"Each cutting is 50 years of grapes." The ex-cavalry officer ran a hand through his blond hair, shaggy from neglect. "That's money to them. They're invested with us – five percent each."

"We replace." The muscles in the younger brother's arms rippled when he crossed them. "From the original."

Paolo nodded. "Let's get them in the ground."

The leftover twine had been used to lay out the rows, scrap wood serving as stakes that the big man had hammered into the softening ground. The brothers held the corners of the burlap sheet, moved it to the center of the planting site. With narrow spades, they began digging, pacing to get the spacing right with each new hole. They stopped after the tenth one and began the planting, the backfilling, the watering-in, the tamping down of the soil.

Watching them work – silent, with no need to comment on a process they each knew intimately – Reg thought of Sgt. Dickson and his stones, the precision of his labor.

"They look so happy," he said.

308

"They're planting life." Paolo switched on the Landini, fed petrol to the sputtering engine, put the machine in gear. "I plow, you keep their water buckets full."

The tractor began discing the upper stretch of the flood plain. Reg picked up a bucket and headed to the river, wondering how many trips he would have to make before all 494 of the cuttings had been planted, like a big family of children tucked into their new beds.

•

They chose the newly tilled area for the picnic because it offered a view of the house, the river and the new plantings, covered now by awnings of burlap suspended from the twine and stakes. From this distance, it looked like an army had bivouacked on the flood plain, soldiers asleep in their tents.

The baby kept crawling off the blanket, too fast for Gabby to catch him before he got into the dark soil. Bits of it clung to his skin and diaper. The dirt wouldn't brush off.

"My son, the explorer." Paolo wore a broad grin. "Let him go."

Watching their cousin crawl away, the girls looked as through they wanted to get on their hands and knees and follow him. Teresa saw that, too. "Stay," she told them. "Help serve the cheese."

Just enough sun was getting through the burlap to keep the new vines warm without burning them. The brothers from Valdobbiadene would come back to take the awnings away as soon as the first buds appeared.

Warmed in the hamper, the Soave tasted heavier, even a bit sour. The ex-cavalry officer studied its pale color in the glass. "The Glera will give a lighter shade," he told the river. "Our Prosecco will be sweeter."

Goat cheese and bread, wine and sugar-coated biscuits. A breeze off the water, the musty smell of dank earth. A view of The Montello and, just south, the tower in Nervesa, somehow spared in the shelling.

"In town they say Ceneda will be called Vittorio Veneto," Reg said. "For the victory that ended the war." He focused his stare across the river. "And that will be Nervesa della Battaglia, for where the victory march started."

Paolo swatted a fly with the back of his hand. "We will go to Rome, get the government to give us the protection zone of origin. As soon as we have the signatures of all the Glera growers."

The winery would be only the first step. Establishing a trademark for the Prosecco made from Valdobbiadene to Conegliano would bring recognition – and a premium price. "Like champagne," the ex-cavalry officer had told each grower he had spoken to. "We make the best, we charge the most."

Denominazione di origine controllata. The designation would cost the growers nothing.

"The maps are nearly ready," Paolo said. "You should buy a suit. For the journey." He winked. "Your investment."

The women paid no attention. To be out here and not cleaning or cooking or washing was too valuable to be spoiled by conversation. The way the breeze played with the ends of Teresa's hair made him think of new grass in Denny Bottom, almost waving back to him each Spring.

The baby had a handful of mud he was patting onto a rock. He glanced back, found his mother smiling at him, then scooped up more mud.

"He never stays clean," Gabby said.

"This soil is in his blood," Paolo told her. "He needs to be in contact with it. Like me." He slapped Reg's arm. "Like us."

Not a rock. Much too yellow for that. And where those little fingers had rubbed, that yellow was shiny.

Bolting from the blanket, hearing the glasses clatter and the voices clamor in confusion, he ran through the soft soil, losing a slipper on the way. The baby boy never saw him coming, so he let out a startled shreik that quickly turned to joy when Reg scooped him up and pulled him away from the unexploded artillery shell, its pointy outline now visible in the top soil.

He stepped back, held up an arm to stop the others from getting too close. "German," he said. "Must have floated up after the tilling softened the soil."

As big as the baby, the shell was aimed directly at the tower in Nervesa.

Gabby took her son, checked to make sure no part of him was missing. Teresa clutched her daughters to her side, refusing to let them move. Paolo fell to his knees at Reg's feet. He couldn't stop staring at the artillery shell. A tear leaked out an eye. He crawled to the yellow object, carefully digging around its edges, then backing away and standing. His long exhale raced toward the river. He turned and pulled Reg into his chest, squeezing him. "First my wife, now my son. I can never repay you."

"You could buy me that suit," Reg said.

310

The big man started to laugh, but he couldn't stop crying at the same time. Gabby was already on the move, heading toward the house, the head of her son bouncing on her shoulder. The way her body moved, Reg realized she was always coming toward him or walking away, never actually there with him.

It all seemed to make sense now. She was the glow of the sun on the water, forever eluding anyone's grasp. He was the bramble on the high bank, cousin to those dark smooth pebbles on the shore that were real to the touch, like the solid feel of Teresa and her daughters.

He took the girls by the hand. "Let's go find my slipper."

With their mother following, they led him straight to it.

•

The men from the moutains never rested, except at mealtime or to shoot a long glance at Gabby when she stepped out of her house, a breeze off the river billowing her sun dress or the twilight putting a glint in her light hair. Hour after hour, these sinewy men hauled logs up the slope, used dual-handled planes to scrape the bark, piled the wood chips on the flood plain for future placing around the base of the vines as mulch to keep the soil moist and to hold back the grasses.

They ate, drank, sang, made hunting trips, lugging back wild boar that they roasted in a pit and deer that they strung upside down for days before butchering, the thick chunks of meat skewered for cooking over an open fire. To them, building the winery was a festival, every day a chance to enjoy each other's company and admire their handiwork.

They stacked the timbers beyond the staked corners, where the footings for the pier foundation were being dug – deep holes that would be filled with rock, rubble and cement, lifting the building's floor two feet above the ground to allow the cool breeze to keep the structure cool. "Heat is our enemy," Paolo had said. "Spoils the grapes. And the wine."

The former cavalry officer had already lost interest in the building site. He was busy now laying out the route for the water line down the middle of the flood plain, allowing branches to run north to the new house and south toward the old cabin, where a tank would be installed to pressurize the system.

To get the water up from the river, a series of three lifting stations had been installed. Each one operated by hand crank, but in the future, wind power would do this job and also pump the water up to the tank. The lifts resembled giant corkscrews, set inside a cylinder.

311

"Archimedes' screw," Paolo had said the first time he tested them. "The Romans used these. They killed him. But he lives still."

"He was a Greek," Reg said.

Paolo nodded. "From Syracusa. Not all great ideas are Italian." He winked. "Only most of them."

In moments like that, the winery owner could envision all of it finished and up and running. The future was already here. His smile each late summer sunset said that much as he watched the mountain men walk back into town to their rooms at the southend of the village, near the garbage heap where vendors tipped their rotting fruit and vegetables from carts.

He brought the rifle out and handed it to Reg. "Shoot it. We can't wait for the army."

The army might never get here to dispose of the artillery shell. It had sat on the shore below the low bank for more than a month now, lurking like a wounded animal, unpredictable and dangerous.

"It could crater the shore," Reg said.

"Then we'll run the end of the new flood channel into that crater." Paolo inspected his vines as he led the march to river. Skidding down the bank, he sidestepped the yellow shell and found cover behind one of the stone arches of the ancient bridge. Kneeling, he pulled Reg behind him. "Use my shoulder to brace your aim. And keep low."

From 30 yards, Barry would have had no trouble hitting the shiny object. "I'm not a very good shot," Reg said.

"We have four bullets," Paolo told him. "Use them all if you have to."

The water was clear of the small boats that took people and supplies across to the Nervesa side. The longer he squinted down the rifle barrel, the more the shell began to resemble a large yellow fish that had beached itself.

"We should let the army take care of this," Reg said.

"If someone dies because of this, on my land, I will feel responsible." The big man steadied himself against the stone rampart, put fingers in his ears to deaden the sound. "Shoot now."

It felt too familiar, taking aim, slowing his breath, quieting his finger on the trigger so that the squeeze came as a slow movement of steady presssure. The sound of the bullet leaving the rifle was followed instantly by the sound of the explosion of the target, as if the echo could be louder than the original shout. Stones pelleted the arch, like hail on a slate roof. Mud showered into the water. Smoke settled

312

over the crater. The river backfilled that hole, tearing at its edges, then hiding it under silt.

"Ben fatto!" Paolo brushed dirt off his clothes and out of his light hair. "Well done! First shot!"

He lost his grin when he saw the blood. The stinging Reg felt made him touch his cheek. A sliver of metal was sticking out of a puncture wound. He yanked the shrapnel out. Blood oozed down the side of his face. "Wounded in peace time," he said. "Perfetto."

"It's nothing." Paolo stuck his handkerchief against the wound, then examined it, his face close to the blood. "I'll stitch you up myself."

"You've done that before?"

"We should cauterize it first," Paolo said. "Kill the bad flesh."

"Sounds worse than the injury."

"It is." Paolo threw an arm over Reg's shoulder, led him up the bank. "But a Ziccardi does what is necessary. Never forget this."

"I'm not a Ziccardi," Reg said.

The hug got stronger. "You are. To me."

•

She tapped the gauze taped to his cheek. "It hurts?"

He shook his head, let it sink into the pillow, but he could still see the two girls standing in the bedroom doorway. "Let them in."

Teresa stood, shooed the girls and shut the door. "This is our room now."

"I'm fine sleeping in the alcove."

"I am not." She sat facing the closet, her clothes at one end, his at the other. "We can put the crib in there, where it will stay warm."

Crib?

She reached back, took his fingers in hers. "January. A winter child."

The throbbing ache in his cheek disappeared. He felt his heart beat louder. His mouth got dry and all the strength ran out of him. It felt like being shot, dying.

He felt like singing.

8

S he refused to come to the celebration or to allow The Mayor to attend. The balding man sat slump-shouldered on her balcony, sulking. Missing out on the taste of wild boar and venison, the wine, the cheese, the music, had made him ponder if this woman was worth the sacrifice.

"Then at least talk to the priest," Reg said. "Or let The Mayor do it."

Amelia shook her head.

"Paolo asked me to give you this." He pulled a note from his jacket pocket. "He wants your help."

Her fingers trembled as she opened the small envelope. Her eyes scanned the words, her lips curling into a snarl. She glared at him. "You would throw away your life, too?"

"I won't abandon her," he said, "like her father did."

She scoffed a laugh, then dropped the note into the fire. "Leave. You are no longer welcome here."

The thick paper wrinkled in the flames before turning to ash. Her footsteps got softer, a door off the hallway shut. The Mayor stood, rubbed the chill off his arms and opened the glass door to come back inside. He opened his mouth, but must have decided against saying anything. With a lame wave, he disappeared down the hall, where that door opened, then closed again.

For all its finery and color, the room felt sterile, as though no one actually lived here, they simply walked through from time to time. The clutter of Mr. Kipling's office, the vast portions of landscape he had left wild, defined Bateman's as his own province. This room could have belonged to anyone with money and no time to enjoy it.

He hurried down the stairs and out into the cool alpine breeze. The new vines would be grateful for this early cold snap. So would the mountain men, whose work on the winery would feel easier and whose appetites would get bigger. He quickened his pace to join them.

•

It resembled a pavillion – all roof and poles. Carpenters from Conegliano and Belluno sat with their legs draped over the cross beams, hand-drilling, hammering, using planes to get a perfect fit. From the river bank, where the second flood channel had been trenched, it looked as if a carnival had come to town. So much noise, so much activity spread out over such a large area, there was no place to go to escape it.

Except in town, but he no longer looked forward to going there. Shunned by villagers now, thanks to Amelia and her gossip, no one requested his help these days. Doors closed as he approached. Faces disappeared from windows. Merchants still took his money, but without small talk. Even the cherry vendor, a man who constantly mumbled to himself, fell silent when dealing with Reg.

The balcony was always empty now. The Mayor was too busy to see him. Ony Luigi's old friends still sat with him, discussing weather, wine and women. "You think Amelia is difficult?" one of the men had said, laughing. "Her father was worse."

Stuck in the middle of the flood plain, the water pipe channel half dug, Paolo and the mechanic finally got the Landini to start. It sputtered, but the engine held and began to purr as it warmed up. The little man from Treviso clapped his hands as he danced around the machine. Paolo climbed onto the seat, put the tractor in gear, drove it toward the winery site.

"We'll try it going downhill," he said, shouting over the motor noise. "Should be easier."

With the mechanic following close behind, the tractor made slow steady progress. The sound of it drew Gabby outside. She waved. Her husband kept his focus on a point in the distance, as if setting a survey line for the pipe. The little mechanic waved back at her. So did Reg. It made her laugh.

The baby crawled between her legs like a cat. She got him before he reached the steps, picked him and turned him around and followed him back inside. Tomorrow, the two brothers from Valdobbiadene would come to remove the burlap shading for the vines, begin pruning, prepare new cuttings ready for rooting.

Leaving the shovel stuck like a stake at the end of the new flood channel, Reg put on his overshirt and began the walk home, taking his now familiar route past the old cabin – little more than a weathered storage shed compared to the new house. A passing stranger would have trouble imaginging anyone had ever lived there. Dying grasses beyond the cabin had been cleared to make way for a water tank, scheduled to arrive on the first or second train over the new bridge later this Fall. By then, the branch of pipe to it would be in place. Sometime next Summer, they would tap into that branch and the small house would have its own supply of water. A vineyard manager would live there, plant a garden, raise a family.

He smiled at the splintering wood of the door, the still shiny padlock holding it fast. "Wait," he told the old stones. "One more winter."

Workers at the winery began cheering as the Landini crept up the slope from the flood plain. The blond-haired man in the driver's seat punched the air in triumph. The little mechanic, out of breath and struggling up the hill, held his arms out straight from his sides like a footballer who had just scored a goal.

There would be meat stew on the hearth, young laughter in the kitchen, wine on the table. And slippers.

•

"He was loud." Propped up by new pillows against the headboard, she picked up flakes of pastry from the bedspread with a wet finger. "He slammed doors, broke things. Gabriella was too young to remember any of that."

Reg watched her breathe. "What did he do?"

"He was old man Ziccardi's accounts collector in Susegana." Grunting as if in pain, she slid down into a reclining position. "Rents, loans. People feared him."

"Your mother, too?"

She shut her eyes, shook her head. "He broke her heart when he left. They said he stole money and took up with a woman in Venice. Uncle Luigi went there, but never found him." More grunts. She rolled on a side, her back to him. "She would take her chair outside to wait for him. Even in the rain."

He pulled the blanket up over her shoulder, blew out the lamp flame, then swung his legs over the edge of the bed. She reached back and grabbed his arm. "No. Stay."

"The girls – "

"They will be fine. Stay."

In the dark, he could feel her smiling as he stretched out beside her. "I would not sit and wait for you," she said. "I would go find you. God help you then."

•

It sounded like thunder. He glanced through the kitchen window, saw no sign of darkening clouds in the bright Fall sky. The builders must have set a charge for the piers of the roadway span that, when finished, would parallel the railroad bridge. In a year's time, a person could walk or drive across the river. Trucks from the new winery would make good commerical use of that.

316

He finished the last of the breakfast pastry, looked in on the girls, still sleeping side by side, and slipped into his jacket, heading out the door. At the top of the little swale, he could see the plume of smoke rising from the flood plain.

He ran.

•

What was left of the Landini lay on its side at the edge of the crater, like a dead horse, bloodied by what was left of its rider. The largest piece − a chunk of skull, straw-colored hair clinging to it, dotted black by the residue of the explosion − was being cradled by one of the carpenters. Several other workmen used hand tools and their feet to stamp out the fire burning on strands of fuel that riddled the soil.

He saw her coming, struggling under the weight of the baby, too heavy to carry the long distance up the slope from the new house, but determined to see for herself. The carpenters cleared a path for her. One of them took the infant. All of them looked away from her bare feet and the blue house dress clinging to her breasts and hips. She saw the piece of her husband's head in the dirty hands of the worker kneeling near the crater rim. Her mouth opened, but no sound escaped. She knelt, took the bloody skull fragment into her own hands, began picking the bits of black powder from the hair. The baby started crying. She acted as though she didn't hear it.

"You'll be warmer inside." He helped her to her feet, turned her toward the new house. "I'll carry Berto."

She nodded, not taking her eyes off the gruesome remains in her palms. Her first steps were in the right direction, then she turned and walked around the four foot deep hole and toward the old cabin.

The carpenters mumured. Their eyes found Reg, the wailing baby thrashing in his arms. "Bring a sledge and a cold chisel," he said. "We'll break the lock and get her indoors."

He followed her, catching up near the tamped down path of the newly buried water line. With her hands cupped, she looked as though she was carrying an offering toward an altar only she could see. He tucked the infant under the flap of his jacket to keep him warm. Muffled by canvas, those sharp cries sounded like the goat.

Three workmen ran past with their tools. They would have that padlock in pieces in no time. The little house, even cold and unswept, must have felt like home to her. Safe.

Once he got a fire going, he could try to figure out a way to pry that chunk of Paolo out of her hands.

The cavalry officers were easy to spot among all the uniformed men ringing the gravesite. Their headgear resembled a tall cake – flat on top, a big emblem stuck in front for decoration. Their trousers were Hunters' britches, puffy above the knee. They wore brown leather gloves, matching their ammunition belts, worn diagonally across their tunics, ending at a scabbarded sabre, a gold fabric knot dangling from the hilt. They could have walked straight out of the Prussian War, copies of those lead soldiers he and Digger had loved to play with.

Other military included several Alpini, the crow feather in their elf-like caps and the green rank ensignias making them stand out. A few were in full dress – knapsacks on their backs, wood staffs as tall as they were in one hand, rifle in the other. Two of them Reg recognized as carpenters who were building the winery.

They were dwarfed by Mountain Artillery soldiers, some of whom had worked the timbers for the building. These men wore caps with feathers, too, but carried their rifles slung across their backs.

Those in uniform nearly matched the number of villagers and grape growers. Some, like the brothers from Valdobbiadene, had traveled from as far away as Belluno, beneath the flat-topped shadow of Mount Antelao – King of the Dolomites, the highest peak overlooking this region. Workers from the railway bridge had also shown up. The only person who wasn't here was Amelia.

Gabby wouldn't have noticed her anyway. She kept staring at her hands, empty and clean now. Reg knew what she saw there. He saw it, too.

Her sister had dressed her in black and told him to lead her to her seat, hold her hand through the service, bring her back home. Teresa had stayed at the new house with the baby and the girls, unwilling to endure the disapproving glances that an unwed pregnant woman would receive, even one widowed by war.

The tall man speaking in Latin must have been a bishop. When he finished, he shook hands with The Mayor and disappeared into a black motorcar parked at the side entrance to the church. That automobile sped over the little hill and out of sight before the rest of the mourners could file out of the cemetary. Most of them walked in a long line down La Via Barca toward the river, resembling a column of soldiers on forced march, advancing toward their objective.

Every door in the new house stood open. Platters of food, pastries and fruit sat on the long table. All the chairs had been moved against

318

the walls. Teresa came out of the kitchen long enough to escort her sister into the bedroom, past the framed painting of Tesoro the stallion, still singed by war, centered over the fireplace mantel, the twisted remains of that melted silver bowl directly below it.

The cavalry officers and the Alpini came inside to eat, but the Mountain Artillery men stayed near the fire outside, where a boar had been roasted, its tusks stuck in the soil like daggers. "Symbol of a clean kill," the mountain man tending the spit said. He meant the animal had been hunted on foot. His compatriots would not eat the flesh of an animal that had been baited or trapped or run down on horseback.

One of the carpenters – a Sergeant in the Alpini – carried a plate out for a taste of boar. His cap insignia depicted an eagle, wings spread atop a round crest, backed by crossed rifles and sitting on what looked like upturned ram horns. Through the open doorway, he could make out Nicoletta chasing the crawling baby. His eyes looked wet. He glanced at the winery building. "We will finish it," he said.

"Not sure we can pay you," Reg told him.

Staring now at the mangled skeleton of the Landini standing near the filled-in crater, a line of idle shovels stuck in the dirt like toothpicks, the carpenter nibbled at the meat. "No need. We discussed it." He put a hand on Reg's shoulder. "All of us – Piave Valley, Second Regiment, Seventh Battalion. We didn't fight our war in snow and ice to let an enemy artillery shell defeat us after the peace."

Inside, a line of uniformed men snaked around the table, filling their plates in silence. Little Sancia sat on the kitchen floor, eating another pastry. Her sister held the baby around the waist while her mother filled water pitchers. No women from the village had come out to help.

The sound of a lute broke the quiet. Rudolfo, Sr. sat crosslegged near the fire, strumming a tune that some of the men must have known because they hummed and sang along with it. His son led a new goat to a tethering post at the back of the house.

"Come in for some food," Reg told him.

The goat man shook his head.

"She won't mind," Reg said.

"Death inside," Rudolfo, Jr. said. "Life out here."

The new vines, the last of the summer grasses, the river, the music – the flood plain was alive with all of it. Reg followed him back to the smoke and a helping of sweet roasted meat.

•

The cavalry left first. The Alpini lingered a little longer. The mountain men sat and ate and drank as if they planned to sleep here. Moonlight silhouetted the carcass of the Landini and the two people standing beside it. Reg walked toward them.

The Mayor nodded on his way to the food. Amelia kept her back to the river, her gaze on the real gravesite, the place where most of Paolo had turned into vapor.

"You must take over," she said. "My cousins and the bankers agree. This official designation zone — you will go to Rome and see to it."

"I don't know anyone in Rome."

"You will have the names." Her eyes narrowed. "Do this or I call in the loans."

His own laugh surprised him. "Then you can run the winery. Good luck."

"His wife and son" — she had a handful of his sleeve — "will lose that house. And you — would you be permitted to stay here if the authorities discovered you had entered without papers?"

"I had a visa."

"Temporary. Expired." She let go of his jacket, refocused on the winery building. "I warned you about the DaPonte curse. It could force your unborn child to grow up without a father." Her small black shoes crunched the soil. She stopped after a few steps, turned toward the river: "You will need a suit. Have it made in Milan. Romans have no sense of style."

He watched her climb the newly widened path toward the big building, its black slate roof bouncing moonlight back into the night. Against an enemy like her, how long could the two DaPonte sisters survive on their own?

"The devil strolls at night." The goat man was watching her, too. He offered a sack, heavy with fresh cheese: "For your family. Don't let the mountain men eat this. Or know where it came from."

His slim figure joined the stoop-shouldered frame of his father carrying the lute. The two of them trudged up the slope, mixing with stragglers in uniform. Reg ran his fingertips over the cold metal shell of the tractor. Except for the bleat of the hungry goat and the crackle of the lonely fire, the flood plain filled with the hush of the autumn river — whispered like an primeval lullaby, serenading this valley, yet all the while hinting of the torrents headed downstream with each

320

snow and ice melt, the terror promised by the mountains every Spring. Only a fool would expect to win that war.

"A dead fool," Reg told the picket of shovels. He aimed his stride at the light spilling out of the windows and doorways, where the women and children were safe, for now, from the darkness all around.

9

Cars, bicycles, slow-moving trolleys, pavements jammed with people. This was not the Milan he had left less than two years ago. It smelled different – like a factory, the perfume of wet wool and silk, the exhaust fumes, the cigar smoke – and sounded louder, as if someone had turned up the volume on the wireless, getting stray squawks cutting into the buzzing static. Just walking along – getting honked at by drivers frustrated with traffic or being jostled by pedestrians in a hurry – felt like being under assault.

He followed Via A. Manzoni past the opera theater. Near the cathedral, he thought about taking a detour to the Red Cross Hospital, but the chilly moist wind convinced him to keep going south, to the newspaper offices another 15 minutes away.

The giant building dominated the corner. Atop the roof, more than eight stories up, tall letters spelled out *Il Popolo d'Italia*. What he had supposed was a small metropolitan paper must have been a substantial economic force. It was warm inside. And surprisingly quiet. A young clerk escorted him up to the Editorial offices.

"Mr. Mussolini will see you shortly," another clerk told him, pointing to chairs in the outer lobby. A copy of today's paper sat on the rectangular table. The front page story criticized the occupation of Fiume, a city in Croatia captured last year by the forces of Gabriele d'Annunzio, a former General who had declared war on Italy. It read like a fairy tale – the impossible now considered normal.

The small chunky man wearing big round eyeglasses walked up the hall and offered his hand. "I am Mussolini."

"No, you're not," Reg said.

"You were expecting my brother." He smiled. "Everyone is." He gestured to the hall. "He is in Pula, giving speeches. You can discuss your financial contribution with me. Arnaldo" – another smile, broader this time – "Arnaldo Mussolini. "

•

Pula, it turned out, was a small city on the Adriatic, on a tip of Croatia closest to Venice, and not far from the major port the Romans called Fiume. There was no telling when Arnaldo's older brother would return. Trains through Trieste were still unable to keep a schedule.

"How much do you wish to contribute?" The stocky man opened a ledger and readied a pen. "Mister – ?"

"Olcutt. Your brother wrote a feature on me."

The eyes behind those thick glasses squinted. "And – ?"

"I was hoping he could help me with a business matter."

The pen got set gently in the crease of the ledger binder. "Let me get Manlio. He's who you should speak with."

The big office was too clean and neat to belong to a real newspaper man. The framed photographs on the wall all showed sour-faced men, some in uniform, some in suits. In one, Benito Mussolini had his chin raised, his lips in a pout. He was wearing a black shirt, medals pinned to it.

The tall man who came back with Arnaldo had a well-trimmed moustache. And a strong handshake. "Manlio Morgagni, director of advertising. What business matter?"

"A protected agricultural zone," Reg said. "For wine."

The grim look on the tall man's face turned into a grin. "Agriculture is one of my main interests. I hope to start a newspaper devoted to it." He sat and crossed his legs. "Where?"

"Colfosco."

"Where?"

"On the Piave River," Reg said. "Opposite Nervesa. The zone would include Valdobbiadene and Conegliano."

Both men were studying his British clothes. "You are not Italian," Morgagni said.

"English."

The tall man's mouth fell open. "Olcutt – The Englishman who forgot his own name!" He slapped the desk, smiled at Arnaldo. "One of our strongest issues for advertising. You have already made us money!" He leaned in closer. "Tell me. Everything."

•

It took three cups of espresso and a tour of the offices. The tall man knew his way around the place much better than Arnaldo did. But maybe the older Mussolini's eyesight was the problem.

The DOC – *Denominazione di origine controllata* – would be simple to establish, but it would have to come from Venice, the province controlling the region around Treviso. If a businessman from Milan were involved in the enterprise, the provincial government of Milan could represent his interest and help the process along. And Morgagni would send a reporter out to do a story on the new winery and the untimely death of an Italian Cavalry officer.

The matter of Reg's expired entry visa would be more complicated. But since he was running the business, and was expecting the birth of a child – an Italian child – the officials in Rome could be counted on to make permanent status official.

"We will give you some names to see in Rome," the tall man said. "And a letter of introduction. Do you know anyone in Milan to join your venture?"

"Just Mr. Mussolini," Reg said. "The other Mr. Mussolini."

Arnaldo shook his head. "Benito could not be part of it. Not anymore. He cannot even be part of this newspaper. He belongs to the country now – the people. They love him."

"Paolo has a wife and son," Reg said. "Couldn't they – ?"

"The infant? No," Morgagni told him. "The woman? No. We can find an investor for you. Come back in a day or so."

Reg eyed the soft wool of the double-breasted jacket the tall man was wearing. "Where did you have that suit made?"

"Beautiful, no?" Long fingers ran down a lapel. He reached for the pen in the ledger. "Trecanni's. See young Alberto Galetti. A genius." He scribbled a note on the back of his business card. "Give him this." A new smile. "And bring your wallet."

•

Young Alberto Galetti no longer worked at the tailor shop on Via Pattari, just two streets east of the cathedral and an easy 10-minute walk from the newspaper building.

"Homesick little boy." The hunched over man with a paper tape measure draped around his neck struggled to lift a bolt of dark fabric into its slot in the wall. "He went back to Venice." He glanced at the note, holding it at arm's length to focus on the lettering. "Tremila lire."

3000? He swallowed the stale air in here. "That's over twenty pounds sterling."

The tailor squinted at Reg's boots. "Shoes, too. Cinquecento."

500 – three quid – for a pair of shoes?

"A shirt and tie, yes?" He held up swollen fingers before Reg could protest. "No cost." He picked up a pencil, found a blank index card at the roll top desk. "Name?"

"I have to think about it," Reg told him.

"You don't know your name?"

"The price," Reg said. "Expensive."

With a shrug of those sloped shoulders, the tailor shuffled to pairs of large scissors at the far end of the long table. "Blame the war for the price" – he waved the scissors like a weapon – "not Trecanni."

The main entrance — a 20-foot high double door with footed columns supporting a balcony above it — led to a wide hall with an art gallery on one side. Stairs led to classrooms and offices. Near the end of east hallway, he found the door marked *E. Valanga*. He knocked.

A muffled voice responded: "No students today."

He opened the door, stuck his head inside the small room. "Come to Rome with me?"

The man behind the desk had to take off his wire-rimmed eyeglasses to focus across the office. Ezio stood. "Can it be?" He rushed around the desk, pulled Reg into an embrace. "How? When? Sit, sit."

There was no place to sit. Both chairs were loaded with books and newspapers and folders with student names on them. It was just as cluttered and dusty as Mr. Kipling's office. The professor grabbed his overcoat and hat — "Outside. We'll walk." — and shut the door behind him. "Rome? Why?"

"Long story," Reg told him.

"You will stay with us. Your luggage?"

Reg jostled the satchel in his hand. "Only this."

The rear stairs led down to a wide courtyard, dominated by a 15-foot bronze standing on a pedestal almost as tall. "Napoleon," Ezio said, "as Mars the Peacemaker."

"Wasn't Mars the God of War?"

Looping an arm through Reg's, Ezio laughed. "*Exactamente.*"

•

They ate a lot of rice and cooked everything in butter. One of the meals Ezio's wife, Ilba, prepared mixed winter cabbage with bangers and pork rib chops. And that apple pie — how did the language and poetry professor stay so thin?

On a tour of the city center, they carried dry salami to nibble on, even in the convent of a church, Santa Maria delle Grazie, where da Vinci's *The Last Supper* was on display. The colors were surprisingly dull, almost faded.

The wide meadow a few streets south of the main cathedral didn't look big enough to house the university that was planned for the site. Ezio had already accepted a position here because he could go back to teaching only poetry. "If it ever gets built," he said. "The government is not so stable."

Squads of five or six black-shirted men strolled the streets by day. Some wore medals and carried swords. Most carried batons. At night, they carried rifles. They wore baggy khaki trousers tucked into tall black boots. They looked as though they owned the streets. Maybe they did.

"If you look like a Socialist," Ezio said, "you could get attacked. And your Mr. Mussolini feeds them."

Reg made eye contact with one of the black shirts, who smiled and nodded at him. "What does a Socialist look like exactly?"

The skinny professor quickened his pace. "Me."

•

He had a suit his wife could alter, but Ezio wouldn't take any money for it.

"You saved me over three thousand lire," Reg told him.

"You make me your business partner," Ezio said. "That is worth more."

"It's only a formality." He sipped the sweet yellow dessert wine. "You won't actually have to do anything."

Ezio raised his own glass. "Even better."

The custard was not as sweet as Reg had expected. It was creamier than the kind his mother made, and darker in color. "Delicious, Ilba," he told the wide woman who had been eating with her apron on. "I've never heard that name before."

She shrugged and spooned custard into her mouth.

"Latin," Ezio said. "From the Greek. For the island. Elba."

The two boys laughed into their dishes, trying to hide their amusement by eating faster. The young girl pushed the last lump of custard around in her bowl, trying to make it last.

Their father ignored them. "Your visas – were you expecting your army to return you to France?"

Reg shook his head.

"These are military," Ezio said, "like the French transit papers. Unusual."

"A problem?" Reg said.

With a sigh, the thin man pushed back from the table. "I think yes." He drained his tiny glass of wine. "Your Mr. Mussolini might be useful after all."

•

His Mr. Mussolini was still traveling.

The government official Mr. Morgagni had sent Reg to see seemed puzzled by the passport and transit papers. The hand stamp – *Commandement des Troupes alliées à Calais – Le Gènèral Commandant* – didn't match the exit visa issued by the Inter-Allied Control Bureau in

Modane or the Italian entry visa in Bardonecchia, re-stamped in Collegno, just before Turin.

"You had military business to conduct?" the cigarette-smoking official said. "But no uniform?"

"It's what they gave me," Reg told him, "when they brought me back to England."

Another cigarette got lit while the one he was smoking rested in the ashtray. "They planned to return you to France and Italy? For what purpose?"

Sharp rays from the winter sun ran in bands through the slatted blinds on the tall window. Reg stared at the visas, tried to swallow. That wasn't a passport after all. It was a ticket for his execution.

"They wanted to shoot me," he said.

Ezio started laughing. "The English, they joke. He was to advise Mussolini. This man is a hero of our war. He saved lives. Italian lives."

The odor of sweat and cigarettes floated off the official, who blew smoke out of the corner of his mouth. He re-read the letter Mr. Morgagni had written. "If Morgagni approves, then Moretti approves." His stubby fingers stamped two new forms, signed them, put them together with the other papers and slid them across the narrow desk. "Take these to Treviso or Venice. They will enter them in the public record."

Afraid to touch the stack of forms, Reg sat up straight. "Then, I don't have to go to Rome?"

"Rome?" The form stamper lit another cigarette. "You want to live in Rome?"

Before Reg could answer, Ezio grabbed the papers. "Who would live in Rome when there is Venice or Milan, yes?"

"Certo," the official said, offering his hand. "Congratulations. And good luck on your business venture."

"And with his child," Ezio said.

"Yes, of course." The official hurried to open the door. "What type of wine will you be making?"

"Prosecco," Reg said.

Those stubby fingers lingered on the door latch. "Never heard of it. Please tell Mr. Morgagni that Moretti was of assistance to you."

"Of great assistance." Ezio ushered Reg through the doorway and rushed him down the long cold hall. Near the top of the stairs, he slowed down and whispered, "We are governed by fools."

He didn't need a suit and he didn't have to go to Rome. "It's almost too good to be true," he said.

"And tonight we have *Cassoeula* again." Ezio slapped him on the back. "We'll stop to buy fresh cabbage. But first, we eat at Café Cova – the oldest and best in Milan. You pay."

Reg grinned as his hand glided over the smooth marble handrail. "Even better."

•

With his eyes closed, he listened to the rumble of the train and conjured the image of Ezio and Ilba standing in their doorway with their three children, waving. The smell of the last apple pie rose from the small box on his lap. He wondered if this was how Mr. Kipling had felt as a young journalist, always leaving some place he knew he would never be returning to.

The track to Brescia was the best stretch. After that, the going was slower. The war battles had not reached Lake Garda or Verona, but so much of the infrastructure there had been pilfered to supply the front line that this area might as well have been shelled. The train wouldn't get back up to normal speed until it crossed the Brenta, just west of Cittadella. The city hall in Treviso would be open by the time he arrived. His new papers, packed on top of clothes in the satchel, would get filed while he ate breakfast.

Home for supper.

He opened the white box, pinched off a piece of pie. Sweet, buttery – but not as sweet as tomorrow.

10

Rain. The kind with ice in it. Nothing like this existed in West Kent. Here, the mountains made the weather, and today, the mountains were angry. Workers huddled in the big room of the winery, waiting for the storm to pass. Sheets of hard sleet obscured the view of the new house and the river. The little cabin would be taking a beating. Its roof might not hold up if this lasted much longer. If the baby came in this weather, how could a midwife get down from the village?

The two brothers from Valdobbiadene came inside with their helpers. They went straight to the wood stove, rubbed their hands, stripped out of their wet clothes, leaving puddles. Anyone walking in now would see five naked men toweling off with the same blankets they would wrap themselves up in, while an audience of a dozen carpenters and machinists sat around them and smoked cigarettes, dousing them in the rivers of sleet now spreading over the floor boards.

"Calzini all in place," the older brother said. "The vines will be warm."

The burlap wraps they had tied over the vines – they called them "socks" – wouldn't keep the wetness out, but they would offer protection from the night wind. By next year, the vines would be strong enough to survive without help.

"You should go home," the younger brother told him. "The baby."

"I wouldn't be any help with that," Reg said.

"Women don't need help," the sinewy man said. "It's nature. Just go and be there."

His older brother nudged Reg toward the door. "No more to do today."

One of the carpenters – the Alpini – handed him a green slicker. "Take. I stay here."

It smelled of tobacco smoke, especially the hood. The waterproof canvas made the rattle of the freezing rain sound like gunfire. He kept his head down and trudged on.

•

She was cooking, the steam off the pot dampening her strands of yellow hair. The girls sat on the floor. They had the baby surrounded, stopping him from crawling beyond their grasp. Berto didn't like this game. When Sancia ran to greet Reg, the baby followed, hoping to escape.

"How did you get here?" he said.

Gabby looked at him as if he were a slow-witted fool. "Same as you."

"With the baby?"

She ladled stew into a bowl, set it on the table for him. "The new house is too big. And he is everywhere."

At first, he thought she meant the baby. With the first taste of the potato and cabbage in the broth, he realized she meant her husband, the man who had built the place, who had put his touch in every detail.

"Mama's sleeping." Nicoletta gathered up the infant, hoisting him into a standing position and moving him back toward the hearth. "The baby comes soon."

He stopped eating, stepped toward the green slicker. "I'll go get someone from the village."

"They won't come." Gabby stirred the soup, then sat at the table and patted his chair. "Sit. Eat. I'm here."

The smile on her face was different from all the other smiles he remembered. This one was determined. Older.

"You sleep with the girls," she said. "I'll be with her."

"How soon?" he said.

She leaned back in the chair, made that little shrug her uncle had perfected and let out an impatient sigh the old man himself would have been proud of. "Just eat."

•

It came down to vats or barrels. The brothers from Valdobbiadene didn't trust the shiny vats. The grapes might take on a metallic flavor. Growers from Conegliano insisted on drawing the wine directly from the vats, the final fermentation in bottles, the way champagne was made. They argued like school boys, louder than the carperters' hammers, and always revolving around what Paolo would have done. Everyone, it seemed, knew exactly what the dead cavalry officer would do – everyone except Reg.

He listened, then walked away. In the big office, the one he was to have shared with Paolo but now had all to himself, it was quieter. Almost as big as the little cabin by the river, this room had high windows. Shut now to keep out the cold and the constant sleet and snow, those casements required a long pole to unlatch and allow the glass frames to swing back, held open in place by chains. Another design feature the big man had come up with, to allow the summer heat to escape, the way the flaps in an officer's tent kept that space cool.

He signed the order for the vats, walked the papers out to arguing men, handed it to the older brother, who glanced at them, slapped them against his thigh. "This is a mistake."

"This is what we're doing," Reg told him.

"Amelia will be angry."

"She's alway angry." He kept moving back toward his office. "Buy the bloody vats."

The growers began clapping. He shut the door to block out as much of the cheering as possible. From the bookshelf, he took down a volume of *The Jungle Books*, opened it to a random page: *Toomai of the Elephants*. The 10-year-old is being told he can't become an elephant handler until he sees them dance.

The sentences made him smile. He knew that fear of failure — that feeling a miracle was needed to succeed. He settled back in his chair and kept reading, hoping to find the answer and hearing the words as if Mr. Kipling were speaking them. And for a long moment, all other sounds disappeared, the same way the loading room at Mr. William's stationer store had become silent, the same way his old bedroom in Rusthall had, when the angry shouts of his father filled the rest of the house. Holding a good book, reading was magic.

•

She wasn't angry about the vats. She was too busy reading over the stamped forms that established the governmental zone of origin for the Prosecco. "If the growers are pleased, my cousins will learn to accept it." She looked up from the forms, allowed a small smile. "Each of us must accept our fate, no?"

At her request, the old priest at San Daniele had ushered two elderly women out of the church and then had retired to the rectory. She stared at the simple altar. "You know the story of the lion's den?"

Reg nodded. "A bit unbelievable, don't you think?"

That sliver of a superior smile again. "They say St. Daniel would have been over 80 years old at the time."

"Even more unbelievable then that the lions didn't pounce on him."

"They always attack the weak one." Amelia handed back the forms. "Your woman's father was a drunkard. He beat his wife. For that, Luigi killed him."

One of the stamped forms slipped through his fingers, floating onto the chipped tile floor like a fallen leaf. He stared at it, unable to move.

"This is the family you are joining," she said.

"How do you know?"

"My father saw it." She picked up the form. "The two of them fought near the little house. Luigi dragged the body to the bank. The river did the rest." She brushed lint from her dark gray dress, let out a soft laugh. "In that way, it's true: he did disappear in Venice." Her gloved hand touch his forearm. "It isn't too late to leave the DaPonte women – and save yourself."

He tucked the folded forms inside his jacket. No one had thought of heating this sanctuary. It felt as cold in here as it did where he had waited for her to arrive, out front by the statue of St. Daniel that had somehow, like this building, survived the war intact. "And you held it over his head all that time?"

"My father did him a favor," she said, "to keep him out of prison."

"A favor?" Reg said. "Or a debt?"

She caught her scowl in time to turn it into a blank expression. "He never did anything with all his land. No DaPonte did. Lazy – all of them."

"So, the land, then."

"He was the last DaPonte," she told him. "And he needed money to raise his nieces."

"He owned over two thousand acres," Reg said.

"Nine hundred hectares, yes."

He watched her keep her body rigid, like a soldier just before the attack. "He could have sold off a small piece."

"The money would do him no good," she said, refusing to make eye contact, "if they hanged him." When she did glance his way, she was squinting. "Who would take care of those young girls then?"

"Paolo told me his family bought Luigi out."

"With our money. It was understood the holdings would pass to our children – the sons I would have with Paolo." She stood, fluffed the black wool muffler high on her neck. "Luigi was brave, in his own way. Poor woman – his sister. She loved that brute of a husband." Her smile evaporated, her face turned cold. "Imagine how her daughters would feel to learn the truth."

Her shoes made a clopping sound on the tile. The moment she opened the big door, those two elderly women scurried back inside, found their pew and resumed their prayers. He took the side door out to the cemetery, thought about finding Luigi's grave, wondered if he might get any clarity by lingering there. But wouldn't that be as foolish as the story of lion's den? Head down against Winter, he buttoned his upturned jacket collar and took the foot path through bare trees down toward the flood plain, avoiding the village.

•

By Spring, he would need new boots. This pair would barely get him to the shoemaker in Conegliano by then.

"Giordano's can re-sole them," Gabby told him. "Next to the butcher."

He could have told her that he didn't want to reward merchants in Colfosco after the villagers had turned their backs on her, her sister, him. She must have known, though, because she didn't argue with his silence.

"How soon?" he said.

She tasted the soup. "An hour."

"I meant the baby."

Her body softened. She turned and smiled at him. "Paolo could never be there. My sister is a lucky one." She looked in on the girls napping in their room with the infant between them. "She says it will be early. Days now."

"Does she know if it's a boy or girl?"

She nodded. "She always knows."

". . .Well?"

She shut the door to the girls' room, stepped to the main bedroom – "She must be the one to tell you" – then disappeared behind that soft-closing door.

The wet wind slathered the window in sticky leaves. It was like watching a painting being made, the colors changing, the shapes wriggling. He added more branches to the fire, listened to the soup bubble, took in the aroma of winter cabbage and wondered what Ilba would be cooking back in Milan. "Ezio's the lucky one," he told the fresh wood snarling against flames in the hearth.

Then he remembered the crowded Milan pavements, the traffic, the stink of petrol, trash, all that cigarette smoke – almost like being back in the trenches – and he started chuckling to himself. He pulled his chair toward the fire, stretched his legs and warmed his stocking feet.

•

The new baby came in the dark. The clatter of pots, the scurry of footsteps, the bumping into furniture awakened the infant. Berto's cries got the little sisters up and out of bed. Reg was the last one in the house to make sense of the noise.

And no one would allow him into the bedroom.

From time to time, Gabby would hand linens to Nicoletta, who would drop them into a big pot of boiling water, which she stirred with a tree branch. Sancia brought cold water to her mother. Teresa grunted, screamed, pounded the table on her side of the bed. Berto's part in this nighttime play was to cry, nap, cry. Anyone passing by would have thought the place was under enemy attack.

Just before sunrise, a sudden silence overtook the house. Even the morning wind got quiet. Then the yowl of a newborn sent tingles across his shoulders, and behind that bedroom door, women were laughing. A moment later, Sancia marched out of the room, took him by the hand and led him to the bed.

Black hair slick with sweat, Teresa looked as though she had lost the fight to whomever she had been battling. But she was smiling. The bundle in her arms was making a gurgling sound, like a swimmer in a summer creek.

Dabbing her sister's face and neck with clean linen, Gabby was crying. But she was smiling, too. "Come meet your daughter."

She looked red. And angry. All those wrinkles. Those wisps of dark hair.

"Elisabetta." Teresa's whisper sounded like sniffle. "After our grandmother."

Appropriate – the baby looked like an old woman. His pinky was too big for her fingers to grasp and have the tips touch her thumb. But she tried and kept trying, squeezing as though she needed to hold on.

Little Sancia rubbed his back and let out a long sigh: "Another girl."

He felt the tears dribble down his cheeks and all the air stay trapped inside his lungs. "I am badly outnumbered," he said, the words turning into sobs he couldn't stop.

"You don't go to work today." Gabby picked up her son and lugged him toward the door. "Sancia, come. Help with breakfast."

He watched Teresa tuck the linen all around the baby, who began to squirm in the swaddling. "This one wants to run already," she said, using a warm thumb to wipe away his tears as if he were a dirty-faced little boy coming in for supper.

He felt like one. Helpless.

"What can I do?" he said.

She smiled the way her uncle did when someone said something nonsensical. "What fathers do," she said. "Everything. And then more."

●

The main story in *Il Gazzettino*, the newspaper out of Venice, wasn't about the fiasco of Fiume or politics or even the first anniversary of the armistice. It was the weather – the constant wetness. Even when it wasn't raining or sleeting or snowing, the air was saturated with moisture. One brother from Valdobbiadene worried about mildew. The other worried about the vines drowning.

Engineers overseeing the bridge building worried about the curing of the cement pilings and the rusting of new bolts and rivets. Rudolfo, Jr. worried about his goats getting mired in mud and dying from starvation or from exhaustion trying to get free. The carpenters worried about the swelling of the joints in the roof joists, the lag bolts splitting the timbers, the roof falling in on itself under a heavy snow load.

By the time La Befana showed up again, the constant sound in the winery was men coughing. Some vomited spontaneously in the middle of a task. One of the carpenters in the Alpini's crew passed out while working on a ladder, breaking his arm and collarbone in the fall.

And still, with all this wetness and cold, the flood plain wasn't close to being as muddy as Flanders or France. Even the river seemed fed up with the rain. Its current roiled and split into choppy dark ribbons, full of silt, speeding south so fast they hissed.

Keeping enough wood dry to heat the house and cook the food proved a challenge until Gabby turned it into a game for the girls. Leaving her son with her sister and the newborn, she ran into the evergreens to hide, the girls giving chase a few minutes later. They had to stack branches in piles to dry under the shelter of the big trees at the same time they hunted for their aunt. They always found her.

"Ten days of firewood drying," she said over supper, "four days in the house. Uncle Luigi's rule."

Nursing the baby, Teresa nodded. "Snow or no snow, the fire – "

"– is always hungry," Gabby said.

Then the two sisters spoke in unison: "Like babies and goats."

They shared a small laugh, knowing they were continuing to live their lives based on the wisdom of the man who raised them – the man who had killed their father.

"I checked on your house," Reg said. "No leaks."

335

Gabby put a wad of mashed carrot into Berto's mouth, watched him gum the red gruel. "And the little place?"

He could have told her he didn't have a spare moment to get down that way, or that a new padlock had been installed there, or that the carpenters had boarded up the windows to keep roaming strangers from looking inside to see what they could steal. She might have accepted all of that. "Still in good shape," he said.

She smiled. "Grazie."

He rubbed his itchy eyes, blew his nose into a handkerchief, took a swig of warm lemon grass tea to stop the cough before it started.

Nicoletta squinted at him the same way her mother did. "Does your stomach hurt?"

He shook his head.

"Mine does," Sancia said.

"Too much cheese," her mother told her. "Finish your broth."

Those big dark eyes stared at him. "It tastes sour."

"It's good for you," Gabby told her. "Don't argue with your mother."

Sancia pouted. "But you do."

He tried to hold in the laugh, but it burst out of him. An instant later, everyone at the table was laughing, even Sancia, now so proud of herself she sat up straight and moved her head side to side as if to the beat of a song.

Startled, Berto began wailing. Reg started coughing. He pushed away from the table and hurried to the door, expecting to throw up his supper. The freezing rain felt good on his skin, making it easier to breathe.

A hand grabbed him by the belt, yanked him back inside. Her arm full of her crying son, Gabby kicked the door shut. "You'll catch your death out there."

"This weather will never let up," he said.

"Of course it will." She nudged him toward the table. A moment after she sat, she stared at Teresa who had the baby on her shoulder, patting its back, her breast still exposed from nursing. The sisters must have been sharing another one of the old man's maxims, probably something about the weather. Whatever it was, it made them giggle like little girls.

Hearing that, Sancia shook her head and forced another spoonful of sour broth past her sulking lips. She grimaced as she swallowed. She glared at him. "You have to finish yours, too."

He tossed her a smart salute, picked up his spoon and got busy with it.

·

Sun warmed the soggy soil, sending steam into the cold. The flood plain seemed to be boiling.

Everywhere he looked, in every direction, he saw DaPonte land. All of it now belonged to a one year-old, the last Ziccardi male. All of it mortgaged.

"Beautiful, no?" The little mechanic wiped mud spatter from the rear fender of the new Landini he had brought down last week and had test-driven this morning. "The best."

"It was more beautiful before," Reg said.

"Scuza?"

"When nothing was here." He climbed onto the seat." Except the river."

"You are well enough to drive?"

He shook his head. "I only want the view from up here."

"Not good to be out in this weather," the mechanic told him.

"This weather? It's warm today."

"Exactamente. It tricks you." He put a muddy boot on the steel step, tried to make out what Reg was looking at. He slammed a hand against the engine housing. "Then, bam!, the freeze comes back and makes everything worse."

The Montello looked so much bigger in Winter, the leafless trees like match sticks, revealing the slope that Summer hid, and the old evergreens, bent by constant wind, exaggerating the mass. The little mountain dwarfed Nervesa, and the way the river bent around the outcropping tricked the eye, making it look as if that giant mound was actually the source of the hard flowing dark water.

Behind him, carpenters were taking advantage of the sunlight and warm air to finish the exterior work on the winery. Workers dropped wood ash around the new vines, the gray dust rising in small clouds and clinging to their boots and trousers.

"Drive it back up to the building." Reg climbed down. "It passed the test. You can return to Conegliano."

The little man shook his head. "The Influenza is there. In Susegana, too." He set the crank at the front of the tractor, then pulled himself up into the driver's seat. "Here is safer. I can stay with the machine."

"Suit yourself," Reg said, heading toward the vine workers.

The engine started, the gears groaned. The tractor lurched forward, then began a wide turn, nearing the skeleton of the machine it replaced before it straightened out and drove up the slope to the winery.

With the two flood channels speeding the swollen river past the flatland, it was safer here. *Safer than ever.*

He wondered what Luigi would have made of all this, if he would have approved, if he would have cared. The last of the DaPontes had never spent any time near the river – and Reg now knew why – and would probably have spent most of his time in town, especially those nights when The Mayor's wife left the back door unlocked.

The image of the old man sneaking into the darkened kitchen off the square and creeping up the stairs and into bed to chase the loneliness from the house made Reg grin. The laugh made him cough. The cough made his eyes itch again, his nose run, the chills race over his shoulders.

"If the weather turns again," he told the dusty vine workers, "stop and take shelter. I don't want anyone getter sicker."

The men murmured and kept tossing shovelfuls of ash around the plantings.

"And stay in Colfosco," he told them. "No trips north. We need all of you healthy."

The slight chill in the breeze this close to the river made him shiver. He turned to hide his sweaty face and runny nose, then slogged toward the slope, staying in the rut of a tractor wheel where the footing was firmer. Mud was seeping into his boots. His socks squished with each step. By the time he passed the new house, he couldn't feel his toes.

He made it as far as the pile of scrap lumber before he had to sit to keep from toppling over. This close to the winery, someone – a carpenter on a ladder, a vine worker on his way up from the flood plain – might see him lying there on his back like one of the planks. He struggled to sit up.

The vomit shot out of his nose and mouth. Breakfast now the color of spring grass slithered away from his boots. Shivering, he used a piece of siding as a brace and got to his feet. The sun felt good on his face. He wiped his mouth, blew his nose, took deep breaths, soured by bile, and started walking, convinced the worst was over.

11

The warm spell lasted four days, broken by hard rain. Snow flurries blew through one late afternoon, but nothing stuck to the ground. Except for his boots, the worst really was over.

He used old burlap from the vines to wrap the thick soles and covered it with the glue paste the carpenters used to seal joints. Once hardened, the repaired boots made a cracking sound. Workers laughed when they heard him coming. They called him *Il Vagabondo*.

He felt like a vagrant, sitting behind the low desk or roaming through the building, watching others do all the work. He could sleep all day on the couch and nothing would change. He could stay home and not be missed.

It was the same at the house. He had no chores, not even with the baby girl. He had become a visitor in both places, and a stranger to the village.

On clear days, he checked the lifting stations at the river, but the little mechanic had those cylinders running as smoothly as the motor in the new tractor. The water tank near the little cabin magically appeared one morning, the result of a mixed work crew of carpenters and pipe fitters getting the structure raised before breakfast with pulleys and cross bracing. Water lines, buried below the frost line, got flushed. A petrol-powered pump got the tank filled by lunchtime. The tap to the cabin was ready for use by sundown.

As boring as his days were, nights were worse. Tired from getting up with the newborn, Teresa had no use for him. Twitching away from his touch, all she wanted was sleep. He stared at the ceiling, wishing for a window like the broken one at Calverley Lodge, so he could at least see the night. Groggy when he got out of bed, he went through the day listening to a drone of voices: at breakfast, Gabby and the girls planning their days; at work, workers discussing tasks, their rooms in town, food, women, wine. At supper, he learned which sister might have gone into the village and what she had brought back and how people he didn't know by name had gained weight, lost teeth, had relatives in Susegana battling The Influenza.

He was not part of any of it.

His only job – tallying hours for the workers and initialing pay slips – took less than an hour each Saturday. He didn't even hand out the slips anymore. The self-appointed foreman – the Alpini carpenter – handled that now. The bank in Conegliano took care of the rest.

One of the vine workers walked into his office without knocking, dumped a pair of old boots on his desk, then walked out without a word. As beat up as they looked, the boots were soft inside. And they fit. He walked through the building, relieved that his steps no longer announced him with the creak of splintering plaster, yet saddened when he realized that now no one would realize he was even there.

Back in the office, he glanced at his desk, so uncluttered and neat, as if he had simply vanished, so unnecessary he would not need to be replaced. Someone had already taken his ugly worn-out boots from the room. He shut the door, stretched out on the couch, listened to the rain. The goat men would be happy to see him. A walk into the foothills would lift his spirits. He debated whether to take the road through the village or the path through the woodland near St. Daniel's.

The door banged against the wall. Gabby rushed in, coatless and sopping wet, her dress sticking to her skin. "She won't wake up!"

•

Despite the rain, he could hear both babies crying from the top of the swale. Wearing a borrowed slicker, Gabby raced past him and got inside first. Near the dying fire, Nicoletta had Berto in her lap, bouncing him. In the bed, Sancia petted the swaddled baby, lying beside the lump under the covers.

He pulled back the blanket. The sheets were damp from sweat. Her wet hair formed black daggers against her skin. The color had run out of her face. But she was breathing.

He handed Sancia his slicker. "Get water."

Before the little one could get off the bed and hoist the canvas over her head, Gabby walked in with a pitcher and a cup. She set them on the floor on her sister's side of the bed, then hurried out to the main room and began feeding branches to the fire.

He pulled the slicker off Sancia. "Towels."

Nodding and coughing, the going-on five year-old slid the closet drape open. She went from one end to the other, searching for linens, her hands over her ears to muffle the baby's wails. "She won't stop crying," she said.

"She's just hungry." Gabby nudged past her, reached up to a closet shelf, pulled down an armful of towels. She threw one to him, then stripped off her slicker and started to wriggle out of her soaked dress. He dabbed the sleeping woman's skin, patted her hair. She felt clammy.

He forced himself not to look at the naked woman in front of the closet, drying herself, shivering. "No fever," he told her.

"We need to move her to the fire." She kicked her wet clothes to the corner, yanked something out of the closet. She had the brown housedress on before she put a knee on the bed and cradled the crying baby. "See if she'll drink. Then carry her."

And she was out of the room, barking instructions to Nicoletta. Something about a blanket bed.

"Mama snores," Sancia said. "But now – "

He couldn't get those thin lips to sip from the cup. His arms under her, he lifted her from the bed and brought her to the hearth, where Gabby was using her bare foot to arrange the blankets, a crying infant in each arm. He knelt and rolled Teresa onto the blankets.

"Take Berto," she told him, then she sat beside her sister, opened the damp nightgown, pulled out a breast and placed the swaddled baby to the nipple. The crying stopped, the suckling started instantly.

"Is that – safe?" he said.

"It's good for both of them." She put Nicoletta's hands on the nursing infant – "Don't let her slide off" – then stood, toweled her hair as if she was angry at it. Frizzy, those blond strands made her look like a mad woman. She didn't bother to smooth it. She wrapped the towel around her head, took back her son. "Sancia, help me strip the bed."

Over her shoulder on the way into the bedroom, she said, "Stoke the fire. Then go get more wood. Nicoletta knows where we stacked it."

The moment he bent to pick up pine branches, he felt full of energy. Even this simple chore made him feel useful. He built a lattice of branches, set small logs on top, watched the flames lick the framework.

"Will she wake up?" Nicoletta said.

He stroked the top of the girl's head, rubbed the nursing baby's back. "Get a pillow. We'll make her as comfortable as we can."

•

The wet rags she had set outside to freeze seemed to help. They crunched when he pressed them to Teresa's forehead. Her breathing was getting deeper. The warmth of the fire and the blankets had stopped her shivers.

"She's been sick for a week." Gabby wet her sister's lips with water. "The bad coughing didn't start until yesterday."

341

"How did I not see that?" he said.

She brushed the limp black hair, fluffed the pillow. "She's good at hiding."

Trying to hold back her cough, little Sancia came out of the bedroom dragging a new pair of boots by their laces. "You need these."

They were oiled leather, with a supple welt. They felt light.

"Where did these come from?" he said.

The little girl shrugged and stepped to her sister to play with Berto on the floor.

"Susegana," Gabby pointed to his slipper. "The same shoemaker who made your slippers. I gave her the money. He would want you to have them."

"She went to Susegana?" he said.

"The boots would not walk here by themselves."

The other pair of boots given to him today were drying near the hearth. He stepped into them, grabbed the slicker and hurried out into the storm.

•

The Alpini carpenter's wife, visiting from Belluno, was happy to look in on the sick woman. On the way down from the village, she listed the curing virtues of clear broth. And mustard plasters, even heated glasses to draw the fluid up from the lungs. A small woman, she must have worn her entire wardrobe for her trip. When she walked, she looked like a bundle of laundry. He couldn't get her to walk fast enough.

Inside the doorway, she removed her coat, muffler, gloves, wool cap, placing each neatly on a chair, the entire time glancing at the house. "So big. Actual bedrooms?"

He guided her to the blankets. Her face went limp. She knelt, felt Teresa's forehead, put her ear to the sick woman's chest. Grim-faced, she waved him to her side. "Sit her up."

That limp frame had to be held in place. The carpenter's wife listened to Teresa's back, then checked the pot on the hearth, waving her hand to catch the aroma. She shook her head. "Water. Another pot." She glanced at him, lowered her stare. "We may have to force her to take the broth." She peered up at him the way Sancia did when her feelings were hurt. "To keep her strong enough 'til you can get medicine. A doctor."

"What kind of medicine?" he said.

342

She took the pot Gabby brought her, ladled a small portion from the pot on the hearth, added water, set the little pot over the fire to boil. "For The Influenza. You should hurry."

•

They had run out of medicine in Susegana. Dozens of villagers had been moved into quarantine within the castle walls. Open fires smoked in the street. People brought clothes and bedding to be burned. All three doctors had gone north to Conegliano, where they were needed more.

It was worse there. Villagers battled to pull screaming neighbors from their houses, stripping them in the street, burning their clothing. Entire structures were in flames. A naked woman and her young sons knelt in the rain, watching their home glow red, fall in on itself. The doctors from Susegana had never arrived. "Gone to Belluno with our own," a man with a rifle said.

"Why the rifle?"

He spat toward the bank and a boarded up surgery. "Quarantine breakers."

Belluno stood half a day's walk up into the mountains. Traveling in the dark, a wrong turn could cost him days. He headed away from the man with the rifle, toward the tractor and implement store. Then he circled back to the rear of the surgery, kicked in the door. He filled his pockets with vials and bottles of tablets on the shelves, and grabbed a thick book from the desk on his way out.

He took the game path through the muddy wood, checking over his shoulder to make sure he wasn't being pursued and that no rifle was aimed in his direction. He quickened his pace, but had to slow down to make sure the rattling glass in his pockets didn't break. Keeping the medical book dry under the slicker, he cut back to the road leading south, trying to remember if there was an alternate route around Susegana and, if there was, how much time he would lose.

The winter sun was already low enough to touch the river. Less than half an hour of light left and over two hours of travel ahead. He remembered he had not eaten and that he had not spoken to Teresa today before leaving for the winery and that he could not remember the last time he had held her or kissed her or even smiled at her. Rain mixed with tears. He opened his mouth, drank from the sky and kept walking.

•

Somewhere along Via dei Colli – the way of necks – south of the creek flowing out of Crevada, the rain stopped. Smoke hovered over

343

the main street through Susegana. He tucked the thick book against the small of his back at the beltline, allowing him to use his hands and arms to keep the medicine vials and bottles quiet. The few people walking on this narrow lane moved out of his way, wary of coming too close to anyone.

Smoke rose from inside the castle, too. The smell of burning hair and flesh floated on the dying night breeze. He headed south to rejoin the road through Colfosco, knowing the streets would be empty, the windows shuttered, doors shut. No one would recognize the blue-green slicker or the beat-up boots. Everyone would assume he was a worker at the winery and be glad to see him disappear down Via Passo Barca – the boat passage.

The last few steps to the front door proved the hardest. He feared what was waiting for him inside. He stopped before entering, listened. No cries from the babies, no sobs of grief from Gabby, no frantic clatter of pots and cups. He pushed the door open.

The carpenter's wife sat at the table, her head bobbing as she dozed. Alone on the blankets, Teresa lay on her side, her back to the fire. He shut the door, startling the round woman.

"Where is everyone?" he said.

"Her sister's house." She put a finger to her lips. "The little one is asleep in her room. I go now."

He looked in, found Sancia under the black and red knitted afghan. "Why?"

"I have a family of my own." She had her coat and muffler on, was pushing her fingers into her gloves. "Stew in the big kettle, broth in the small one. Keep trying to get them to eat something."

"But I have medicine!"

She pulled her cap down over her ears and hurried out of the house, her lumpy figure wobbling up the swale into darkness.

He lined up the vials and bottles on the table. At the hearth, he filled a bowl with stew. Eating, he tried to find the names of the medicines in the index of the book. The small puddle of water near the rear window, where his bed used to be, must be from a new leak. It was the only thing he knew how to fix.

•

Most of vials contained herbs. The bottles held elixirs made from herbs. They treated aches and pains and upset stomachs, nervousness, insomnia. One of them was a foot powder. The thick book carried no mention of The Influenza.

344

In the girls' bedroom, little Sancia grunted every now and then, especially after a coughing spell. She took broth, but couldn't hold it down. A dark brown stain soiled the bedding near her pillow.

Teresa slept. He wet her lips, toweled her dry, kept the fire going through the night. He crawled into the bed nook in the alcove, kept the drape open to see the room. Alert to every cough, moan and sharp breath, he listened to the stillness settling all around him.

•

The smacking of lips awakened him at first light. She was pawing at her eyes, turning her head on the pillow, shifting under the blankets. He jumped out of bed and shot to her side, cradled her into a sitting position, fed her warm broth straight from the ladle. She swallowed, sighed. Her eyes fluttered open.

"Where is Elisabetta?" she said.

"With Gabriela."

Her smile filled her face. "You like your boots?"

He hated them. They were the reason she had gone to Susegana, the reason she got sick. He would never wear those boots. "A wonderful surprise," he said.

Somehow, that smile got bigger. She squeezed his hand holding the ladle. "The roof is good?"

She wouldn't be able to make out the puddle across the room. He fed her more broth. "Holding up fine."

"You fix everything." She turned her head, coughed up the last mouthful. Suddenly, her body felt heavier, as if she was sinking into his grasp. Those dark eyes tried to find him. "You can't fix this."

He held her, kissed her damp hair. She was sleeping again, her breath easier than it had been, but still shallow. He fed the fire, stepped outside to see how much new wood remained in the stack under the roof overhang. By midday, he would have to get more. He took a cup of broth into the small bedroom. Sancia lay soaked in sweat. Steam actually rose from her skin. He picked her up, brought her out to the blankets, covered her with the afghan.

At the table, he leafed through the medical book, hoping to find a miracle.

•

The berry jam in the dugout cellar outnumbered all the other jars, thanks to a bumper crop. That sugary taste might give both mother and daughter the energy to sit up and take more broth. He carried two jars into the house, cut into the wax seal on one of them, pried the wad of wax off the jam. He brought a spoonful to the blankets,

345

spread some dark shiny jam on Sancia's lips, then on Teresa's. Neither one of them reacted. With a finger, he poked the sticky stuff into that small mouth. The little tongue didn't move.

Neither did her mother's.

He set the spoon on the floor, sat cross-legged facing them and the fire, watched their quick, strained breaths. He waited.

●

They burned everything, including the mattresses. They scrubbed down the floors and walls, tables and chairs with the same vinegar and salt mixture they used on the winery. They wouldn't allow him to do any work.

"You should go to your daughter." The carpenter's wife patted his hands near the well pump. "We can walk together."

A good father would have thought about his own daughter. "Does she have it too?"

The small woman shook her head. "They are all fine. You should see for yourself."

A good father would want to do that.

He wanted to stay here until the men from the church came to cart the bodies off. The village had its own undertaker, but the man and his son had both been killed in the war. Housewives cleaned the bodies of their dead relatives and made the shrouds now. The church elders saw to the burials, overseeing the lone gravedigger, a man so frail he looked too weak to swing a pick axe.

"There is nothing left for you to do here." The Alpini carpenter put his arm around his wife. "We'll see to everything."

A good boss, a good friend, would be grateful and show it. He just stared at the vials and bottles and the thick book that had been set outside by the ladder. "I should have stayed here. There might have been something – " He turned, studied the evergreens. "I'll walk with them to the church."

One of the workers set his new boots and slippers on the side of the doorway. Another carried an armful of clothes – small dresses and coats – out to the fire near the garden fencing.

"They should burn mine, too," he said. "No chances."

With a long sigh, the Alpini led his wife back to the house, where he told a worker to burn the clothes from every closet. There would be nothing left inside. Except that rain puddle.

Overhead, the sun broke through clumps of clouds, then hid again. And down the swale, three men guided a flat bed hand cart toward the house.

12

few vine workers and carpenters surrounded the gravesite. The Alpini's wife had already gone north to her home in Belluno. Her husband, looking exhausted from taking over Reg's chores at the winery, stood next to The Mayor, who seemed lost, his stare on the wispy clouds circling the valley.

It was over in 15 minutes. No one waited around, no one expected a feast. The group simply turned and walked away, nodding at him on the way out of cemetery. Except The Mayor. He was staring at Reg now, his hand trembling. In it, a small white envelope. He took careful steps around the grave, put the message in Reg's hand. With a pat on the shoulder, the balding man lowered his head and walked off.

The letter inside came from lawyers in Venice: *Ombelli – Tessatta Studio Legale*. The loans Amelia held on the winery and the land were being called in:

> The heir of Paolo Ziccardi has 30 days to make payment in full or vacate the premises and surrender the assets.

It was dated three days ago, two days after the deaths of Teresa and Sancia.

His first instinct was to crumple the note, toss it into the open grave. He slipped it back into the envelope, put it in a jacket pocket and stared at the two bundles wrapped in white at the bottom of the grave. The old grave digger trudged up the walk, adjusted his cap, drew a deep breath and spat into his hands.

Reg took the shovel from him and began filling the grave. The rail-thin old man removed his cap, bowed his head, moved his lips in mumbled prayer, and watched the moist soil spatter over the shrouded bodies.

•

"Too big." She finished nursing the baby girl, lifted her son to her other breast. "Like everything he did. Leaving this house will be a good thing."

He put the legal notice back into its envelope. "You don't want to fight them – for your son's future?"

"No one needs this future." She pulled her shawl down to cover herself and all but Berto's face. "The little house will be fine for us."

"They're taking that, too."

347

Her face tightened, her lips pressed together. "Paolo and Uncle Luigi had an understanding."

"And they're both dead. Amelia will take everything. You have to know that."

She stared at the little seven year-old sleeping on the spotted hide in front of the fire. "If something happens to me, you would take care of the girls and Berto, yes?"

"You're not feeling sick, are you?"

She shook her head. "Sad. Worried." She rubbed her thumb on the baby's cheek. "So much loss."

The half moon scattered patches of light over the flood plain out the side window. Except for Digger, everyone he had ever cared about had been lost within eye sight of those vines and this river.

"You must wear the new boots." She put her son down in the deep dresser drawer she had pulled out to use as a cradle. "Wear them out. For her."

He kept staring at the broken light on the damp soil.

"And stop blaming those boots for her death," she said.

Her words knifed through him. He felt his fingers tighten into fists. "Paolo wouldn't have worn them to her funeral."

Focused on the dozing babies, she fingered her mother's rosary beads in a small dish on top of the dresser. "You are not him."

"He was everything I'm not." He walked toward the back door and that cold moon. "Everything I could never be."

A large night bird skimmed the surface of the river, heading south. It could have been an eagle. More probably a buzzard. So many of the native birds had been killed, their nesting grounds and habitat destroyed. Just seeing that wingspan hug the water made him think that the grasses and woodlands would return, just as that writer John Masefield had predicted. He wondered what the river valley would be like filled with bird song.

Lost in thought, he didn't hear her come up beside him. She wore her shawl and carried his jacket, helped him into it. The spot he had been staring at was empty of night birds now. She put her hand in his. "He loved you for who you are. So did Uncle Luigi. So did she." She squeezed his fingers. "All of us do."

He glanced over her hair at the new house, the lamplight spilling out of the back window. "You better get inside. The babies."

"Asleep," she said, swinging her gaze from The Montello to the high bank where the ancient bridge footings would be half-submerged in the swollen river. "This is always my life. Not even

348

Amelia Ermacora can take that." She pointed south. "I found you there."

Her fingers slipped out of his and she was walking back toward the orange glow in the window. He watched her until she got inside, then studied the running water, waiting for new wings.

•

The Alpini carpenter came into the office with a white envelope. "It says you cannot be here. Can this be true?"

He put his feet up on the desk, stared at the new brown boots from Susegana. "What do you think of them?"

Nicked fingers felt the soft leather. "Made for a prince."

"It's business as usual," Reg told him.

"But The Mayor handed this to me himself."

He checked the new invoices for the water filtering system. "We'll need the tanks and lines tested by late Spring."

The sinewy man stood at the edge of desk, staring. "Biaggio. My name. Biaggio Abbadelli."

Reg nodded. "Schedule the testing – Biaggio. And thank you. For running things here when I was – "

"Compagni d'armi," he said. "Una volta e sempre."

Comrades in arms. Once and always.

He watched the former Alpini soldier stroll through the big room toward the new vats. At his desk, Reg stripped the rifle, cleaned the chamber with a dry rag, the barrel with an oiled rag on a stiff wire, snapped the ammo clip into place. That familiar click made him smile. He removed the clip and, wondering if those old bullets would explode in the chamber, set the weapon on the empty low table behind his chair.

Luigi's rifle would need cleaning and oiling, too. For the first time in days, he looked forward to walking home.

•

The pry bar popped the boards from the window. The crossbar over the door proved more stubborn, but he got it off. He swept the floor, brought in fire wood, tested the new pump outside under the window, laundered the bed linens and hung them over bushes to dry in the sun. Then he made a list of things to be brought to the little house: bowls, cups, spoons, the kettle and stew pot.

The note paper stuck to the table top. He scrubbed it down, then used the same rag to rub grime off the chair.

349

Leaving the old man's rifle in the same spot by the door where the shotgun once stood, he shut the door and headed across the flood plain, sensing her surprise with every step.

•

She didn't know why they were carrying pots and plates and cups past the new vines. Halfway there, she stopped, looked at him, her eyes getting glassy. She quickened her pace.

Inside the little house, she put the baby girl on the bed, placed her palm flat against his cheek and took her son out of his arms. Her whispered "grazie" sounded like a soft breeze.

Nicoletta dumped spoons and forks on the table, startling the babies. "It's so small."

"Yes, isn't it wonderful?" Gabby started twirling around the room, dancing with her half-awake son. "You can see the river from every corner."

Tugging on his pant leg, the seven year-old was frowning. "We won't live here, will we?"

"You'll stay here for a little while," he said. "So you can help your aunt."

She bowed her head, nodded. "When can I visit Mama and Sancia?"

"Soon," he said. "I'll take you myself."

She sat on the floor in front of the hearth. "Cold."

He banked two logs on the bed of branches, lit the kindling. The dry wood snapped with the flames, providing a crackling beat for the tune Gabby was humming.

•

The workers hauled the bed from the new house and Biaggio himself built the inside cross brace for the door. The thick slat pivoted silently on a bolt in the jamb, rising like a stout arm and falling into a metal bracket on the other jamb. It would take three men to break through that door now.

He brought in the last of the berry preserves from the dugout cellar. Gabby was nursing his daughter at the table. "You feed her, too?"

"She doesn't know who I am. Or care." She stared out the window. "My mother must have nursed us here."

Nicoletta slept on the small bed by the hearth. Tired of crawling, Berto rested against his mother's leg, barely able to keep his eyes open.

"The warmth puts them to sleep," she said. "The new house never gets this cozy." She pulled the baby's lips from her nipple, covered herself with the hand that tucked her breast back into her dress. "Why do you sleep in your office and not your house? They scrubbed it safe, no?"

He nodded. "It's Teresa's."

"And she was yours."

He stopped adding branches to the fire. "I came back for you."

"I know." She had his daughter over her shoulder, patting the tiny back. "Teresa knew that, too. And Uncle Luigi. Only Paolo did not."

He turned toward the stew pot. "I wanted him dead. In the war."

Her sigh ran through him. "After they took you, I was sure I would be alone. Always." The chair legs groaned against the floor when she shifted positions. "He was going to ask you to take his family name. Make you a Ziccardi."

"Bloody hell," he told the fire.

"*Come?*"

"I'm an awful human being," he said.

"You saved my sister's life. And my son's. My uncle's. Mine."

Rust-colored streaks lined the inside of the empty stew pot. "One of the vine workers was eating a cream puff this afternoon. I couldn't stop crying."

"I think Sancia missed you the most," she said. "She kept looking for you, convinced you were hiding."

He ran a finger over the warm rim of the black pot. "I can't cry for Teresa. What's wrong with me?"

She was nodding. "I tried to cry for Paolo. I was his, but never felt he was mine. Does that make sense?"

"Sometimes, nothing makes sense."

A tear rolled down her cheek toward that sliver of a smile. "We are both awful human beings."

He laughed. He wanted to kiss her. He stepped to the door. "Don't forget the crossbar."

Her fingers wiggled a wave. Everything she loved was within reach of those fingers. He envied her.

It was cool outside, but it felt colder. He followed the recently filled-in water line trench back to the new house, where no bed and no fire would be waiting for him.

351

13

With her hair bunched up in her small red hat, she looked like a bloodied bullet marching toward the office. The Mayor had been unable to match her pace, so she had to wait for him to reach the door and open it for her.

"You are trespassing." Amelia said.

"I work here," Reg told her.

"You were served notice by my lawyers."

He pretended to look through the invoices on his desk. "Never saw it."

She glared at The Mayor, who had removed his hat and was busy turning the brim in his hands. "The winery was also served," she said.

He stood and waved through the open doorway, gesturing Biaggio to leave his schematics and come to the office. "Did we get anything from lawyers?"

Those slender shoulders shrugged. "I received nothing."

"I handed it to you myself," The Mayor said. "I gave the letters to both of them," he told her. "As you requested."

"You will leave now." She pointed a black-gloved finger at him. "Or we'll have you arrested."

He sat, put a foot on the desk. "Arrested by whom?"

"The authorities." She nudged The Mayor's arm. "Ercole will bring them."

"People dying in Susegana," Reg said. "Conegliano, too. Takes a brave man to risk The Influenza."

Beads of sweat began to dot that balding scalp. The Mayor found his handkerchief, mopped his brow.

"You'll be deported," she told him.

He reached back, slid the rifle into his lap. "You need new lawyers. First they fail to deliver these notices you keep talking about. Then they don't check with the province clerk in Treviso about my visa. My permanent visa."

She pressed her lips into a tight frown. "I can get an army here."

He swung his legs off the desk, stood and tossed the rifle to the former Alpini in the doorway. "I have an army here."

Baggio caught the weapon and, in a smooth single motion, pulled the bolt, checked the bullet chamber, snapped the bolt shut. "German. Well-oiled."

With a growing smile, he found the ammo clip in his desk drawer. He lobbed the dull metal case to Baggio, who snatched it out of the air and clicked it into the rifle. "We're going to paint a Z on the roof," Reg said. "For Ziccardi. So big they'll see it in Nervesa."

She was grinding her teeth behind that scowl. Spinning on a heel, she stepped toward the door. Reluctantly, the sinewy man with the rifle moved out of her way. The Mayor picked his hat off the floor and followed her.

"His name is Ercole," Reg said.

Baggio snapped the ammunition clip out of the rifle and grinned. "It suits him." He set the rifle on the low table, the ammo clip on the desk. "Is this a good idea? To go against her and her money? She's from the northeast – Friuli. The Julian March. Ruthless. Some are savages there."

Opening the desk drawer and sliding the clip into it, Reg sat in the big chair. "Do we have anyone with family in Milan?"

"I'll see. Why?"

"I need someone to go there and bring one of our investors back," Reg said. "To handle this."

The slender man sat on the edge of the desk. "And what is – this?"

He could have told him about how the war dead had produced such a shortage of men, crippling provincial authorities who had no troops to enforce private actions, how the outbreak of The Influenza had all but eliminated travel from the north, how the winery had enough ex-soldiers to defend itself against any force a coward like The Mayor might scrape together. Instead, he leaned back in the chair, put his feet on the desk. "This," he said, "is us."

"The two of us? Against all they might bring?"

"All of us," Reg said. "The growers already own a share in the winery. I'll assign half of the Ziccardi family share to be split among everyone on payroll. In writing." He sat up straight, offered his hand. "Congratulations. You're now an owner."

With a knowing nod and smile, Baggio gripped his hand with both of his. "I'll tell them, but they may not believe me. They will believe you." He laughed. "Us. Perfetto."

•

They would come by the river road from Casonetti and Valdobbiadene – if they were coming at all. He scouted the terrain all the way to the big bend in the Piave, opposite The Montello. Strands of barbed wire lay rusted and half-buried within spitting distance of the water. He couldn't be certain of the exact spot where Barry had

353

been shot, but in two different locations, he thought he recognized the young tree the small raft might have been tied to.

Most of the mountain men and all of the former Alpini would have their own rifles or shotguns. Five decent marksmen could discourage a small private army. Ten could defeat them. Over 30 worked at the winery.

Scanning the low bank and the islands in the current to the north, he knew no one would be coming. The two brothers from Valdobbiadene had too much at stake in the new plantings to risk losing their shares. The other growers, already reluctant to join anyone who disrepected Paolo's memory, would feel the same way.

He wiped mud off his new boots, turned and, whistling the same tune Gabby had been humming the other night, followed the river south.

•

She was singing inside the cabin, joined by a higher voice, one that didn't know all the words. He knocked on the door, pushed it open. Nicoletta stopped singing and ran to him, hugged him. Both infants lay asleep on the small bed near the hearth. When he sat at the table, Gabby spotted his new boots and grinned. She walked out to the well pump.

He left the seven year-old inside and stepped to the blond-haired woman. Taking hold of the handle, he started pumping. "If anything happens to me," he told her, "There's a man coming from Milan – Ezio. He'll know what to do. Listen to him."

She watched water gush into the bucket. "What will happen to you?"

"Nothing. But I don't want you and your son cheated out of Paolo's dream. Ezio will take care of you and Berto."

"It's not our dream," she said.

"It's your son's future. You're both entitled to it."

"And Nicoletta and Elisabetta?" She unhooked the bucket from the spout. "You are their future. They are entitled to you."

He followed her back inside. "Ezio will be here in a day or two."

"More war?" she said, glancing at her uncle's rifle against the wall and setting the bucket on the table. "You like it. All of you men do."

She wasn't going to turn around. He knelt beside the bed, watched his daughter sleep. "You didn't use the crossbar," he said.

She wasn't going to talk to him now – maybe for the rest of the night. Or week. She stood at the window, staring at the river.

Outside, he drew in a long breath. "Smells like Spring."

354

"That's what Aunt Gabriella says," Nicoletta told him, taking his hand and leaning against his leg.

He could make out her face reflected in the window pane. "Then it must be true."

•

Down the narrow street, his rifle slung over a shoulder, he found the village square before the rising sun did. The obelisk near what had once been a fountain had a small circular wall around it. He sat on the cold stones, his eyes on her balcony, the rifle at his side.

The only thing moving was the mountain breeze, still chilled by night. He listened to it kissing the buildings. Then he heard the footsteps.

A slender woman in a heavy robe carried a small tray from her door. A tiny cup of coffee and a hard biscuit sat on the tray. She put it down next to him.

"I was sorry to hear about Teresa and the little one." The Mayor's wife dug into a robe pocket, pulled out a ring, placed it on the tray. The small blue oval caught the first light. "Blue lace agate," she said. "His sister's. His niece, and your daughter, should have it."

Set in a plain gold setting, the stone had a darker wavy pattern running through it, like slender rivers.

"The color of the Adriatic," she said. "Where his people come from." She glanced at the empty balcony. "The color of his eyes."

He sipped the hot bitter coffee, tried to bite into the biscuit.

"Dunk." She moved his fingers to the small cup, putting the tip of the biscuit in the coffee. "He always said the lines in the stone were the waves in his sea."

The warm liquid made the sweet biscuit edible. How many of these had she fed to Luigi? How many mornings had she worn this ring?

"His sister left it on the table the night she. . . left us." Her finger turned the ring. "Such a simple setting. He thought of himself as a simple man." She allowed herself a remembered smile. "He wasn't."

One more glance at the balcony. She lowered her head, traded him the cup for the ring, then picked up the tray and walked across the square to her front door, disappearing inside.

He couldn't fit the ring over his pinky. He tucked it deep into a jacket pocket.

More footsteps. The workers were surprised to find him in the square. He waited for the stragglers. Biaggio was one of the last to arrive.

"Since you're all part owners now," he said, "I wanted to give everyone the day off. With pay."

The men cheered, slapped each other on the back. The Alpini carpenter was grinning and nodding.

"Maybe you can take your rifles and go hunting today," Reg said.

More mumbled cheers. The men began to turn and head back to their lodgings.

"See you all tomorrow," he said. "Bright and early."

A few of the workers shook his hand. One of them patted him on the shoulder. Biaggio had his stare fixed on the balcony. "She saw," he said.

Resisting the urge to look up, Reg nodded. "Might be a good idea to have them bring their rifles to work from now on."

The ex-Alpini soldier widened his grin. "In case you want to give us another day off."

Reg met his smile. "Good game outside Casonetti. At the big turn in the river."

With a laugh, Biaggio snapped a salute and walked away, trailing his co-workers. A corner of the red drape moved in the window door on the balcony. Reg shouldered his rifle and started the slow walk back to the flood plain.

•

The round woman shuffled into his office. Biaggio ushered both boys and the girl in behind her, handed a letter across the desk.

The agreement making Ezio part owner in the winery looked as fresh and new as they day it had been signed and filed.

Ilba began sobbing. "The black shirts," she said. "They attacked him. He's dead."

14

Primo, now 14, liked to build things. His sister, Mira, two years younger, already read in three languages, not including Latin, which she claimed was no longer an actual language spoken anywhere, except at mass. The little nine year-old, Roberto, kept silent, preferring to run ahead like a scout, then scurry back – always in motion. Their mother stopped crying long enough to gasp at the size of the main room, stare wide-eyed at the two bedrooms, nod at the width of the hearth and test the pot hooks set in the mortared bricks.

"So quiet," she said, standing at the well pump, watching water gush into a bucket. "Everything sleeps."

A country girl from Nosate, along the Ticino River separating Lombardy from the Piedmont, she grew up near a canal. Even Milan, a full day's walk to the east, wasn't as noisy. She learned to cook in kettles at a hearth like the one in this house. When she saw the stacked piles of branches and small logs, she seemed to calculate how many meals she could make before needing more wood.

"Where do you sleep?" she said.

"Another house," he told her. "By the river. This is my wife's."

She studied her scuffed black shoes. "We cannot pay."

He carried the bucket back inside, set it on the ledge by the sink below the window. "I'll have bedding brought in. And food from the village. Do you eat goat cheese?"

Her children stared at her, expecting her to speak. When she didn't, the girl helped her sit in the chair at the table. "Cheese, yes," Mira said. "And bread?"

He nodded. "There's a garden on the side of the house. Ready for planting."

The youngest ran out the door to find the vegetable patch. His older brother followed at a slow walk. The girl looked in each bedroom. "You have no books?"

"Someone will be bringing your luggage," he said.

"The neighbors are selling our furniture," the girl said. "Even the plates."

Ilba put her head in her hands. A soft wail escaped through her fingers.

•

The new cheese was creamier than the last batch.

357

"The goats have no fear now," Rudolfo said. "A good Spring will triple the herd."

His father had already started sleeping outside. Neither goat man went into the village anymore. Villagers came to them, trading bread, wine, dry goods and jams for cheese. "Better than money," Rudolfo, Sr. said. "Money we cannot swallow."

The high pasture, spotted by early grass, stretched out against the rocky foothills, waiting for the first flowers. The rifle slung across his back, he lugged the sack of cheese down the path, hoping the baker would still have loaves to sell.

•

They had not tasted this kind of cheese before. And they had not heard the details of how their father had died. With their backs to the small fire in the hearth, they watched their mother's lips, not believing the words were coming from her.

A rally near the site where the new university would be built. Speakers demanding rights for workers, education for girls, food and shelter for the hungry poor, an end to the talk of colonizing Slovenia in a quest to recreate the *Spazio Vitale* – the vital space, the old Roman map of Italy. The black shirts attacked from two sides, with clubs.

The newspaper claimed the Action Squads only meant to break up the rally, not the heads of Socialists there. Four were clubbed to death. A fifth man, trampled by the fleeing crowd, was left in the field, bleeding from internal injuries.

"A long time in the weather," Ilba said. "In his best suit. The one he wanted you to have for Rome."

Reg couldn't block out the image of the skinny Italian soldier, lying in the dirt pen outside the castle at Susegana, his buttonless uniform stained with his own blood. Ezio had seemed at peace with death then.

"They took his shoes," she said.

There was more – the university took care of the burials, the city promised a public memorial service, *Il Popolo d'Italia* scolded the unlawful attackers in print, the police vowed to find them – but Reg paid more attention to the tight faces of the three children, wondering how long their father had suffered before he died, how much pain he had had to endure, fallen in the meadow of his future.

"The roof leaks in that corner." He stared at the water-stained floor under the back windows. "I'll make sure it gets fixed."

From the front door of the new house, he could see the workers file into the winery just after daybreak, their rifles and shotguns catching first light. Every morning, Amelia would see these same men carry their weapons under her balcony. She would fume, but soon enough, she would come to realize the need to negotiate a reasonable agreement. He began thinking about what terms to insist on. He smiled as he crossed the flood plain toward the little house, early sun painting the river gold.

Over breakfast, he studied Gabby, sitting at the table in her mother's chair, wearing her mother's ring. Telling her the story of that blue stone, he had watched her expression flatten, as if the years since she had last seen her mother had suddenly stretched the skin on her face.

"The color of your grandfather's sea," she told Nicoletta. "The color of his eyes."

"Your eyes," the girl said.

With a smile, Gabby put the ring back on her finger. "One day, it will be yours. And Elisabetta's."

"He was really our mother's uncle," Nicoletta told him, "not ours. Sancia wasn't old enough to understand."

He kissed the top of her head and took careful steps toward the door so the sleeping infants would not awaken. Luigi's rifle leaned against the wall, the ammunition clip sitting on the floor near the stock. "You should keep them separated," he said. "For safety."

Gabby nodded, picked up the clip, dropped it into an apron pocket. Walking out into the morning light, she turned the polished blue agate on her finger. "She had dark hair, my mother. Like Teresa."

His could see his life sitting on a single line, from her through the open doorway to the little girl eating dried fruit at the table, to both babies sleeping on the low bed in front of the hearth, to the back wall, where that small black dress once hung from a peg. Hypnotized by that image, he didn't see her kiss his cheek. But he felt it.

"Teresa was your mother's dress," he told her. "You are her ring."

She glanced at the empty peg, where that dress once hung. He strode toward the big slate roof of the winery, anxious to get to work.

•

The quilt had been keeping him warm for the last few nights, but it had not softened the floor or his dreams. The new wood of the big house Paolo had built felt harder than the ground inside the wire prison pen in the shadow of Castle San Salvatore. The murmur of the night river reminded him of the struggling breath of half-starved soldiers. Sleep, when it came, didn't last.

He could smell Spring in the river now. Musty, raw, not anything like the fresh-washed scent of winter ice or the sweet perfume of summer grass, the sharp aroma of rot in Autumn. Even indoors, sleeping in Spring felt and smelled like sleeping in a new meadow.

What he smelled now wasn't Spring.

Petrol. That acrid tang.

Then smoke.

He rolled toward the odors. Flames danced around the window, orange tongues began sneaking under the door jamb, riding narrow rivers of fire. New wood siding groaned, pine cones exploded like grenades in the kindling bucket outside the dining room. He scrambled to his feet, pulled on his boots, yanked the quilt out of the way of the streams of flames making their slow, steady way toward fireplace.

The front door would be too hot to open, and a wall of fire would likely blow in on top of him. He raced to the back door, but the flames and smoke had found the kitchen. Grabbing the quilt and wrapping it around his head and shoulders as he moved, he ran head first through the window in the big bedroom. He never heard the glass shatter, rolling clear of the house and into a stack of slate roofing tiles that clattered like shrapnel showering into trenches to strike metal helmets.

A shard of window pane had made it through the quilt and into his hip. He pulled it out, held his palm over the wound, checked for more damage. Flames had reached the roof. How long had he been sleeping through all of this? The copper nails would expand and crack the tiles they were holding in place. In a few minutes, it would be raining slate. He limped toward the river.

She was standing near the high bank, her black dress glistening from the shine of the flames, an edge of her long red muffler fluttering in the breeze. A handcart sat between her and the house. A tall petrol can stood in the cart bed, glimmering and reflecting the orange flicker like a mirror.

When Amelia spotted him, her eyes widened. "I thought the house was empty!"

He kept moving toward her. "You thought she was here. With her son."

"No!"

She looked around for something to defend herself with, began taking backward steps along the bank. Then she turned and ran, that scarf billowing like a flame on the wind she created. He quickened his pace, moving away from the heat of the fire, but she was faster, getting smaller, then disappearing. He followed her footprints in the dark soil. They stopped just past the water lifting cylinders, short of the ancient bridge footings.

He made his way down the low bank, onto the pebbled shore, scanned the old stones, waiting for his eyes to adapt to the darkness. "You can't get past me."

Something whizzed by his ear.

"They'll hear me screaming!" she said.

He used the sound of her voice to narrow his search. "No one's here."

"In Nervesa. The sound will carry on the water."

It was coming from the broken arch near the middle of the island. He took careful steps, making sure of his footing.

Another object whizzed past his head. He stopped, crouched.

She hurled another river rock at him. It was the size of a cricket ball. Behind her, the river was lapping at her shoes – black velvet and lace. "They will hang you!"

Another rock, easier to dodge. He inched forward.

"You don't have to do this," she said, ducking back behind the arch.

"A Ziccardi does what is necessary. Always."

He could hear her swallow. Then that nasal laugh. She stepped out from behind the stones. "You are no Ziccardi."

He smiled. "Tonight, I am."

Sensing he was about to lunge at her, she ran toward the north end of the island and the other bridge remnants. "I'll let you back in the winery. You can still run it. For wages. Good wages."

Water separated the tall arch from the smaller one. *Trapped.*

"No way out," he said. "No escape. Surrender."

She lowered her head, stared at those small shoes. Her shoulders slumped. All the breath ran out of her. He reached for her.

Her head snapped up and her arm shot forward. The river rock struck him in the temple, knocking him to his knees. He felt her run by him toward the bank, but he couldn't close his arms fast enough to grab anything but air. He was sinking into the pebbles. Blood from the gash flooded his eye. Dazed, he struggled to turn and stand. The

361

moment he tried to straighten his knees, he felt dizzy and dropped back down.

But she had stopped. Her back was to him. If he could crawl, he could reach that long muffler. The smooth rocks hurt his knees. His hip burned. He could taste the blood from his scalp now.

And on the low bank, like a sentry in moonlight, Gabby aimed the rifle at the woman in black. She wore her dull white sleeping gown. No shoes. She squeezed the trigger. A dull *snap*.

He swallowed blood and drew a breath. "Pull the bolt."

Amelia was moving again. Toward her. And Gabby kept squeezing the trigger, unable to get the rifle to fire.

"Pull the bolt!" He crawled faster. "Get a bullet into the chamber!"

"No part of Paolo must live." Amelia picked up a river rock in each hand. Those black shoes toed into the moist soil of the low bank, digging steps for an easy climb. "You and the boy should have burned. It would have been less painful than this."

One last trigger pull, then a throaty moan. Those light blue eyes wide with fear, focused on the black arm cocking, readying a throw.

Swinging the rifle by the barrel, she crashed the stock into Amelia's head. The dark-haired woman fell. And Gabby was on top of her, slamming the rifle butt into the face of her prey, over and over. Stopping to stand, she lifted the weapon, swung it like an axe, landing two more blows. Then she tossed the rifle to the side.

She took a long look at the crumpled woman in black, the bloodied face, then grabbed the dress by the collar and dragged her over the stones to the river's edge. Using her bare feet, she shoved the body into the water. Grasping handfuls of limp limbs, she pulled the torso until she herself was knee deep in river. One final kick sent the black figure into the current, that red muffler riding behind like a dead sail.

It took less than 10 seconds for the Piave to swallow it whole.

She splashed water over her arms and walked out of the river. At his side, she tore a piece of hem from her nightgown, pressed the wad against the gash in this temple, put his hand on it to hold it in place. Then she reached under his armpit and helped him to his feet. Over bloodied stones, she guided him up the low bank.

The little mechanic was hosing down the flames at the new house, now a bonfire against the vines and the river. Reg wanted to call out and tell him it was no use. He couldn't find the breath.

"You belong with your daughters." Gabby steered him toward the little house. "And me."

362

EPILOGUE

THE FLOWER OF GRASS

11 MARCH, 1936

He read Mr. Quaite's letter several times before he believed it. Mr. Kipling and King George V had died within days of each other. The news, now almost two months old, didn't match the sunny winter day, the last swelling of the river glistening cold on its way toward a new growing season.

He glanced at the bookcase built into the back wall of the little house. The middle shelf, reserved for inscribed copies, held *A Farewell to Arms, Mrs. Dalloway, The Collected Poems of John Maesfield*, both *Jungle Books*.

Above the nook where Gabby once slept, faces in framed photos stared back at him. Mr. Quaite and his sister stood with Mr. Kipling in front of Bateman's. Scrawled in the gray space next to a now famous novelist's grin: *To my pal, Reggie – We lived this – Ernie.* The note from Virginia Woolf, expressing her gratitude for his input that Mr. Quaite had arranged when she was visiting a friend, some baroness in Kent, bore a big signature and a curious, unnecessary period at the end of her last name. A signed copy of *The Gods of the Copybook Headings* poem carried Mr. Kipling's thanks and encouragement: *For Reg – Your idea, remember? Where is your novel? – Kip.*

Closer to his desk, cluttered with stacks of notes surrounding the black Olivetti M2 typewriter with its raised feet and open sides, a copy of Mussolini's newspaper feature about him hung off a peg. That frame went lopsided each time he shut the door. He didn't look anything like that young soldier seated on the hospital bed. He ran a finger over the hard groove in his scalp, just above the V-shaped scar at his temple.

The photo of Sgt. Dickson, standing with his bride-the-night-nurse in front of a handsome stone house, had been a casualty of remodeling, when one of the carpenters had left it outside, to be stepped on, stained by paint, dirtied by weather. He missed the proud smile on that stone mason's face.

At Middlesex Hospital, after surgery for an ulcer, Mr. Kipling had died on January 18th. *A Saturday*, Mr. Quaite had written. *With a full moon he would have admired. A mere 19 days after his 71st birthday.*

The King passed away at Sandringham in Norfolk two days later. *His favorite place*, the letter said. Mr. Quaite claimed doctors had injected lethal doses of morphine and cocaine at 11:30 p.m. that Monday, so that the King's death at 11:55 p.m. would be first announced in *The Times* morning edition and *not in some less dignified evening journal*. His son, Edward VIII, ruled the empire now. Mr. Kipling had worried about that. Rumor was, the King himself had worried about it, too.

He left the three-page letter on the desk, stepped to the open door. Gabby was using a hoe to turn over wet earth in her old garden. Her work dress, once white, had been dulled by stains and washing. It made her look as though she had grown out of the dirt, a golden flower, bending back to the soil. Their son, dark-haired Vittorio, now 10, muddy and still her little helper, stood at her side with his own cut-down shovel.

Reg wanted to tell her about Mr. Kipling and how his cousin, Mr. Baldwin the Prime Minister, was one of the pall bearers, and that his ashes had been placed in Poets Corner at Westminster Abbey next to Charles Dickens and Thomas Hardy, and that a dusty-faced lad from Rusthall had been allowed to call him Kip. None of that would have meant anything to her or their son. What mattered here was weather and the current.

Beyond the little garden, gray-brown Glera vines stretched beyond his sight, all the way to the big bend in the Piave, where a stone marker now stood in the approximate spot where Barry fell. Yorke Grove always budded first. In less than a month, it would signal Spring again.

The newest new house – a much smaller version – seemed to squat among the rows of vines. Up the slope, trucks rolled in and out, taking bottles to market at a premium price. Primo would be checking each shipment, clipboard in hand, glasses at the tip of his nose. His sister Mira would be in the big office overseeing the accounts while Baggio pretended to help. The giant gold Z on the winery roof bounced sunlight back at The Montello across the river and the Dolomites upstream.

A blond-haired teen ran along the high bank chasing biplanes on their noisy way south. One of them pulled up and rocked its wings, as if to salute him. Berto came racing up from the river. "Did you see that! He did that for me!"

Reg nodded. "They fly too low."

"They know what they're doing." He looked so much like her, those pale blue eyes, the golden hair. He was studying the air those biplanes had left empty. "That's what I'm going to do. It's the new cavalry."

"It would break your mother's heart. And mine."

Already taller than the ex-cavalry officer, Berto smiled at his mother. "My father would want me to enlist. We're at war."

The Second Ethiopian War had pushed Mussolini even higher in popularity. The stocky dictator didn't resemble the scholarly newspaper editor from Milan these days. Empire had made him tubby and dour. In photographs, he was never caught smiling.

"Those planes are dropping mustard gas," Reg told him. "You don't want any part of that."

The tall teen laughed. "Those were Fighters. Fiat CR 32s − water-cooled V-12 engine, 600 horsepower!" He shook his head. "With twin 7.7 machine guns. They don't drop bombs."

Reg put a hand on the boy's shoulder. "War lives on inside you."

"What do you know?" The teen recoiled from his touch. "You're the stupid 'Englishman who forgot his own name'."

"I remember everything," he told the river.

Spinning toward the new house, Berto marched across the flood plain, muttering under his breath. His mother watched him go, then squinted and cocked her head. Reg shrugged. She nodded and wiggled dirty fingers in a wave that still made him smile. The small boy at her hip raised his shovel. Reg waved back, then headed for the cabin.

Ilba would be making her famous cabbage and pork stew − *Cassoeula* − at Teresa's house, waiting for Nicoletta and her two boys to cross the river from Nervesa for dinner, and for her youngest, Roberto, to come down from the goats and cattle in the foothills with new cheese and fresh milk. A Sunday feast in the middle of the week − Elisabetta's idea: *"Sunday is too good to celebrate only once a week."* Having just turned 16, she had been setting the family schedule for almost two years. There was no arguing with her. Ever. Even Berto kowtowed to her orders. "The Berto and Betta show," Gabby called it − a daily ballet since they were both able to walk, always producing the same outcome: girl one, boy zero.

There were times, especially in the early mornings, when she walked across a room that he would swear she was the mother she never knew. Elisabetta would be the only one who could talk her brother out of rushing down to the air base at Istrana, east of Treviso, to enlist.

Inside, he found his mother's bible on the top shelf. Her name, *Irene Vannes Olcutt*, written in her own hand, had blurred from moisture. He opened to the First Book of Peter, chapter 1, verse 24:

> *For all flesh is as grass, and all the glory of man as the flower of grass. The grass withereth, and the flower thereof falleth away.*

On a piece of note paper, he scribbled in Italian, now the language he dreamt in:

> *My Elisabetta — If you can help me convince Berto that there is no glory in war, that glory is like the flower of grass, we can save him from risking his life*

He thought of adding, *for nothing,* but knew she would scold him, remind him of how The Great War had brought him here, of the life it had opened, how without him, nothing here would exist as it did today. He jabbed a period to end the sentence, closed the bible on the note, set it at the edge of the desk, where over 100 pages sat face down in a tray labeled, *Three Women and the River, a novel.*

He studied the sharp light pouring through the window, then fed a blank sheet of paper into the Olivetti and began writing.